ZERO-G

My suit has gone completely stiff, like I'm encased in ice. All I can hear is my breathing, thick and rapid, causing condensation to form on the inside of the helmet. There's no other sound.

I'm upside down, looking at the tug as we fly away from it. It's so small – a little metal bubble, nothing more, vanishing into the distance.

"—ley, get—" Carver says, his voice crackling in and out.

"What?" I shout. My eyes are locked on the tug.

"We need to— away. The thrusters—"

I collide with Carver.

I didn't even see him. He just slams right into me. We're knocked away from each other, tumbling out of control. My breathing has never been so loud. I can hear the details of every inhale and exhale, and each one tastes sour in my mouth.

There's another fizz of static, and then Carver's voice comes again. "—losing you. We—"

"Carver, can you hear me?"

"—sters!"

"Carver! Where are you?" I can barely get the words out. Outside my helmet, the world is a spinning nightmare. I see him, just for a second, and then he's gone, spinning out of view.

By Rob Boffard

Tracer
Zero-G

ZERO-G

ROB BOFFARD

orbit

www.orbitbooks.net

ORBIT

First published in Great Britain in 2016 by Orbit

1 3 5 7 9 10 8 6 4 2

Typeset in Palatino by Palimpsest Book Production Limited,
Falkirk, Stirlingshire
Printed and bound in Great Britain by Clays Ltd, St Ives plc

Papers used by Orbit are from well-managed forests
and other responsible sources.

MIX
Paper from
responsible sources
FSC® C104740

Orbit
An imprint of
Little, Brown Book Group
Carmelite House
50 Victoria Embankment
London EC4Y 0DZ

An Hachette UK Company
www.hachette.co.uk

www.orbitbooks.net

For Mom and Dad

Prologue

Outer Earth

A huge ring, six miles in diameter, its cooling fins slicing through the vacuum. The Core at the centre of the ring, the sphere containing the station's fusion reactor, shines in the glowing sunlight. Three hundred miles below it, the Earth is dark and silent.

To generate gravity for the million people who live on board, Outer Earth spins – just fast enough to keep everything inside Earth-Normal. The spin is almost imperceptible, the rockets on the station firing at intervals to maintain it. It has been in orbit for over a hundred years.

The side of the station explodes.

A great wound opens up in the hull, like skin parting under a knife. The hole expands faster than the human eye can register, ripping apart until the gash is half a mile long. The pressure loss rips out everything inside, forming a cloud of glittering debris. Shreds of metal collide, bouncing off one other.

And there are bodies. Dozens of them. They tumble through the wreckage, crashing into the larger chunks of debris as they hurtle away from the station. Some of them are still moving, limbs clutching at nothing, fingers hooked into claws. One by one, they go still.

All of this happens in the purest silence.

1

Riley

Two days earlier

"We've got hostages."

Royo's voice echoes around the narrow entrance corridor. The big double doors to the Recycler Plant are behind him, shut tight. A rotating light spins above them, casting flickering shadows on the assembled stompers.

"Roster says twenty sewerage workers were on duty today when it happened," Royo says, jerking his thumb at the double doors. "It's our job to get 'em out."

"How many hostiles?" I say.

A few of the stompers look round at me, as if they can't quite believe I'm actually wearing one of their uniforms. I can't quite believe I am either. Six months ago, I'd be doing my best to get as far away from the stompers as I could. I've never liked cops.

Royo glances at me. His bald head reflects the spinning light perfectly. "We don't have any intel on the situation inside. That's the problem."

"What about the cameras?" says a voice from behind me.

I turn to see Aaron Carver jogging up, the top half of his black stomper jumpsuit tied around his waist, his perfectly styled blond hair swept back. He's wearing a bright red vest, exposing his toned upper arms. Behind him is Kevin O'Connell, a head taller than any other stomper here, with a closely shorn head and dark stubble across his cheeks.

All three of us used to be tracers – couriers who took packages and messages across the station. That was before Royo got us onto the stomper corps.

Royo shakes his head. "Nice of you to join us, Carver."

"Wouldn't miss it for the world, Cap."

Royo turns back to the group. "There were two working cams on the floor, but whoever did this shot 'em to pieces the second they got in there. Locked down all the exits, too."

Carver comes to a stop alongside me, breathing hard. "Was over on the sector border when I got the call," he says to me between breaths.

"Worried about us starting without you?" I say, out of the corner of my mouth.

He puts a hand on my shoulder, uses it to pull himself upright. "Only worried you'd make us look bad. Lucky I got here when I did."

"You got something you want to say, Carver?" Royo shouts. Heads turn to look at us. My stomper jumpsuit is made of thin fabric, but right then it feels too tight around my shoulders.

Carver gives a huge smile. "Not at all, Cap. Carry on."

"What are their demands?" says one of the other stompers, a heavily muscled woman named Jordan, leaning up against the corridor wall. Her ponytail is pulled back so tightly that it looks like her hairline is going to tear her face apart.

"Before they killed the camera," Royo says, "they held up a tab screen with a name written on it."

"A name?" says Jordan, her eyes narrowing.

4

But I know already. We all do. I grit my teeth, without really meaning to.

"Okwembu," says Kev. His voice is quiet, but it cuts across the hubbub in the corridor.

Royo gives him a crooked smile. "Big man gets it in one."

Janice Okwembu. Our former council leader, who nearly destroyed the station in a twisted attempt to gain more control for herself. A lot of people want her dead. More than a few have tried to break into her maximum security prison to do just that.

I guess whoever took the plant got tired of waiting.

Royo raises his voice. "We don't negotiate with hostage takers. Never have, never will. But, right now, what we don't have is – *hey*! Get those people out of here!"

I look back towards the entrance. The corridor leading to the Recycler Plant backs out onto the main Apogee sector gallery, an enormous space with multi-level catwalks running all the way up the station levels. This much stomper activity has attracted a crowd, blocking up the entrance to the corridor. They're craning their necks, looking for action. I see workers in mess kitchen uniforms, tech jumpsuits, a few people with tattoos who look like they run with a tracer crew. One man on the side is covered in filthy rags, holding on tight to a pushcart full of gods know what. Three stompers break away from our group, shouting at the crowd to fall back.

"As I was saying," Royo says. "We need intel. That means we need people inside. So while Jordan here takes point on the assault, I need our new tracer unit—" he points at us, and I feel a nervous prickle shoot up my spine "—to get inside, and see what we're dealing with."

"All right," says Carver, rolling his shoulders. "About time we had some action."

"Wait, hold on," I say, raising my hand. "You said they locked down the exits, right? So how *do* we get inside?"

5

Royo smiles that crooked smile again. A few of the other stompers are sniggering.

"That means the only way in . . ." I trail off, and, as one, Carver, Kev and I look down at the floor. The metal plating is perforated, and just then I realise what's below it.

Pipes. Conveying human waste from every hab in the sector to the plant. Pipes which we're now going to have to pull ourselves through.

Carver raises his eyes to Royo. "You have *got* to be kidding me."

2

Knox

Morgan Knox stands on the edge of the crowd, watching Riley Hale.

Everybody gives him space. Nobody wants to go near the man with the crippled leg, the man wrapped in filthy, stinking rags. Knox barely notices the sideways glances, the muttered insults. He just stands and watches Hale, with his hands on the handle of his cart, his knuckles bloodless and white beneath the dirt.

It's not the first time he's seen her – he's been thinking about her for months now – but it's the first time he's had such a long look. He'd gone out to get supplies, and was surprised to see Hale running across the gallery in front of him, sprinting for the Recycler Plant, where the rest of the stompers were assembling.

She's got her back to him. Her dark hair falls to her shoulders in ringlets. Her black stomper uniform is a little too small for her, like it was made for someone else, and he can see the tight contours of her toned shoulders and upper arms. The bottoms of the pants show a flash of ankle above her off-white tracer shoes.

She turns to say something to one of her companions. For a moment, he sees her in profile, caught in the corridor's flashing light. Not for the first time, he catches himself thinking that she's quite beautiful.

No, he thinks, and squeezes the cart handle even harder, as if he can pulverise the thought itself. *You're not beautiful. And you never will be.*

He spits, a giant gob of saliva spattering across the ground. He feels the crowd moving further away from him, as if he's infectious. Fine by him.

He hears shouting. He looks away from Hale, to see stompers pushing the crowd back, ordering them to move along. It jerks him back to reality, and he spins his cart, using his good leg as a pivot. The cart's wheels are old and rusted, and they squeak as he pushes it across the gallery floor. He glances upwards, at the catwalks silhouetted by the vast banks of ceiling lights, and keeps moving. He can't get distracted. There's still a lot of work to do.

3

Riley

The noise in the corridor has gone from loud to deafening. Orders are being shouted, weapons checked, tab screens sought out. Royo strides towards us, ignoring the disgust on Carver's face.

"There *has* to be another way," I say, glancing down at the metal grate.

Royo shakes his head. "There isn't. It's like I said. Exits blocked off." He keeps walking, heading back down the corridor, and we fall in behind him.

"How do you know they haven't shut off the pipes, too?" I say.

"We don't. But, right now, it's the only way in we haven't tried yet. Which means you're up."

"Cap, come on," says Carver. "You are *not* thinking of sending us down there."

Royo stops at a metal plate at the side of the corridor. Black lettering across it reads WASTE PIPE ACCESS AUTHORISED PERSONNEL ONLY, with smaller writing in Hindi and Chinese below it. There's a keypad on the door, its numbers faded with age. Royo crouches down and keys in a code, the beeps drowned out by the noise from the other stompers.

"You're going to get in there, you're going to get to a vantage point, and you're going to report back," Royo says. He taps his earpiece. "I want regular contact at all times, understand?"

I'd almost forgotten about my earpiece. Every time I think I've got used to it, I realise it's still there, clogging my ear canal. The earpiece is moulded plastic, designed to fit snug in my right ear. It links me to SPOCS: the Station Protection Officer Communication System. The stompers had it before we joined up, but it was a badly maintained network, full of glitches and dead spots. Carver's big mission over the past few months has been to fix it – his first big contribution to what he calls his straight life.

"Send someone else," Carver says, folding his arms. "I didn't sign up to crawl through shit."

"I second that," I say.

Royo gets to his feet. "Tracers go where other people can't. That's the whole point of your unit. That's why we recruited you." He taps the metal trapdoor with his foot. "And by the way, try and remember that we have twenty people being held at gunpoint right now. Let's help them out. What do you say?"

Carver and I glance at each other. After a long moment, we both nod.

I look around, and something occurs to me. "Where's Anna?" I say.

"Miss Beck is currently on a staggeringly important mission further up the ring, my dear," says Carver, imitating Anna's accent perfectly, adding the twang that people get when they grow up in Tzevya sector.

Royo glances at me. "Some punk group of tracers are getting themselves into the drug trade. She's getting dirt on them for me."

My anger flares at his words. Not too long ago, we were a punk group of tracers, too. But, secretly, I'm glad she's not here. The fourth member of our little unit is the last person I want to deal with right now.

"We've already stopped the flow into one of the pipes," Royo says. "It'll back up nasty down the line, but Level 3 is just going to have to deal with it."

He reaches down and hauls open the trapdoor. The space beyond is as black as space itself. A second later, the smell nearly takes my head off.

"Gods," says Carver, his nose and mouth buried in the crook of his elbow. Kev makes a strange noise, half retch, half disgusted groan.

"Tell me you've got some full-face filters," I say to Royo.

He shakes his head. "Those are back at HQ. We're only supposed to break them out for emergencies, not bad smells."

I close my eyes, willing the contents of my stomach to stay put. Royo calls out for a tab screen, and another stomper brings one over. As he passes it to Royo, I catch him staring at me. I meet his gaze, and he looks down, disappearing back into the chaos further up the corridor.

Six months on, I'm still the woman who had to kill her own father, plus the leader of her tracer crew, to save Outer Earth. Six months on, people are still treating me like a freak, or a saviour, or both. That includes other stompers. I don't mind the stares – I've got used to them. They're part of the job, and the job is what takes my mind off what happened. It's what makes going to sleep easier.

I turn back to Royo. With a few taps on the screen, he calls up the schematics of the plant.

"There are access points for maintenance here, and here," he says, pointing at the outline on the map. "My guess is the hostage takers won't know about them, but it won't stop them from spotting you if you get careless. I want to know how many, their approximate positions, what they're armed with. Once we've got that, we'll hit the door with shaped charges and come and get you."

He snaps the tab screen off. "Carver, Hale, get going. O'Connell, you come with me."

"Wait – what?" Carver says. "Since when is Kev exempt from shit-pipe duty?"

"Since he's too big to fit in the shit-pipe," Royo says. "Besides, we don't want him getting an infection."

"Oh come *on*," says Carver. "His op was months ago."

He jabs at Kev's midsection, aiming for the spot where the scar is. Kev dodges back, smirking.

It took us a while to recover from the insanity of a few months ago. We were all injured – cuts, bruises, deep muscle strains. Carver's shoulder was dislocated, and it took quite a few physical therapy sessions before it was back to full strength.

Kev got it the worst. The ligaments in his ankle were torn, and while the surgery to fix them went OK, there were complications. Pulmonary embolism, Kev told us – a blood clot that originated in a leg artery and travelled upwards, lodging itself in his lungs. He collapsed a few days after the first op, spilling a cup of homebrew all over the floor of his family's hab. Emergency surgery, followed by months in hospital – that was his reward for helping save the station. It's only in the last few weeks that he's been back at full strength.

I was worried about him for a while – and not just because of his physical injuries. His closest friend, Yao, died last year. But he's thrown himself into his new life. Out of all of us, he's the one who's settled in the best. It's like he was born to be a cop, and being a tracer was just an interlude. I actually heard him telling some of the other stompers a joke – when we were tracers, he hardly ever spoke unless you asked him something first.

Royo looks Carver and me up and down. He steps in closer, lowers his voice. "I send any of my guys in there, they'll get caught. You've got agility, you've got speed, you've got your stingers, and you've got each other. We'll be right on the other side of the door if things go wrong."

I nod, suddenly aware of my stinger, the small pistol holstered on my left hip.

Royo claps his hands. "O'Connell. On me."

Kev fist-bumps Carver, squeezes me on the shoulder. "Stay in touch," he says, tapping his ear, and then jogs off after Royo.

"Riley," says Carver quietly, as soon as they're out of earshot. "I can take this if you want. You don't have to go down there."

I look up at him, surprised, thinking he's suggesting I can't handle it. But there's nothing but concern on his face, and my irritation drains away.

"Not a chance," I say, forcing a smile. "If I'm not there to help out, you'll make us look bad."

He returns the smile, then digs in his pocket and hands me a stomper-issue torch. Its grainy metal surface is ice-cold. I click it on and off, and he winces as the light flicks across his face.

"Want some after-market gear?" he says.

"Like what?"

He digs in his pocket, and hands me a small box. It's a good thing the bottom is covered with sticky adhesive, because I nearly drop it when I realise what it is.

"I can't carry a *bomb*," I say. Carver raises his eyebrows, motioning at me to stay quiet. I look over his shoulder, but nobody appears to have heard me.

I thrust the box back at Carver. When we were tracers, he was the one who built us gadgets, who designed our backpacks and shoes. And, occasionally, he'd make something a little more deadly.

The box is a sticky bomb. It's palm-sized, modified from a small plastic food container with a tight-fitting lid. Inside the lid is a sharp spike, tipped with chemicals. Just below it, on the other side of the box, is a wad of explosive putty. Slam your hand down on the box, and you've got four seconds to clear the hell out.

"Relax, Ry," Carver says. "This one's self-assembly."

He holds out his hand. The explosive putty is in his palm, a shiny blue glob. "Totally inert," he says. "Until you combine them."

"And what exactly do you think we're going to need these for?"

He gives me an evil grin. "Use your imagination."

I shake my head, but I know he's not going to take them back. I put the box in my left jumpsuit pocket, and the putty in my right, as far away from each other as possible. The gunk has left a little residue on my hand, and I wipe it on my leg, which does nothing more than add a thin layer of lint to my skin.

Carver nods at the pipe. "Ladies first."

I lean away from the smell, taking a last breath of cold air. Then I slip down into the darkness of the tunnel.

Prakesh

Prakesh Kumar takes the stairs two at a time, his arms pumping.

Suki is screaming at him to hurry. He can see the intense lights from the Air Lab ceiling through the open door at the top, and he raises a hand to his face, shielding his eyes.

He takes the last step and explodes out onto the roof of the control room complex, jogging behind Suki. Her hair – green this month – flares out behind her. Prakesh still has his heavy lab coat on, and he rips it from his shoulders as he runs, letting it fall to the ground behind him. They're running down a narrow canyon, bulky air-conditioning units on either side humming quietly.

"This way," Suki says over her shoulder. He can see the tear tracks down her face, gleaming under the lights. He nods, trying to control his breathing.

They sprint out of the mouth of the canyon. There's an open area on the roof, and Prakesh sees that there are other techs there, huddled in a small group off to one side. Prakesh doesn't know all of them, but he recognises Julian Novak from genomics, and the new guy, Iko, from maintenance. Prakesh isn't particularly fond of Julian. The man's lazy, prone to taking shortcuts in his work. He gives Prakesh a guarded nod. His dark hair hangs down over his face, and he's chewing something, his mouth moving mechanically.

Suki comes to a clumsy stop, pointing to the other side of the roof, beyond another bank of aircon units. "He's over there. We found him when we . . ." she trails off, doubling over and clutching her side.

"It's OK," Prakesh says. But it doesn't feel OK. Not by a long shot. He can feel his heart pounding, the sweat soaking into his shirt. "Do we have a name? Do we know who it is?"

"It's Benson," says Julian, talking around whatever he's chewing.

Prakesh's eyes widen. James Benson. Quiet, cheerful, hard worker. He's been at the Air Lab forever – Prakesh remembers working with him on some project years ago.

"Did he say why he's doing this? Did you talk to him?"

Julian shrugs.

Prakesh's anger flares. How can the man be so calm? He has a sudden desire to tell him to handle it, see if he keeps that smug look on his face then.

But he can't. He's in charge of the Air Lab now, and that means this is his show.

"How long's he been up here?" he asks Suki.

She takes a moment to answer. "Twenty minutes," she says. "I think."

Prakesh grabs her shoulder "I want you to get a Mark Six and jack it all the way up. Make sure he doesn't see you doing it."

"It'll never work!"

"Just do it, Suki. And do *not* put it in place before I tell you."

He strides off without waiting for her to reply. The aircon units run right up to the edge of the building. The control room

16

complex is in the corner of the hangar, six storeys high, and Prakesh can see the Air Lab stretching out below him. He can see the enormous man-made forest dotted with algae pools. From up here, it seems like every square foot of extra space has been given over to growing food. Prakesh sees dark soil, brown climbing frames, the emerald green of the plants, the blinking lights of the hydroponic systems.

He looks down at the edge of the roof. There's less than a foot of space between the aircon units and thin air.

Prakesh takes a deep breath, holds it, then lets it out through his nose. He puts one foot on the edge, slipping his body around the aircon unit, his hand hunting for a hold.

Benson is a little way along. He's middle-aged, with the lean body and huge arms of someone who has spent years carrying heavy sacks of soil and fertiliser. His face is ashen-grey, his eyes closed. He's facing outwards, his hair buffeted by a stream from the aircon unit, and beyond him, a single step away, is a sixty-foot drop to the ground below.

5

Riley

The smell in the drained pipeline is like a living thing. It crawls into my nose and squats there, prickly and burning. I almost gag, manage to keep it down. The floor in the pipe is uneven, criss-crossed with ridges and bent metal, spotted with puddles of soupy water.

I'm on all fours, a few feet into the tunnel, when I hear Carver come down behind me. I flick on my torch as he lands, illuminating walls stained with gunk.

"Well, Royo was right," Carver says. "Kev would *never* fit down here."

I look back, playing my torch across his body. For me, the space is tight, but for Carver it looks as if he's been squeezed into the pipe, his shoulders bumping up against the roof.

We start forward. As I push myself around a corner, forcing my body into the wall for balance, my hand slips. My forearm slides into the muck, which soaks through my jumpsuit. It takes every ounce of willpower I have not to start hammering on the walls.

"Everything OK?" Carver says.

Rob Boffard

"Couldn't be better," I say through clenched teeth.

Another right turn, then we'll be in the plant itself. The next T-junction should have a grate which we can lift up.

It doesn't take us long to get there – the *patoosh-patoosh* of the machinery in the plant is coming down into the pipe, more felt than heard. The smell has grown stronger, too – something I didn't think was possible. The inside of my nose feels scoured.

There's a crackle in my ear. Royo. "Tracer unit, come back."

I look down at my wrist, at the thick flexible rubber band with the small digital display. It's the companion to my earpiece – each stomper unit gets its own dedicated channel on the system, and ours is 535.

I touch my wrist, keying the transmit button. "Copy. Loud and clear, Captain."

"Report."

I keep my voice low. "We're getting close. We should be inside the plant in two minutes."

"Good. We've got a team standing—"

There's a burst of static on the line, fading and vanishing inside a second. It's loud enough to make me wince.

"—static, Carver. When are you fixing it?" Royo says. If anything, he sounds even more annoyed.

"Gimme a break," Carver say from behind me. "I'm still trying to find out why it's even there. The frequencies on SPOCS are supposed to be discrete, so we don't pick up any radio—"

"*Carver.*"

"Fine, fine," he mutters. "Hope you and Kev are having *fun* up there."

I crawl round a corner, and suddenly there's a grate above my head, sending thin strips of light down into the pipe.

"We're here," I whisper. "Gotta go."

"Copy that," says Royo.

Someone walks across the grate.

The light blinks out. I see boot soles, and footsteps boom down into the tiny crawlspace. I wait until the owner of the boots recedes into the distance, then keep crawling.

I can see the exit up ahead – it's another grate, with pinpricks of light leaking in. I look back over my shoulder as I get close; Carver catches my eye, and nods. Very slowly, I put a hand on the grate and push.

The metal grinds as it lifts up, and I freeze.

There are no shouts, no running feet. I lift it up the rest of the way and haul myself out.

I've come up behind one of the waste vats. It's an enormous metal cylinder, one of dozens dotted around the walls of the room, gleaming under the spotlights in the ceiling. The vats form a loose U-shape around an open area on the plant floor. The smell here is a little better, the stench of waste cut by the tang of disinfectant.

I pad to the side, moving on the balls of my feet, and Carver slips out of the grate behind me. He gets to his feet, hugging the wall as he moves into the shadows.

I rest a hand on the cold surface of the vat. I can feel it humming and vibrating as it churns the wastewater, separating out the good and the bad. They mix the water with bacteria to eat the waste, sending the oxygen produced back into the system. When the water's clean, it recirculates, flowing to water points across the lower sectors.

I sneak a peek around the side of the vat. I don't see the hostages. What I do see is a man with a stinger coming right towards our hiding place.

6

Prakesh

For a terrifying second, Prakesh doesn't know what to say. If he startles Benson, the man could slip right off the ledge.

Benson saves him the trouble. The eyes in that grey face slide open, and he looks over.

"What do you want?" he says. His voice is calm, as if he's asking Prakesh to deal with a routine lab matter. But Prakesh can't stop looking at Benson's feet, the toes already out over the edge.

"Hey, James," he says, going for nonchalance and failing. "I was, um . . . I was hoping I could talk to you."

"Oh yeah? About what?"

About what? Prakesh almost laughs. He can feel his palm sweating against the metal aircon unit. There's no manual for these kinds of situations, no step-by-step procedure you can rely on.

"Let's talk about why you're up here," Prakesh says. "How about it, huh?"

"Do you know how long I've been at the Air Lab?" Benson says, looking out at the vast hangar.

21

Prakesh's mind whirs away, trying to remember. "I don't—"

"Twenty years. I was here when old Xi Peng was running the place, long before you came along." He says it without malice, as if it's just a fact he's learned to live with. Prakesh supposes he has.

"Twenty years," Benson says again. "And I've hated it for nineteen and a half of them."

"We can change that," Prakesh says. He can hear noise on the ground below. He has to keep Benson's attention. If he jumps before the Mark Six is ready . . .

"Really?" Benson actually laughs. "How? You think changing my role or putting me at a better time on the shift roster is gonna make me *happier*?"

Prakesh starts to speak, but Benson talks over him. "I got nobody. Never had nobody. Didn't think I needed them, neither. But it wears you down, you know?"

He jabs a finger outwards, pointing at the hangar wall.

"They," he says. "Them. They take us for granted. We give them food, all of them, and they treat us like dirt."

"James," says Prakesh. "You have to listen to me. We need you. *I* need you."

Benson ignores him. "Even you. Especially you. With that genetic breakthrough of yours, they should have put you in charge of the whole damn station. How do you stand it?"

"They made me head of the Air Lab," Prakesh says. "That's enough for me." He's feeling embarrassed somehow, like he shouldn't be talking about his success. He desperately wants to look back over his shoulder, hoping against hope that a stomper or a councillor or *someone* will appear on the rooftop, ready to step in.

"I always respected you," Benson says. "You seem like a

decent guy. But I don't want to do this any more. You can't make me."

And before Prakesh can do anything, Benson closes his eyes and steps forward off the roof.

7

Riley

The man is my age, his face pockmarked with acne scars, wearing an old flannel shirt under a khaki jacket. When he comes round the side of the vat, Carver and I are pressed up against it, deep in the shadows.

The man stops, looking back over his shoulder. The stinger in his hands is homemade, cobbled together from spare parts, but perfectly capable of ruining your day.

I feel Carver tense beside me. I'm already working out the angles, the fastest and quietest way to take him down. If he gets even a single word off—

"We don't need any heroes here," someone says from across the room, out of my field of view. The man in the flannel shirt turns, striding back across the floor. I breathe out, long and slow.

The voice is faint, but I can just make out the words. "Everybody just stay on the ground, and we all walk away."

I sneak another peek round the side of the vat, taking in the floor of the plant. I can see some of the hostage takers, their backs to me, and a few people lying face down on the floor, but I can't get a clear look at the whole plant. Carver slips past me, placing a hand at the small of my back, moving silently to the next vat along.

I hear another voice – one of the hostages, I think. There's a muffled thump, followed by a groan of pain.

"Ivan," the first voice hisses.

"Sorry, Mikhail."

Carver puts up a closed fist: *Wait*. He takes a look of his own, scanning the plant, then pulls back into the shadows.

I catch his attention, pointing in the direction of the hostage takers, then hold up six fingers, three on each hand.

He shakes his head, quick-quick, then holds up a fist and two fingers. Seven.

I risk another look. There he is: he was out of my field of view, standing off to one side, over by the far wall. I can't pick out his features from here, but he has a massive beard, falling all the way to his stomach.

Carver taps his ear, looking at me questioningly. I nod, then key the transmit button on my wristband.

"Captain Royo," I say, keeping my voice to a low murmur. "This is Riley, come back."

"Copy, Hale. What do you see?"

Carver has moved further along the back of the vat, and is peering round the far end. He looks back at me, flashes seven fingers again, then a thumbs-up.

"We've got seven of them. They're carrying stingers, home-made. I don't see any other weapons."

"And the hostages?"

"They look OK for now."

Mikhail speaks again. "We don't want to hurt anyone. Not unless we have to," he says. He's just in my field of view. His accent is syrup-thick. The set of his shoulders and his posture speak of a man in his thirties or forties, but he has an ancient

25

face, jagged with wrinkles and scars. His head is ringed with grey hair, long and greasy.

"Confirm seven hostiles," says Royo. "Can you—"

As he speaks, the earpiece gives off a burst of static, so loud I almost tear the unit from my ear.

My heart starts hammering. I slip around the back of the vat, praying the sound didn't go further than my ringing eardrum. I flick the SPOCS to a dead channel.

"You hear that?" someone says. Whoever it is starts walking towards my hiding place, his footsteps getting louder. Not good. I shrink back against the tank, willing myself to be as still as possible. Carver has dropped to one knee, so deep in the shadows that I can barely make him out.

"What is it, Anton?" says the leader from the other side of the room.

"Heard something," Anton says. "Just checking it out."

"OK. Be careful."

The man is going to be on me in seconds – and this time I can't count on him turning away. If I run, he'll hear me. If we take him out, if the others don't see him again in a minute or two, they'll come looking for him. I hear his footsteps, getting closer, see his shadow growing larger on the wall.

And then, all at once, the idea is there.

I can see Carver getting ready to move, a shifting shape in the shadows. I signal him with a raised hand, then shake my head.

The gap between the wall and the vat is maybe four feet. I push my back against the vat, facing the wall, then raise first one leg, then the other. When I'm locked into position, suspended a few feet off the ground, I start to push my upper body a little way up the side of the vat. One leg at time, I walk myself up the wall, always sliding my upper body first, always keeping my feet below waist level.

Being a tracer teaches you about friction. Friction maintains grip. Friction keeps you defying gravity in places you shouldn't be able to. Friction – perfectly calibrated pressure between two surfaces – can keep your hand on a wall, or your fingers on an edge for the extra half-second you need to pull yourself over. Friction keeps us alive.

I try to keep my movements smooth. When I'm on a run, sprinting through the station, I don't worry too much about making noise – matter of fact, the more I make, the longer people have to see me coming, and get out of the way. But if I make a sound now, I'm dead.

"If anybody's back here, come out now," Anton says again, the word given a metallic edge in the tight space. "We won't hurt you."

I'm ten feet up, but it's not enough – he'll see me. I force myself to keep sliding upwards. A foot. Another. The muscles in my thighs are starting to burn.

Anton comes into view. He's a tall man, heavily muscled, wearing a ragged blue jumpsuit. He's right underneath me. I can feel sweat pooling in the small of my back. If he looks up, he can't possibly miss me. He won't even have to aim. I feel a burning need to look at Carver, to see if he's still there, but I don't dare turn my head.

Just as these thoughts run through my mind, my shoe slips on the metal wall, giving off a tiny screech.

He had to have heard that. He must have. Any second now, he's going to look up and put a bullet into me.

But he doesn't. He looks everywhere, except above his head.

The burn in my thighs has become a raging fire, adding to the ache in my knees and ankles. I can't stay where I am – if I don't go up, or slide down, I'm going to fall right on top of him.

I will my legs to stay locked, keeping me in place.

He turns, and begins to walk the other way, intending to check behind the other vats. If Carver doesn't move, the man is going to trip right over him.

Carefully, I look to my left. Carver isn't there. He's moved away, slipping down the vats. I can just see him at the far corner of the room. "I'm OK," he says, his voice barely audible on my SPOCS.

My lungs feel like they're going to rip through my torso, but I exhale as quietly as I dare. I'm about to slide down when I stop.

Climbing is quiet. Getting down is always noisy. No matter how carefully you do it, there's always sound. I might bring the man back this way, even more determined.

But if I go up, I can stay quiet, and get an even better view of the plant

Slowly, ever so slowly, I begin sliding up the vat, walking up the wall, treating each step as if there's crushed glass under my feet.

"What are you doing?" Carver says. I don't answer.

It seems like hours before I reach the top of the vat. Getting onto it isn't easy – I have to stretch out as I come over the lip, and for a minute the edge digs painfully into my lower back. But then I slide onto it, face-up, pulling my feet off the wall.

The air up here is just as dank, slick with the stink of human waste. The voices below me are muffled. Not knowing what's happening in here must be driving Royo insane. He'll be pacing, furious at us for going silent on him.

You're in a world of shit, I think, and have to force myself not to laugh.

"Carver," I whisper.

Carver speaks almost immediately, frantic with worry, abandoning SPOCS protocol. "Riley, talk to me."

"I'm up on one of the waste vats. They haven't seen me."

"You need to stay where you are. They've got two of them looking for us now. They know something's wrong."

Royo must have been listening in. "Tracers, report. We're ready to go out here. Give me hostile positions, *now*."

"Standby," I whisper. I slide across the top of the vat as I talk. The surface is convex, and as I near the edge I have to work to keep myself in place, but I finally get a good view of the plant.

The waste vats line the walls, surrounded by a ganglia of pipes and valves. The hostage takers are spread across the floor, talking in low voices. Two of them are patrolling the vats on my right, looking for Carver. Two more stand over the hostages, all lying in a small cluster on the floor. Mikhail is over by the main door.

"You find anything back there?" one of them yells.

The answer comes from below me. "Nothing, man. I don't like this."

The questioner nods, turning to the others. "Spread out. There's someone else here."

I look down. And that's when I see a woman, one of the hostage takers, staring up at me.

29

8

Prakesh

"*Now, Suki!*" Prakesh shouts. "*Do it now!*"

Everything happens at once. Benson screams – the scream of a man who realises what he's done, and desperately wants to take it back. He throws his arms out as if he's about to hug someone. At the same time, Prakesh hears metal on metal as Suki, or whoever she's with, shoves the Mark Six into place.

Benson vanishes. A half-second later, there's a strange sound, as if a giant has been punched in the stomach. It's followed by a crack so sharp that it reverberates off the walls of the Air Lab. Benson screams again, and this time it's a scream of pain.

Prakesh closes his eyes for a moment, then looks over the edge.

The Mark Six is destroyed, its surface pushed inwards. It's a transparent, inflatable greenhouse, six feet square, a light-weight alternative to the steel and plastic ones they used before. Suki did what she was told, pumping it up out of sight, then pushing it into place when she heard Prakesh call out.

Benson hit hard enough to rip the surface. If it had been pumped up even a little bit less, he would have gone straight through it. But it was enough to bounce him sideways, stopping the fall. He's broken his leg – Prakesh can see the bone poking up through the fabric of his pants. Benson is writhing in pain, surrounded by techs, who are calling for stretchers and medkits. No one is looking at him except for Suki, who looks like she wants to throw up.

Slowly, very slowly, Prakesh finds his way back onto the roof. He puts his hands on his knees, bending over. He's curiously light-headed. *Depression*, he thinks, not entirely sure what the thought is connected to until he remembers what Benson said. *That can't happen again. I need to pay more attention to the techs. I'll get Benson help, whatever he needs . . .*

He hears applause and raises his head. The group of techs on the roof are cheering, running towards him. Only Julian Novak hangs back, still chewing, his expression entirely neutral. Then Prakesh is surrounded by beaming faces and eager voices, and he lets Julian slip from his mind.

9

Riley

Before I can pull myself back onto the vat, the woman raises her stinger. "Up there! On the tank!" she shouts.

"Where?"

"Third from the right! By the pipes."

"Just one?"

"Watch the hostages."

"Somebody fire!"

I hear the crack of the stingers, and the bullets pinging off the metal. I'm on my back, frantically looking for an escape route. I have to move – a single ricochet off the roof or one of the pipes could end me.

Carver's in my ear again. "Riley! I'm coming!"

"No!" I say, shouting over the gunfire. "I got this."

I regret the words the second they're out of my mouth. A stinger bullet slams into the vat ahead of me, spitting up sparks. The bullets aren't designed to go through metal, but they'll make a real mess of anything softer. Another bullet whips by, scoring a hot line above my ankle, only just missing.

Royo is barking in my ear. "Hale, we're hearing gunfire! I need an update!"

I'm trying to stay as low as possible. Maybe I can slip off the back of the vat, drop down, make a run for it. I could draw my stinger, return fire. But I'm an awful shot, always have been, and finding a target under fire will just get me killed. I dig in my pockets, feeling for anything that could help. Half a protein bar. A tiny battery. I'm going by feel, and I'm about to admit defeat when my fingers grasp something else.

The box. Carver's sticky bomb. I'd forgotten all about it.

"The sticky," I say, hoping SPOCS picks my voice up over the gunfire. "How big's the blast?"

"Not big enough to take out seven people with guns!"

"Just humour me."

"You set that thing off, you're looking at a powerful, concentrated blast of three or four feet. Maybe less. But I don't see how . . ."

I've already flipped myself, and begun to move on all fours towards the edge. There's a seam, running down the middle of the vat, a vertical weld joining the two halves. Before I can even think about it, I'm scooting around on my stomach, ducking as another stinger bullet hits the metal above my head.

"Hale!" Royo shouts. "Get to cover. We're breaching now."

I fumble with the box, popping the lid off and squashing the putty down. I replace the lid, then slam the whole thing down on the seam.

I roll right off the side of the vat. A second later, the sticky explodes.

10

Riley

The sticky doesn't just blow a hole in the vat. It *ruptures* it, ripping the welded seam apart.

The bang hits my ears right as the shock waves ripple across my falling body, followed a second later by the sharp stench of shit and piss. I hear the terrified shouts of the hostage takers as a tidal wave of waste rolls towards them. An image flashes into my mind of the hostages, caught prone, submerged in the filth.

I twist in mid-air, tuck my arms, hit the ground, roll, come up on all fours in the torrent. There's not enough sewerage to flood the plant, but it rolls out in a great, sluggish, frothing wave. It's a dark brown, almost black, with misshapen lumps floating in the slurry. In the distance, an alarm is blaring.

I'm up on my feet, bursting into a run, when there's another enormous bang. The door to the plant explodes inwards, and stompers surge into the room. Kev is among them, sprinting to the side, trying to flank the hostage takers. His feet kick up huge waves of liquid as he runs. He hits one of the gunmen shoulder first, knocking him flying, then swings a punch at

34

another. The floor is a confusion of brown sludge and screaming, scrambling, sliding bodies. Carver is roaring in my ear

Mikhail. It takes me a minute to pick him out in the chaos. He's raised his gun, taking aim at the nearest stomper.

He's the one. I can't take down every hostage taker, not on a floor that's this slippery, not in the chaos of a firefight, but if I get their leader . . .

I'm already running, the sea of muck rising up my shins, soaking through my pants. Mikhail fires. The stomper gives a strangled cry, flying over backwards as the bullet takes him in the chest.

My foot connects with something loose and slippery, and with a sick horror I feel myself flailing forward. On instinct, I tuck for a roll. The wet muck soaks through my jumpsuit and the shirt beneath it to touch my bare skin, shockingly cold.

But then I'm through the roll and on my feet, still running. For a moment, I can't see Mikhail – just stompers and hostages, diving and slipping across the floor. Then I spot him. He's almost at the doors, elbowing stompers out of the way when they try to grab him.

"Move!" I yell, dodging past a hostage. Her huge, panicked eyes are the only thing in her face not slick with filth.

Mikhail is past the doors now. Two stompers are giving chase, but they're not fast enough, and they can't risk firing – a missed shot would go right into the gallery.

I bolt through the doors, now no more than shredded chunks of metal. As I pull free of the muck, as my feet kiss solid ground, I lean forward and drop my centre of gravity, swinging my arms, pushing myself into a full sprint.

Think you're fast, Mikhail? Let's see if you can outrun me.

The shadows from the catwalks cut the floor into pieces. The area past the plant is filled with the crush – the people that pack the floor of every gallery and corridor in Outer Earth, a slow-moving morass of humanity. Mikhail is still shoving people out of the way, powering through the crowd. I do the same, trying to keep sight of him, shouting his name as I elbow people aside.

No one tries to stop him. They're all gawking at the scene in the plant. He's at the edge of the gallery, pulling away, sprinting into one of the corridors leading off the floor. I see him look back over his shoulder as he does. I'm still fighting my way through the crowd. If I don't get free in the next five seconds, I'm going to lose him.

"No!" I scream as he slips out of sight. I'm furious with the people in the crowd. They stand there like statues, not moving until I put a hand on their chests or pull their shoulders to the sides.

My SPOCS unit is filled with shouted orders from dozens of stompers, coming across the all-channels setting. "Carver?" I shout, hoping that I can be heard through the chaos.

The noise vanishes, replaced by his voice, calmer than it should be. "Copy, Ry."

My words are rendered ragged by my running. "I'm chasing Mikhail. We're on the bottom level, heading towards the furnaces. I need you to cut him off for me."

"No can do. I'm *way* behind you."

"Kev?" I can feel a stitch creeping down my left side as I run, jabbing me with every step.

"He's here. Beating someone to a pulp with his own stinger."

I don't respond, partly because I'm trying to save my breath, and partly because I know what he's going to say next and don't want him to say it.

"You'll have to call Anna."

There's a sharp turn in the corridor. I'm coming up on it too quickly, and jump towards the wall, using it to arrest my momentum and change direction in one movement. I see

36

Mikhail, pushing past a group of people standing outside the door to the furnaces. He's sprinting past, heading for the stairwell at the far end.

"She's on a different channel today. Uh . . . 349," says Carver.

I have to glance down at my wristband as I flick through the channels. I spin past 349, and have to pull the dial back.

"Anna, this is Riley, come back."

For a moment, there's no sound except the pounding of my feet. "Anna," I say again. "Riley here. You copy?"

"What do you want?" Anna says, her crisp accent coming through on the line perfectly. She sounds like she just woke up from a nice doze.

"Where are you?" I say.

She pauses before answering. "Level 6 in New Germany."

Mikhail hits the stairs, taking them three at a time. I'm closing, but nowhere near fast enough. "I've got a runner heading your way," I say. "He's climbing the stairwell on the Apogee border side. I need you to take him out."

Static explodes in my ear, and I nearly tear the SPOCS unit out and hurl it at the wall.

The noise dies, and Anna snickers. "What's the matter? Too fast for you?"

"Just do it," I say, as I sprint past the door to the furnace. A blast of dry heat whips by me as I pass, and then I'm at the stairs.

"If you're going to give me orders, I'll let you keep chasing him."

I can hear Mikhail above me. His thundering footfalls shake the stairwell.

"Anna, now is *not* the time," I say, the words burning a stitch in my side. Above me, Mikhail's thundering footfalls shake the stairwell. "He's coming from below you. Middle-aged, long hair, dark overalls, backpack."

Anna yawns. I hear it come over the comms, a little swelling exclamation mark, and I want to reach through the frequencies and smack her.

"I'll see what I can do," Anna says.

The bottom of the stairs is littered with garbage and scraps of twisted metal. I take the steps as fast as I can, dodging around wide-eyed onlookers, tracking the noise of Mikhail's thundering footsteps above me. He's got too much of a head start. Anna might get there in time, but she might not. I need to close the gap.

I climb as fast as I can, my legs pistoning out in front of me, my thighs screaming. The stairwell is a dark, tight space, with half the lights missing from their sockets. There's a woman working a plasma cutter just below Level 3. I smell her before I hear her, the scent of ozone sharp and pungent, and I have to shield my eyes as I dash past. I'm already looking up towards the next set of stairs, and that's when I see it.

The landing above me isn't flush with the wall. There's a gap. Five feet wide, an open space beyond the railing at the landing's edge. I didn't realise I was on this particular stairwell – the gap reaches all the way from Level 1 to Level 6, something the construction corps used to get building materials between the levels, back when the station was built.

There's a railing, waist-high and flecked with rust, separating the landing from the gap. Before I can even think about it, I jump. My right foot lands square on the rail, and I use it to launch myself at the wall, flying into space.

If I don't pull this off, if I don't swing my body a hundred and eighty degrees at just the right moment, I'll fall, screaming, all the way to the bottom.

My left foot connects with the wall, sending a shock wave up into my knee.

Time slows, then stops.

I can pick out every detail. The rough texture of the metal. My pants stretched tight against my leg as my knee bends. The feeling in my hips as I start to twist.

The word running through my mind is *friction*. My foot needs to stay in immobile contact with that wall. If it doesn't, I'm finished.

And then, as time begins to speed up again, the yell escapes my lips, forcing its way out as I push back off the wall and spin my body, injecting that tiny bit of extra energy into my movements. I throw my hands up, as high as they can go.

My palms slam into the edge of the landing above. There's a split second where I'm scrabbling at it, but my body takes over. I swing forward, then on the way back I use the momentum to thrust myself upwards. A second later, I'm up and over the railing. My arms are burning, and I can actually feel the blood powering through my veins, but I'm alive. And I can hear Mikhail, closer now. His breathing echoes off the walls, hot and ragged.

I ignore the pounding in my own chest, ignore the stitch which has turned my side to a searing flame, and charge after him into the corridor. I'm frantically scanning my mental map of New Germany – where does the corridor lead? The hab units? Or is this the sector where they've got the mess hall on the upper levels?

The lights above us flicker, then die completely, plunging the corridor into darkness. When they click back on, Anna Beck is there, in front of Mikhail, running right at him, her slingshot raised in front of her like a shield.

She fires, the slingshot strips snapping forward with a high-pitched *crack*. Whatever she's loaded it with whips through the air, too fast to see, and takes Mikhail dead in the chest.

11

Knox

Knox strips naked, then washes his hands, holding them up so the water drips down his arms. It's scalding hot, and the industrial detergent he uses makes his skin feel as if it's been scoured.

He shakes the water off into the metal basin, then turns his attention to his chest. Two strips of tape, their edges peeling, form an X above his heart. He peels the tape off, wincing, using one finger to hold the tiny transmitter underneath it in place.

Two thin wires run off the transmitter, terminating under his skin, and he touches the entry wounds gingerly. No infection. Good.

He replaces the tape, smoothing it down, then washes his hands again. The skin on them is red and raw, peeling away on the ball of his left thumb. He bites down on a stray piece, tearing it off and spitting it into the basin, then gives his thumb and forefingers another quick scrub.

The cart, and his rags, lie behind him, pushed into a corner of the storage room, below the shelves that line the walls. He hates that he has to keep them here, but he doesn't have a choice. He's lucky to have this place: these tiny, forgotten rooms on the bottom level of Apogee. And he needs his cart, the rags that keep other people away from him. It's his protection, his shield. The only way he can pass through the rest of the station unnoticed.

He pulls a set of clean scrubs from a hanger next to the basin, and slips them on. His mind is racing ahead, checking and rechecking, making sure he hasn't forgotten anything, and the cool cotton soothes him.

His hand darts through the air, plucks an object from a shelf. He cobbled it together from scratch – his electronics knowledge is passable, at best, but he worked at it until he had it right. It's a misshapen metal box, a foot square, an antenna sprouting from it. He made sure that all the messy wires and circuit boards were packed away, out of sight.

He hits a switch on the front of the box. A light flickers on, and a dial leaps into life. The storage room fills with static, words pushing through it, barely audible.

"—Go left! On your left!—"

"Confirm we have the hostiles in custody, repeat, confirm we have—"

"—Drop your weapon!"

He snaps it off, satisfied.

He exits the storeroom, leaning on his good leg. The space beyond is in darkness, but his hand finds the bank of switches on the wall to his right. The lights flicker on, one after the other, illuminating a room so clean that the floor shines. Banks of medical equipment line the walls, their surfaces spotless, and his eyes land on the wheeled tray with his tools: the forceps, the clamps, the retractors, the syringes. His lone good scalpel, its edge still razor-sharp.

In the centre of the room is the operating table, its metal

surface glaring under the lights. Knox limps towards it, running his hand across its cold surface. He should clean it again. It wouldn't do for his patient to get an infection.

12

Riley

Mikhail's breath explodes out of him. He stumbles, trying to right himself, but his feet get tangled up with each other and he crashes to the ground.

His backpack splits down the side, disgorging its contents. A stinger flies out, skittering across the metal plating. A canteen, its top popping open, paints the wall dark with water.

Mikhail tries to get up, but Anna is already there. She drops a knee into the small of his back, locking him to the floor. He tries to roll over, swinging his arms behind him, striking at Anna.

"Nice try," Anna says, and drives a fist into the side of his neck. His body crumples. When I reach him, he's wheezing and clawing at the floor, his face a horrified grimace.

Anna flashes me a self-satisfied smile. She's sixteen years old, her blonde hair spilling out from under a green beanie, pulled down to just above her eyes. Her stomper jumpsuit is immaculate, with only the merest suggestion of dirt on the knees and elbows.

She waggles the slingshot in the air. It's a Y of welded metal, with a thick rubber strap hanging off the top end, bouncing off her wrist. One-Mile, she calls it.

"There," she says. "Easy."

Mikhail lashes out. Before I can yell a warning, he grabs Anna round the ankle and yanks her towards him. She topples backwards, howling in pain as her coccyx hits the deck.

Before Mikhail can rise, I'm on top of him, slamming my knee into his back. I reach for his arms, yanking them behind him. With my other hand, I reach into the pocket of my jumpsuit, then pull out a plastic zip tie and slip it around his wrists, cinching it tight. Mikhail's yelling is incoherent now, nothing more than cries of fury.

I keep my knee in the small of his back. Anna has risen onto her elbows. "I had him," she says, speaking to me but staring angrily at Mikhail.

"No, you didn't," I say.

"If I hadn't been here, you would've lost him."

"If *I* hadn't been here, he would've got away."

I grab Mikhail by the arms and pull. He groans as I yank him upwards, first to his knees, then to his feet.

"Mikhail, right?" I say. "You're under arrest. You don't have to say anything right now. You're entitled to a trial within three days. You're entitled to space in the brig until your trial. If you resist further, I'm authorised to subdue you. Have I made myself clear?" The words sound odd in my mouth. But I know I've done it right, just like Royo explained.

"Are we clear?" I say to Mikhail, when he doesn't answer. The look he gives me could turn a planet to ash, but he gives a terse nod.

I gesture to Anna. She rolls her eyes and grabs him by the other arm. As she holds him in place, I shove as much as I can back into his pack – may as well check for anything we could use as evidence. There's the canteen, plus a homemade stinger

44

that looks like it would explode if you tried to fire it, and a broken tab screen. There's a small cloth bag, and when I shake it over my palm a tumble of seeds fall out. Bean seeds, from what I can tell.

Anna picks up one up, shrugs, then drops it back into my hand. I shove everything back into the pack, zipping it shut. We march Mikhail back towards the stairwell. I call Carver, let him know where we're taking our prisoner. He says he'll meet us there.

Anna and I don't speak, but, then, we've never really had a lot to say to each other. She was Royo's final recruit to the tracer unit. To hear him tell it, she made waves up in Tzevya, where she was running with her own crew – *fresh blood*, he called her. And right from the start, she made a point of getting in my face.

The first time we met, at the stomper headquarters in Apogee, she walked up and challenged me to a race, right in front of everybody. She wouldn't leave it alone, even when I told her no. Royo had to tell her to can it before she backed off. Even then, she's always been distinctly cool towards me, always quick with a snide comment.

We're at the top of the stairs when Mikhail makes a break for it.

Anna's holding his right arm, and I've got his left. He hurls himself forward, out of our grip. Of course, he happens to be at the top of a flight of stairs with his hands bound behind him, so all he does is lose his balance, crashing down the steps. He comes to a skidding halt on the landing below, groaning in pain.

Anna has collapsed against the wall, bent over with laughter. I'm about to head down to him when she puts a hand on my shoulder. "No, wait. I want to savour this," she says between gasps for breath. "The worst escape attempt in history."

Despite myself, I can't help smiling back. We walk down and haul Mikhail to his feet. Anna leans forward and sniffs the air delicately.

"You smell," she says to me.

I reach up to rub my face without thinking. There's a streak of shit caked on my cheek, already dry and hard. I wipe it off, embarrassed, especially since Anna's skin is almost completely free of dirt. How she keeps herself clean in this place, I have no idea.

When we get to the brig, Mariana is on guard duty outside, leaning up against the wall. Carver's with her. He flashes me a thumbs-up when he sees Mikhail.

"Who's this?" Mariana asks. She's as squat as a turnip, with broad shoulders and piercing blue eyes. Unlike the other stompers, she doesn't carry a stinger, preferring an enormous iron bar strapped to her back in a homemade scabbard.

"He took a bunch of people hostage in the Recycler Plant," I say, pushing Mikhail towards her. She and Carver grab him, and Mariana taps at the keypad by the door.

"Oh yeah," she says. "A few of your friends are already inside, *hijo de puta*. Move."

Mikhail says nothing. Mariana glances over her shoulder at us. "Nice job."

"Nothing to it," says Anna, her arms folded. She sees my look, and rolls her eyes, before handing Mikhail's pack to Carver. He roots around inside it, muttering to himself. He takes the homemade stinger, the canteen and the little cloth bag, dropping them into his own backpack.

"Are you *trying* to get me fired?"

It's Royo. I turn to see him and Kev walking up towards us, and I've never known him to look more like a stomper than he does at that moment. He points a thick finger at me. "I asked you to go in and observe, not blow things up. It's

46

going to take *months* to repair the damage. And what the hell is that smell?"

"What do you think it is?" I say, too weary to argue. Anna smirks.

"Captain Royo," a voice says from behind us.

Royo looks up, and his eyes narrow in disgust. I look round, and realise why.

13

Riley

Han Tseng is striding towards us, hands clasped behind him.

The acting council leader for Apogee wears a long brown coat, buttoned to the neck. His eyebrows are like beetles, close together, always moving. Acolytes trail in his wake.

"What's he even doing here?" Carver mutters, turning away.

"Acting councilman," Royo says, as Tseng walks up.

If Tseng notices the tone, he doesn't say so. He doesn't even look at us. "That did not go well, Captain. I want a full briefing. Immediately."

"I'll have one of my men take you through what happened," Royo says, turning back to us. "Now, Hale—"

Tseng puts a hand on Royo's shoulder. The captain slowly turns around. His face is stone.

"What did they want?" Tseng says. "Food? Better accommodation? Whatever it is, this can't happen again. With the *Shinso Maru* coming back into our orbit, we're not going to have much chance to pander to these people."

"What's the *Shinso Maru*?" Carver whispers to me.

"Asteroid catcher ship," I whisper back. "Do you even *listen* in briefings?"

"They want Janice Okwembu," Royo says to Tseng.

"Then we should have given her to them. It makes no difference in the end. If we could just . . ."

Royo's look pins him to the spot. "How many people are on the new station council at the moment, exactly?"

Tseng's mouth flattens into a thin line. "The representatives from Tzevya and Gardens should be chosen soon. Until then—"

"Until *then*," Royo says, "there'll be no decision on any prisoners. You might want to read the station constitution sometime, acting councilman. Everybody's entitled to a fair trial by a full elected council. That includes her."

Right then, the lights above us flicker, and die, plunging us into darkness. Everybody goes quiet for a moment.

A moment later the lights flicker back on.

"I were you, I'd stop getting involved in hostage situations, and start worrying about the lights," Royo says to Tseng. He jabs a finger at the ceiling. "They're getting worse."

Tseng seems about to interject, but Royo pointedly turns his back. The councilman's eyes fall on me, and after a moment he stalks off.

"See what I have to deal with, Hale?" Royo says, lowering his voice. "I've got Han Tseng crawling up my ass, along with a pissed-off crew of waste technicians who now have to put an entire plant back together. Care to explain?"

"I'd like to hear this, too, actually," says Anna.

"Shut up, Beck," says Royo.

"How many hostages died?" I ask him.

"Don't get smart with me, Hale."

"How many?"

Royo gives a long sigh. "It's not just about getting the minimum amount done, Hale. You don't win just because everybody's still alive at the end of it."

"I'm going home now," I say, then turn and start walking, heading back towards one of the corridors.

"I'll come with you," says Carver.

My first instinct is to tell him no. After the chase I've just been through, I could use a few moments by myself, a slow jog back to my hab to warm down my muscles and calm my mind. But he's going in the same direction I am anyway, and I don't have the energy to protest.

Carver flips Kev a salute, nods to Royo and Anna, and jogs to my side. Nobody tries to stop us.

We accelerate to a jog. Carver sticks close, saying little, letting his breathing match mine as we head back towards Chengshi. As we reach the sector border, he indicates a nearby water point, its lone light gleaming in the darkness of the corridor. The water is cold and crisp, much better than it should be.

"Sorry about earlier," I say, wiping my mouth.

"Huh?"

"When I decided to climb on top of the vat in the plant. That was a really dumb idea."

"Oh. That." He gives a lopsided grin. His tugs at the goggles around his neck. "If I'd tried to stop you, you'd have just called me names and done it anyway."

"True."

"I have to admit I'm impressed. That was a very cool use for a sticky bomb."

"Thanks."

"Kind of genius, actually."

I can feel myself blushing. "Well, I wouldn't say *that*."

"Oh, I wasn't talking about you. I was talking about the bomb. Only a true genius could have constructed it."

"Really?" I say, raising an eyebrow.

"And you should see what I'm working on now," he says. "It's big. I mean, when this thing is done, it's going to change *everything*."

"Like SPOCS?"

Carver grimaces. "Forget SPOCS," he says. "It's not right yet. Too much static, and I can't figure out where it's coming from. No, this other thing is much cooler."

I think of Carver's requisitioned workbench at Big 6, the stomper headquarters. "I haven't seen you building anything at HQ?"

His smile gets wider. "Who said I've been building it at HQ?"

"So what is it?"

He opens his mouth – and then stops. His eyes drop. "Not ready yet," he says.

We fall silent as we walk away from the water point. When we cross the border, he turns to me. "Wanna go on an old-fashioned cargo run with me?" A small package appears in his hand as if by magic.

I look at him. "You serious? Being a stomper isn't good enough for you?"

"I—" He looks away. "I miss it. I didn't think I would, but I do. There's something about taking cargo jobs that's just *easier*."

I don't have a response to that, and I don't like the way he's looking at me.

"Do you ever go back to the Nest?" he says.

I get a flash of memory just then: a room, hidden between levels in Apogee, where our crew, the Devil Dancers, lived. Carver's workbench, Yao's mural on the wall, the pile of mattresses and blankets where we slept.

I shake my head.

"Would it make you feel better?"

51

I squint at him. "What?"

"Ever since the thing with your dad . . ."

"Don't."

He stops, aware that he's gone too far. Remembering what happened to my dad is still enough to stick a sour lump in my throat.

In order to save the station from Okwembu's insane scheme, I had to kill him, detonating his ship before it could collide with us. It's a memory I try to keep locked away, deep inside me.

He clears his throat. "I guess I'll see you tomorrow."

"Yeah."

He turns and jogs away, not looking back.

That's when the fatigue really hits me. It's all I can do not to slump against the corridor wall. But I know if I do that I'll never get up again. Better to keep going, to make it all the way home, where there is Prakesh and food and soft, cool blankets.

My SPOCS unit bleeps once. "Hale, come back. Dispatch calling Riley Hale."

It's a man's voice, one that I don't recognise. I toy with not answering, but that would mean pointed questions later. Royo's already pissed at me, and this wouldn't help matters.

I close my eyes and key the transmit button. "Copy, this is Hale."

"We have a 415 with your name on it, confirm code."

"A 415?"

The dispatcher pauses, as if he can't quite believe that I don't have all our call codes memorised. "Domestic disturbance. A woman's been hurt, keeps asking for you. Location is A1-B22."

Of all the things I've had to get used to as a stomper, it's how they talk about locations on the station. As a tracer, I thought of places with pictures and memories, but stompers think of them in terms of letters and numbers. My mind whirls

52

as I try to decode the dispatcher's words. A1 – that's Apogee, Level 1. And corridor B, junction 22 . . . that would be over by the heat exchangers, past where the silkworm merchant sets up. Not too far from here.

I really don't want to take this call. For a second, I nearly tell the dispatcher no. Then I see Royo's face in my mind again.

"Confirm code," I say. "On my way."

"Copy. Out."

I avoid the gallery floor, not wanting to run into Royo again, or any of the crew who have to clean up the Recycler Plant. It takes me a little longer than I'd like, and by the time I reach the silkworm merchant, the fatigue has settled into my legs, intertwining my muscles with cords of lead.

"Get 'em hot," the merchant intones, not looking up from the sizzling platter on his cart. "Hot silkworms, get 'em hot." I ignore him, jogging past, turning left at what I'm pretty sure is junction 22.

I thought I knew the station well enough, and that goes double for my home sector of Apogee, but I'm in a corridor I've never seen before. The walls are covered in a mess of red graffiti, tag on tag on tag. There's an odd smell, too – at first I think it's the silkworms frying, but it's sharper somehow, more unpleasant.

There's no woman here. There's no one at all.

I frown, slowing to a walk. The corridor splits again at the far end, and there's a door set into the wall. As I get closer, I see it has a faded sign bolted to it. ROOM 18.

I tap my wristband, annoyed. "Dispatch, this is Hale, come back."

Silence.

I look down at the wristband display – I'm on an open channel. I should be hearing sporadic stomper chatter, bad jokes, bursts of static.

Something's not right.

"Dispatch?" I say again. "Dispatch, I need a check on the location of that 415."

Movement. Behind me. I feel it before I see it, feel the air shift. I spin round, dropping into a fighting stance, and see a dark shape looming over me, a man, his features in shadow.

Every muscle in my body explodes with pain.

I go rigid, trying to scream. There's static everywhere now, crackling in fury, and then I'm gone.

14

Knox

Knox doesn't like the taser. It's a crude, ugly weapon, but it gets the job done.

Unlike the old models, which used electrode darts and conductor wires, this one is completely wireless – it uses field induction, with a ten-foot range. Put 2000 volts through someone, and the loss of neuromuscular control is instantaneous. He flexes the hand-held taser in his fingers, ready to give Hale another blast if she shows signs of coming round. She twitches, conscious, but only just.

Knox looks round to see if he's attracted any attention, but the corridor is silent. He drops down onto one knee, an awkward movement that nearly unbalances him. The syringe goes into Hale's neck – a sedative, not suitable for long procedures but more than enough to keep her down after the taser effects wear off.

He grabs her under the arms. Hale is heavier than he expected – he nearly drops her, and, with his bad leg, it's all he can do to lift her up. He has to pause, taking a few deep breaths before rolling her into his cart.

She hits the bottom with a thud, her body contorting. She groans, and he can see the muscles in her neck standing out. How could he ever think she was beautiful? She's as ugly as the rest of them, flawed, imperfect.

Working quickly, he buries her under the stinking rags. She becomes nothing more than a shape at the bottom of his cart, a piece of trash that no one but him would ever want. In the distance, he can hear the merchant's refrain: "Hot silkworms, get 'em hot, hot silkworms."

He looks up and down the corridor again, then swings the cart around, its wheels squeaking on the metal floor as he pushes past the wall of graffiti.

"Hey, you."

He closes his eyes, astonished and furious, then looks around. Three people have appeared in the corridor behind him. Two women and a man – gang members, judging from the identical black tears tattooed on their cheeks. The man is munching silkworms, stuffing them into his face from a dirty cloth bag.

One of the women tilts her head. "What you got in there?"

She and her companions start sauntering down the passage towards him, spreading out. He tries to keep any expression of his face. His hand is already in his pocket, where he keeps his knife. *There's no way you can fight them off, not a chance.*

But he can't let them discover Hale. He's worked too long and too hard to get her here.

The woman stops, wrinkling her nose. "Gods. You shit yourself or something?"

The other two pick up the scent. "Oh, that's rough," the man says, swallowing a mashed mouthful of silkworm.

Morgan Knox puts all the confused anger he can into his face. "Leave me alone!" he shouts at them. "They're listening to me! I'm talking to them right now!"

He's babbling, saying the first things that come into his head, but it's working. They're laughing, making exaggerated expressions of disgust. One of them digs in the bag, rooting up a handful of worms, then throws it at him. They smack into his cheek, dribbling down the front of his coat.

But they're leaving, still laughing among themselves. Knox waits until they're around the corner, then lets himself relax. His mask worked. It always works. Show the world your real face, and they'll tear you to pieces, but if you can disguise yourself, if you pretend you're not a threat, they'll let you pass on by. Pathetic.

He pushes the cart, shoving it with his thigh, getting it moving again. His surgery is close, and it's prepped and ready to go. Under the rags, his patient is silent.

15

Prakesh

It's only when he shuts the door to his office that Prakesh finds he can breathe again.

He sits down on the edge of his desk, letting his chin touch his chest. *That could have gone very, very wrong.*

After a moment, he drops heavily into his chair. The room itself is tiny, with no windows. The desk is battered and ancient, covered with tab screens and old drinks containers, taking up half the room. The only luxurious item is the chair behind it, a curved combination of mesh and black straps that fits his frame perfectly. It's much too comfortable – he doesn't think he'll ever get used to it.

The Food Lab used to be run by Oren Darnell, but he was killed in his insane attempt to torture the station. After it was all over, after Darnell was dead and Okwembu arrested, Outer Earth was hit by the worst food shortages in its history.

Prakesh and the other techs had already been working on creating genetically modified plants, and they stepped up their programme, working impossibly long hours to make plants that would grow faster, stronger, with more fruiting bodies.

And Prakesh was the one who cracked it. He'd worked all night on a hunch, focusing on the telomere caps at the ends of the plant nucleotides. He planted a single runner bean seed, then passed out, exhausted, leaning against one of the algae ponds. When he woke up, the bean plant was exploding out of the soil. A few hours later, still not entirely sure it wasn't a dream, he bit down on a fresh green bean.

After that, even Prakesh was amazed at the progress they made. The Food Lab was still being rebuilt, but the floor of the Air Lab became a tangled mess of grow-ops, and every day it seemed like there was a new plant variety. For the first time in months, Outer Earth had more food than it could ever need.

The techs told Prakesh that they were putting him in charge of the Air Lab, and they told the current head, a sleepy man named Archer, that he'd better step down. They even offered him Oren Darnell's old office: a huge space above the control room, with massive glass windows that looked out onto the trees.

He turned it down. Darnell had nearly destroyed Outer Earth and Prakesh didn't feel like occupying the man's old space. The office is now the most well-appointed storeroom on the station, which suits Prakesh just fine.

He doesn't need much space to work, anyway. He glances across the three tab screens on his desk: monorail shipping manifests that need signing off, fertiliser test results, a message from a tech asking him to resolve a work dispute. He picks up the test results first. If he can power through all this, he can go home, forget this day ever—

"Anybody home?" Suki says, sticking her head around the door. A frizz of red hair tickles her cheek. "We're going for drinks. All of us. That includes you, 'Kesh."

"I don't feel much like Pilot's," Prakesh says, thinking of the grimy bar in the station dock.

"Who said anything about Pilot's?" Suki says. "My brother's got these watermelons, right? He's been soaking them in home-brew for like a week."

Prakesh smiles. "You go on ahead. I might see you down there later."

He looks down, intending to get back to the test results, half of his mind already thinking about the dispute message. He looks up when he hears Suki crossing to his desk.

She perches on the end. She's one of the only techs – scratch that, one of the only people on the whole station – that he's ever seen wearing a skirt. It peeks out from the bottom of her lab coat, over black leggings. He can smell the soil on her as she leans in.

"You did good, boss," she says.

"Benson – is he—"

"Already took care of it. He's on suicide watch, and the psych docs are on it. He won't be back until they give him a clean bill."

He smiles thanks. "Good job with the Mark Six, too."

"How did you know that was going to work?"

He shrugs. "Didn't, really."

She smacks his shoulder, then hops off the desk. "Be down-stairs in ten, or I'll come and drag you out of here."

"I'm really OK."

"No way. You need a drink."

"I said *no*, Suki."

He doesn't mean for it to be harsh. But he can't control it – his tone just changes, dropping his voice low. He's instantly sorry, furious with himself.

But the last thing he wants to do is go and socialise, and Suki's closeness, the smell of her, has just made him think of Riley.

Suki looks like she's been slapped, but only for a second.

She composes herself, a neutral expression sliding back into place. "Well," she says. "I guess I'll see you later, then. You should bring Riley by sometime."

Her last sentence is said without enthusiasm, more of a reflex than anything else. The door clicks shut behind her.

Prakesh turns back to his tab screens, but finds he can't concentrate. He sits back, rubbing his eyes.

He'll never get used to Riley as a cop. Every time she suits up, it's like she becomes a different person. She moves with purpose, like the last six months haven't happened, and there's a look in her eyes every time she heads off to work. Like she can't wait to get out there, can't wait to *move*.

But when the jumpsuit comes off, she changes. Everything that's happened to her – her dad, Janice Okwembu, Amira – all comes rushing back. She's quiet at home, her mind off somewhere else. Prakesh has done his best, tried to fill her world with colour and love and as much good conversation as he can, but it's never enough.

And going home at the end of the day has lost its spark.

For the hundredth time, he bites back on his frustration. He tells himself to ease up. She just needs time. He shuts off his tab screens, one after the other. They can wait. He's going home, and he's going to see Riley.

He leaves the office, snapping the door closed behind him. As he walks down the passage, he wonders idly what she's doing at this moment.

16

Riley

I'm stuck in the nightmare again.

I'm running down the middle of a long, dark corridor, moving faster than I ever have before. There's a man standing at the end, his body cloaked in shadow. I can't see him clearly, but I know it's my father. It always is.

Any moment, I tell myself, I'm going to wake up. I'll be in our bed, with the blankets knotted at my feet and the mattress drenched in my sweat, Prakesh's arm around me and his hushed voice in my ear.

But it's different this time – the darkness isn't the darkness of a dream. And the pain rippling up from my legs isn't the dull, distant pain of exertion. It's horrible, needle-sharp, bigger than life.

My father raises his head towards me. His eyes – angry, confused, terrified – lock onto my own. I see my name appear over his face, blinking bright orange. *Riley. Riley. Riley.*

I jerk awake, a strangled cry bursting out of my throat. The dream vanishes. The pain doesn't.

This is all wrong. There's too much light. The surface under-

neath me is hard, nothing like the soft warmth of our bed. I
don't have to reach my hand out to know that Prakesh isn't
with me. I'm lying face down, one arm tucked underneath me.
My tongue is a dry, dead thing, and my throat screams for
water. I can feel my heart pounding, pulsing in my chest and
neck.

Slowly, my surroundings come into focus. I'm lying on a
metal table, gleaming under a single harsh light. The light is
focused, a tight circle on the table, and the rest of the room is
in darkness.

The pain in my legs chooses that moment to really wake up.
It's in my knees, biting and tearing. Before I can stop myself,
my hand is moving down towards my right knee.

My jumpsuit is gone. I've still got my tank top and my
underwear, but the flesh on my bare legs has risen in heavy
goose bumps. I push my fingers down my right leg, my movements jerky and shuddering. I have to find the source of that
pain. If I do that, I tell myself, I can get through this. My fingers
track across my skin. The pain isn't in my kneecap, it's deeper,
somehow . . .

Then I touch the tough, spiky thread of a stitch, and I scream.

I twist myself around, my fingers exploring in horrified
bursts. The stitches are on the back of my knees: tiny, thick
lines buried just under the surface of the skin, as if a parasite
has wormed its way into my flesh. The stitches run horizontally, tucked between the bones. They zigzag back and forth,
and the thick ends jut out at awkward angles. The flesh is
horribly tender, and even touching it lightly makes the pain
spike.

Get them out. Get them out now.

My fingers snag the end of the stitch on my right knee. I
grit my teeth, getting ready to pull.

"I wouldn't do that."

The voice is cold and businesslike, coming from the darkness at the edge of the room. I freeze, trying to squint past the light.

"Who's there?" I say

No answer.

How did I get here? My memory is in fragments. I was on a run – what was I doing? Was I delivering cargo? No – that's wrong. Then I remember the call, the empty corridor, the movement behind me.

Something flies out of the darkness, bouncing off my chest. I grab it just before it skitters away. It's a small bottle, off-white plastic, the blue label faded and peeling. Whatever's inside gives a dry rattle as I turn the bottle in my hands.

"You should take one," the voice says. It's a man's voice, soft and precise – the same voice as the dispatcher who called me over SPOCS.

The hell with this. I swing my legs off the table, calculating how far away the voice is, already lining up the angle of attack. I'm going to get whoever's out there and drag them into the light, make them take back whatever they—

The second I touch the floor, there's a horrid, searing explosion in my legs. I collapse, howling in pain, the pill bottle locked in my hand.

I raise myself up on one elbow, sweat pouring down my face, staring in horror at the stitches. They're already beginning to bruise, the skin fading from red to a sick, mottled purple.

My eyes are growing accustomed to the darkness beyond the pool of light. The room we're in is small, the surfaces dull metal and clean, white ceramic. There are banks of equipment lined up along the wall to my right: water basins, blank tab screens, shelves stacked with bottles and medical instruments. There's a small storage area leading off the main room, its shelves groaning with even more equipment.

The table I was lying on isn't a table, but a hospital bed, minus the mattress. There are restraints hanging off it, wrist and ankle cuffs, soft fabric hanging open. Dark brown stains run over the edge of the table. Blood

My blood.

Movement, at the far side of the room. I finally spot the owner of the voice. He's older than me, in his forties at least. He has thick black hair and a neatly trimmed beard. His right hand grips a battered cane, the metal worn down in places and the rubber foot cracked and peeling. His scrubs are white, and, except for the dots of dried blood on the front, they're impossibly clean. He wears dark pants underneath them; they hang loose on his left leg, as if it doesn't fill them properly.

He limps over, the cane hitting the floor with a soft thud at every step. He crouches down in front of me, his bad leg folding under him. Before I can move, his hand darts out, grabbing my right knee in a pincer grip, his thumb digging into the stitches.

I snap my head back and scream. It rips around the room, turning it into a horrific echo chamber.

"Take your medicine," he says.

He lets go of my leg. I scrabble at the bottle cap, hating myself for it. The tablets are blue, chalky and bitter in my mouth, accenting my raging thirst.

The man glances at my bare leg with a grimace. Before I can do anything, he produces a pair of surgical scissors, and calmly snips the stiff ends of the stitches off. The cool metal of the blade just touches my skin.

"There," he says. "Perfect."

He lifts his other hand. He's holding a thin, black, rectangular box, with a single raised button in the centre. No – not holding. It's taped to his hand. *What . . .*

"At the back of the knee," he says, tracing the stitches with the tip of his finger, "is a gap in the muscles called the *popliteal fossa*."

"I don't—"

"An object of up to half an inch in diameter can be inserted in the *popliteal fossa*, without interfering with the normal movement of the leg."

His eyes find mine. "There is a device in each of your *popliteal fossae*. Each device carries a small but extremely powerful explosive charge. If the devices detonate, there will be significant damage to surrounding tissue: bone, muscle, blood vessels, nerves. Assuming you survived the resultant blood loss, you would almost certainly lose both your legs below the knee."

I can't move. I can't look away from the box taped to his hand.

"Don't worry," he says. "The trigger mechanism takes quite an effort to push. I won't hit it by accident. But if you try and attack me, or do anything other than *exactly* what I tell you, I *will* push it. And when I do, it'll make that little squeeze of mine feel like a flu shot."

He stands, then limps over to one of the machines in the corner. "And the operation went perfectly. As I said, the devices will not inhibit your normal running motion in the slightest. There'll be some pain, but it might even be manageable – if you keep taking your medicine."

The sob comes out before I can stop it. He's lying. He has to be. I'm staring at my knees, as if I can make the stitches melt away.

"And just in case you're thinking about running to the hospital to have another doctor remove the devices, don't bother," he says. "I'm the only one who could do it without setting them off."

My lips are forming words, and I have to will myself to turn

66

them into sounds, pushing them past my shredded throat. "And what if I kill you first?"

In response, he pulls at his scrubs, undoing the knot at his side and lifting them away from his bare chest. There's a second box taped to his skin, nestling in thickets of wiry black hair. Two red wires run out of the box, burrowing into his skin, right over his heart. There are tiny, crusted rings of blood around the edges of the insertions.

"That wouldn't be a good idea," he says.

Very slowly, I get to my feet. Every movement sends a dull boom of pain echoing through me, radiating out from the stitches.

"Every second," he says, "the devices inside you send out a signal. The device on my heart answers it, and it only works as long as my heart does. If your devices don't receive that answering signal, they'll detonate. Keeps things honest, wouldn't you say?"

He turns back to the machine, bending over it.

"Look," I say. "I don't know who you are, or what you want. I don't understand why you're doing this."

"Do you remember Amira Al-Hassan?" he says, not looking round.

Amira. My crew leader, my mentor, my friend. The head of our tracer crew, the Devil Dancers – the fastest package couriers on the station. The woman who tried to murder me on Janice Okwembu's orders, who I killed in self-defence.

He looks at me, and taps his scrubs over his heart. "My name," he says, "is Morgan Knox."

I can just see the words stitched into the fabric, so faded they're all but vanished. "Amira and I were in love," he says. "And you took her away from me."

I stare at him. "Amira didn't have a . . ."

"You think she told you everything?" he says. His voice is

67

nothing more than a hiss, the hatred in his eyes spreading out onto his face, twisting it into a rictus of anger. "You think she shared every part of her life with you?"

His fingers twitch, brushing the detonator button. I choose my words very carefully. "She never said anything to any of her crew. I swear."

I pause. Could Amira have had a secret lover? It's possible – she certainly kept a lot of things from us.

"She loved me," Knox says after a moment, looking away. "I know she did. She delivered cargo to the hospital I was working at."

Remorse has crept into his voice. "She was beautiful. I felt like we could talk for hours. Every time I saw her . . ."

I can fill in the blanks myself. This is not good. Not good at all.

"It took me months to find out what happened, but I did," he says. "You killed her."

I take a deep breath. Every word feels like a step on a tightrope, like a single wrong move could send me plummeting into the abyss. "She was trying to kill me, so I fought back," I say. "It's what she trained me to do."

"I know," he says. "It's why I'm giving you a chance to make it through the next few days."

"I don't get it. You got to put these . . . these *things* inside me. What more do you want?"

"You?" he says. "You're not what I want. You killed her, and you deserve everything that's coming to you, but I'm after a bigger prize."

For the first time, he smiles. "I want you to bring me the person who brainwashed my Amira. I want you to bring me Janice Okwembu."

17

Riley

His words hang in the air between us.

"No way," I say.

"You're not exactly in a position to refuse."

"No way, because it's impossible. She's in max security. There's no way to get her out."

I can already hear Royo's words in my mind: *Everybody's entitled to a fair trial by an elected council. That includes her.*

"You'll just have to figure it out," he says. He turns, his leg making the motion awkward and jerky, and limps over to the other side of the room, yanking open a drawer and rummaging through it. "After all, if you can travel all the way through the Core and take out Oren Darnell, a prison should be no problem."

I screw my eyes shut, hoping that when I open them it'll all go away. It doesn't.

"If you feel you need more motivation," he says, "I could always perform the same procedure on one of your friends. Except in their case, I'd implant the charges directly into their brains. I haven't done neurosurgery in a while, however, so I may not remember which parts are safe to cut into."

The thought of Carver, of Kevin, of *Prakesh* being subjected to this monster gets my legs trembling again, and I have to consciously force them to stop.

"I need time," I say.

"You've got forty-eight hours," he says over his shoulder.

"It's not enough."

"That's your problem," he says conversationally, as he turns and walks towards me. "You should be grateful I'm giving you even that."

He hands me a small tube of cream, the surface cold to the touch.

"Of course, as your doctor," he says, "I advise you to get plenty of rest and keep yourself hydrated. You need to be performing at full capacity."

He gestures to the cream. "Apply that three times a day, and keep taking your painkillers. I like to make sure my patients are comfortable after an operation."

It's all I can do not to lash out at him. I have to contain my anger, my frustration, locking them away behind clenched teeth. "I run, OK?" I say. "I run, and roll, and knock into things. If I hit my knee too hard—"

"And are there many situations where you take a blow to the back of your knee?"

"You think I can run with these things inside me?"

"Of course. I designed them that way. Or were you not listening when I explained about the *popliteal fossae*?"

He points. "Your clothes are under the table."

As if in a trance, I pull my jumpsuit out, then sit down again to put it on. Bending my knees all the way hurts, an electric sting shooting up through my legs.

Knox tilts his head to one side, looking at me as I slip my arms into the sleeves. "Tell me – do you miss being a tracer?" he says. "Do you miss not being able to run where you like?"

When I don't respond, he says, "You couldn't keep the Devil Dancers together, could you? After Amira died. You didn't have her spirit. You had to go begging to the stompers."

"It wasn't like that. They—"

I lower my head. I'm not giving him anything more. He has way too much already.

"Here," he says. "I've charged it for you. You shouldn't have to worry about running out of power."

I turn back to look at him. He's holding out my SPOCS unit. It's strange that in the time I've been awake I haven't noticed its absence. I guess I still haven't got used to it.

"I need the wristband," I say. Knox hands it to me, and I snap it on.

"I'll turn that back on for you after you leave," he says. "I made a few changes to the basic design. I can listen into your conversations whenever I feel like it, and I will, so please keep it in your ear at all times. I've also added a small external microphone, so I'll know what's happening around you. I like to know that our little arrangement is just between us."

I stare at him. "How did you . . ."

He ignores me. "Don't take it out. Not ever. And don't think you can switch channels to get rid of me. Whatever you hear, I hear."

"And if I have to talk to you?"

"Just say my name. If I hear you and respond, it'll lock out anybody else on the channel. They'll think it's a glitch, and we'll be able to talk."

He gestures to the door. "Get going."

I don't need an invitation. But as I walk towards the door, each step sending prickles of pain shooting through my legs, I get an idea.

"You're bluffing," I say, turning back to face him.

"Am I?"

"I think it'll take a lot for you to hit that button. You want Okwembu, and so you need me."

He nods, as if he expected me to say this. "I need you functional, that's true. But go ahead. See what happens."

His smile is one of the most terrifying things I've ever seen.

"You won't do it," I say.

"But what else will I do?" he says. "You think I've told you everything? Test me, and you'll suffer in ways you can't even imagine."

With that, he closes the door in my face.

The sound of the door shutting fades away. I look around me: the walls in the corridor outside Knox's surgery are caked over with rust. A beam of light cuts across the darkness ahead of me, picking out dust motes hanging in the air.

I close my eyes, listening hard. I can just make out the cries of the silkworm merchant, far in the distance.

With my heart in my mouth, I go from a walk, to a jog, to a sprint. I expect to feel the devices Knox put inside me – in my head, I picture them grinding up against the bone, making themselves felt with every step. But he was right: they don't stop me moving. Not even a little. There's stiffness, and the pain is still there, only partially dulled by the drugs, but that's all. It's only when I hit the corridor with the red graffiti that I stop, one hand on the wall, nausea doubling me over.

This isn't happening. It can't be. *Knox is lying. There's nothing inside you.*

But I only have to focus on my knees to realise that that isn't true. It's not just the stiffness: there's a *pressure*, a feeling that wasn't there before.

I stand up straight, breathing deeply, taking my hand off the wall. The dust sticks to my fingertips, and the edge of my palm.

Write it down.

How could I not have thought of that? I can't talk about what's happened to me out loud, not with him listening in over SPOCS, but I can write it down – hell, I could use the dust on the wall if I had to. I could find Carver, or Royo, and tell them. After all, Knox can't *see* what I'm doing, and if I keep talking while I do it . . .

Then I remember what he said. That if he found out that I told anyone he'd blow the bombs. And then go to work on whoever I told.

Can I risk that? Can I put other people in danger?

Not yet. If it comes down to it, if time starts running out, then I'll tell someone. But for now, this is on me to handle.

I make myself focus. Okwembu. Just the thought of her – of what she did – causes a little bubble of hatred to rise up through me. Sometimes I go days without thinking about her, but she keeps coming back, like a cut on the roof of my mouth that I can't stop touching with the tip of my tongue.

I clench my hand into a fist. It's still on the wall, and my fingernails scrape across the metal. I pull it away, tiny jolts of pain shooting up my fingers, and jog away down the corridor, thinking about where I have to go next, and hating myself for it.

It doesn't take me long before I reach the max security brig. I have to work hard to convince the guards outside that I need to get in – there are eight of them, wearing full body armour. Can't say I blame them. There have been plenty of pissed-off people trying to get in, to take revenge for what the occupant put Outer Earth through.

But, for once, my reputation helps. The guards know me, they know what I've done, and they know my history with the person inside. It helps that I can fabricate a plausible reason to be there: I make out like it's to do with the Recycler Plant, that we need to make absolutely sure that it had nothing to do with *her*.

The inner door opens up into a narrow corridor. There are four cells in this particular brig, two on either side, spaced at wide intervals. The lights are harsh, not even letting a shadow escape, and the frosty air bites through my clothes. It's easy to find the cell I need. It's the only one that's occupied.

I reach the cell, and see her lying on the bed, her arms under her head. I rap hard on the transparent plastic covering the front.

Janice Okwembu rises up on her elbows, staring at me.

18

Riley

"Ms Hale," Okwembu says, moving to a sitting position on the bed.

The last time I saw her was in the control room in Apex, right after I had to kill my father. She looks, like she always does, as if she's in complete control. As if she was in a council meeting, or broadcasting a message to the station, rather than locked away in a cell. She was a computer programmer before she became a councillor, and it's easy to imagine her parsing real life like she did computer code, cool and logical and unhurried.

"I hear they're close to reforming the council," she says. "I assume that means I'll be on trial soon. I'd be lying if I said I was looking forward to it, but perhaps I can show people what I was trying to do. Tell them that I was acting in their best interests."

I barely listen to her. I'm scanning her cell, looking for any weak spots. The plastic is sealed tight into the walls and ceiling – no cutting through. The door release mechanisms are by the entrance, but there's no way I could spring them, and get her out, before the stompers outside gun me down.

She sees where I'm looking. "I assure you, I'm most secure in here. Just as well."

I don't look at her. "Shut up."

"Didn't I give you a choice? Didn't I acknowledge your sacrifice? Isn't that worth more than hatred from you?"

"It's worth nothing to me," I say, instantly furious at myself for letting her draw me in. The scar on my left wrist starts itching, and I have to force myself not to scratch it. Hell of a choice. Cut your wrists and be remembered as a hero, or take a bullet and go down in history as a traitor. Okwembu's twisted way of making things right.

Too bad I'd turned on the station's main comms and unlocked the entrance to Apex. Everybody heard what she'd done, and they came for her.

Just in time. I'd almost bled out.

She folds her arms. "I can only tell you how sorry I am so many times before it becomes pointless. If it were up to me, you would never even have been involved. All I wanted was to bring peace to Outer Earth."

"With you in complete control."

She laughs. "Do you know how the moon was formed, Ms Hale?"

I don't respond. There's got to be a weak link, something, *anything* I can use to get her out of there.

"A long time ago," she says, "another planet collided with the Earth. It shattered our newly formed crust. It turned every part of the Earth's surface into magma. An ocean of lava. And it created an enormous body of material orbiting our planet – rock, dust, debris."

I want to tell her to stop. I can't quite manage it. Okwembu seems to sense this, and takes a step towards the plastic barrier.

"Over time, that debris came together as one object – a ball of rock known as the moon, orbiting Earth and changing the surface. The oceans, when they formed, had tides. The impact from that other planet knocked our own a little off its axis, angling it towards the sun. From chaos, Ms Hale, comes life. From adversity, comes strength."

"That's a great story. I'll tell it to the people you nearly wiped out."

"I was only—"

"You can talk as much as you like. You're still in there, and I'm out here. All you have to look forward to is a trial, and the firing squad."

Okwembu says nothing. My shoulders are too tense, and it takes me a moment to realise that I've got closer to the plastic. I'm almost right up against it.

She raises her chin. "*That's* why you came to visit me."

"What?"

"You want me to be evil. You want me to be insane, because it would absolve you. It would mean that killing Amira and Oren Darnell and your own father wasn't your fault."

Okwembu puts a hand on the plastic. "Do you dream, Ms Hale? I do. And I'm sure my dreams are easier than yours."

My right hand twitches. Before I can stop myself, I slam a closed fist on the plastic barrier. The bang rockets around the cell block. Okwembu takes a step back, startled, a flash of fear appearing in her eyes. It vanishes an instant later, replaced by that cold stare.

My hand is humming with pain. I shake it out, not looking away from her, only becoming aware of the guards when one of them puts a firm hand on my shoulder.

They yank me away from the cell, pulling me by the arm towards the entrance. Then they shove me outside, and close the barred door behind me.

19

Knox

The picture of Amira Al-Hassan is old, taken when she was still a teenager. She hadn't yet developed the high cheekbones, the dark eyes. But it's unquestionably her. There's a warning in her face – she's staring back at the camera as if daring it to make a move.

It's the only file photo they had, and it took Knox a long time to track it down. He has it maximised on his tab screen, and his thumb traces the delicate curve of her jawline. What he wouldn't give to have a more recent picture of her. What he wouldn't give to have seen her one last time.

He puts the tab screen down, then pushes himself up from the hard chair in the corner of his surgery. He knew this would be the worst part of the entire operation. The waiting. Hale is in play now – sufficiently motivated, he hopes – but even she will take a few hours to come up with a plan.

His hand finds the tab screen again. Amira's photo has shrunk back down, and for the hundredth time he reads her file information, lined up alongside the photo. Born in Apex. Orphaned at an early age. Recognised by the council for bravery and personal sacrifice during the lower sector riots. Declined council post. Last known affiliation: Devil Dancers tracer crew, Apogee.

There's nothing else in the file. As he always does, Knox feels a surge of anger. The file doesn't record how she died. It doesn't record how she was *murdered*.

He should have said something to her when he had the chance. He remembers when he first saw her – over time, it feels as if the memory has grown sharper, new details popping up. The way she strode through the hospital doors, the way her eyes picked him out of the crowd instantly – and never left him. He remembers the impossible curves of her body, the shrug of her shoulders as she shucked her pack, the touch of her fingers when she passed him the cargo. He couldn't say anything, could do nothing but nod a mute thanks.

And, as it always does, the anger gives way to blind fury.

Riley Hale might have been responsible for Amira's death, but she was only in that situation because of Janice Okwembu. Okwembu got to her, poisoned her mind, twisted everything good about her. Hale was just the one who pulled the trigger.

His finger brushes the button on the unit taped to his palm. For a moment, the desire is there, burning hot. He wants to press it, right now, and listen over the SPOCS channel as Hale screams and screams and screams.

He lets his hand fall to his side. Not yet. He'll give Hale a little more time, then he'll use the hacked SPOCS receiver to call her. He hopes for her sake that she has something to tell him.

20

Riley

After the situation with Okwembu and my father, the few interim council leaders made a big deal about giving me my own place. Prakesh and I now live in Chengshi, on Level 3, a few minutes from the mess.

We were there maybe two days when the tributes started arriving.

I can see them now, even as I jog down the corridor. A sea of flowers, bags of food, trinkets and tokens, pushed up against the wall and stacked around the door. People just keep bringing them, and no matter how often Prakesh and I ask them to stop, they won't. Some even hang around, wanting to speak to me, to thank me for saving the station. I try to be as polite as I can, hating myself for wanting to tell them to go away, feeling selfish and petty for wanting to be left alone.

Then I see it. Graffiti, sprayed on the wall next to our door. HONOUR HALE.

That's new.

It's not the hastily sprayed, ragged graffiti you see elsewhere on the station. The letters are carefully formed in blue ink, with minimal drips. I stare at it, a mess of feelings mixing in my stomach. My chest is heaving, though whether in exhaustion or anger I can't tell. There's a tightness in my chest, too, and an odd tickle in my throat. Like I'm getting sick. The stitches in my legs feel bigger than they are, throbbing with pain, despite the pills.

I wait until my breathing has calmed, then push open the door to our hab.

It's a tiny room, no more than a few yards across, with an even smaller washroom attached. We haven't got around to decorating the bare metal walls, but we've filled the room with plants. Every spare surface is covered with pots and sprouting greenery.

My eyes are drawn to the pot by the wall. It holds an orchid, with bright red flowers and leaves curling like old paper. A twenty-first-birthday present from Prakesh. Genetically engineered. He said it would last years before losing a single petal, but it's already shedding.

Prakesh is sitting on the double cot, propped up against the wall, flicking through a hand-held tab screen. The hab is hot, as it usually is at this time of day, and he has his shirt off. A couple of rivulets of sweat run down his dark chest, pooling in his abdominal muscles.

"Hey you," he says, swinging his legs off the bed. I bury myself in his arms, resting my head on his chest. I can hear his heart pumping against my ear, and a bead of sweat tickles my cheek. I don't mind.

"Long day?" he asks.

"You have no idea."

"Same here."

The urge to tell him everything wells up again, and it takes me quite an effort not to say anything. Knox might be listening. Right now, just being close to him is enough.

I look up at Prakesh. "Don't kiss me, by the way. I think I might be getting sick."

He wrinkles his nose. "Kiss you? When you smell like that? What happened?"

"I'll tell you while you feed me."

"And if you're getting sick, you need to get checked out. You know how fast bugs spread in here."

". . . And when I get sick for real, I will."

"I'm not kidding, Ry. You might even be infectious already. How many people did you come into contact with today?"

I rub my eyes. "I don't know. A lot."

Truth is, he's right. Annoyingly so. Outer Earth is a million people packed closely together. You get so much as a cold spreading around, and whole sectors can get quarantined off.

"I promise I'll go get checked out," I say. "But I really am starving."

He rolls his eyes. "So demanding. Fine."

We eat sitting cross-legged on the bed. Crisp green beans and tofu, slathered with salty, tangy beetle paste Prakesh managed to score. The normality of it, the routine, makes me breathe a little easier. I can forget the stitches, forget the devices behind them.

I tell him about the siege – he grimaces when he hears about how close I came to being discovered, but he's known me too long to get angry or anxious. He tells me about what happened to the tech, Benson. Halfway through, I put a hand on his leg, squeezing tight. He puts his over it.

After he's finished, we're silent for a few moments. "There's new graffiti," I say.

"I saw. Maybe now they'll do an HONOUR KUMAR sign."

"They should." I'm not kidding, either. Before his break-through with the genetically modified plants, I barely saw him. There were times when he would come home, mutter two words to me and crash out for four hours before trudging back to the Air Lab. He and his team worked on the problem for months, struggling to get plants to grow fast enough to feed a million-plus people. For a while, the big joke was that prisoners in the brigs ate better than everyone else – they got the dud batches, the ones where the genes weren't quite right. Prakesh told me that it usually made them taste terrible.

After Prakesh cracked it, he was the centre of attention. For a while, I could slip into the background, which was just fine by me. But masterminding a new food supply isn't as flashy as saving the station from being smashed to pieces, and pretty soon the tributes started coming back.

"We sent out a new batch today," he says, swallowing a lump of tofu. "The fruiting bodies are even better this time around. Did you know that they've now got as much energy in them as two protein bars?"

"Oh yeah?" My mind is drifting, drawn back to that graffiti.

"Right. And—"

"How long do you think it'll be before they find someone else?" I ask.

He frowns. "How do you mean?"

I nod towards the hab entrance.

"It's not so bad," he says. "I get to live with a hero."

"I don't feel like a hero." I feel selfish admitting it, the words bitter in my mouth.

He sighs. "Riley, we keep going through this. *None* of what happened was your fault. You don't have a single thing to be guilty about."

Suddenly, I want nothing more than to be under a blanket, with my arms wrapped around him. I reach out and stroke his cheek. "Come to bed."

"Oh no," he says. A little bit of the spark has come back into his eyes. "First, you need to clean up."

"I hate air showers."

"And I hate going to bed with someone who smells like shit. Literally. And then you're going to go and get a throat swab at the hospital."

I know better than to argue. I slip the top of jumpsuit off, then pull my sticky tank top up over my head. It gets stuck, and Prakesh has to help me yank it over my arms. Before I can bring them down, he reaches in, his fingers brushing my face—

—And plucks my SPOCS unit from my ear.

I freeze, my eyes wide. Then I snatch the unit back, jamming it in. I can't describe the terror I feel at this moment. All I can think of are Knox's words: *Don't take it out. Not ever.* My legs are itching – I came this close to pulling off the bottom half of my jumpsuit. If Prakesh had seen the scars . . .

Prakesh gives me a weird look. "You're off duty, right?"

"Don't ever touch my SPOCS. Not *ever*." It takes a moment before I realise that I'm shouting, mimicking Knox's words. I fumble in my jacket, yank open the bottle of pain pills, shove one into my mouth, not caring that Prakesh can see.

"Whoa," he says. "What's going on? What's got you angry?"

"I'm on call," I say, my mind scrambling for a reason. "I can't be out of touch. Gods, Prakesh, you should know that."

I'm too embarrassed to look at him. My reaction came from the gut, a jagged bolt of animal fear that shot through me before I could stop it. What's worse is that Morgan Knox doesn't deserve that fear, especially since I'm still not completely convinced he'll really blow the bombs.

I lie back on the bed, staring at the ceiling, willing my legs to stop hurting.

"What are you not telling me?" Prakesh says.

"Nothing. I'm fine."

"The last time you said that, I ended up getting kidnapped by Oren Darnell. Remember?"

It sounds like a joke, one of his snappy lines, but when I look over I see that there's no laughter on his face. There's another expression – one I don't like a bit.

"Don't keep secrets from me, Riley," Prakesh says. "I don't keep any from you. What's going on?"

"Just stomper work. You know I can't tell you everything we do."

"More like you can't tell me *anything* you do. And you've spent more time with Aaron Carver than anyone else. Even I know that, though of course you won't tell me."

I stare at him. "The hell is that supposed to mean?"

He lies back, his eyes closed. "Nothing. Forget it. I just didn't like you yelling at me, is all."

"Carver's a friend. We work together. You know that."

I lie down, and put a hand on his chest. He wrinkles his nose at the smell, but says nothing.

"I'm sorry," I whisper.

At that moment, the tiredness crashes down on me. I can feel Prakesh's chest rising and falling, and the rhythm calms me. It occurs to me that both of us forgot about me going to the hospital, but then I decide that I'm just too tired to care.

I try to sleep, and don't quite manage it. I get up, have an air shower, slip into clothes that aren't caked with dirt, then slide in next to him to try again.

You've got to be able to tune out to sleep on the station. It's never truly quiet here, and even now I can hear the vast metal hull groaning and clicking as Outer Earth continues its slow, spinning orbit. Let your mind drift to the edge of sleep, and it can sound like a living thing, breathing and hissing and stretching blackened metal limbs.

Just before I drift off, there's a whisper in my ear, horribly alive.

"Are you there, Hale? Answer me."

Knox.

Moving as carefully as I can, I swing my legs off the side of the bed. My head is pounding, razor blades scraping across my throat. I stumble to the door, then slip out into the corridor. It's deserted, and I sink down against the wall.

"I'm here."

Another burst of static. Then: "You need to respond faster next time. Something we're going to have to work on, aren't we?"

"I was asleep. That's all."

"Sleeping? I do hope that means you've figured out a way to bring me what I want."

I rub my eyes. "I need more time."

"You're not getting it. Tell me your plan." The eagerness in his voice makes my skin crawl.

"Working on that," I say.

"Work faster."

"Go to hell."

"Go to hell, *Sir.*"

I shut my eyes.

"Say it."

My hand has strayed to my right knee, touching the unbending end of the stitch. He won't blow them. He can't. They might not even be explosive. They might be dud pieces of metal, put there to trick you.

Keep telling yourself that.

"Go to hell, Sir," I mutter.

"Better. You'll have to learn respect if we're going to work together. Go back to sleep, Riley Hale. You have a big day tomorrow."

The line cuts off, leaving me in the black silence of the corridor.

21

Riley

I don't think I'll ever get used to the noise in Big 6.

That's what we call the stomper headquarters. It used to be the operations centre for all six station sectors, but now it's just a satellite office. A mess of fizzing lights and mouldy food containers, a place that nobody bothered to rename.

The stompers stand around desks, lean back on chairs, scream out orders and jokes and questions. The sound is like a forgotten engine, one which has spun up to a furious roar. Snatches of speech whiz past me as I cross the floor.

"Hey, Sanchez, you got any info on that pusher in—"

"—teenage girls up in Tzevya. He was whoring 'em out for tofu, if you can believe that."

"We need six bodies to run a show-and-go in Gardens. Don't make me ask for volunteers."

Anna's the first tracer I see. She's drinking from a canteen with her feet up on one of the desks, her ankles crossed and her shoes unstrapped. She ignores me, but Royo doesn't. He and Kev are standing on the other side of a battered desk. The

87

wall behind it is so smudged with marker that it doesn't even reflect the glaring fluorescents any more.

"You're late, Hale," he says.

"Sorry," I say. Kev winks at me, a gentle smile on his face, then turns back to Royo. I grab the canteen out of Anna's hands and take a long slug of water.

"Get up on the wrong side of the bed this morning, did we?" she says.

"Bad dreams," I reply, wiping my mouth and tossing back the canteen.

It's not even close to the truth. The dreams weren't bad at all. They didn't even exist. I just stared at the ceiling all night, running over the layout of Okwembu's prison again and again, looking for any possible way to break her out. Twice I had to get up to take another pain pill, and it was all I could do not to burst into tears.

When I woke up, Prakesh was gone. The other side of the bed was cold.

At least I don't feel sick any more. As I got out of bed, I noticed that the tickle in my throat was gone. The flesh on the back of my knees has swollen slightly – not enough to stop me running, but enough that I feel it every time I move.

"What's on the board today?" I ask Anna, more out of habit than anything else.

"Now she's talkative," she says to herself. "No idea. I haven't talked to the Captain yet."

"Wouldn't advise it on an empty stomach," says Carver, sauntering in through the door with his jacket tied round his waist. He tosses me a protein bar, handing one to Kev as he walks past. I smile thanks. The slab is sickly sweet, but it fills me up.

Royo waves us over. "Everybody here? OK. We've got the *Shinso* coming back into orbit tomorrow, so I need everybody on high alert. You know what this place is like when there's a fresh asteroid. Now, the regular officers're taking care of most things today, but we've had a report of a disturbance up in Gardens."

Gardens. I feel a pang of concern for Prakesh, but it passes as quickly as it came. If the last year has taught me anything, it's that he can take care of himself.

"Why can't the stompers in that sector deal with it?" says Anna. "Why do we have to clean up their mess?"

"We already had officers go in, but they haven't reported back. Probably a glitch on the feed, but we're not taking chances here."

"Any word on our Recycler Plant guys?" says Carver

Royo shrugs. "Not that I've heard. The one in charge, the one Beck and Hale took down. He hasn't said much. Anyway, we've got more pressing things to deal with."

Royo turns back to the wall. "After you see what's going on in Gardens, I need you to . . ."

I'm not listening any more. An idea is slowly starting to take root in my mind – maybe the first good idea I've had since this all started.

"Captain?"

He doesn't look round. "What?"

"I was thinking. Why not let me stay on the hostage case?"

"I see I'm going to spend the day repeating myself," he says, looking over his shoulder. "It's a waste of time."

"What if they were just the start? There's a lot of hate for Janice Okwembu. Maybe this isn't the last hostage situation we'll see."

"No way, Hale. You go where you're needed. And, right now, that's Gardens. I'll assign someone else to the hostage thing."

"Just let me do a little digging. I'll head right up to Gardens afterwards, I swear. Surely three tracers'll be enough?"

I have never longed more to tear the SPOCS unit from my ear and smash it on the ground. I have to make this work. If I'm going to make it through the next twenty-four hours, I *need* to get away from regular stomper duties.

Royo sighs. "Fine. Do what you have to do. It's not like you idiots listen to me half the time anyway."

"Now that isn't fair, Cap," says Carver. "We listen to you at least three-quarters of the time. Maybe more."

Royo points at me. "But when you're done, Hale, you get up to Gardens double-time."

While Carver and Kev fill up the reservoirs in their packs from the Big 6 water point, I sit down in front of one of the tab screens. There's a bank of them on the wall – probably the largest number of working screens on the station, outside of the control room in Apex. I grab one of the battered chairs from a nearby desk. Its wheels have long since been cannibalised for other things, and its legs screech as I drag it across the floor. That's when I realise that I don't have my stinger with me – I must have left it back in the hab. I feel a guilty relief. I never liked the thing, never liked feeling it against my hip.

Carver puts a hand on my shoulder and squeezes. "See you in a few?"

I put my hand on his. "You know it."

They head out. Pulling the chair up to a screen, I call up our database.

Back when I was just a tracer, I thought I knew a lot about how the stompers worked – I'd tangled with them often enough. But I didn't know about their database. The official name for it is SCRD – Station Criminal Records Database, as the logo flashing up in front of me says – but you won't find a stomper on the station who calls it that. To us, it's just the Wall of Shame.

Aware of Royo hovering, I tap the name 'Mikhail' into the system. It's not a lot to go on, but as the results pop up, blinking onto the screen one after another, it becomes clear that there are only a handful on the station. It takes me no more than a few seconds before I'm looking at the right one – that snide face framed with greasy hair is impossible to miss.

"Mikhail Yeremin," says Royo from over my shoulder, making me jump. He scans the rest of the information – what little there is. "Forty-six years old, born Tzevya sector, no known kin. Dock worker. That's the thing about the Wall, Hale. It hardly gives you anything useful. He's only in the system because he's been arrested before." He leans in closer. "Water racket."

Royo taps his knuckle twice on Mikhail's picture, accidentally making it full-screen.

"Stop that," I say, minimising the picture.

Royo clears his throat. "Sorry. I'll leave you to your detective work."

I stay on Mikhail's entry until I can see that Royo is absorbed with what he's doing – giving another stomper hell, it looks like – and then I bring up the search bar. I tap KNOX, MORGAN into it and hit *Go*.

Until now I've been focused on doing what Knox says. What if I can find something on him? A weak spot I can use? Not that I'm holding out much hope. I'm almost certain that he won't be in the system.

But, to my surprise, there's an entry – and the Wall has far more on Knox than it did on Mikhail.

I scan the words. Knox, Morgan Joseph. Forty-two years old, born in New Germany. Qualified as a medic from the sector hospital at age twenty-two, specialising in musculoskeletal surgery. Assigned to work in Medical Unit 262, wherever that is. And he has a record: stole drugs from the same hospital he qualified at. It's recent – no more than a few months ago. Spent a few days in the brig, medical licence revoked. Last known habitation is a corridor code close to where his current surgery is. No known kin. Arresting officer: Royo, Samuel.

I glance over at Royo. He's talking with another stomper, bent over one of the desks. The only person I know who's had contact with my nemesis, and he may as well be a million light years away.

The idea unrolls itself slowly. What if I could take Knox out of action from afar? Once he's in the brig, he won't have that remote any more.

Putting out an arrest warrant for Morgan Knox is the work of a few taps. So is entering the last place I saw him, and the reason for the warrant – drug trafficking, of course. I punch in the corridor and level location, and sit back, exhaling deeply. There. At some point today, a dispatcher will get over SPOCS and ask a couple of stompers to swing by that room of his.

The question is whether he'll blow the bombs as soon as they do. I don't think he will, not if I'm still out there. That's *if* his threat is actually real in the first place, and he isn't playing me.

It's a gamble. But it doesn't feel like a reckless one.

I stare at the screen, thinking hard. The arrest warrant is a start, but I still need to work on breaking Okwembu out, just in case.

My eye lands on *Medical Unit 262*. Something about it kicks my mind into gear.

Working quickly, I pull up the location. It's in the Caves – the run-down, cramped, overcrowded part of the sector that anybody who wasn't born there tries to stay away from. Kev's parents live there, but his family aren't the only people I know in that part of the station. There's someone else.

He might not know how to take down Knox.

But if it comes to it, he might be able to help me break Okwembu out of prison.

22

Prakesh

The first thing Prakesh sees when he walks into the Air Lab is Suki looking apologetic. The second thing he sees is Han Tseng.

The councilman is standing over by one of the algae pools, his arms folded, a thunderous expression on his face. Prakesh groans inwardly. His sleep was full of ugly dreams, and it's left him groggy and irritable.

And now he has to deal with Tseng. Great.

No point avoiding it. He squares his shoulders, then walks over. The councilman watches him approach – he's actually tapping his foot, as if Prakesh is an errant student. Above them, the leaves of the giant oaks move gently in the blowback from the air exchangers.

"Councilman," says Prakesh.

"No more putting this off, Kumar," Tseng says. "I want you to show me the new security measures now."

"You've picked a bad day, Sir." Prakesh keeps walking, moving between the algae pools. "We've got test results due in from a new strain of soya, and I have a dozen other things on my desk that need attention."

"Three months ago, you said you'd be implementing stricter controls," Tseng says, striding after Prakesh. "Chain-of-custody signatures, technician background checks, closer collaboration with the protection officers." He ticks each item off on his fingers.

Prakesh has to suppress the urge to roll his eyes. "If you make an appointment with Suki, I promise I'll give you a full briefing." He looks for Suki, but she's vanished.

"We can't afford another robbery," Tseng says. "The people of this station need to know that it's unacceptable behaviour."

That's one way of putting it, Prakesh thinks. Three months ago, just before Prakesh had his breakthrough with the genetically modified plants, a shipment of food was stolen. In this case, it was a dud batch, a failed experiment, destined for the brigs in each of the station sectors. A group of assailants managed to board the monorail, stop it in the tunnel and make off with several crates of food. Prakesh was amazed that it hadn't happened sooner.

They never caught the people who did it, and as far as Prakesh was concerned it hardly mattered. With more than enough food for everybody on the station, securing shipments had slipped way down the priority list. But still Tseng had been onto him, demanding that he take steps.

Tseng is still speaking, lecturing him on how to do his job. "Actually," Prakesh says, cutting the councilman off in mid-flow. "I have a meeting with the local protection officer captain this week. We'll be addressing these issues." Thinking: *Better make an appointment as soon as this idiot leaves.*

Tseng folds his arms. "Really?"

"That's right." He places a hand on the councilman's elbow, starts guiding him back towards the entrance.

"Yes. Well," Tseng says. "I expect a full report by the end of the week."

"You got it," Prakesh says, as they reach the open area by the entrance. The sliding door is twenty feet high, hastily cut through the existing wall. Before Oren Darnell, you got to the Air Lab by going through the equally cavernous Food Lab. That changed when Darnell torched the latter.

The councilman stalks off, not bothering to say goodbye. Prakesh watches him go, then rubs his eyes, massaging away the gritty sleep. He would do anything to blow off today. The thing with Riley is still going round and round in his mind – he can't understand what got her going last night. He's never seen her lash out like that before, not at him, anyway . . .

Raised voices, outside the doors. Prakesh looks round, and sees two stompers talking with Tseng. They're pointing to the Air Lab, and Prakesh doesn't like the looks on their faces.

He starts walking, picking up his pace. He's thirty feet away when Tseng charges towards him, shouting, "Seal the door! Seal it now!"

95

23

Riley

By the time I get to the Caves, a deep itch – so ingrained it feels like a part of my body – has set into the backs of my knees. It takes every ounce of will I have not to yank the stitches out.

As I get close, I slow to a jog. My skin crawls at the thought of having to talk to Knox again, but it has to be done. He'll still be there – I've issued arrest warrants before, and they take a while to move through the system.

I turn to what I hope is a dead channel. "Knox," I say, as quietly as I can. The SPOCS unit hums and clicks in my ear. There's a burst of static, and then a stomper says, "Come back? Didn't catch—"

Then Knox's voice is in my ear, cutting the stomper out. "What?"

"I'm going to get help for the thing you asked me to do," I say. Then, taking a deep breath: "Someone I think might be able to . . . you know."

"No, I don't think I do," he says, and his voice is deathly quiet. "My instructions were that you were to tell no one else. You need to learn to listen."

"I'm serious," I say, dropping to one knee. There's a pool of liquid – oil, judging from the colours on its surface – puddling on the floor, and I only narrowly avoid it. "I can't do it on my own. And I won't tell him about you, I swear."

"Who?"

"You won't know him."

"Answer the question."

When I tell him, Knox barks a laugh in my ear. "Him? He's useless. He'll never help you."

"I'm going to ask him anyway."

"Tell him whatever you want. Just remember: time's running out, Riley."

Not if the arrest warrant catches up with you, I think. I rise to my feet, and walk on.

When Amira and I tried to get into the Caves a year ago, we were met with suspicion and bared weapons. They've always seen themselves as slightly apart from the rest of the station – anybody who tries to muscle in, any gang that wants to get a foothold, finds themself going home minus a few members and a couple of important body parts.

When Oren Darnell took over the station, Caves drew in on itself, full lockdown. This time, the big metal door – the only way in or out – is wide open. The corridor beyond it is poorly lit, the walls marred with ancient, scabby graffiti.

I step through. A hand comes out of the darkness, grabbing my shoulder.

"Stomper," says the person attached to the hand. He keeps his face in the shadows.

"I'm not here on stomper business," I say.

His grip tightens. "Better not be." He releases me, pushing me backwards, and goes back to where he was sitting, on what looks like an upturned barrel. I still haven't seen his face.

"I'm looking for Syria," I say.

97

The man in the shadows waves a hand in the general direction of the rest of the universe.

I hold my ground. "Help me out here."

The man grunts. "You need Syria's help? You must be in bad trouble."

"The worst kind."

There's a long silence. Then he says, "1-E. Down by the water point."

As I walk away, he shouts, "Better *not* be stomper business, or I stomp you, you get me?"

"Got you," I mutter, pushing my way through a group of sullen women milling around a corner in the corridor.

The water point is the closest thing that the Caves have to a gathering place. The lights in the ceiling burned out a long time ago, never to be replaced, and the only illumination comes from small fires, scattered across the floor. The big water tank bolted onto the wall towers over a line of people topping up their canteens. Small groups hang around nearby, playing cards, talking, laughing in quiet bursts. I can feel eyes on me the second I draw close, and not all of them are friendly.

Syria has his head bent, greasy hair falling over his face, shoulders bent and angular. Down on one knee in a card game, every other player watching to see what he does. As I get closer, I see they're playing acey-deucy, and that Syria already has three twos down. One more, and he wins the game.

"Show 'em," mutters one of the players.

"He got nothing but odds," says another.

"Odds and faces."

"I got what I got," says Syria. "You just sit there while I think it over."

It's impossible to make out his face, hidden under the strands of greasy hair. I hover on the outside of the circle, willing people not to notice me. I'll talk to him when the game's finished, when he's—

Syria looks up and sees me.

"Everybody clear out," he says quietly.

The other players have seen me by now, eyeing me warily, but now they turn back to Syria, cursing and complaining. He silences them with a wave. "I *said* clear out."

In seconds, they melt away. And I become aware of something else: no one is looking at me any more. I've gone from being an object of interest to not existing. That's what happens when you go and speak to the single most powerful person in the Caves – a man who, if you believe the stories, has never set foot outside his sector.

I don't know if Syria is his first name, or his last. He's not a gang leader, or a power-hungry maniac like Oren Darnell. He just keeps the Caves safe. I did one or two deliveries for him while I was with the Devil Dancers, although he's not what I'd call a regular client.

Syria folds his feet under him, sitting cross-legged. He shuffles the cards, and I see he's wearing a thin, highly polished silver ring on his hand. It seems out of place amid the dirt and grime on the rest of his skin. I sit opposite him, my legs complaining as I do so. He says nothing.

"How are you, Syria?" I say.

It's a few moments before he replies. "You're a stomper now. Got nothin' to say to you."

"Come on, Syria," I say, feigning bravado I don't feel.

He says nothing. I exhale slowly. No point trying to convince him that the stompers aren't about to come busting in here. Better just to be out with it.

"I need your help," I say.

"And what exactly do you think I can help you with?" He

looks up at me again. The spark in his eyes has faded a little, replaced by an amused curiosity.

I look behind me, at the queue of people by the water point pretending to pay no attention to us. "Can we go somewhere private?" I say.

"Don't get cute." His eyes find me again. "You got two choices. You can speak your piece here, the whole of it, no lies, or you can get out. There's a third option, but it's not one you want to pick."

I lean in as close as I can. "I want your help to break Janice Okwembu out of the brig."

Syria rockets to his feet. Before I can react, he grabs me by the arm, marching me away from the water point.

"What's the deal?" one of the men yells.

"Back later," Syria says. He rips open a door, and shoves me inside. It's a dormitory hab, with neat rows of bunk beds lined up along the walls. Drying clothes hang from lines strung wall-to-wall, and there are kids' toys underfoot. The air is thick and muggy.

Syria leads me to a bed, and pushes me down to sit on it. He stalks around the hab, and, when he's satisfied that we're alone, he sits down opposite me.

For a long time, neither of us says anything. My SPOCS unit is completely silent.

"Do you have any idea," Syria says, "of what would happen if any of my people heard you say that?"

"I—"

"They've been wanting to take a crack at her for months. It'd be like putting a torch to a line of fuel."

"I don't understand."

"Oh, don't you? A stomper, with inside knowledge of the whole system, comes into Caves talking about a prison break. They'll either think you're on a sting operation, in which case

Rob Boffard

you won't make it out of here alive, or they'll go off half-cocked, and get themselves killed. Not to mention bringing every stomper on Outer Earth into the Caves, looking for payback."

He sits back on the bed, his shoulders sagging, as if he used up all his energy on the outburst. "What are you doing, Riley? I know what happened to you. Everybody does. But you aren't thinking straight."

I look down at the floor. There's a chalk drawing on it, a child's drawing, all big heads and misshapen eyes. A man and a girl, holding hands.

I stare at it, picking my next words carefully. I don't dare tell him about Knox – not yet. But I have to make him help me. It's the only idea I've got.

"And why shouldn't we go get her?" I say. "She's been in there for months. There's no council to convict her. It's time she got what's coming."

"Were you not—"

"Your guys are right. I *do* have inside knowledge. I could protect you. I could make sure the stompers never come near the Caves."

He looks at me, his eyes giving away nothing.

Eventually, he shakes his head. "Sorry. There's no way. You get safe passage out of the sector, but that's all I'm—"

Someone starts yelling for him in the passage outside.

"Busy," he shouts.

But there's more sound coming from outside. Panicked voices, the noise of running feet. Syria looks towards the door, starts to rise off the bed.

The shout comes again. "Syria, get out here!"

Syria takes off, sprinting out of the room. I'm right on his heels.

The line by the water point has scattered, people running in all directions – all except one man, on his hands and knees. He wears a dirty, tattered flight jacket, his long hair hanging down around his face.

He's coughing – huge, hacking bursts. And every time he coughs, he sprays thick, black, shiny tendrils from his mouth.

24

Prakesh

Prakesh gets to the doorway a second before Tseng does. He knows what Tseng means to do – there's a control panel on the other side of the door. You need a code to access its functions, but you can use it to seal the Air Lab. A safety precaution, built in when the door was installed.

"Whoa, hey," Prakesh says, slamming his hand around the door frame. "What's going on?"

Tseng stumbles to a halt, staring daggers at Prakesh. Stompers are closing in behind him – there are more now, Prakesh sees, at least half a dozen.

"Emergency situation," Tseng says. "Step aside. We need to seal the lab."

"Not a chance," Prakesh says. He knows he's on shaky ground – technically, a station council member can make that particular call. But there's no way he's letting them seal the techs in. Not without knowing why.

"Step *aside*, Kumar," Tseng says, looking over his shoulder at the stompers. "This isn't your concern."

"Yeah, don't care," says Prakesh. It's then that he sees the

103

tracer unit, running towards them from the far end of the corridor. Kev is in the lead, elbowing his way past the other stompers. Carver is trailing him, along with the other girl Riley works with – *Anna, that's her name.*

All three of them are wearing face masks. The masks are thin plastic, covering their mouths and noses and chins.

"Sir," says one of the other stompers – a thin man with an even thinner mouth. "We need you to step back, and secure your employees."

"Not until—"

"*Now.*"

Prakesh can feel the other technicians congregating behind him. He looks over his shoulder; they form a loose semicircle, dozens of them, staring in confusion at the standoff. They've seen the masks, too, and they're whispering to each other, already nervous. He has to get control of this now.

"Look," he says, spreading his hands. "You need to tell me what's going on. If you're going to shut us in here, then we should at least know what's happening."

"Virus."

Everyone turns to look at Anna Beck, jogging to a halt. She rests a hand on Kev's shoulder, bent over, holding her other hand at her side.

"Officer," Tseng says, all but hissing the words. "You're not authorised."

Anna ignores him. "It's bad," she says, looking at Prakesh. "People coughing up black gunk everywhere. It was in the mess first, but we're getting reports from all over."

Prakesh hears gasps from behind him. He lets out a shaky breath. "Just in Gardens?"

"Other sectors, too."

"Might not be a virus," says Kev. He shrugs when everybody turns to look at him. "Just saying. Might be a bacterium."

Prakesh briefly closes his eyes. It's a nightmare. Virus or not, even non-lethal diseases can spread like wildfire in Outer Earth. This one does not sound like a non-lethal disease. And if there are multiple infection sites, multiple vectors . . .

He flashes back to the previous night, to Riley's sore throat. He dismisses the thought immediately, refusing to entertain it. *She's OK. She has to be.*

"Listen," he says. "No one's infected here, right?" He looks around at his team, who shake their heads. "If you give us face masks, we can keep working."

"P-man," says Carver, and Prakesh rankles at the nickname. "You shouldn't have this door open. We can't afford to have any techs coughing up black slime. They're too important."

"We're fine, Aaron."

"Don't be an idiot."

"You're *not* locking us in here."

Before Prakesh can blink, Carver is in his face. He crosses the floor in seconds, fists clenched.

"Get inside. Now." Carver says. His voice has gone deathly quiet.

"Or what?" Prakesh says. Deep down, he can see Riley's face.

Tseng is almost apoplectic. "That's enough!" he says.

Anna steps between them, turning to Carver and putting a firm hand on his chest. "We do *not* have time to argue over something like this. Let them shut the doors, and we can get out of here." The other stompers are crowding in, as if they trust Carver to handle things, but only to a point.

"Stay out of this, Anna," Carver says, trying to push her aside. She plants her feet, not moving. He pushes harder, and, this time, she shoves back, her hands balled into fists.

Carver stares at her. "Are you insane? This should not be this big an issue. We need these people to keep us alive, so we have to get them locked down. It's the most important thing we can do."

"Important?" Anna hisses. "More important than what's happening in the rest of the station? In Tzevya? My *family* are up there, Carver . . ."

Kev steps in. "And mine are in Caves. We all have people we need to take care of."

"You heard your friends, Aaron," says Prakesh, pointing a finger at Carver over Anna's shoulder. "Go find the ones who actually need your help. Don't bother the ones who can handle themselves."

The impasse is broken by several sharp beeps. Tseng is at the door's control pad, his finger hammering on it. There's a longer beep, and then the door plummets towards Prakesh.

Carver acts fast. He plants his hand on Prakesh's chest and *shoves*. Prakesh flies backwards, his feet tangled, landing hard and skidding across the floor into the Air Lab, just as the massive door slams shut.

25

Knox

Knox is spooning beans into his mouth when he hears his name over the hacked SPOCS line. When he does, he nearly spits them across the room.

He drops the food container, grabbing his stick and limping across the floor of his surgery, turning up the volume on the transceiver.

"Suspect last spotted in A1-B22. Richards, we have you and Olawole on duty in that area, confirm?"

"Come on, dispatch," says an irritated stomper. "It's almost the end of my shift."

The dispatcher ignores him. "Repeat, your suspect is Morgan Knox, forty-two years old. Physical description is dark hair, Caucasian, six feet. Pronounced physical disability."

Knox grips the sides of the transceiver. *This can't be happening.*

"Copy that, dispatch," the stomper says, resigned. There are a few seconds of silence. Then: "Dispatch, this is Richards. I'm getting a lot of chatter on the private channels about a situation in Gardens, and another in Caves. You sure you don't want us to help?"

"Negative. We need continued stomper presence in the other sectors. Go and do your job."

"Copy," Richards mutters.

For the first time in months, Knox doesn't know what to do. Did he make a mistake somewhere? He's committed plenty of crimes in the past, but the stompers never caught on – why is he being targeted *now*? He has to leave. He has to—

Richards' voice bursts through the SPOCS transceiver. "Sarah, you read me?"

A crackle. Then: "Danny Richards. What's up?"

"You in Big 6?"

"Affirmative."

"Look up something for me on the Wall, would you?"

"Sure. What do you need?"

"We just got an arrest request on a Morgan Knox. I want to find out who issued it."

Knox stiffens, turning his head back towards the transceiver.

"OK . . . why?"

"Because it's keeping me from my homebrew. I'm at the end of my shift, and dispatch hits me with this. Whoever wants this son of a bitch arrested, I'm gonna—"

"Yeah, yeah, yeah. Here we go. Morgan Knox. Warrant issued by Junior Officer Hale, R."

"Damn tracers don't know how things work around here. I'll have to show her."

"Good luck."

"Hey, you got anything on what's going on up in Gardens?"

It's all Knox can do not to swipe the transceiver off its shelf. *Hale.* Did she think he'd go quietly? Did she think he wouldn't fight back? His fingers caress the remote taped to his hand. One push, that's all it would take.

He should leave. He should get far away from here. If he's

arrested now, then he'll never get near Okwembu. He can deal with Hale later.

But as he looks around the room, Knox realises that he doesn't want to leave. His surgery is perfect. It has everything he needs, everything he ever *could* need, and he worked very hard to make it this way. Out there is chaos, ruin, disaster. In here, he is fully in control.

No, he's not going to run. Hale isn't going to chase him out. He'll wait, and he'll deal with the stompers she sent, and then he's going to make her realise the exact consequences of failure.

26

Riley

"Everybody get back," Syria shouts.

The man tries to stand, but his hands slip, sliding in the black gunk. He falls face down in it, shivering uncontrollably. A bubble of black slime expands in one corner of his mouth, popping gently.

Syria turns away. His eyes pass across me, but it's like I'm not even there. He points at two men standing nearby. "Bruno, Tamir," he says. "Get everyone inside. I don't want to see a single person in the corridors."

A yell comes from behind us – a man's voice, thick with fear. "We got another one!" We all whirl to see a teenage girl stumbling down the far passage, her back to us. She half turns, and I see the shimmering black threads hanging off her face. Her eyes are rheumy, unfocused.

Panic is starting to crackle through the Caves. There are shouts about something in the water. Doors are slamming shut, and running feet form a thundering undercurrent. Syria and his men take off, moving at a brisk walk, barking instructions.

My thoughts race ahead of me. I'm thinking about what

Prakesh said the night before, when I thought I was getting sick. No matter what Syria does, other stompers'll be here soon. And if they close off the Caves with me still inside, then I'll never meet Knox's deadline.

I don't waste any more time thinking. I just run.

The cramped corridors pulse with bodies as the word boils up the line. People come scrambling out of the habs, heading for the exits. They begin to push tighter around me, slowing me to a jog, then a twisting, stumbling push through the packed crowds. An elbow jabs into my neck, another into my stomach. The noise is horrific: a screaming roar that the corridor magnifies and turns into a huge blast of white noise. *One exit. How could they design this place with a single exit?*

There are more people piling into us from behind, more hands raised, as if they can pull the exit towards them. The air is hot and sticky, and less and less of it is reaching my lungs every time I take a breath. Parts of the corridor are pitch-black under the burned-out lights. I have to look ahead, plan my angles, work out where each person is going to be two seconds from now. My legs move of their own accord, powering me forward as I dodge and weave through the corridor.

I'm not moving fast enough. A man goes down, his arm raised in one final plea before he vanishes under a sea of stamping feet. There's a hand in my face, pushing against my cheek and nose, a finger jamming into my mouth, arms against my back, too hard, way too hard . . .

And then, all at once, the bottleneck breaks. The crush surges forward. The hand whips away from my face, and then we're all running again, tripping and stumbling through the corridors.

Ahead of me, someone falls – a tall man, with no shirt and a pair of ragged shorts. What little light there is is reflected on his bald head. In half a second, I'm going to crash right into him. It'll send me sprawling across the floor, trampled underfoot.

I jump, flying over his body even before he hits the floor. I stumble on the landing, pitch too far forward, and have to throw my hands out. My palms scrape metal. As I look up, an arm swings at my face, the elbow rocketing towards my forehead. I twist to the side, and the elbow rushes past me.

There's only room in my mind for one thought: *Keep moving.*

The crowd has bunched up again, fighting for space. They've done it at a corner, where the passage narrows slightly. The door to the galleries is just ahead – I can see the light from it bathing the walls of the passage. Beyond it, two stompers are sprinting for the doors, guns up.

Amira's words whisper in my mind. Her presence is unwelcome. Her advice isn't. *Don't just run on the floor. Run on the walls and the ceilings. You can use every surface on the station to get where you're going.*

I look up at the roof. There's a fluorescent light bar, running from wall to wall, the glass thick and dusty. The bulb itself is burned out, which means the bar will be cold to the touch. I tic-tac off the wall, jumping towards it, leading with my left foot and using it to push myself off it. In the same instant, I reach up, stretching as high as I can, and grab the light with both hands. The glass cracks under my fingers, a tiny splinter needling my skin.

I exhale, and as my swing hits its apex I push my legs out so I'm parallel to the ground. Then I piston my arms, and let go.

If I miscalculate this, if I'm off by even half a foot, then I'm going to hurt a lot of people. Including myself.

The crowd is moving beneath me. The gap I'm trying to launch myself through, between the tops of their heads and the ceiling, is maybe a foot and a half. I feel their heads brush my back, raised hands across my legs.

And then I'm through. There's an *absence*, a feeling of space below me. I lean to one side, tuck my legs and hit the ground rolling.

The world goes upside down for a split second, and then I'm up and running, my muscles twanging, the cold shock of impact spreading through me.

At that instant, a transmission comes over my SPOCS, crystal clear through the static. "All points New Germany, quarantine Caves. Repeat, quarantine Caves."

No.

But the stompers ahead have heard it, too. They're already moving, guns up, and the few people still ahead of me come to a stumbling halt. I push past them, spinning around their bodies, keeping my balance as I hurl myself at the door. Not fast enough. It's already closing, one of the stompers pushing against it.

I'm ten feet away when it slams shut.

27

Riley

I'm hammering on the door even before the rest of the crowd get there. It refuses to budge. Even when other hands join me, other voices pleading to be let out, it doesn't move. Locked tight.

I find a spot against the wall and collapse against it, chest heaving, vision blurred. I feel like I've got up too quickly from a chair – like all the blood is rushing around my body, unsure of where to settle. How many hours do I have left? Eighteen? Less?

"Quiet!"

Syria. I don't know where he came from, but his presence shuts the crowd down instantly. He turns his glare on them, and they shrink away, forming another crush as the ones at the front try to back up.

"Get back to your habs," Syria bellows. "Get in there, stay in there."

They head back down the corridor in twos and threes, muttering among themselves.

Syria turns, looking down at me. "You're OK," he says,

reaching down and pulling me to my feet. His skin feels calloused and worn. Once I'm up, he strides away.

"Hey." The word barely makes it past my lips. I have to clear my throat to make it come out right. "Hey!"

I jog up behind him. Syria doesn't look in my direction, but when I put a hand on his arm, he stops, his shoulders heaving.

"There has to be another way out of here," I say. "There has to be."

Syria finally looks over his shoulder at me, firmly removes my hand from his arm. "My advice? Find somewhere to hunker down until this is all over."

I try to pull my thoughts into some kind of order. Prakesh would know what to say. He'd know how to convince someone like Syria.

Then, inspiration. "If it wasn't for me, you'd all be dead."

"Excuse me?"

"What I did . . ." I swallow. All at once, I'm back in the nightmare, seeing my father's face, my name splashed across it in orange letters. "With the *Akua Maru*. I saved this station. You *owe* me. So get me out of here, and we'll call it even."

It's the first time I've used what happened to me to get something. It feels weird, like I'm breaking a rule.

Seconds tick by. Shouting echoes through the Caves corridors, along with more doors slamming shut. Somewhere, very distant, the station hull is creaking and groaning.

"Follow me," says Syria. Before I can say anything, he strides away, slipping into the shadows. I bolt after him, jogging right on his heels. In my ear, SPOCS hums with traffic, almost all of it about the Caves lockdown.

He stops at one of the doors, nestled next to a giant 1-B spray-painted on the wall. He has to knock hard a few times before the door opens a crack.

A voice comes from behind it. "You get out of here now or – Syria. You OK?"

"Fine, Jamal," Syria says. The door opens wide, revealing a skinny guy with no front teeth and a shorn head. Three children cower behind him, huddled on a battered single cot, wrapped in thick blankets. The hab is cloaked in shadows, lit by a lone electric light bulb, hanging off the end of the cot. The floor is covered with patches of wet grime.

"Who's she?" Jamal says, pointing to me. Syria ignores him, picking his way across the floor to the wall at the far end. I follow, nodding at Jamal, hoping against hope that there really is another way out of here.

One of the kids slips from the bed and walks alongside me. She's a tiny girl, no more than five, wearing a dirty pair of pants and a red sweater so huge that it hangs down to her knees. She stares up at me, her brow furrowed.

Her eyes light up. "You're the lady who blew up her dad."

"Ivy!" says Jamal.

I'm too stunned to respond. Before either of us can say anything more, there's a huge screech. Syria has lifted a panel from the wall. Grunting, he sets it down. "There," he says. "It's a tight fit, but it'll pop you out by the power couplings on Level 2."

I look back once more at Jamal and Ivy, still not sure what to say. At that moment, the stitch in my left knee starts itching again, as if to hurry me along, and I step into the wall.

"Thank you," I say, as Syria lifts the panel again. Ivy has taken Jamal's hand, staring at me in wonder.

"Just go," Syria says.

Then he slots the panel back into the wall with a clunk, leaving me in darkness.

116

28

Knox

The two stompers – Richards and Olawole – walk up the passage towards Knox's surgery. Richards is lean, more gristle than flesh, with a gaunt face. Olawole is a foot taller than him, massive, with a trim goatee. His left eye is gone, the socket sewn shut.

"Morgan Knox," Richards says, as he slams his fist against the door a second time. "Station protection. Open the door please."

Silence. In the distance, a merchant is yelling about hot silkworms.

"This is bullshit," mutters Olawole, as Richards hammers on the door again.

"Knox!" Richards shouts. "Respond, or we're breaking in."

To Olawole he says, "Damn right. Hale is going to be one sorry piece of ass tomorrow, I'll tell you that."

Olawole smirks. "Hey, tell me something. Would you ever hit that?"

"Who? Hale?"

"Yeah."

117

Richards thinks for a moment. "Nah. Not my type."

He steps back, removing a tiny hand-held plasma cutter from his belt – useless for thick steel, but easily capable of melting a lock. "Knox, last chance," he shouts. "Open this door now."

There's a barked voice from behind them. "Not there."

Richards and Olawole spin around, their hands automatically going to the holsters on their belts. Olawole pauses, the fleshy part of his thumb resting on the butt of the stinger. Then he relaxes. It's just an exile – a vagrant, someone without a hab to go back to. You can recognise them a mile away, usually by the stench. The first whiffs of it reach the stompers now, thick and foul. Richards wrinkles his nose.

The exile is dressed in rags, his face lowered, as if in defer-ence to the stompers' authority. He has a thick coat, caked with dirt, the collar pulled up around his neck.

"Move along," says Richards, his hand still on his gun.

"Not there," the exile says again. He's mumbling, like he's got a mouth full of something. "Saw him go out a few hours ago."

"You hear that?" Richards taps the back of his hand on Olawole's chest. "He's not here. Let's call it in and go home."

But Olawole is standing stock-still, his one good eye locked on the exile. The man twitches, scratches his neck, and Olawole can see the dirt caked under his nails.

"You listening to me?" says Richards. But Olawole is already moving, and in moments he's standing over the exile, towering over him. The man shrinks against the wall, cringing. He still hasn't looked up.

"Kind of interesting, you just showing up here," Olawole says. He leans in close – the smell scours the back of his throat, but he ignores it. "Knox say where he was going?"

The exile shakes his head, a furious back and forth, still

staring at the corridor floor. "He didn't say anything to me, man. Anything. But I saved you the trouble right? Of knocking the door down? Right? So you can look after me?"

"What's your name?" Olawole says.

The exile mumbles something, more to himself than to the stomper. Olawole frowns, leans in a little closer. He turns his head to one side slightly. "What was that?"

He doesn't see the taser until it's too late. The exile pulls it out of his jacket pocket and activates it in one movement. Olawole rockets backwards, his arms flailing, and there's a crack as his teeth smash together. His one good eye rolls back in his head, showing nothing but white.

"Shit!" Richards says. He's already pulling his weapon from its holster, already gauging the distance, but Morgan Knox is one step ahead of him. The field-induction discharge sends him slamming into the corridor wall, barely conscious, every muscle burning with white-hot fire.

Knox checks the taser. Still at three-quarters charge. He has to move quickly – they won't stay down for long. He limps over to the big one, the stomper with one eye, then points the taser at him and holds down the trigger until the horrid smell from his rags is chased away by the smell of cooking flesh.

Richards is starting to come back as Knox walks towards him. He can move his mouth, but he can't form words yet. Drool leaks down his chin. He swivels his eyes towards Knox, but all he can see is the bulbous end of the taser, two feet from his face.

Knox drains the taser battery. When it clicks off automatically, he notices that the stomper's jacket is smouldering. He puts a foot underneath the body, then rolls it over to starve the fire of oxygen.

He looks around the corridor, but he's alone. He pockets the taser, and walks back to his surgery. There's a furnace nearby, rarely manned – he'll get his cart, dispose of the bodies, and then he'll finally get to deal with Riley Hale.

120

29

Riley

Syria wasn't kidding. At times, the passage through the wall is so tight that I have to shuck the top half of my jumpsuit to make myself thinner, trailing it behind me. Dust is everywhere, tickling the back of my throat, and the only light comes from cracks in the panelling.

The exit comes sooner than I anticipated. I have to crawl to reach it, flattening myself under a coil of power cables, and I nearly bang my head against the wall as the passage dead-ends. But the panel is unsecured, with no screws in place, and I lift it gently away. It's at floor level, and I can see feet in the corridor beyond. Nobody's running, which means news of the disease hasn't spread yet.

Working quickly, I slide my way out, getting to my knees and slotting the panel back in place. I'm unsteady on my feet, my body trying to process the insanity I've put it through over the past hour. The corridor thrums with activity around me, but nobody notices me slipping out of the vent. Just as well.

Royo hails me over SPOCS, and I key my wristband to transmit. "Copy, Hale here," I say.

"New orders," he says. "Rejoin the unit at the hospital in Chengshi, Level 2. Beck can brief you on the way. Confirm."

I try to ignore the prickles on the back of my neck. "Everything OK in Gardens?"

"It all went to shit," says Carver. "People spewing black gunk out of their mouths. We've got hotspots popping up all over the station."

"What?" The prickles have spread, fizzing up onto my scalp and down my spine. It couldn't have made it out of Caves. Not this soon.

Royo tries to say something, but I cut him off. "Is it in Gardens? The Air Lab?" I try to disguise the worry in my voice, and fail miserably.

"Negative," says Royo. "Han Tseng shut it down."

"What do you mean *shut it down*?"

"Locked the techs inside," says Anna.

"Can't risk whatever this is getting into the Air Lab," Carver says. "And before you freak out: Prakesh is fine."

"Well, Carver nearly knocked him out," Anna says, "but generally speaking, everything's OK."

I take a deep breath. "Could someone please explain to me what the hell is going on?"

"*Tracers,*" Royo says. "Hospital. Chengshi. *Now.*"

"We'll tell you when we get there, Ry," says Carver. I don't waste time trying to argue. I take off, pushing my body into a sprint.

30

Riley

My throat is already burning, but I don't dare stop running.

The strange thing is seeing how normal the rest of the station is. Everybody's going about their business, still unaware that there's any kind of outbreak. I pass a group of men sitting on the benches in one of the galleries, talking among themselves. One of them is at the climax of a story, and they burst into laughter as I dash through the middle of them.

The motion of running calms me, like it always does. My body comes first, the muscles relaxing into well-oiled routine, burning brightly as I run through Apogee. My mind follows as I climb the stairs towards Level 2 on the Chengshi border, dodging around the small clusters of people standing on the mezzanine.

I might be sick, too. Whatever this . . . *thing* is, it might be cooking in my lungs right now. Maybe my scratchy throat last night was just the start. I lick my dry, cracked lips. There's nothing I can do about it. If I so much as hint that I was in an infection zone, they'll quarantine me, lock me away, just like Prakesh. At that, I get two shots of guilt at once: one for possibly being a moving disease carrier, and another for how Prakesh and I left things. At least he's safe. At least he's with his people.

It occurs to me that Knox might be behind this. He's certainly got the skill to do it. But it doesn't make sense – he doesn't care about the rest of the station, just me and Okwembu. He's not like Oren Darnell, who was quite happy to take himself out along with the rest of us. He wants to live just as much as I do.

The area around the hospital entrance is quiet. It's in a larger corridor than most, better lit and free of graffiti. The other tracers are standing over by the closed double doors, and the metal surfaces reflect my body as I run towards them.

Carver gives me a wordless wave, and it's only then that I see that he and the others are wearing flimsy white face masks over their mouths.

Kev looks over. Above his mask, his eyes are more alive than I've seen them in months. "Got one for you, too," he says, digging in his pocket.

"Glad you could make it," Anna says, folding her arms.

I ignore her, slipping the scratchy mask over my face. "Where is everybody?" I say, gesturing to the empty corridor. The mask makes my voice sounds weird

"On the way," Anna says. "We just got here first."

"The Air Lab. What happened?"

"Your boy was—" Carver says, then doubles over with a coughing fit, his paper mask ballooning out. He looks up to see us all staring at him. "Would you relax? Gods."

"Prakesh is fine," Kev says. He puts an enormous hand on my shoulder. "Air Lab is secure. No disease, no nothing. Not that I could see. You're good."

I smile up at him, then remember that he can't see it under the mask. Instead, I tilt my head pressing it against his hand. "OK."

Kev squeezes once, then lets go.

"We talked to the docs?" I say, gesturing to the doors.

Anna nods. "Stay indoors until the shooting stops."

"This thing's nasty, Ry," says Carver. "And it's everywhere. Air Lab might be the only place we *haven't* seen it."

My SPOCS unit crackles, and a dispatcher comes over the line. "This is a priority call," he says. "We have a medical update on the disease. The next voice you hear will be Dr James Arroway, chief medical officer in Apex."

Anna starts to speak, but Carver gestures her to be quiet. His head is tilted slightly, listening hard.

There's a pause, another painful crackle of static, then Arroway comes on.

"I'll be as brief as I can," he says, his voice tinny over the comms. "We've tested some samples, and it's not good. It's a virus – we've taken to calling it Resin. We don't know where it came from, but we do know that once it hits the human body, it works fast. Our drugs don't seem to have any effect on it, and patients aren't producing strong enough antibodies. Unconsciousness occurs at twelve hours. Extrapolating from the cases we're seeing, death occurs within eighteen."

"Holy shit," Anna says.

"Yup," says Kev.

"It attacks the lungs and the nasal mucosa," Arroway says. "We do know that it's airborne. Anybody with it is a walking cloud of infection – touching someone, or even just being in close proximity to them, will cause the virus to enter your system. The virus does not – I repeat, does *not* – survive in water. You can treat all water points as active.

"We're working on a cure now, or, at the very least, a mix of drugs to slow the spread of the virus in the body. We're also working on our processes and manufacturing equipment to produce it as fast as possible, but we don't know if we'll be able to keep pace with the infection. Until then, keep your masks on, keep—"

At that moment, the hissing static in my SPOCS unit cuts out, and Knox says, "Riley."

I turn away from the others, trying to ignore the fear in my gut. "Not a good time," I say, keeping my voice low. Anna and Carver are deep in discussion, and Kev is staring into the distance, eyes scanning the corridor.

"Do you know what I'm looking at right now?" says Knox.

The fear in my stomach grows colder, sending tiny chips of ice through my body.

"Two stompers," he says. "Two *dead* stompers. They came to arrest me. Why do you think they did that?"

This isn't happening. This *can't* be happening.

"I don't know," I say, through gritted teeth.

"You must think I'm simple," he says. "It's the only explanation. They mentioned your name when they were told to bring me in, by the way." His voice turns mocking. "*Warrant issued by Junior Officer Hale, R.*"

And, right then, I decide I've had enough. I'm sick of his games. I'm sick of his poison voice in my ear. Time to call his bluff.

"Go ahead then," I say. "Do it. I don't think you can. I think you still need me, because without me you'll never get Okwembu."

"Who are you talking to?" says Carver. I can feel him and Anna looking at me. The corridor is deathly silent, as if the station is holding its breath.

"Tell me," says Knox. "Is Kevin O'Connell with you?"

The chips of ice expand, freezing the blood in my veins. My eyes find Kev. He sees me looking, and gives me a quizzical glance. When I don't look away, he slowly pulls his mask down.

"Everything OK?" Anna says, looking between us.

126

Knox's voice is as smooth as silk in my ear. "I want you to watch your friend Kevin very closely."

"Riley?" says Kev.

The words come out of me as one long, agonised howl. *"Kevin! No!"*

There's a wet, distant thud. Kev doubles over, clutching his stomach, as if his hands are trying to cover up the red stain spreading across his shirt.

31

Riley

What happens next is difficult to follow.

I'm at Kev's side, kneeling over him, my hands hovering above his body. There's blood on the floor, soaking through my jumpsuit.

At the same time, I'm seeing him running with his partner Yao, seeing him swing her into the air to catch the edge of a catwalk. She's sitting on his shoulders, legs dangling, talking non-stop while he shakes his head at her bad jokes.

I'm being shoved aside by Carver. He flips Kev over, grabbing his shoulders, shouting his name.

In my memory, Kev is sitting against the wall of the Nest, reading our copy of *Treasure Island* for the tenth time, his lips moving ever so slightly.

I see Anna, her hands over her mouth, staring down at Kev's empty face. I see Kev smiling, lopsided and goofy, feel his hand on my shoulder.

And in my ear, I can hear the very quiet hiss of Knox's line.

"Move, Riley!" Carver pushes me back a second time, so hard that I tip over backwards. He looks up at Anna. "Get a doctor."

She doesn't move. He jabs a finger at the hospital doors. "Get a fucking doctor!"

She turns and runs, slamming through the doors. The bang echoes around the empty corridor. Carver's hands track across Kev's stomach, hunting for the source of the wound. Blood soaks his forearms. He's talking to himself – no, he's talking to Kev, telling him to stop it, telling him to say something, anything.

And then there's a doctor, a white blur with wrinkled hands, and he's lifting Kev's tattered shirt, and the look on his face shocks me to my core. By now I'm standing, staring in mute horror at Kev. My face is wet from tears. I hear words like *internal*, and *organ damage*.

It all falls into place. Kev's operation – the one he had to remove the pulmonary embolism after they fixed his ankle.

He was operated on in Caves, where he could be close to his family. Was it at Medical Unit 262? Knox's old hospital? It had to be – it's the only way Knox could have sneaked the explosive into Kev's abdomen. Maybe he even performed the operation himself. He must have been planning all this for months, planning far enough ahead to know who I ran with, to figure out how to get to them. He saw an opportunity, and moved on it.

The doctor vanishes, calling for more help, for a stretcher. But it's far too late.

Then there's silence. The corridor is still.

"What happened to him, Riley?"

Carver's voice is different: brittle, fragile, like a thin pane of glass with nothing but the blackness of space beyond it. He stands slowly, one movement at a time, and turns to look at me.

"You knew what was going to happen," Carver says. "You and whoever you were talking to."

Anna's eyes are huge under the edge of her beanie. "This –
I don't—"

"Tell me," Carver says. His voice hasn't changed. But there's
no mistaking the raw fury in his eyes.

I say the only thing I can think of.

"I can't."

And then before either of them can react, I turn, and run.

130

32

Riley

By the time I reach the Chengshi border, the stitch in my side is an inferno, and Outer Earth is coming apart around me.

I expected Han Tseng to announce Resin on the comms. He doesn't. Not that it matters – by now, rumours have spread around the station, helped along by the tracer network. Even if people don't know exactly what's happening, they'll know that something bad is going on. I'm expecting panic, but the corridors are emptying. People are withdrawing into their habs, shutting themselves away. Nobody wants to come into contact with anyone else.

I can't think about the confusion and betrayal that Carver must feel. It's beyond words. He and Royo keep trying to call me over SPOCS. Their voices are eerily calm.

I make it as far as the Apogee gallery before I have to stop. I collapse against the railing on the Level 4 catwalk, sinking to the floor. Around me, the cavernous gallery is shockingly empty, and so quiet that I can hear the clanking of distant pipes. Someone has left a child's toy, a patchwork doll, in the middle of the catwalk, as if its owner decided not to go back for it.

The sobs are coming fast now, the tears streaming down my face. I keep seeing the blood, and Kev's face.

"You son of a bitch," I say, not knowing – not *caring* – whether or not Knox is listening. My voice is thick and gummy.

"Now do you see?" he says. His tone is quiet, almost regretful.

"I'm going to kill you," I say. "I'm going to rip your head off and stick one of these bombs down your throat."

"It had to be done. You had to see that your actions have consequences."

"He didn't do anything to you!"

I shouldn't be yelling. I shouldn't attract attention. But right now I don't have a choice in the matter. I think of Kev's family, in the Caves. His parents. How am I going to face them? How am I going to tell them that their son is dead because of me?

"You were at his operation, weren't you?" I say. "That's when you did it." I don't know why I'm asking him. I don't need confirmation – it's the only way that Kev could have had that *thing* inside him.

"He was harder to get to than you were," says Knox. "He had a prototype version of the device – a bulkier model. I put it next to his right lung, and sent him on his way. And that was months ago."

"Are there more?" I say. "Others?"

He actually laughs. "Maybe. Maybe not. Either way, you're running out of time."

"I don't have anything," I say. "Do you understand me? She's in a maximum security cell, and I can't get her out."

But he's gone.

I get to my feet. My legs are trembling – I don't know whether it's from exhaustion, or terror. I have to do it. I have to find a way. If I don't, then Kev will have died for nothing. Whatever happens, I have to get Morgan Knox what he wants. But it's too big a job – I can't get a handle on it, can't stop my mind from dashing itself against the problems.

Wait.

I pause, staring off into the distance. A man runs across the floor below, gesturing at someone else to hurry. His shadow tracks its way up the wall, as black as the fluid coming from the lungs of the infected.

Resin, whatever it is, is spreading. That means more quarantine zones. More quarantine zones mean more stompers will be needed to enforce them. Which means fewer stompers guarding Okwembu's cell.

That's it.

That's how I save myself.

33

Knox

It takes Knox longer than he'd like to dispose of the stompers' bodies. By the time he's finished, his bad leg is on fire.

He limps back into his surgery, teeth gritted, prickles of sweat standing out on his forehead. As he digs in one of his cabinets, hunting for a bottle of pain pills, he realises that the room is mess. Hale's blood, dried to a thin black crust, still speckles the operating table. The wheeled surgical stands, usually lined up against the wall, are out of place, tilted at crazy angles to each other. A tray of surgical tools is on the floor, and he can't remember how it got there.

He finds the pills, and dry-swallows two of them, the bitter taste rolling around in his mouth. He should clean up – put everything back in order, scrub the table, make the room perfect again. But before he can act on this thought, a wave of exhaustion crashes over him. He's not used to physical activity – as if anybody could be used to dumping two bodies into a furnace. He limps to his chair, finds it with his right hand, then sinks into it. A minute. That's all he needs.

His mind drifts back to Amira. To the woman he loved. He

had to work hard to see her again – he couldn't be sure she'd ever visit his hospital, and he might have spent months without seeing her. That was unacceptable. He began to use every excuse he had to get out of his shifts, throwing himself into finding out who she was. His supervisor, a pallid, careful man named Goran, tried to discipline him, but he barely noticed.

He saw her for the second time in the Apogee gallery. He was up on the Level 1 catwalk, and she was passing below him, sprinting across the floor. He couldn't take his eyes off her. It couldn't have been more than a few seconds before she vanished into one of the corridors, but those seconds are etched into his memory. Every movement she made, every turn of her head, every adjustment of her pack. It's all there.

He gropes for his tab screen, a sudden longing shooting through him. In a few taps, the sketch program appears. The drawings are right where he left them – his finger is a clumsy tool, but he was always skilled at anatomy, and he's drawn her perfectly. The curves of her muscles, the sharp angles of her jaw. The only thing he couldn't get right are her eyes, but he doesn't blame himself for that. No painter could. Her body was perfect, as if a goddess had decided to walk among humanity. Even her missing fingers, taken from her by the sub-zero temperatures in the Core, seemed to enhance her beauty.

He zooms in on the drawing, scrolls down. What would her thighs have tasted like, he wonders. He tries to imagine it, imagine *her*, naked, opening her legs to him, beckoning him . . .

No. He shuts the tab screen down, lets it drop onto his lap. Best not to. He'll never get that chance. Not after Hale and Okwembu snatched her away from him. The familiar anger returns, burning hot. Hale should have thanked him for being merciful, for sparing her life. That won't happen again.

He gets to his feet and stands, swaying. For a moment he feels dizzy, and puts out a hand to steady himself against the wall, then coughs. His chest feels a little tight.

34

Riley

"No way," says the stomper.

The stomper I'm talking to is holding two stingers, one in each hand. His jacket is off, and he wears a brown undershirt, soaked with sweat. His mask is slightly askew on his face. The outer door, made of criss-crossing metal bars, is locked shut. His partner leans against the wall, arms folded.

I was right. There are no longer eight stompers outside the maximum security brig. There are only two. Doesn't look like it's made things any easier for me.

"You think Captain Royo wants me to go back empty-handed?" I say. "It's like I said: I *have* to check the prisoner for Resin exposure."

The lie sounds ridiculous even as I say it. But it's the best I have. Two stompers is as good as my chances are going to get, and I have to get inside.

"Will you relax?" the first stomper says. Tomas, I think his name is. "We're all fine down here. No virus, inside or out."

I can feel the eyes of his silent partner on me, studying me, like I might start coughing myself.

137

"Orders have changed," I say, through gritted teeth.

"Until I hear it direct from Royo, orders stand. If you were coming, he would have called us."

"He's a little busy right now. In case you hadn't noticed, there's a bug going around."

Surprisingly, he seems completely unmoved by my death glare, staring down at me over the top of his mask.

"Royo's going to be pissed when I tell him you didn't listen," I say, but Tomas is ignoring me, his gaze somewhere over my shoulder. Inside, I'm screaming at myself for not coming up with something better. After all I've been through, *this* is the best I can come up with?

I trudge away. Amira's face jumps to the front of my mind – for her, it would have been easy. She took down eight guards breaking me out of a brig, like it was nothing. She'd go through these two in about five seconds.

I could probably do the same – I've fought bigger men before – but even if I did, all they'd have to do is broadcast one alert over the comms, and stompers would swarm all over us. And with no more than a dozen hours left on Knox's deadline, I need to come up with something. Fast.

Think, Riley. Think.

Slowly, I turn around, and get right in Tomas' face.

"The hell are you still—" he starts, but I cut him off.

"Listen to me carefully, *stomper*," I say, channelling the tracer I used to be. "Do you know what's going to happen if we don't uncover where Resin came from? Total anarchy. I've been ordered to eliminate this prisoner from the investigation."

I jab a finger on his chest. "Now, I could call Royo," I say, tapping my SPOCS earpiece. "Ask him to reconfirm his orders. I'm sure he'll be *thrilled* to hear from you. After all, it's not as if he has a lot going on at the moment. When this whole thing blows over, he's going to remember that you insisted on checking in. But, hey, you want to spend the rest of your career cleaning out the toilets back at Big 6, you go right ahead."

Tomas glances back at his buddy, who hasn't moved from his place against the wall. Without another word, I turn around and start walking.

It didn't work. They're not going to let me in. I have to think of something else. Maybe I can knock them out somehow . . .

"Hold up."

It's Tomas. "One minute, in and out. Then I don't want to see you back here."

Speechless, I just nod. We walk back to the entrance. The other stomper taps a keypad on the wall, buzzing me in. As I step through, the first door closes behind me. The control pad to open the cell doors is on the wall to my left, but I don't dare touch it.

There's a beat, and then the inner door slides back.

I jog down the cold passage towards the far end. If anything, the brig is even colder now – when I breathe, the air burns on the way in, and becomes crystal-white vapour as it comes out. The block is in darkness – I can't tell if it's another power failure, or if they're turned off deliberately.

The light's off in Okwembu's cell, too. But then there's a shifting form in the darkness, and I see her asleep on the cot, her body curled under a thin blanket.

I need to get the stompers to open the door to Okwembu's cell. I need her ready to go, not fast asleep. And, somehow, I need to surprise the stompers before they can transmit an alert call, and take them down. Preferably without killing them.

I have absolutely no idea how I'm going to get all those things done.

I rap on the plastic barrier. The shape under the covers shifts slightly, curling in on itself, as if caught in a bad dream. "Okwembu," I say.

That's when I hear shouting from outside – shouting, and gunshots.

I stop, hardly daring to breathe. There are scuffling sounds, another two gunshots, and then silence.

My body reacts before I can think about it. I have to hide. I spin in place, looking for somewhere to hunker down, but there's nothing. I'm in a short corridor surrounded by locked cells. Not good.

There's a bang, and the inner door slams open. In surprise, I lose my balance, skittering backwards, only just managing to stay upright.

I slip into the shadows at the far end, pushing back against the wall, hoping that I'm not too noticeable. My hearing comes back slowly. Okwembu's up, her hands on the plastic, staring at me.

I look back down the block. There are people stepping through, silhouetted from outside. There's no way to make out their features, but I count six at least. One of them turns to the keypad that controls the cell doors.

"Which cell?"

"Doesn't matter."

"Open 'em all."

There are several clicks, and then all the cell doors slide open, vanishing into the ceiling. I don't waste any time. I slip into the cell opposite Okwembu's, pressing up against the wall, hoping the darkness keeps me hidden.

Footsteps pound down the passage. Okwembu has shrunk back into her cell, her body nothing more than a dark form against the far wall. She has to know why they're breaking in, and what it means for her. Someone's had the same idea as me – they're using the chaos to get to Okwembu. But, unlike me, they'll be wanting her dead.

Do something.

Rob Boffard

The men find Okwembu, crowding around her cell. Their shapes are dark silhouettes, but I can see their shoulders slump in relief, and I hear a couple of exhausted cheers. I have never wanted to be holding my stinger so badly, to feel its weight in my hand and the rough edge of the trigger on my index finger.

I shrug my stomper jacket off my shoulders. I'm wearing nothing more than a tank top underneath it, and the cold air cuts right through the fabric. It dances across my bare arms, raising thousands of tiny bumps.

With no weapon, with nothing to hold them off, I have exactly one option. It's a terrible, terrible idea, but it's all I've got.

I bolt from the shadows, running right towards them.

35

Riley

In the split second before I reach the man at the back, I have
just enough time to be grateful that he's the same height as I
am. One arm goes around his throat, the other slams into his
temple. He gives a strangled cry of surprise, and I feel his body
go rigid as I pull him close to me.

The others spin around, guns up, pointing right at us.
"Anton!" someone shouts.

"Don't move," I yell, trying to keep the tremor out of my
voice. "Come any closer, I'll snap his neck."

But my mind is reeling. I've heard the name Anton before.
He was back in the Recycler Plant – the one who I had to hide
from by climbing up the vat. Are these the same people?

Can't worry about that now. I squeeze tight, and Anton cries
out. Snap his neck? What was I thinking? Now I have to sell
it, to make them *believe* that I can do it. I can barely make the
others out – just dark forms with raised arms. My heart has
climbed up into my throat. At any moment, I'm expecting to
see muzzle flashes, to feel bullets tearing through us.

"Easy," says one of them.

142

Anton tries to pull away from me, attempting to shrug out of my grip. I pull harder around his throat, and he gives off a horrible choking noise. "Bad idea," I hiss into his ear, before raising my voice. "Okwembu! Get out here."

There's no movement. The men stand frozen, not knowing where to look. My eyes have become accustomed to the darkness, and I can see that they've got scarves over their noses and mouths.

Janice Okwembu glides through, passing between them like a knife through ribs. Her face is blank, expressionless, as if being broken out of prison is the most natural thing in the world.

She stops in front of me. "What comes next, Ms Hale?" she says, clasping her arms in front of her.

I jerk my head behind me, and without another word she steps in that direction.

"I can take her," says someone from the edge of the group. From the sound of his voice, he's younger than the rest. I can see his gun trembling slightly in the air.

"Quiet, Ivan," barks one of them. Before they can react, I start dragging Anton backwards, following Okwembu. He takes awkward, stumbling steps as he walks, and I have to fight to keep him upright.

"Where do you think you're going to go?" says one of them, spreading his arms. "You can't drag him forever."

"Watch me."

"Outer Earth's finished. People are dying out there. Why don't you come with us? We can protect you."

"Not convinced. Sorry."

"What else are you going to do?"

I'm no more than a single step ahead of them, the plan forming in my head as I go. With their stingers raised, the men start to take hesitant steps towards us.

Okwembu speaks from behind me. "If you've got a plan, Ms Hale, now would be the time to share it."

Ivan's stinger goes off.

The bullet ricochets off the floor in front of me, dinging off the metal. Without thinking, I shove Anton forward. Choking, he stumbles into the group, knocking another man off his feet. They all start firing, muzzle flashes lighting up the dark cell block, the bangs echoing off the walls. I grab Okwembu by the shoulder and run, head down, heart jackhammering in my mouth, my shoulders itching as I wait for a bullet to slam into my back. Some pass so close to me that I can feel the blowback.

We've got no more than a couple of seconds' head start, and I can already hear running feet behind us. I shove Okwembu through the door to the brig – out of the corner of my eye I catch sight of Tomas and his partner, laid out on the ground, dark pools of blood around their bodies. I jab the keypad by the doors, hitting every button, hoping it'll do something.

With a metallic buzz, the barred gate slams shut. A second later, a man slams into it, snarling in anger.

We take cover, flattening ourselves against the wall. I glance over at Okwembu. She's looking around her, squinting in the bright lights. Her eyes widen as she looks in my direction. "Behind you!"

I'm just in time to see someone's hand, clutching a stinger, thrust out of the bars and point in our direction. Its owner twists his arm around, hoping he might hit us when he pulls the trigger.

I dart forward, gripping his wrist. In one movement, I jerk upwards, twisting as I go. His wrist snaps cleanly, and he screams in agony. The stinger clatters to the floor.

I don't have it in me to thank Okwembu, or even to meet her eyes. "Move," I tell her, pointing back down the corridor.

We bolt, putting distance between us and the brig. I can hear her breathing as she runs beside me, low and even.

It's a few minutes before we stop. We duck into a side room, an abandoned hab of some kind. No telling if its owners are dead or have simply walked away, but the place has been stripped. Bare metal cots and overturned lockers make the place look as if the station stopped spinning, let the resulting zero gravity lift everything up, then kicked back into gear.

Okwembu sits down on one of the lockers. Her shoulders rise and fall in huge, juddering gasps. I lean against the wall, breathing hard. I did it. I got her out.

Now I just have to get her all the way across the station to Knox. Without being seen.

36

Prakesh

Prakesh is on the other side of the lab when he sees Julian
Novak leading a group of people for the doors.

He ignores them at first, looking back down at the rows of
soybeans planted in the giant troughs which run along the
wall. He told the techs to carry on as normal, and he's trying
to do the same.

He looks up again. There's something about the set of Julian's
shoulders that he doesn't like.

"pH levels are good," says Yoshiro, frowning over a tab
screen. "I could adjust the lights a little, get the soy to repro-
ductive stage even faster."

"Yeah, yeah, fine," Prakesh says. He straightens up, dusting
off his hands on his lab coat. "Back in a sec."

He strides across the Air Lab, cutting across the pathways
between the giant oaks, keeping his eyes on Julian. The tech
has at least ten people trailing in his wake. Two of them are
carrying something, swinging it between them – there are too
many bodies there, and Prakesh can't quite see what it is.

He knows that the shutdown code Tseng used sealed off all

the Air Lab exits, including the ones at the monorail docks. There used to be plenty of other entrances – little access points dotted here and there, loose panels and ventilation shafts and forgotten corridors. Prakesh used one of them himself, during the Sons of Earth crisis. Tseng, of course, doesn't know about them.

When Prakesh was made head of the Air Lab, he thought long and hard about whether to leave them open. In the end, he gave the orders to have each and every one of them closed off. The Air Lab was the single most important part of Outer Earth. Despite what Tseng thinks, he does take its security seriously. He checked each of them himself, Air Lab and the old Food Lab, checking the welded seals over the panels and the steel bars over the ventilation ducts. *No way in. No way out.*

And as much as he hates to admit it, it has to stay that way. It doesn't stop his mind from being drawn to Riley – it's impossible not to think about her, impossible not to feel sick with worry about what she's facing out there.

And because he's thinking of Riley, he can't help but think of Carver. His anger rises, and he pushes it away. Nothing he can do about that now.

He reaches the open area near the front of the lab, and moves diagonally across it, heading right for Julian. He's picked up an entourage of his own – Suki and a few of the others are jogging towards him. Yoshiro trails behind them, still carrying the tab screen.

Julian has stopped a few feet from the doors. "Bring it closer," he says to one of his followers, and that's when Prakesh sees what they're carrying. It's an old plasma cutter – one of the models that relies on an external fuel source, a big, heavy box that needs two people to carry it. Julian himself has the cutter head, a long tube with a red handgrip on the end. Prakesh can see the metal nozzle, gleaming under the lights.

147

"Julian," says Prakesh, ignoring the flutter of fear in his chest.

Julian looks up and sees him, along with the rest of the techs. For an absurd moment, they freeze. The plasma cutter quivers, held a few inches off the floor. Prakesh recognises one of the men holding it – Iko, who was up on the roof the day before, when Benson took his plunge.

Julian gives him a tight nod.

"Want to explain what you're doing?" Prakesh says. He keeps moving, getting himself between Julian and the doors.

Julian tosses his hair back, then raises his chin. He's not heavily muscled, but he's tall, and looks down at Prakesh along the bridge of his nose. "Getting out. What do you think?"

"No, you're not," Prakesh says, folding his arms. Suki and Yoshiro and the others are standing off to one side, waiting to see how this plays out.

Julian half smiles. "I quit. There. I don't have to take orders from you any more." He looks behind him. "I think everybody here's had enough of being ordered around. Right?"

There are nods and murmurs from behind him. The plasma cutter fuel container drops, its clanging echoing off the door.

"Doesn't matter," Prakesh says, holding Julian's gaze. "You're not leaving. Turn around, take that thing back where it came from."

"What do you care?" Julian says. "Weren't you trying to stop them sealing it off in the first place? You just rolling over and letting it happen now?"

Prakesh opens his mouth to tell Julian about the closed ecosystem again, and the variables at play, and the probability of infection, and stops. He's remembering James Benson. His words on the roof of the control room, just before he stepped off. *They take us for granted. We give them food, all of them, and they treat us like dirt.*

148

Maybe Benson was right. But it doesn't matter. Being head of the Air Lab may be difficult, it may not be perfect, but Prakesh loves it. He loves being here, among the soil and the trees and the algae pools.

If he lets Julian through, if he opens up the sealed Air Lab, Tseng will see him fired. He'll never set foot in the Air Lab again. He should have thought of that before, when he and Carver nearly got into it. He wasn't thinking straight.

He can't lose this job. He won't. *If Julian wants out, he's going to have to go through me.*

Prakesh walks up to Julian. "Last chance. I don't care what you do, but you leave that cutter here, and you walk away." He raises his voice. "All of you."

He can feel Suki and Yoshiro stepping in behind him, along with a dozen other techs, and a small smile slips across his face. Julian's group are muttering among themselves, casting dirty looks in his direction.

Julian turns away, and Prakesh feels a surge of elation. "That's right," he says. "Move on."

Julian turns back. He's holding a stinger in his right hand.

Suki lets out a strange noise – a squeak and a cough, melded into one. Yoshiro spits a hushed curse.

Slowly, Julian raises the stinger and points it at Prakesh's face.

37

Riley

My right knee groans in pain. Without thinking, I scramble in my pocket for the pill bottle, twisting it open and pulling down my face mask.

Last one. The pill rattles around the bottle, and I knock it back, swallowing it quickly, getting only the barest hint of bitterness. The mask goes back on, covering my mouth and nose. I throw the bottle behind me, and it clatters off one of the lockers and out of sight. I'd do anything for a drink of water. Sell my firstborn. Trade a kidney. Anything.

"Why are you—" Okwembu takes a ragged breath. "Why are you wearing a mask? And why did those men have scarves around their faces?"

I swallow. "Disease," I say. "They're calling it Resin. It's going through the whole station."

Okwembu looks away. "Perhaps I should have stayed in prison," she says to herself.

I glance at the door. "We need to keep moving," I say. "There's a place on the sector border. We'll be safe there."

"Why did you get me out?" she says.

"Don't worry about that," I say, keeping my eyes on the door.

"How do I know you aren't planning to kill me, Ms Hale?"

"I just saved you. Or weren't you paying attention back there?"

"Yes, but you still haven't told me why. You, a station protection officer, just broke me out of the brig. You're risking everything to do this. And if you don't want me dead, then what exactly *do* you want?"

I want to bring you to Morgan Knox. I want him to take these things out of me. I want my life to go back to normal.

I lean forward, looking her right in the eyes.

"If you try to run from me," I say, "I will chase you down and snap your neck."

"Would you? After all you've gone through to get me here?"

"Try me. Find out."

She goes silent, staring at me. Eventually, she says, "So why shouldn't I have gone with the others? The ones we're trying to run from?"

"Because they *definitely* want to kill you. With me, there's a chance you might actually survive. Logically, which one would you pick?"

"Oh? I have to say, Ms Hale, for people who wanted me dead, they seemed very intent on marching me out of there alive."

We fall silent. Okwembu watches me. Ever since I've known her, she's been able to do that – find the weak spot in any argument, pin it down, drill right to the heart of a problem in a second. It's as if she still views the world like it's made up of code. Like humans are just strings in a program, designed to be shifted around at will. Her eyes make me think of camera lenses, capturing everything, storing it for later use.

"This isn't a negotiation," I say. "I don't owe you a damn

thing. You either go where I tell you, or I'm going to chase you down, knock you unconscious, and then we'll get there anyway. Your call."

"And drag me through the station? Hardly becoming for a lightning-fast tracer."

I take a step towards her, and she raises her hands. "I can help you. We can work together."

There's a long pause. Somewhere, in a distant part of the station, there's a deep bang, turning into a rumble as the sound travels through the levels.

"Someone wants to talk to you," I say. "He asked me to get you out." A cold shiver runs up my spine, but whether in fear or anticipation I don't know.

"He must have been offering something very important to you," she says.

"You have no idea."

She walks to the door, peering out into the corridor. It's a deliberate move, but I can almost see the cogs in her mind turning, weighing the odds.

She turns back to me, gives me a tight nod. "All right. I'll come with you. Lead the way."

The old Riley couldn't do it, couldn't lead her to her death, would never have even considered it. No matter what crimes Okwembu had committed, the old Riley would have found a way around it, done everything she could to stop it happening.

The new Riley? She's thinks a little differently.

Okwembu did worse things than you ever will. Than you could ever think of doing.

But the guilt comes anyway, surging up through me, hot and acidic.

"Wait," I say. I head to the back of the room, hunting around the smashed lockers. Earlier, I spotted a pile of what looked like clothing. It's now little more than rags, ripped and shredded,

152

but perfect for what I need. I select a long strip of rough fabric, dark blue in colour. I hand it to Okwembu.

"Wrap it around your face," I say. "Resin is airborne. This'll keep you safe." *And anonymous.*

She takes the cloth, holding it awkwardly in her hands. "Thank you," she says, after a moment.

I walk out into the corridor, my centre of gravity low, ready to bolt at the first sign of trouble. It's empty, and I relax, but only a little.

"She trained you well," Okwembu says from behind me. The sound of her voice is muffled by the fabric. "That move, back at the brig, where you broke his wrist – you could have been Amira."

Unwelcome memories fight for attention. With an effort, I force them back down.

"You run in front," I say, pointing. "One wrong move, and I'll end you."

38

Prakesh

The techs scatter.

They just bolt, heading for the algae pools. Prakesh feels an urge to go with them, to get as far away as he can.

He doesn't.

Keeping his eyes on the stinger, on the black hole of the barrel, he raises his hands. He immediately feels stupid – Julian knows he doesn't have a weapon, and really, what is he going to do, block the bullet? But it's an instinctual reaction, and when he tries to put his hands down, he finds that his arms aren't listening to him.

He sneaks a look over his shoulder. Suki and Yoshiro are still behind him, and Suki's face has gone completely white. Prakesh looks back at Julian, trying to meet his eyes.

"Put it down," he says.

Julian shakes his head. "No. I don't think I will." He's moving slowly towards the three of them, almost sauntering. Behind him, one of his followers breaks and runs. It unbalances Julian for a moment, but then he sees that the rest of the group isn't moving, and he relaxes.

154

Prakesh tells himself to stay calm. He tries to remember everything he knows about stingers: their range, their velocity, their stopping power. They're designed to go through soft targets, like humans, and not to penetrate metal – useful for a space station hanging in orbit, with the vacuum on all sides. Prakesh knows that the rounds are small-calibre, but can still make a real mess of whatever they hit.

On the other hand, actually getting a hit with one is a trick in itself, especially if you don't fire them regularly. Could he disarm Julian before the man takes a shot? What if he's wrong? Where did Julian even get the stinger in the first place?

He keeps very still. "Julian, listen to me—"

"Move aside," Julian says, jerking the gun.

"Think about what you're doing. They'll put you up against the wall in front of a firing squad."

Julian hangs his head. For a half-second, Prakesh thinks he's got through, but then he sees that Julian's shoulders are shaking with laughter.

"Oh man," Julian says, his fingers flexing around the stinger. "You don't understand what's happening here? The whole station's finished."

"You don't know that."

"Whatever. I'm not spending my last few days trapped in here with *you*," Julian says, ignoring Prakesh. "I got friends out there. Me and mine. So does everybody here." He jerks his head at the group behind him, then starts walking towards Prakesh. Prakesh feels Suki stiffen behind him.

"Now move," Julian says.

Prakesh shakes his head. "Not going to—"

Julian smashes the pistol into his face.

Prakesh's head snaps sideways, and it's as if someone has let off a firework right in front of him. Sparks fizzle and crackle in his vision. The pain wipes them away, huge and sudden,

155

expanding outwards in a slow-moving wave of fire from his right cheek. There's something loose inside his mouth, one of his teeth, scratchy against his tongue.

He's lying prone, and pushes up onto his right elbow. Yoshiro is cursing every god he can think of, backed up against the wall. Prakesh blinks, unable, for a moment, to move.

"Last chance," Julian says. The barrel of the stinger seems to swell as Prakesh looks at it. He can see a slick of blood on the tiny spike of the stinger sight.

Yoshiro runs at Julian. He explodes off the wall, sprinting towards him, his arms pumping. Julian swings the stinger around.

"Don't!" Prakesh shouts. But the booming gunshot drowns out his words, and when the report fades away, all he can hear is Suki screaming.

39

Riley

Any hopes I had about not being recognised vanish with the first person we come across.

It's an old woman, a few corridors down. She's sitting against the wall, her threadbare dress pooled in her lap. She either doesn't have a place to live, or doesn't care about Resin, because she looks blissfully unconcerned as she spoons a thick soup into her mouth.

Unconcerned, that is, until she catches sight of us. Her eyes hesitate on me, but grow huge when they hit Okwembu. The spoon pauses, quivering by her mouth.

"Oh gods," she says, rocketing to her feet.

"Hope you can run," I say to Okwembu, and charge into a sprint. No time to keep her ahead of me now.

More people are looking out of their habs, spilling out of the doors. Arms reach for us, trying to grab hold of our clothing, and we duck under them or knock them away, sending their owners flying. Under my face mask, my skin is slick with sweat.

As we burst out into the gallery, onto the Level 4 catwalk, we see a large group up ahead of us. Like the men back in the brig, they've got fabric wrapped around their faces and they're all holding weapons. I even see a few children there, hefting steel bars as big as they are. They look from me to Okwembu, not sure what to do, not sure how to take seeing me running with someone like her.

"Wrong way," I say, already starting to turn. My mind is racing ahead. If we double back, we can drop down two levels by the power couplings. There's a gap we can slip through, so it should be easy to—

Okwembu puts a hand on my shoulder and shoves me towards the edge of the catwalk.

I see the railing coming towards me in slow motion. I'm already off-balance, and the railing will take me in the waist. I'll topple right over it, right off the edge.

The railing collides with my stomach, not my waist, knocking the air out of me but keeping me on the catwalk. At that second, I feel something whoosh past my back and bounce off the far wall of the gallery. It rebounds onto the catwalk, skittering to a halt.

I get a look at it as Okwembu pulls me upright. A spear. A metal pole, filed to a rough spike. If Okwembu hadn't pushed me out of the way, it would have skewered me in the small of my back.

For a moment, I marvel at how quickly the crowd decided I was a threat. They jumped straight to that conclusion, without even trying to talk to me, acting before I could stop them. The thoughts are strange, like broken puzzle pieces that can't quite fit together.

Okwembu doesn't give me a chance to really process it. Just drags me along until we're running again, away from the crowd. They give chase, but there are too many of them, and they get bunched up at the entrance to the corridor. Their angry shouts vanish behind us.

A few minutes later, we reach a gap between the power couplings, leading down to the level below. I drop first, then help Okwembu down.

"Thanks," she says. It's hardly a word – more like an exhausted exhalation.

"I owed you one," I say before I can stop myself.

I've lost track of the number of Resin hotspots, but it's everywhere now. New ones keep being reported over SPOCS. Apogee, Level 2. New Germany gallery. Outside the habs in Gardens. For now, only Apex and Tzevya remain unaffected. Hospitals and furnaces across the station are full to bursting. Whatever this thing is, it's eating Outer Earth alive. More than once, we come across a body, sprawled across a corridor, or curled into a foetal position in a corner. Black liquid is spattered on the walls and floor, shining like foul oil. And at each one, I have time to think the same thought: *why am I not sick yet?*

"How much further?" Okwembu says. Surprisingly, she's managed to keep up.

"A few minutes. Keep moving."

The words burn my throat. I focus on the image of a bottle of water, letting myself imagine the condensation dripping down the side. More than once, I hear Royo trying to hail me. He sounds worn out, like he doesn't care whether I respond or not. News of the jail break hasn't found its way onto SPOCS yet, not that I can hear. I guess with everything going on, two stompers not reporting in from maximum security has got lost in the shuffle.

As we get closer to Knox's surgery, I look back at Okwembu. She's spent. Her face has gone a strange grey colour, and she keeps coughing – quick bursts, like gunshots. My legs are hurting again, but I don't care.

I've done it. Gods help me, but I've done it. He can get these things out of me. I don't know how I'll square things with

Carver and Anna, with Royo, how I'll explain my role in breaking Okwembu out. But I'll get to see Prakesh again. I picture his face, keep him uppermost in my mind.

Thinking about him leads my thoughts onto Kev. That only lasts for a second. It's too painful, too raw – I squeeze my eyes shut, shaking my head, as if to physically dislodge the memory.

The door to the surgery is shut when we arrive. It gives me a moment's pause – did he tell me a way to get in if it was locked? But I can't think of anything, and after a moment I rap hard on the door.

"Knox."

No answer. I knock again. "Knox, it's Riley. Open the door."

Nothing. Frowning, I grab the handle and pull.

The door slides open easily, taking me by surprise. Knox is nowhere to be seen.

The blood on the operating table has dried to a dark, crusty brown. Okwembu stares down at it, but for once I'm not paying attention to her. There's a canteen on one of the shelves, dark green against the grey metal, and before I can even think about it, it's in my hands. It's wonderfully heavy, full to the brim. I drink most of it in three seconds flat, gulping it down. The relief is exquisite.

I wipe my mouth, then, without thinking, offer it to Okwembu. She's still by the operating table, her finger just touching one of the streaks of dried blood.

"What is this?" she says. She's gone very quiet, her eyes locked on mine.

"Nothing. He's a doctor, that's all."

She turns and runs.

I drop the bottle. The water bursts out of it as it hits the floor, splashing across the metal. I barely notice. In two strides I'm on her, gripping her shoulders just as she reaches the threshold. She gives a howl of fury and tries to twist away, but

I hold on, throwing her backwards. She stumbles across the room and slams into the far wall, sliding down it as her legs give way. Her prison jumpsuit is soaked with sweat. The cloth around her mouth and nose has come away, hanging around her neck like a noose.

I walk towards her, ignoring the guilt surging through me. She shrinks back against the wall, like she's trying to vanish into it. Reaching down, I yank up the leg of my jumpsuit, exposing the stitches, then turn to show her.

"Bombs," I say. "I deliver you, he takes them out. Sorry, *Janice*, but your life isn't worth losing my legs for."

A part of me is recoiling in horror at my own words, but on one level it feels good to say them. It's good to have *her* scared for a change.

"So this was all about saving yourself," she says, and shakes her head. "Of course it was."

I have to hold her here. She's already taking little glances at the door, and I can see her trying to work out how to get past me. I can't turn my back on her, not for a second.

The operating table. The restraints hanging off it are padded fabric, flexible and strong. More than enough.

I grab Okwembu, pull her to her feet. She starts fighting me, clawing frantically at my skin, but she's too exhausted from the run. I jam her body into the head of the table. It knocks the air out of her, and she doubles over, moaning in pain.

I lean over her, using my own body to keep hers in place. I pull her arms across, cuffing them. Secured as she is, her hands are far enough apart that she can't use one to free the other, and the fabric cuffs are tight enough that she won't be able to pull away from them.

Okwembu goes still. She lies under me, trying to get her breath back. As I pull the final strap, she mutters something.

"What's that?" I say.

"You're not the Riley Hale I knew," she replies.

For a reason I can't quite figure out, that hurts worse than anything else.

I shake it off. Knox. Shouldn't he be here by now? This place isn't *that* big. I wasn't thinking about him while I was dealing with Okwembu, but now . . .

He must be in the other room. The one off to the side. I haven't even looked in it yet, and it's shrouded in darkness.

"She's here," I say, raising my voice. The darkness doesn't answer back. Behind me, I can hear Okwembu tugging at her restraints.

"It's over," I say, walking to the storeroom, stepping over the threshold. "I did it. Take them out."

Still nothing. I fumble for a light switch, my hand questing across the wall. It takes me a second to find it, but the lights are still working, and they flicker on.

Knox is in the middle of the floor, lying face up, unconscious. His cane is trapped underneath him.

And around his mouth: black slime, spattered across his lips and chin.

40

Prakesh

Yoshiro dies before Prakesh even gets to him.

The side of his neck is gone, torn away. His blank eyes stare at the ceiling as his blood pools on the floor around him and Suki screams and screams and screams.

Prakesh shuts his eyes. This doesn't seem possible. Five minutes ago, he and Yoshiro were discussing soybean plants, debating soil quality. He wonders if he's dreaming, if the blow to his head caused some kind of hallucination. But Julian is shouting at him, waving the gun in his face, and it feels far too real.

"See what you made me do?" Julian is furious, his face blood-red. His whole body is shaking. He swings the gun from Prakesh to Suki, who cringes, holding her hands up to her face. "You see what happens?"

"Take it easy," Prakesh tries to say. The words feel as if each one is wrapped in thick layers of gauze.

"Gods," says Iko. Prakesh turns his head to look at him – it seems to take a long time – and sees that he's gone white. "You killed him."

Julian is shaking his head, as if he can bring Yoshiro back to life. Suddenly, he raises the gun, jabbing it in Iko's direction. "Shut up!" he shouts.

Ṣuki has started screaming again, dissolving into hysterics. Julian hears, and Prakesh sees him tensing, ready to swing in the other direction. Fear brings clarity, chasing away the fuzz in his head. If he doesn't get control of this, Julian is going to shoot Suki.

He could let them go. He could promise not to interfere, take Suki away and join up with the others. But something burns inside him – an anger, hot and fierce. Maybe it's Yoshiro, or maybe it's the sight of Suki, cowering and helpless against the Air Lab doors, but he doesn't want to let Julian win.

He gets to his feet, moving slowly and carefully, making sure Julian has plenty of time to see him. It's just enough to pull the man's focus off Suki, but it means that the gun is now pointed at Prakesh. He swallows hard, choosing his words carefully. "There's another way out of here," he says. "You don't have to cut through the door."

Julian's eyes narrow in suspicion. He knows that Prakesh had all the other exits sealed shut. Prakesh speaks before the thought can get a grip in Julian's mind. "I left a way open. Thought it might come in handy one day. I'll take you there, right now. Just . . . just don't hurt anyone."

He's lying, and he desperately hopes that Julian is too wired to see it. There's no secret exit. But his first job is to get Julian away from Suki, away from anyone he could hurt. And he knows that Julian will take the easy way out, just like he does with his lab work.

"Where?" Julian says.

Prakesh points. Julian's eyes flick to the side, following his finger. He's pointing to the wall nearby, to the sealed double doors leading to the destroyed Food Lab.

"You're lying," Julian says, training the pistol on Prakesh.

"No," Prakesh says. "I kept one open for myself. I'll tell you where it is."

Julian smiles. His teeth are bad, brown and craggy, and they look strange in his flushed, sweaty face. "Of course you did. Of course. It's just like you, isn't it? Keeping things from everyone else."

Prakesh doesn't know what to say to that, and doesn't get a chance to. Julian steps towards him, wrapping a hand around his arm above the elbow. He jabs the barrel of the stinger into the small of Prakesh's back.

"You're not going to tell us," he says, as he pushes Prakesh towards the Food Lab. "You're going to show us. Iko! Roger! Bring the cutter. We're not leaving it here."

Prakesh's head is pounding. His sense of balance is shot, and he struggles to stay upright, nearly falling, correcting himself just in time. *Don't do that*, he thinks. *You fall, and he'll put a bullet right through you.*

Julian leans in close, whispering. "You'd better be telling the truth. If you aren't? I'll come back for Suki after I do you."

Rob Boffard

41

Riley

I can't take my hand off the switch.

It's stuck there, as firmly as if it's been nailed down. Knox's chest rises, holds, trembles and then slowly falls, like a deflating balloon. I'm holding my breath, and as I force myself to exhale, I manage to pull my hand off the wall.

I drop to my knees next to Knox, my hands gripping his shoulders, shaking him, yelling at him to wake up. My voice sounds like it's coming from a long, long way away.

After a while, I sit back, cradling my head in my hands. After everything I've been through, after everything that happened in the past day, I'm going to lose. The second his heart stops beating, the return signal will stop firing and the devices will detonate.

I stand up, getting to my feet slowly, like an old woman. I walk back into the operating room, where Okwembu is still bent over the table. Her eyes are narrowed, vicious, brimming with fear and anger. Gods know what I must look like.

I reach for her cuff, intending to release her. There's no point now. I don't even want revenge any more. I just want to find somewhere warm and dark, and crawl inside and wait for it all to be over. I want someone's arms around me – Prakesh, Carver, anyone. I want to bury my face in their shoulder and have them tell me it's going to be all right, even if it isn't.

"You're letting me go?" she asks, disbelief fracturing her voice.

My hand stops, my finger just touching the cuff. I think of my father, of how he reappeared again after seven years, screaming towards Outer Earth, intent on destroying us all. I think of how I stopped him. Right at the end, when it looked like there was no way I could do it.

Knox isn't dead yet. All I have to do is find a way to keep him alive, to make sure the Resin doesn't stop his heart. I could find somewhere to hide and wait for death, or I could do what I always do. Run. Fight. Find a way.

Doctor Arroway must have made some progress by now. He said they were working on drugs to slow down Resin. It's the slimmest chance in a universe of slim chances, but so was getting Okwembu out of the brig.

There's no way I'm making it all the way to Arroway's lab, then all the way back here, by myself. Not with every stomper looking for me. I need help. And with Knox out of commission, I might just be able to get it.

Okwembu sees my hesitation. "Ms Hale – Riley," she says. "If you leave me here, you're condemning me to death. That's not you. You'd never—"

"Shut up," I say.

Okwembu starts cursing, yanking at the cuffs, the rough fabric abrading her skin and leaving thin red weals as she pulls at them. I grab her arm, gripping it tight.

"I'm going to make a call," I say, gesturing to my ear. "Don't say a word. You may just make it out of this."

She shakes her head, looks away.

I don't want to speak to Carver right now – that's a conversation I'll have another time – but I can still find Anna.

Our channel is filled with the soft hiss of static. I take a deep breath. "Anna, this is Riley, come back."

Nothing. A drop of dread lands in my stomach, sending ripples across my body. I'm gripping the operating table with my free hand, so tight that it hurts.

"Royo? Anyone? This is Riley, come back."

The line crackles.

I stop, hardly daring to breathe. For a second, I'm sure I imagined it, but then the crackle comes again, louder this time, and I hear someone speak.

"Where are you?" Anna says. She sounds awful – not sick, just tired, her cut-glass accent shattered.

"Never mind that," I say. "I've got a problem, Anna. You're the only one who can help me."

This kind of flattery usually works with Anna. This time, however, she just sighs, a horrible, rattly sound that seems to resonate with the static. "Not this time. Not unless you tell me what happened to Kevin."

"I'll tell you when I see you. I swear. Anna, I'm running out of time. I need you to help get me to Arroway."

"*You're* running out of time?" Her voice drips with scorn. "Clock's ticking for all of us, my dear."

Okwembu speaks up from behind me. "Ms Hale, I can help you. Let me go, and we can solve this together."

"Who's that?" Anna says.

"Nobody. It's nothing," I say, turning and walking back towards Knox's body.

Anna is silent for a long moment – so long that I think the channel's got cut off. When she speaks, her voice is brittle. "Before everything went to hell," she says, "there was a snap on SPOCS about an assault on one of the brigs. We couldn't respond to it, not with the number of people we had left, but I heard it was the max security prison."

She pauses. "Please tell me it wasn't you, Riley. Please tell me you didn't do what I think you did."

I open my mouth to reply, but what am I even supposed to say?

"Oh gods," she says. I can even see her, standing there with her eyes screwed up tight and her hand massaging her neck. "You did, didn't you?"

". . . Yes."

There's a long silence on the line, broken by Anna letting her breath out in an equally long sigh. "Riley, I know you want revenge, but please trust me, this is not the time . . ."

"It's not about revenge," I say, cutting her off. "Look, why don't you meet me somewhere? I'll explain everything."

"I doubt it. With you gone, and Kev out of the picture—"

Her voice hitches, and she stops. There's a silence over the comms. Then: "What did you do to him, Riley? Why did you run?"

I close my eyes. When I speak, the words are pushed through gritted teeth. "It wasn't me. You have to believe me – I would *never* hurt Kev. Never."

"Then who?"

I glance over at the still unconscious Knox. Then I take a deep breath, and tell her, going as fast as I can. Knox, Okwembu, all of it.

When I'm done, Anna draws a shaky breath. "Well, this explains a lot," she mutters.

"How bad is it out there?" I say, trying to bring the subject back around to Resin.

"It's hit the whole station," Anna says.

"What about Tzevya? Apex?"

"Not yet, but soon."

I push the thought out of my mind. "What about the *Shinso*?"

"The what?"

"The asteroid catcher. The ship that was due back."

"Oh. That. I heard Royo say he'd told them to hold their position in station orbit. They must be getting pretty worried out there."

At least there's one pocket of humanity with no Resin. If it really does get as bad as I think it's going to, then at least they'll survive. At least they're used to each other's company: asteroid catcher ships run on a skeleton crew. They're built for utility rather than comfort, and most of their body is given over to the enormous engines needed to bring an asteroid to a halt, and the machinery to reel it in. They tow it behind them, anchored with enormous cables.

"Why aren't we sick?" Anna says.

"Huh?"

"Have you been coughing? Got a tight chest, anything like that?"

"No, but . . ." I trail off, not sure if it's worth mentioning that I *was* sick, but got better.

"Me neither. You, me and Carver. We're not sick."

This is harder to process than I thought. If it's not just me, then what the hell is going on?

"We're wearing masks, Anna," I say.

"So were a few of the stompers, and they're all down. Royo's not sick yet, but they've switched the stomper commanders to full-face respirators."

She takes a breath. "Listen – you're right about Arroway and the other doctors. They haven't cured it yet, but they've made something that can slow it down. Some kind of drug mix that's keeping people alive."

170

I breathe a long, slow sigh of relief. So Arroway came good. "OK. Tell me more."

"How long it lasts depends on who you give it to – some people only get a few hours, but others have lasted a lot longer." She pauses. "Can you bring this Knox person to us?"

"Not a chance. I'll have to come to Apex and bring the drugs back here."

There's silence for a moment. "I'll do you one better," Anna says. "You know the broken bridge in Gardens?"

I do. It's a Level 6 catwalk on the border of Gardens and Apex, named for its railings, torn and shredded in a long-forgotten attack.

"I'll meet you there," she says. "It'll save you going all the way."

"OK," I say. "And listen, Anna . . . thank you."

"Don't mention it. Just get here."

"Copy. Out."

Okwembu, silently listening to my half of the exchange, speaks up. "Will you at least tell me what's happening?"

I ignore her, stretching my legs out, doing my best to work up my tired muscles into something resembling a fit state to move. I'm going to have to run faster than I've ever run before – and I've already run so much today.

My eyes are drawn to Knox's hand, lying splayed out on the other side of his body. The remote unit is still held in it, secured to the palm with thin strips of tape. I walk over and crouch down, yanking it back and forth. After a few moments, it rips free. Knox groans, his lips twitching, sending a drop of Resin running down his chin.

One less thing to worry about. But what to do with it? I can't just leave it here. And if I have it on me, and accidentally hit the button during a roll or something, I'm done.

I cast around the shelves, looking for something to use. My

eyes land on a small box, made of hard plastic. It's almost identical to the ones Carver makes his stickies out of, only slightly bigger.

I pop the lid off. It's got cream in it, white and glistening. I rinse the box out over the basin, then wipe it off, making sure the inside is completely dry.

I jam the remote into it. It barely fits, but I tell myself that that's a good thing – it means the unit won't rattle around inside while I'm running. I slip the box into my pocket. It's uncomfortable, but it'll have to do.

Okwembu clears her throat. "Can you at least pull the scarf over my mouth before you go?"

She nods at Knox. The tendrils of Resin creeping out of his mouth are shiny under the storeroom lights, shimmering wetly.

I walk over and pull the scarf up, knotting it loosely behind her head. She's still bent awkwardly over the table. Her back's going to start hurting before long. Tough.

The canteen is still in my hand. I take a long drink from it, then set it down in front of Okwembu, between her bound hands. I spotted a length of rubber tube earlier, coiled in a box on one of the shelves. I retrieve it, then slip one end into the bottle and drop the other close to her mouth, hanging off the end of the table. All she has to do is bend down to drink.

She leans back, giving me some space. "Someone you love has got sick, just like him," she says, nodding at Knox. "It's written all over you."

She's wrong, but I don't say anything, just fiddle with the rubber tubing, adjusting its position on the edge of the table.

"It's Prakesh Kumar, isn't it?" she asks. "I'm so sorry, Ms Hale. I hope you find what you're looking for."

I don't bother to correct her. "So do I."

Suddenly, she leans forward, planting her elbows on the table, her face inches from mine.

172

Rob Boffard

"Your expression barely changed when I said his name," she says, her eyes glinting. "It's worse than that. Someone is dead. And since you don't have any family to speak of, that must mean someone other than dear Prakesh has become important to you. Was it Kevin O'Connell? I heard you say his name earlier. What about Aaron Carver? Maybe even Samuel Royo? Are you going to be able to save them, Ms Hale? Or are you just going to save yourself?"

Before she can say anything else, I'm running, charging out of the door and taking off down the corridor, heading towards Gardens.

42

Riley

I run. Faster than I've ever run before, pushing my body to the limit. The few people still in the corridors have to dodge out of my way, cursing as they flatten themselves against the walls. I don't care. I can't stop. Not now.

A smell has crept into Outer Earth. The air is thick with it, cloying and sweet. It tickles the back of my nostrils, and I can't escape it no matter which route I take. My paper mask does nothing to stop the stench. The mask itself is drenched with sweat, starting to tear. I don't even know if it's worth keeping, but I don't dare take if off yet.

When I cross the Chengshi gallery, high up on one of the catwalks, I'm startled to see black smoke curling in the air. Looking over the side, I see a pile of bodies being burned, attended by stompers wearing full-face respirators.

Standard procedure on the station is to cremate dead bodies, but this . . . have the furnaces given out? This kind of manual cremation won't work forever. Will we start putting them out of the airlocks? Leaving them where they fall?

There's too much to think about, too many questions I'd rather not answer.

I make good time, reaching the broken bridge in just under an hour. If I get the drug mix from Anna now, I might just be in time to save Knox.

She's waiting at the far side, in the shadows of the corridor entrance. She looks up as I approach, waving me over. She's abandoned her face mask – guess she decided there was no point, since she's not getting sick. Her cheeks are stained with dirt, black rivulets running down them like tears. Strands of hair stick to her forehead under the lip of her beanie. There's no sign of Carver. Probably a good thing.

"You took your time," she says as I come to a halt. "I thought you weren't going to make it."

I lean against the wall, breathing hard. It's a moment or two before I can raise my head to look at her.

"I'm just fine," I say, throwing a weary thumbs-up.

"Any Resin symptoms?"

"Not with me. Did you bring the drugs? I need to get going."

"Riley, you can barely stand."

I don't want to admit she's right. My legs are trembling, like a baby standing for the first time.

"Doesn't matter," I say, holding out my hand. "I don't have a choice."

But instead of handing me the vial or test tube or whatever it is, she places a hand on the corridor wall, and shakes her head. A ringlet of blonde hair, stained with sweat, falls over her face, and she pulls it back. "It's not just Resin. There are other things now, too. Dysentery." She says it *die-sentree*. "The last time we had someone with it was over two hundred years ago on Earth. *On Earth*, Riley."

"Anna, give me the drugs. Please."

"Do you think it's us?" she says. She keeps looking back over her shoulder, and over mine, to the other end of the catwalk. "Do you think we've got something to do with it? Why else wouldn't we be getting sick?"

What little radar I have is starting to ping repeatedly. I reach forward, grip Anna's shoulder. "Just give me the drugs, and let me take care of this."

"Stop being so bloody selfish. Come in. Let the doctors test you. They got nothing from my blood, or from Carver's, but maybe yours will be different. And they can take the bombs out."

"Are you insane? If I don't get those drugs to Morgan Knox I'm as good as dead." I jab a finger at my shaking legs. "And there's no taking them out. If I try, then what happened to Kev . . ." I trail off.

She stares at me, her eyes hard. "In that case, I'm sorry Riley. I didn't want it to be this way."

They're at the other end of the corridor, just where it takes a turn. Stompers. Grey-clad, with full-face masks like the heads of beetles, all tubing and shining faceplates. Stingers out, pointed right at us.

Royo and the others must have listening in when we spoke over SPOCS. They lured me right in.

Anna flattens herself against the corridor wall. She doesn't look at me.

I'm already moving, sprinting back the way I came, but there are stompers on the catwalk, their feet pounding the metal as they run towards me.

Something deep inside me snaps.

I want it to be over. Not just the bombs, but everything: the guilt, the nightmares, the days of trying and failing to make any sort of difference at all. Because, the truth is, Outer Earth doesn't need me. Maybe I saved it once, but I can't save it now. I can't stop Resin, any more than I could save my father.

Turning in mid-stride, I put one hand on the railing of the catwalk, then get a foot up on it. We're high up enough. It'll be quick.

I try to picture Prakesh's face in my mind, but it won't come, like the connections have been severed. Carver's, too, and Kevin's. Right then, as I feel myself going over, it's my father's face I see. The look in his eyes, right before I executed the on-screen command that killed him. My name, glaring orange over his face.

The stompers running towards me on the catwalk are in another universe. Gravity takes hold of me, caressing my stomach, getting ready to grip tight and *pull.*

43

Riley

But there are hands on my back, my shoulders, my arms. Gravity's grip loosens as they pull me back, hauling me off the railing. I'm airborne for a split second before slamming into the floor of the catwalk.

My head cracks the metal, turning my vision grey. I'm shouting: not even words, just inarticulate yells which turn into sobs as the tears run down my face, staining my face mask.

I'm hauled to my feet, hands gripping my upper arms tightly. Royo is there, staring daggers through the faceplate of his mask. Through a gap in the stompers, I see Anna. Her face is cold, set with purpose, but her eyes tell a different story.

"I thought I could trust you, Hale," Royo says, his words distorted by the mask.

I swallow. "Sam," I say, using his first name. He does nothing. I continue: "You don't understand. I had to—"

"You split from your team. You break Janice Okwembu out of the brig. You're not getting sick from Resin. You are possibly responsible for the death of Kevin O'Connell. You're damn right I don't understand."

"You know about what's inside me," I say. "You heard me talking to Anna, and you know what'll happen if I don't get back. Sam, *please*."

He talks over me. "You're under arrest, Hale. And if you try to run, then so help me I will put a bullet in your head and walk away whistling."

I'm hustled past them, marched so fast down the corridor that my feet barely touch the ground. I try to find some energy. Maybe I can fight them, make Royo put that bullet in me. But there's nothing. My legs feel like pieces of lead, dead and useless. They take my wristband, pull my earpiece out.

"Where are we going?" I say eventually.

"Apex," says the stomper on my right. "We need to get a blood sample."

I don't remember half the journey to the hospital. We have to pass through multiple checkpoints, each one guarded by stompers with full masks. They've locked down the entire sector, surrounding it with stompers – the last stand against an encroaching tide of Resin.

The walls of Apex are a dazzling white, glaring under the ceiling lights. The harsh light brings back bad memories – the last time I was here, I'd just run through the Core, almost hypothermic with cold.

What little order there was in the sector's hospital is gone. Beds have spilled out of the doors, makeshift mattresses littering the floors of the wards and the surrounding corridors. There are huddled shapes on them, wrapped in blankets, shivering. Several are still, with the fabric pulled over their faces. Doctors move between the mattresses, bending down to their patients, occasionally rising to glance at each other and shake their heads.

They take me to a small ward by the main offices. It's strikingly similar to Knox's operating room; there are the same units and basins lining the walls, the same hospital bed in the middle.

The bed is a little more comfortable than the one Okwembu is currently chained to, with a padded mattress and a raised head-rest, but there are the same wrist and ankle cuffs hanging off the side. Before I can argue, the stompers lift me up onto the bed, strapping me down, pulling the velcro tight. I can move my hands and feet a little, but not enough to make any difference. The mattress feels rough and clammy on my skin.

One of them brings over a canteen with a straw attached. The water soothes my parched throat, and I can feel my body relaxing into the bed.

At least I don't have to run any more.

Han Tseng walks in, along with a doctor. It's Arroway – he doesn't identify himself, but he's still wearing his name tag. He looks familiar, and I remember running a hospital job for him before, back when I was still with the Devil Dancers. I remember him looking tired back then – right now, he looks like he's about to fall over.

"Don't look so terrified," he says, washing his hands in the basin. "It's not as if we're going to operate without anaesthetic. I just need a blood sample."

"Do you think there's any chance it'll work?" I ask. But he doesn't meet my eyes, just raises a syringe to his face, tapping the needle to knock the air out. My arm is swabbed with alcohol, icy-cold, followed by the bite of the needle as it goes in. I hiss, failing to clamp the noise down in time.

"Of course it won't work," says Han Tseng. "You'll have the same things in your blood as your friends Beck and Carver. Just a lot of highly complex antibodies that we can't replicate. But we have to at least try."

Arroway draws the needle out. The blood in the syringe – my blood – is a red so dark it's almost black.

"I heard there was a way of stabilising people with Resin," I say.

Arroway shrugs. "It's a mix of furosemide and nitrates we cooked up. Stops the lungs filling completely with fluid. But it only slows Resin down. Eventually, everyone dies."

"Did they tell you about the bombs?" I ask.

Tseng shakes his head. He's not saying no – he's shaking it in disbelief. When he looks back up, there's contempt on his face. "You use Resin as an excuse to settle a score with Janice Okwembu? And then you cook up this story? What do you want me to say here?"

Anger surges through me. "It's not a story. Pull up my pants leg. Look for yourself."

His eyes linger on my legs for a moment, but he makes no move towards them. "You can't put remote-control bombs in someone. It's insane."

I try to keep the fury out of my voice. "Just look. You'll see the stitches. Or better yet – there's a control unit in my left pocket. It's right there."

Han Tseng loses it. He walks over, slams his hands down on the bed, stares right into my face. "We've lost *everything*. The only thing I can do now is try to save what's left. See him?" He points to Arroway. "He and his colleagues are working overtime, trying to figure out how we beat this thing. Do you imagine for a moment that I'm going to pull him away from that so he can perform exploratory surgery on your say-so?"

"*My friend* is dead. His name was Kevin, and he was killed the same way."

Tseng turns, and strides to the door, not looking back.

"Just put me under then," I say. "Knock me out. I don't want to feel it. *Knock me out!*"

But he and Arroway are gone. The stomper standing outside the door looks in, his gaze lingering on my prone body. Then the door shuts, sliding closed, and I hear it lock with a click that

181

echoes off the walls. I yank at the restraints, but they stay strapped tight.

It doesn't take long for me to wear myself out. There's nothing I can do now.

Distantly, I wonder how long I have before Knox's heart stops beating and the signal is transmitted. An hour? Two? I still can't quite believe that the drugs to keep him alive, to keep *me* alive, are right here in this hospital. They may as well be on the other side of the moon.

I can't even work up any anger against Anna. She may have betrayed me, but it feels like something that happened a long, long time ago.

Will Carver come and see me? What will he say? And when it's all over . . . will they stick me on one of those funeral pyres? Will they tell Prakesh?

The room is quiet – even the hum of the station is muted here, reduced to a low hiss. Time passes – I don't know how much. There's a security camera in the top corner of the wall by the door, flashing a tiny red light every few seconds, its black lens staring down at me. I can see the hospital bed reflected in its gaze. I expect Royo to come and question me, but it doesn't happen.

I close my eyes. The light in the room turns orange under my lids. I try to picture myself on Earth, running through that field of grass that I've dreamt about so often, under a warm sun, and a sky so blue that it hurts to look at it.

There's a loud click.

Just as I open my eyes in surprise, the lights in the room flicker and die, plunging me into darkness.

44

Prakesh

They cross the hangar in silence, heading for the Food Lab. Prakesh is acutely aware of the stinger jammed in his back, but even more aware of the man holding it.

Julian is hanging on the end of a very thin thread, and Prakesh doesn't want to think about what will happen if it snaps. He isn't crazy – at least, Prakesh doesn't think so. But he's very scared, and that means he'll be quick to do something stupid.

"That's it," Julian says, as they pass under the oak trees running along the side of the lab. "Keep walking."

The men carrying the plasma cutter – Iko and Roger – walk behind them. Prakesh can hear them struggling with it, swearing under their breath as they lug it across the floor. The other people in the group walk ahead of Julian, as if scouting the way. Prakesh can tell that they're on edge as well, can tell from the set of their shoulders that they don't like this. Then again, they aren't the ones with a stinger in their backs.

This isn't the first time Prakesh has been in danger. He was abducted by Oren Darnell, nearly lost his life. And he and

Riley have been in plenty of other scrapes. But something about this is different. Maybe because it's his own techs holding him hostage – people he worked with, people he trusted. Whatever it is, it's enough to make cold sweat break out across his back.

"So this exit," says Julian. "Tell me about it."

Prakesh has to hunt for the words. Then he has to work his swollen mouth hard to try and form the words. "Wall of the Food Lab."

"I know that." He sounds bored. "Where does it lead?"

"Out into the ventilation system."

"OK." Julian digs the stinger barrel into Prakesh's back. "And where does the ventilation system get us? Where's the nearest exit point?"

"The water point on Level 2. Near the hospital."

Instantly, he realises his mistake. Julian stops dead, then grabs Prakesh's shoulder, spinning him around and jamming the gun into his cheek. "You're sending us to a *hospital*? Where do you think the disease is? I don't feel like dying today."

That's when Prakesh sees them.

There are five – six – Air Lab techs, crouching behind one of the algae pools that run alongside the trees. They're armed: Prakesh can see fire extinguishers, metal rods. He doesn't know how long they've been following Julian's group for, but it's clear what they plan to do. They're going to attack. And even if they succeed, not all of them will make it. Julian won't hesitate before shooting them, just like he shot Yoshiro.

Julian's stinger is still in his face. He speaks as fast as he can. "You won't get infected," he says. "I said it's *near* the hospital. You can just go the other way. Besides, for all we know they could be containing it right now."

Julian looks around, as if hunting for support among the others. Prakesh looks over his shoulder, over to the algae pools.

184

He can just see Suki's terrified eyes looking over the top. Prakesh gives a very gentle shake of his head, desperately hoping that Suki understands.

He doesn't get a chance to find out. "I say we use the cutter on the main door," says Iko. "I don't like this one bit, Jules."

Prakesh can see Julian thinking. He closes his eyes. If Suki and her group attack, if Julian doesn't lead them into the Food Lab, then this could go very badly. He looks at the gun, held tight in Julian's hand, now pointing slightly away from him. *I could take it*, he thinks. He feels a sudden urge to reach out, pulls it back just in time.

Julian shakes his head, then spins Prakesh around again, putting the pistol in its accustomed position in the small of his back. "Let's go," he says.

They resume their march towards the Food Lab, the doors looming large. Prakesh knows what's beyond them: a dark, soot-stained hangar, filled with scaffolding and building equipment. Construction stopped a few months ago – they need building materials from the asteroid, the one the *Shinso Maru* is bringing into orbit. The ship might be ancient, barely functional, but it's still got enough juice to bring an asteroid back. Once they've got that, they can start rebuilding.

Assuming we're still alive, Prakesh thinks.

Julian pushes him over to the doors. There's a keypad set into the wall. Prakesh set the code himself, months ago – another part of his plan to keep the Air Lab secure. He punches it in now: 0421. Riley's birth date. Easy to remember.

Prakesh pauses for a moment before hitting the final number. He would do anything right now to be back in his hab with Riley. He doesn't care about their fight any more. He just wants to hold her.

"What are you waiting for?" Julian says.

Prakesh shakes his head, and hits ENTER. With a hiss, the

doors to the Food Lab slide back into the wall. There's nothing but darkness beyond them.

"We're going to need some light," Prakesh says. He glances at Julian. "They turned off the power couplings. Overheads won't work."

"Oh, we got light," says Julian. He looks at Iko, who lifts the hooked nozzle of the cutting torch. He flicks a switch, and the end of the nozzle sparks to life, a point so bright that Prakesh has to shield his eyes.

Julian shoves Prakesh with the small of his hand. "You're in front," he says.

186

The blackness is total. There isn't even any light coming from under the door to the outside. The whole hospital must be down – I can hear confused shouts from somewhere in the corridor.

I expect the emergency lighting to come on. It doesn't. I yank at the restraints again, as if the velcro was somehow only strapped shut because of the power. It doesn't give, and I slam my head back on the pillow in frustration. There's hammering on the door, and I yell at them to let me out, but then I hear running footsteps, getting fainter. Doesn't matter – not to me anyway. I'm still stuck here. Still dead.

I hope Han Tseng feels really shitty afterwards, I think, and surprise myself by giggling. It's a weird sound, tiny in the darkness. I shut my eyes; apart from a few muffled voices, somewhere in the distance, the hospital is almost completely silent. I could be lost in space, drifting further than any human has ever gone.

There's a noise above me. A grinding sound.

My eyes fly open, but I see absolutely nothing. Just pitch

darkness. My breath has caught in my throat – I imagined the sound, I had to have. But then it comes again, directly above me. A sound like metal on metal, as if someone was—

Pushing back the plates in the ceiling.

Whoever it is chooses that moment to drop. One of their feet takes me in the breastbone with the force of a meteorite impact, sending a huge shock wave of pain slamming through me. I yell out, half in surprise, half in total agony. My attacker's other foot has landed on the mattress; they're off balance, and their arms windmill as they fight to retain it.

The foot digs into me, jabbing hard. "Who the hell is—" I manage to say, but my next word is swamped as a hand clamps over my mouth.

I whip my head from side to side, trying to shake it off, grunting frantically, even trying to open my mouth so I can bite down on one of the fingers. Right then, there's a voice, next to my ear.

"If you don't stop thrashing around," says Carver, "I'm going to suffocate you with a pillow."

I'm breathing hard through my nose. Only when I'm completely still does he take his hand away. He does it slowly, as if I might start yelling again. No chance of that – I'm still working out what I'm actually going to say to him.

I finally settle for "What are you doing?"

"Practising my landings."

I feel his hands moving along my right arm, until he finds the cuff. He rips the velcro away. I start on the other, while Carver works his way round to my feet. Halfway there, he knocks his shin on something and swears loudly.

"Carver, why are you doing this?"

"Has anyone ever told you that you ask far too many questions?" he says. I feel tugging on my right ankle, hear the rip of velcro. "I'm getting you out of here."

"But what happened earlier. With Kev . . ."

"So what, you don't want me to get you out?"

"I didn't—"

"I still don't understand what happened to Kev. But I'm not letting it happen to you, too."

He keeps working on my cuffs. "We all agreed that if you tried to contact anybody, we'd get you to come in. It was just luck that you got through to Anna first, really. I don't think Royo would have managed it – he was never very good at asking nicely."

"Luck? Anna betrayed me."

"Don't start with that, Riley. She did what she had to do. And I still can't believe you wouldn't tell me what was happening to you."

I try to make my reply strident, strong, but it doesn't feel that way. "I didn't want you to get hurt. I had to handle this myself."

"How'd that work out for you?"

The last cuff falls loose. I stand carefully, putting my feet on the floor as if the bombs will trigger from the slightest impact.

"They tested your blood," Carver says. "You and Anna are both immune to Resin."

"What about you?"

"Same thing," he says. "They're not sure why. We've got the right antibodies, but they don't know why, or how to replicate them. Anyway, doesn't matter. Tseng's not letting anyone leave."

"He thinks if we can hold Apex, we can save the station. That about right?"

"Uh-huh. But, right now, we're the only ones who could get anywhere – any stomper with a respirator wouldn't make it ten steps before being killed for it."

I hear another sound from where he's standing – like liquid in a small container being shaken.

"Furosemide-nitrate compound," he says. "Single dose. Got it from one of the labs. If this Knox person is real, and if you really die when he dies, then it'll buy you some time."

I feel myself smiling. It's a tiny chink of light in a very dark world, but it's there.

"We'll have to force the door," I say, stepping my way around the debris.

"Actually, if I have my timing right, we can use the handle."

There's another loud click from above. The room is flooded with dim red light – the emergency power, finally kicking on.

Carver's face, hair and stomper jacket are streaked with sticky, oily dirt from the ducts. "Deactivate the emergency backup, smash the main power coupling, slip into the ventilation system before they arrive," he says. "Easy."

He slips past me to the door and tries the handle. It doesn't move. His brow furrowed, he tries again, rattling it harder.

"Problem?" I ask.

"This should be connected to the emergency power, right?"

"It's a manual door, you moron. They all are."

"Yeah, I see that now, thanks. What do we do?"

I think for a moment, casting my eyes around the room. In the corridor outside, I can hear running feet and urgent voices. How long will it be before they check on us? No way to tell.

My gaze falls on one of the units lined up against the wall. It's about chest-high, the metal shelves stocked with pill bottles and plastic containers filled with viscous liquid. I step towards it, pulling it away from the wall on its casters, struggling to keep it straight. "Help me with this," I say to Carver.

He's shaking his head. "If you're trying to reach the ceiling vent, it's no good. It's too high up."

But for the first time in what seems like a year, I'm smiling. "Better idea. There's a guard outside the door, right?"

He nods, confused. "There should be. Why?"

190

I point to the unit. "Just help me. Then get on one side of the door."

Puzzled, he complies, pulling the unit over to the door, then pressing his back to the wall on the right. I take the left. "Ready?" I say.

"Ready for what?"

"This."

I put one foot on the unit, and shove. It topples over with a colossal crash, sending bottles flying across the floor. Almost immediately there's a startled cry from outside. The door flies open, and a stomper runs into the room. He's got his stinger out, but before he can turn around I hit him in the back of the neck, right in the pressure point.

He goes limp on his feet, and I shove him to the floor. He turns his face up to the light, his eyes clouded, and just before Carver pulls me out of the door I recognise him. Sanchez – one of the guys from Big 6.

There's no time to feel bad. He'll live, and that's good enough for now.

The corridor is bathed in the red emergency lighting, turning it into something from the depths of hell. There's a strange buzzing sound, like the power cables are frying in their rubber insulation, cooking the entire hospital.

"How did you know there was only one stomper outside?" Carver says over his shoulder.

"I didn't."

"You could have told me."

"You had a better idea?"

"Not really," he says.

As the words leave his mouth, two stompers materialise in front of him, stingers out. I see their eyes widen above their masks, see them raise the stingers. Carver drops to his knees, skidding along the corridor.

191

I know what he's doing. It's a move Amira taught us, years ago, and I wasn't even aware that I'd remembered it until now. I take off with one foot, planting the other firmly on Carver's back and launching myself upwards, going so high that my forehead taps the roof of the corridor. I fling my legs out in front of me, as if I'm sitting in mid-air.

My feet hit the stompers at the same time. My left foot takes one of them in the throat; his gun goes off, the bullet slamming into the floor somewhere behind us. My right foot hits the other stomper square in the face, the heel smashing into the faceplate of his respirator. I hear it give under my foot with a *crack*.

They're both down before I land. I barely manage to get my feet under me before I do, but as I make contact I see the one I smashed in the face try to rise. Carver jams a fist into his neck, sending him sprawling. Then we're both up and running, charging down the corridor.

The buzz in the walls is louder now, like the hospital is angry at us for overcoming its guards. We don't see any more stompers – wherever the rest are, we seem to have slipped past them. We sprint out into the hospital atrium, heading for the exit. The atrium has high ceilings, going up at least two levels, with balconies clustering around it – another one of those vastly impractical designs that our ancestors seemed to specialise in. There's an admissions desk in our way, between us and the door, a chest-high slab with overturned chairs scattered before it. We vault over it in unison, landing with a bang on the other side, no more than a few strides from the doors.

We're almost there when we hear a shout from behind us.

"Hale!"

It's Royo. He's standing by the desk. His respirator has been ripped off, hanging on his chest, a tangle of black tubes and straps. His bald head is shiny with sweat under the lights.

And the stinger in his hand is pointed right at us.

It's only when he fires that we stop. We're nearly at the doors, and we skid to a halt. Carver nearly tumbles, his feet catching under him. Royo fired upwards – a warning shot, buried in the ceiling.

"Next one finds its target," he says.

His gun hand stays steady, but there's something in his eyes. Like he doesn't quite know where he is. We're too far away to jump him – and too close to run.

I shake my head. "We're on the same side, Cap."

"And what side would that be?" he says.

"Yours," I say. "Outer Earth's."

"No. No, no, no, no. You and Janice Okwembu. You're all in this together. You made the virus. It was you."

Carver steps in front of me, his hands held out in front of him. "Put the gun down, Captain."

Royo takes a step forward, the stinger aimed right at Carver's chest. Above and around us, the darkened balconies stare down. "You're helping her, Carver? Can't say I'm surprised."

A tiny flash of anger crosses Carver's face, but he doesn't move. Instead, he says, "Whatever's stopping Riley and me from getting sick, they can't build it in a lab. There's nothing more we can do here."

"You're wrong. We have to hold the sector."

"With who?" Carver says. He raises his arms, pointing to the empty balconies. "Where's your backup? How many stompers have we lost today?"

"I don't care."

"Cap, listen to me," I say. I can feel the stitches in my legs burning, like lit fuses. "Everything you heard me and Anna talking about was true. If I don't do this, I'm dead."

"It's the *Shinso Maru*, isn't it?" he says. "That's your plan. Kill as many people as possible, then capture the ship."

"Captain . . . Sam . . ."

"You're trying to go back to Earth. Finish what your old man started, all those years ago. Okwembu got in your head, just like she did with your crew leader. You shouldn't have listened to her, Hale."

His words aren't true, aren't even close to being true, but they cut deeper than they should. I'm about to say something very stupid when I freeze. What I see stops the words in their tracks, cutting them off as effectively as someone grabbing me round the throat.

A line of thin black liquid has started to run from Royo's nostril. It reaches his lip, moving almost imperceptibly. He coughs, reaching up to wipe it away almost absent-mindedly. It leaves a black streak on his face.

"We're going now, Cap," Carver says quietly.

Slowly, he turns, and starts walking towards the doors. After a moment, I turn and follow. Behind us, I hear Royo take a step forward. "Don't make me do this," he says.

Carver jabs at a button by the doors, and they slide soundlessly into the wall.

"Is this how you want it to end? With a bullet in the back? Hale, I am your commanding officer, and I am ordering you to stop. *Now*."

And then another voice speaks, from the shadows. "Put it down, Captain."

Anna Beck steps out, One-Mile raised high, her fingers clenched around the steel bearing in the cup. She walks towards us, never taking her eyes off Royo, tracking him with the slingshot.

He lowers the gun, just slightly. "So it's like that, huh?"

Anna nods. "It's like that." She's at our side now. I can't look at her. I want to tell her to stay away, that I'll only get her killed. Instead, as one, we turn and start to make our way out. Our walk turns into a jog, then a run.

194

"Dammit, *stop*."

Even without looking round, I can tell that Royo has raised his stinger again. Anna isn't aiming at him any more – she's moving with us, away from Royo. Then we're into the corridor, the lights in the ceiling whipping past above us, the passing struts in the walls punctuating the beating of my heart.

Royo howls – it's a cry of agony, like he's being tortured, like he's going through the worst pain imaginable – and pulls the trigger.

46

Prakesh

The harsh light from the cutting torch throws the structures in the Food Lab into sharp relief. Scaffolding rises above them, ladders and pipes etching rigid shadows onto the walls. The floor is smeared with soot, with tools scattered across it, hammers and welding masks and angle grinders. The greenhouses, destroyed in the fire, are nothing more than shells, their thick bases almost melted away.

The door to the Food Lab whines shut behind them, clicking into place.

Prakesh coughs. Even now, months after the fire, the air is still thick with a sour chemical tang. Julian gives him a shove and he stumbles forward, almost tripping over a welding mask. He whirls, on the verge of anger now, but Julian has the stinger pointed right at him. Iko sweeps the cutting torch from side to side, the shadows moving with it.

Prakesh starts walking, keeping his hands visible at his sides. The group falls silent as they move through the hangar, stepping single file between the melted greenhouses. Prakesh's mind is on fire, anxiety poking holes in his plan. He should make his move now. *No.* He's still an easy target. But the longer he waits, the further he gets from the Food Lab entrance . . .

"I don't like this place," Roger says.

"Same here," Iko replies. "Hey, Prakesh," he says, raising his voice. "Weren't you here when the fire started?"

Prakesh says nothing.

"Sure he was," Julian says. "He watched old Deacon go up in smoke. Didn't you?"

Prakesh keeps his eyes fixed on the floor ahead of him. He'd rather not think about that particularly day – the day when Deacon, one of Oren Darnell's co-conspirators, strapped on a vest containing packs of flammable ammonium nitrate and then set himself on fire. Prakesh nearly died in the inferno. So did Riley; she ran in there to save him.

If I get out of this, he thinks, *I am going to hug her so hard she won't be able to breathe.*

His shin smacks into something hard. A piece of sheet metal, laid between the remains of two of the greenhouses to form a low, makeshift table. He lands on it hands first, soot scratching at his palms, scattering the tools lying across it.

There's shouting from behind him. Julian is there instantly, jamming the gun into his neck, a sweaty hand against his hair.

"Watch where you're going," he says, hissing the words into Prakesh's ear, then hauling him upright. Prakesh can feel blood soaking into his pants, oozing from where the metal edge sliced through them.

Julian kicks the table aside, the crash echoing off the walls. They keep marching. This time, Julian makes Iko and Roger take the lead, keeping the stinger wedged firmly in Prakesh's back.

He directs them to the end of the hangar, to the massive structure that rises almost to the ceiling. The walls still stand –

the support struts are made of thick steel, and they managed to withstand the fire. But the inside is a tangle of melted metal and plastic, and there's another smell in the air now, earthy and sour.

"The Buzz Box?" says Julian. "Your exit's in the *Buzz Box*?"

Prakesh meets his eyes, and nods.

"And you had to lead us here? You didn't think to mention that this was where we were going?"

"You didn't ask," Prakesh says.

Julian falls silent, staring up at the structure. The Buzz Box. Ten million beetles and twenty million silkworms – the station's single best source of protein, before they were all burned to cinders. It deserved its name. Prakesh remembers the noise, a hum so intense that it vibrated your stomach. It's darker inside than it is on the hangar floor, as if the light from the cutting torch can't quite penetrate.

"At the back," he says. "There's a loose panel on the wall."

Julian pushes him inside. "Show us."

The top sections of the structure have burned out, collapsing inwards, and the floor crunches underfoot. At first, Prakesh thinks it's just debris, but the fragments are too small. It's only when Iko plays the light over it that he realises what they're walking on: dead insects. Millions of them, frozen in puddles of melted plastic.

I'm in a nightmare, he thinks, and almost laughs. He expects someone to make a joke, Iko maybe, but nobody says a word.

He's running out of time. But Julian has the gun at his back, and Iko's cutting torch is just a little too close. Sweat beads on his forehead, dripping into his eyes.

After what seems like an age, they reach the back of the Buzz Box. Julian lets him go, and Prakesh makes a pretence of moving along the wall, running his hands across the panels. *Please, please let this work.*

"Here," he says, nearly swallowing the word. He raps on

one of the panels – a panel he knows has nothing wired behind it. "This one."

Nobody moves.

Julian gestures with the stinger. "OK. So open it up."

Prakesh crouches down, pretending to work on the bottom of the panel. He looks over his shoulder, finding Iko's eyes. "I need some more light."

Iko glances at Julian, who shrugs. He steps forward, raising the tip of the cutting torch so it's above Prakesh's head.

Now.

Prakesh reaches up, grabs the cutting torch cylinder, and wrenches it out of Iko's grip. Before the man can do anything, Prakesh pulls it downwards, his fingers hunting for the ON switch.

He finds it just as the nozzle touches Iko's thigh. The plasma slices through fabric and skin and flesh. Iko howls, more in surprise than pain.

Prakesh hears the stinger go off, drowning out Julian's shout of surprise. But he's already gone, sprinting back the way they came in.

199

47

Riley

The bullet buries itself in the wall somewhere behind us. There's no second shot. We turn a corner in the corridor, and Royo is gone.

None of us says anything as we run. There's too much to deal with: Anna's betrayal, what happened to Kev. My body feels like a canteen, drained of its last sip of water.

The time I spent in the hospital, off my feet, has restored some of my energy. Carver drops behind the more we run, first alongside me, then behind me. Initially, I think it's because he's letting me lead the way, but then I realise it's more than that; he's not as fit as me, and not as fast over long distances. I can hear him breathing, ragged and quick.

Anna is hurting, too. I can see it in her stance, in the set expression on her face. But she keeps pace with me, refusing to drop back.

When we slip through the door into the surgery, Okwembu is still strapped to the table, bent over. The bottle I put in front of her has been knocked onto the floor, and, judging by the red marks on her wrists, she's been trying to pull loose. She gives us a cold look, tight-lipped.

Carver stares at her for a moment, fascinated, as if he's never seen her close up. I guess he hasn't. Anna leans up against the door, trembling, pushing against the stitch that's trying to bend her in two.

Carver points to Okwembu. "You actually managed to get her all the way here without killing her?" he says. "Not sure I'd've managed it. Not after what she did."

"I was trying to save Outer Earth, young man," Okwembu says.

Carver leans forward over the table, so close to Okwembu's face that their noses are almost touching. "My crew leader died after you and Darnell got in her head. Didn't save her, did you?"

"Carver," I say. I can't even look at the other room, where Knox is. Not until I have the drug compound.

He shakes his head, then reaches inside his jacket and pulls out a small bottle and tosses it to me. It's about the size of my palm, filled with something that looks like thick urine. Spotting a syringe on one of the shelves, I grab it and yank the cap off before jamming it into the mesh stopper on the top of the bottle. My hands are shaking so hard that I almost drop the syringe. I sprint into the other room, skidding to my knees in front of Knox.

For a long, horrible moment, I'm sure he's stopped breathing. Then he gives a tiny exhalation, almost like a cough, his chest fluttering. There are more Resin strands on his face, fresh ones over the dried tracks. I don't waste another second. I grab his arm, pull back his sleeve and jam the needle into a vein. I push the plunger, and dark blood wells up alongside the wound.

Knox's arm jerks, sending the needle flying. He coughs, then groans in pain, twisting his legs, his back arching so far that it pushes him off the floor. His breath is coming in short gasps.

"Did it work?"

Carver is standing in the doorway, his arms folded, Anna peeking over his shoulder. I can see Okwembu behind her, straining for a better look.

Knox's breathing has settled back to a regular tempo – shallow, but consistent. His eyes flutter open, fix on mine. A capillary in his left eye has ruptured, staining the white matter bright red.

"I was . . ." he starts – but another coughing fit overtakes him, grabbing his body in a giant fist and shaking.

Carver speaks from behind me. "You awake yet, asshole?"

"Carver," I say. "How long?"

"What?"

"The drugs. How much more time do we have?"

He shrugs. "Half a day, maybe? I don't know. Resin's tough to figure out."

"Resin?" says Knox, rising up onto his elbows. He nearly makes it, but his body starts trembling and he collapses. "Is that what it's called?" He rolls onto his side, pulls his legs up to his chest. "Throat hurts."

"Get used to it," I say.

He glances towards Carver and Anna. "You brought someone else in here?"

"They're friends. And they helped save your life, in case you're wondering."

"Not that you deserve it," Anna says.

He doesn't respond. He's bathed in sweat, and every cough sets his body trembling like a leaf in airflow.

"I did what you asked, all right?" I say. "I broke her out. Time to hold up your end."

He stares at me, uncomprehending.

A tiny seed of panic begins to flower, deep inside me. "I brought her to you, just like you wanted," I say, as if repeating

202

it enough will get it through his skull. His pupils are unfocused, his mouth slightly open. When he licks his cracked lips, I see his tongue is almost completely black.

"Who?" he says. "Amira? You brought me my Amira?"

Carver rockets off the door frame, fists clenched, mouth set in a thin line. Anna grabs him, pulling him back.

"No," I say, forcing myself to stay calm. "Okwembu. Janice Okwembu."

I jerk my head towards the operating table. He glances behind me, sees the former council leader strapped down. She stares back at him, refusing to let fear show on her face.

"Very good," he says. He closes his eyes and lets his head fall back on the floor.

I grip his shoulder. "Take these things out. Now."

"Ah yes," he says. "I should keep my promise."

He raises his hands, and with a kind of dull horror I see that they're shaking. He can't keep his fingers still. I grip his right hand – it's ice-cold under my fingers, the skin damp with sweat, and, no matter how I squeeze, it won't keep still.

"I could take the devices out," says Knox, "but doing it without setting them off? Or leaving the surrounding tissue intact? That I'm not sure about."

I throw his hand down. It bounces off his chest, coming to a rest by his side. His eyes are closed. I want to scream at him. But he's right – there's no way he can carry out any sort of surgery.

Carver leans over him. "Then tell us how to deactivate them. There's gotta be a way."

But Knox is gone – fallen back into unconsciousness, his chest rising and falling. No telling how long he has left. How long *I* have. I'm back to the beginning. I walk past Carver and pick up the pills, then lean on the edge of one of the basins lining the wall. I hang my head, trying to focus on my breathing.

"Riley," Anna says. "What exactly was he going to do to Okwembu? Please tell me this isn't what I think it is."

I backhand her across the face, my body moving before my mind registers what's happening. It knocks Anna backwards, the sound cracking around the room. I grab her by the front of her shirt and slam her into the wall. Her beanie falls over one eye, and the other one looks back at me in fear and incomprehension.

"*None of this* is what you think it is," I say. "Being a tracer, being a stomper, all of it. You treat it like a game, but in the real world people die. People we care about."

She struggles in my grip. "All I'm saying is that we should—"

"You wanna trade places?" I say. "Fine. *You* can be the one who gets turned into a walking bomb. You can make the decisions."

Carver pushes between us. When I resist he shoves me away, and when I try to rush back he puts a hand square on my chest. "Everybody just calm down."

"Why did we even let her come?" I say through teeth clenched so hard that my jaw clicks.

"Riley, I—"

Carver pulls me away. I try to wrench free, but he wraps me in his arms, burying my head in his shoulder. That's when I realise I'm crying. The tears are ice-cold against my skin.

"Easy now," Carver whispers. "Easy."

"Kev was my fault," I say, amazed that I can still find words. "I killed him."

"*No*. You didn't. You understand me? That was all Knox. And when this is all over, we'll go and talk to Kev's parents together. Promise."

The oddest feeling comes over me then. It's the same feeling I have when I'm close to Prakesh, when we're lying in bed and I have my head buried in the side of his neck. At first, I think it's just me missing him, but it's more than that. Being this close to someone, being *held*, feels good. Good enough that I don't want to let go.

When I look up, after what seems like entire minutes, Okwembu is watching me intently.

"Riley," Anna says, her voice very small. "I'm so, so sorry. Captain Royo told me that we had to bring you in, so I . . . I mean, if I'd known, I would have . . ."

"It's OK," says Carver. "Everybody screwed everybody. We've balanced the karma."

I take a deep breath. "Yeah."

I glance at Anna. Carver's got no family to speak of, but she's different. "If you want to get back up to Tzevya, look after your folks, that's fine."

She opens her mouth to speak, pauses, shakes her head. "If my father knew I left you, he wouldn't let me back in anyway."

"What's the word on SPOCS?" I say.

Anna tilts her head. "Oh, right. You don't have yours. Resin's all anybody's talking about. We've dropped right down the priority list."

"Good to know."

She narrows her eyes. "Okwembu – she hasn't got sick either?"

Anna's right. I look back at the former council leader – bound, but healthy.

Carver thinks, then shakes his head. "There's a connection, but not one that I can see. Anyway, it's not important right now – we've *definitely* been exposed to Resin, we *definitely* aren't sick and we can *definitely* move faster than anyone else. So what do we all have in common?"

Anna sucks in a breath. "*Of course.*"

Carver and I stare at her. She looks back at us, her eyes wide.

"Mikhail," she says. "He's what we all have in common. He's why we aren't sick."

Neither of us responds. She looks between us, back and forth. "Think about it. Riley and I arrested him, and Carver, you were there when we brought him in."

I shake my head. "So was Royo. And he's got Resin."

"And Mariana," Carver says. When he sees Anna looking confused, he goes on. "The guard at the brig. She died earlier."

"Right," says Anna, grimacing. "But name *one other thing* that connects us. It's him, I'm telling you."

An idea flickers at the edge of my mind. Something I saw. Before I can get a fix on it, it's gone.

At that moment, there's a noise from the corridor outside. The sound of people trying to be quiet and failing. A single glance between Carver and me is enough.

We start moving. But we're barely halfway to the door when it flies open, and people with guns charge into the room.

48

Riley

I let muscle memory take over.

The closest attacker is a woman, her long brown hair pulled back into a ponytail, her lower face hidden by a green scarf. I knock her gun aside, and follow it up with a jab to her throat. She crumples, retching. I'm dimly aware of Carver moving alongside me, grunting as he takes another one of them down.

I drop and spin, lashing out with my left leg, catching another one of them in the shin. I get a glimpse of Anna. She's grabbed a scalpel, and has thrown it, flicking her hand out. It fails to connect, bouncing off a jacket-clad chest. Okwembu is shouting, pulling at her restraints.

I use my momentum to spin myself upright, ready to take out the rest of them. I don't know who they are, or what they want, but they're not getting it.

Too many of them. They're pouring through the door, stingers out, eyes flashing in triumph. Carver and I are slammed up against the wall, and one of them has his arms around Anna, lifting her off the ground. She's screaming and kicking, but her hands are held tight against her waist.

I look around, and a stinger barrel is inches from my nose.

"Stop moving," says the owner. It's the woman I attacked first, the one with the ponytail, and her voice is hoarse from the blow across her throat. Above the green scarf, her eyes are murderous. I subside, breathing hard. Carver does, too – he's got three guns on him. The surgery is packed with people.

That's when I recognise them. Even with their faces covered, I pick them out. There's Anton, holding a gun on Carver. And Ivan, his arms wrapped around Anna. These are the men who took hostages in the Recycler Plant, who later interrupted my attempt to rescue Okwembu, back in the maximum security brig.

Who the hell are these people?

Anton glances at me, and under the rag he smiles. "You left a trail a mile wide," he says. "Would have been here sooner, if you hadn't locked us up."

"There's someone back here," a man says. He's over by the storeroom, standing above Knox.

Anton glances over. "Resin?"

"Yup. Dead." The man nudges Knox with the heel of his boot.

The room falls silent. And, finally, all eyes turn to Okwembu. Their prize, the person they've been hunting across the whole station. She stares back at them. She's still cuffed, still bent over the table, but there's defiance in her eyes.

Anton walks up to Okwembu, his hands clasped behind him. "I've waited a long time for this," I hear him say.

She's finally going to get what's coming to her. Anton's going to kill her in front of all these people, and I'm going to have to watch. It's strange – now that I know it's actually going to happen, I'm not sure I want it to.

Anton leans over her. He undoes her cuffs, ripping the velcro off.

208

"You have something we need," he says. "You're going to give it to us, whether you want to or not."

"And what is that?" Okwembu says, massaging her wrists.

Anton grins. "The Earth."

49

Riley

Dead silence.

Okwembu looks from Anton to Ivan, and back again. "And how exactly do I give that to you?" she says, her tone apparently one of honest curiosity.

"Not here," Anton says, shaking his head. "I'll explain later. You come with us, and you do what we say. Understand?"

Okwembu rolls her wrists, stretching them out. "And if I do . . . you'll guarantee my safety?"

"That's right."

There's a long moment of silence. My mind is reeling. What can Okwembu possibly have that will give these people . . . *the Earth*? What does that even mean?

Okwembu nods. "Fine. Let's go."

"Good." Anton barely looks in our direction. "Put the rest up against the wall and shoot them."

Anna starts howling, twisting in the arms of the man holding her. Carver and I are marched at gunpoint towards the storage room. Knox hasn't moved a muscle. A thin line of Resin has trickled down from his nose, pooling on the floor. My heart feels like it's about to stop.

"Why don't we take them with us?"

It comes from one of the others, a woman, leaning up against the wall. She's wrapped a scarf around her entire head, so that only her eyes are showing.

Nobody says anything for a second. Then Anton says, "We don't need them, Hisako. Anyway, I told you back at base. We're stretched thin enough as it is."

"Right, right, I know," says the woman. "But think about it – if we could bring them over to our side, we'd have people with inner knowledge of Apex." She shrugs. "After all, they're stompers. They've been there. We haven't."

Carver and I exchange a glance. Just what are these people planning to do?

Anton walks over, conversing in whispers with Hisako and two of the others. They pull Okwembu in, too, and she talks quickly and quietly. More than once, I hear the words *kill* and *important*. Anna's eyes are huge.

After a minute, the huddle breaks and Anton walks over to us. "Hisako's right," he says. "Much as I hate to admit it. You're coming with us."

I let out a thin breath. Anton smiles, revealing crooked and broken teeth. "I do owe you one for the Recycler Plant, though."

He leans back, and throws a punch across my face.

There's enough force in the blow to snap my head back. My teeth clack together, and I feel one of them break, almost delicately. There's blood in my mouth, and my cheek is already starting to hum with pain.

Carver shouts in anger. Our arms are pulled behind us, twisted sharply backwards. My hands are snapped together, and I feel something hard and sharp-edged being slipped over them – a zip tie of some kind. It's yanked tight, cutting into my wrists, and I grunt in pain.

Hisako tears a strip of cloth from her scarf. She blindfolds me with it, knotting it tightly behind my head, plunging me into darkness.

50

Knox

Morgan Knox isn't sure if he's awake or not.

At first he thinks he's dreaming. Or hallucinating. Hale and her friends are restrained, blindfolded, and his room is filled with strangers. One of them leads Okwembu to the door. She looks back at him in the instant before she crosses the threshold. Her eyes meet his. Triumph sparkles in them, and she's actually smiling.

It's that smile that jolts him fully awake. It's not a dream, not a hallucination. They're taking Okwembu and Hale both, and it's happening right in front of him.

He tries to move, to cry out. But the only sound he can make is a gurgling wheeze, and it costs him dearly. Pain radiates through his body, boiling up in his throat.

Resin. That's what Hale called it. He must have got it from those stompers, the ones who came to arrest him. Or perhaps he got it from Hale herself. Knox claws at the floor, breaking his nails on it, leaving thin smears of blood behind. He coughs, and it's such an awful sensation that it nearly knocks him out. He can't get enough air into his lungs – they feel stretched, like a rubber bladder, filled to the brim. He's dimly aware that his nasal passages are blocked, jammed solid with muck.

He opens his eyes again. His surgery is empty. Okwembu and Hale are gone.

Anger explodes through him, blocking out the pain. He won't let that happen. Hale is going to learn what it means to fail.

The remote. It's in the pocket of his scrubs. It takes him a minute to work up the strength to roll over, another to lift his hand to his body. His fingers fumble at the hem of the pocket, but when he finally pushes them inside, he feels nothing.

No.

Perhaps he got the wrong pocket. He shuts his eyes tight, willing his arm to move, but there's nothing in the other pocket either. *She's taken it.*

He coughs again, and something rolls inside him: a long, slow movement that tears his chest wall apart. This time, he screams. The world goes dark.

When he comes back, his thoughts are a little clearer. Hale gave him something, he remembers that. Some kind of intravenous fluid. Whatever it was, it's had some effect – he's still having trouble breathing, but he *is* getting air into his lungs. That means he has a chance.

But for how long? He may need another dose, and it doesn't seem as if he'll be getting one any time soon.

His medical training takes over. It's as if he's standing above his own body, looking down on it, another doctor assessing a patient. *He has fluid on the lungs, and in the pleural space behind them. We need to drain them.*

Standard procedure is to do a tube thoracostomy, inserting a static drain in the chest to release the fluid. No chance of that. He can barely move, let alone carry out a surgical incision. He'll have to use a syringe. He can insert the needle into the

214

Rob Boffard

cavity, draw out some of the fluid. It'll hurt like hell, but he doesn't have any other choice.

He could let himself die. It would be easy. All he has to do is lie here. The transponder is still attached to his heart – he can feel the wires itching beneath his skin. That means Hale's devices would detonate. The thought gives him bitter pleasure.

But then he looks up, and sees Amira.

He knows it isn't real. It can't be. Amira is dead. And yet there she is, sitting on the edge of the operating table, her legs swinging back and forth. Her dark eyes are locked on his. Her tank top is soaked with blood. She runs a finger along it, and it comes up dark and shining.

"Help me," he says. His voice is nothing more than a whisper.

He blinks, and she's gone.

They killed her. Hale and Okwembu. They took away the only perfect thing in his world. He can't let them get away with that. He won't.

The syringes are in his surgery, on one of the wheeled stands next to the operating table. Every movement is agony. When he rolls himself onto his stomach, it's as if he's falling from a great height, slamming into the ground with the force of a meteor.

He lies there, breathing hard. After a moment, he tries to rise. He barely makes it to one knee before his muscles fail, sending him crashing back down. He tries to slow his breathing, tries to ignore the horrid sucking feeling in his chest.

There's no way he's going to be able to walk. He'll have to crawl. He gets one arm out in front of him, then the other and pulls.

He makes it three feet before another cough explodes out of him, spraying the floor in front of him with sticky black fluid. He stares at it, bewildered. Blood? Pus? Whatever it is, he has to drain it, and soon.

215

He pulls himself through gunk. It's sticky, like snot. He has to stop to rest more than once. On the third time, a coughing fit nearly tears him in two. But somehow he keeps moving, putting one arm in front of the other.

The stand is in front of him. He's going to have to get to his knees again.

He moves as carefully as he can. A single cough, a single tremor in his fragile lungs, could unbalance him, and he doesn't know if he can get up a third time. Slowly, oh so slowly, he gets his right leg underneath him, then raises himself up on his knee like a sprinter at the block. He can see the tray of instruments on the stand, see the scalpels and forceps. The syringes, he knows, will be in a small plastic case, just out of sight.

He touches the tray, and that's when the cough explodes out of him.

His hand comes down on the tray's edge, sending the instruments flying through the air. He tumbles onto his side, retching, as they roll and skid across the floor away from him.

51

Prakesh

Every step Prakesh makes is as loud as an explosion. He stumbles into one of the Buzz Box supports, bounces off it, nearly loses his balance on a pile of loose metal pipes. Behind him, Julian's stinger fires a second time, a third, the bullets ricocheting off the floor behind him. Iko is still screaming.

Julian stops firing. Without the muzzle flash, Prakesh is instantly cloaked in darkness. But his retinas haven't adjusted yet – he's running through a bright, black void, hands out in front of him, hot breath tearing his chest apart.

"Find him!" Julian says.

Not if I can help it, Prakesh thinks. The thought is interrupted as something collides with his shin.

It could be anything: a piece of scaffolding, a stack of metal sheeting, a machine battery. It hits him in the same spot as before, when he was walking through the Food Lab. The first time, he was moving at walking pace – now the sensation is so sharp that he's convinced his legs have been sliced right off. He tumbles end over end, landing on the floor beyond the obstacle, cracking his skull so hard on it that the black void blossoms with colour.

He pushes against the pain, telling himself to get up. He rises to his knees, fingers bent on the slimy floor, and stops.

The Food Lab has gone silent. No explosions of sound. No crashing of metal. As long as he stays down, he can control his movements. Adrenaline made him run, but he can see past it now, and it's a much better idea to stay hidden.

There's a flicker of light from the Buzz Box – Julian, sparking the plasma cutter back to life. Prakesh sees the obstacle he tripped over. It's a corrugated metal sheet, propped horizontally between two supports. He ran right into its leading edge. His fingers find his right shin, and he feels a slick wetness. The wound is skin-deep, nothing more, but he still has to bite back a hiss of pain.

Iko is moaning now, and Prakesh hears Julian telling him to shut up. "Roger. You, Owen and Jared spread out. Sweep the floor. *Find* him." To Prakesh's ears, he sounds insane: someone at the very end of a very long tether.

Roger says something Prakesh can't quite hear. "Neither does he," Julian replies. "You find him, and you beat the shit out of him."

They only have one stinger, he thinks. Should he make a run for it? All he has to do is get to the entrance to the Air Lab, and he can seal them inside. No. From where he is, it's too risky. He can't track them all, and he doesn't know how fast they can move.

He can hear them now, their footsteps crunching on the melted plastic. He closes his eyes, trying to pinpoint them on the floor, but there are too many echoes. The sounds fold in on themselves, multiply, coming from a dozen directions at once.

Prakesh opens his eyes. The metal sheet he's crouched behind is long – fifty feet, at least. He can move along it, and then . . . yes, there, a stack of yellow plastic barrels he can hide behind.

He doesn't know what he'll do when he gets there, but it's the best chance he's got.

Keeping his head down, Prakesh moves on his hands and knees, listening hard, trying to time his movements to coincide with the hunters'. He feels like the only thing louder than his hands on the grimy floor is his heartbeat, thundering loud enough to blow a vein in his neck.

"Come on out," Roger says. His voice is distant, coming from the other end of the floor. The light has grown dimmer, as if the search has moved away. With any luck, they haven't spread out too far.

Ten feet away from the end of the metal sheet. Five. Still nothing. Prakesh stops a foot from the end, dropping down onto his elbows. The barrels are a few feet away. To reach them, he's going to have to cross a gap on the floor – a gap dimly illuminated by the flickering light of the plasma torch.

Prakesh listens hard. He can hear them: footsteps, a bang followed by a muffled curse, Iko's helpless whimpering. He *thinks* they're at his four o'clock – no way for him to tell if they're looking in his direction or not. Nothing for it. He can't stay here.

He looks up at the barrels, takes a deep breath. He'll move on the balls of his feet, like he's seen Riley do, staying low and quiet. He tenses his thighs, preparing to move.

He sees the shadow a second before he leaves his position. He freezes, and that's when the voice comes, shockingly close, no more than three feet above his head. "He's not here!"

The speaker is standing on the other side of the metal sheet, his filmy shadow stretched out across the gap in front of Prakesh. Slowly, very slowly, Prakesh turns his head and looks up. It's Roger – Prakesh can just recognise the shape of his head and shoulders. He's looking back towards the Buzz Box, and as Prakesh watches, he idly rests a hand on the metal sheet. It shakes slightly, just touching the edge of Prakesh's shoe.

"Keep looking, then." Julian sounds hoarse and anxious.

Roger drums his fingers on the metal. Prakesh can't look away. If Roger turns his head, even a little, and looks down, there's no way he'll remain undetected.

Roger grunts in frustration, shoving off from the metal sheet. Prakesh breathes a long, low sigh – then chokes it back when he sees where Roger is going. The man is coming round the end of the metal sheet, between Prakesh and the barrels. There's nothing Prakesh can do.

52

Riley

The blindfold is hot around my face, and my fingers are already starting to go numb from the biting pain of the cuffs. I can't stop running my tongue over my jagged tooth, and my cheek is still burning from Anton's blow.

My entire sense of balance is gone, destroyed by the blindfold. My feet are constantly tangled up, and my captors have to hold me upright to stop it happening. A few times, I really do start to fall – my stomach lurching as my centre of gravity topples – and they have to pull me back.

I don't know how long we walk for, or where we go. For a while, Anna and Carver are alongside me – I hear them spit the occasional curse as they, too, struggle for balance – but after a while they go silent. My imagination runs away from me: maybe we've been split up, our captors taking us to different places so they can break us individually.

Whoever they are.

My legs are burning. It's been a long time since I took any pills, and the stitches have become hot lines, flipping back and forth between bright sting and maddening itch. There's nothing

221

I can do. I try to ignore the burning, pushing other thoughts to the front of my mind. *Prakesh*. He's never felt further away than he is now. At least he's safe – I don't like that he's sealed away, but the Air Lab is a lot less chaotic than it is out here.

After a while, the sound around me changes – it feels muted somehow, like we've moved away from the main body of the station. I start to hear other noises – people shouting orders, the clanking of machinery. A few minutes later, we come to a stop. The noises have got louder now – it's as if I'm in an enormous factory. Every muscle in my body feels ready to collapse.

"What do we do with her?"

"Take the blindfold off. I don't think it matters now."

I feel the material being unwrapped, light slipping in as the layers come off, and when the last one falls away I have to squint against blinding overhead lights. My eyes fill with tears, and, as I blink them back, I see Carver standing alongside me. His blindfold is being pulled off, too. Anna is being brought up behind us. Okwembu is there as well, her hands clasped behind her.

I look around, and my mouth falls open.

We're in one of the old mineral-processing facilities, where they bring asteroid slag and turn it into something useable. There are dozens of these places across the lower sectors, so it's impossible to figure out the exact location. Smelting kilns line the walls, bracketing enormous centrifuges. They'll spring to life when the *Shinso Maru* comes in, delivering its asteroid cargo. The space construction corps will break it down, and the tugboats will bring the pieces in to be turned into slag, which will be processed to get the minerals out. The asteroids are our building material, our fertiliser, our chemicals.

A metal frame for holding heavy equipment runs around the walls of the rectangular room, reaching to a ceiling that must be sixty feet up. Right above us, I can see a smaller gantry, a set of tracks with what looks like a miniature train car on it, just as high up but with a tangle of cables hanging down from the body. The cables end in a shredded mess of torn wires.

The place makes me think of Big 6. Same energy, same movement. There must be more than fifty people – men, women, children, entire families. Everybody is moving, everybody is doing something: shifting crates, wheeling pallets of equipment. Even the kids.

A few people glance in our direction, but nobody pays much attention to us. Off to one side, a group of them stand around a table, checking weapons. There are homemade stingers, more than I've ever seen before. Other weapons, too: long metal tubes, lined up alongside a strange type of ammo, black and squat. As I watch, one of them hefts the tube onto his shoulder, as if to aim it.

Resin has sucked Outer Earth dry of life, but it's like this one little room has managed to fight it off – to stay alive in all the chaos. I don't see anybody sick. It's like they're preparing for something, a journey maybe.

Or an invasion.

I glance over to the man holding my left arm. He's pulled down the cloth over his face, and I can see that he's not as old as I thought he was. Stubble coats his face, but the eyes above it are young – a bright, anxious blue.

I wriggle my arms. "Any chance you could take the cuffs off? I can't feel my hands."

He shakes his head. "Sorry."

"How about some water, then? We could really use a drink."

He seems about to respond, but then he suddenly snaps to attention. I feel the other man holding me do the same, jerking me more upright.

Mikhail is walking towards us.

223

They must have sprung him from the brig. He looks less gaunt, his prison jumpsuit exchanged for a dark blue jacket and pants over a patched, untucked cotton shirt. His hair has been swept back, pulled into a neat ponytail, and he's wiped the grime off his face. He stands erect, too, with the bearing of a ship's captain. Something about it bothers me, and it takes me a second to realise why: it's the same posture my father had, before he left on the Earth Return mission. Straight-backed, chin up, daring the world to test him.

A ghost of a smile flickers across his face. "We meet again," he says, his eyes finding mine.

The words sound odd in his mouth, as if he read them somewhere and is trying them on for size. I want to ask him about Resin – about why nobody here is sick, and what they're preparing for.

The man with the blue eyes jogs my shoulder. "They're just stompers. We should—"

Mikhail silences him with a look.

"If you're thinking we're going to help you break into Apex," Carver says, "then you need to think a lot harder."

Mikhail glances at Carver. He takes a step closer, and I feel the grip on my shoulders tighten. "I'm going to give you a few minutes to think about what you wish to contribute to our cause. I would think hard, if I were you. Hisako can be very persuasive."

He holds Carver's gaze a moment longer, then turns away, looking towards Okwembu. "You," he says. "My colleagues tell me you were a computer programmer. Before you joined the council."

It's an odd thing to say, out of place in the current circumstances. Okwembu barely blinks. "I was," she says.

"What operating systems did you train in?"

"Operating systems?"

224

"When you were at the academy."

Okwembu frowns. "Ellipsis. Deep-OS. But those are outdated systems. I don't see what—"

Her eyes go wide. She stares at Mikhail, understanding dawning.

Not that it helps the rest of us. The names mean nothing to me. I look round at Carver, but he's just shaking his head, as confused as I am.

"You're going *back* to Earth," Okwembu says, her voice filled with wonder.

Mikhail smiles. "And we need the *Shinso Maru* to do it. You're going to deliver that ship to us, whether you want to or not."

He's talking about the asteroid catcher, the one currently in orbit around the station. And with Resin out there, they'll never have a better opportunity to take it. The pieces are starting to slot into place. The *Shinso Maru* is one of the oldest ships we have. It's a dinosaur, a relic, something that should have been replaced decades ago.

Those operating systems – they must be what the ship runs on. Somehow, these people are going to use Okwembu to gain access to the ship.

"Why me?" Okwembu says. "There must be dozens of people who can use Ellipsis."

"There aren't. We've looked. If there's anyone around who still knows how to use it, we can't find them. Dead or missing, we don't know." He shrugs.

"This is . . ." Carver says, trailing off.

"But I don't understand," Okwembu says. "We've run data on Earth before. There's nothing down there any more."

Mikhail doesn't answer her, and she bows her head, as if thinking hard. Then she composes herself, locking eyes with Mikhail.

"I'm done with this station," she says, and it's impossible not to hear the bitterness in her voice. "It doesn't want to be saved."

"So you'll help us?" says Mikhail. He sounds wary, like he's expecting a trick. Like it shouldn't be this easy.

"Gladly," Okwembu says. She cocks her head. "Tell me about Earth. Tell me what you've found."

Mikhail turns to the men holding us. "Get them out of here."

"Hey!" says Anna. But we're hustled away, marched off as Okwembu and Mikhail huddle together. Someone is working with a plasma cutter above us, and, as we pass underneath, sparks prickle my face.

None of this makes any sense. They can't use the *Shinso* for re-entry. It's got no heat shielding, nothing that'll stop it from burning up in the atmosphere. And even if they make it down, how are they going to survive? We *know* Earth is a dead shell: a world of dust storms and frozen wastelands. That's why my father went down there in the first place – to see if he and his crew could make a part of the planet habitable again.

But he didn't succeed. The mission was a failure. So why does Mikhail think humans will be able to survive down there? What have he and his people found?

I want to talk to Carver, see if he can help me figure this out, but he's too far ahead of me.

My eyes are drawn to something at the back of the room – two people, hunched over a machine of some kind. At first, I think it must be a bomb – my mind kicking into overdrive – but then I see it's something else. There are old-fashioned screens on it, displaying odd shapes, like spiky blots of ink. And there's a keyboard, jutting out from the main body. There are two antennae on top, swaying gently. Before I get a better look, the machine is out of sight.

226

Another piece of the puzzle, and I have no idea where it fits.

Our captors march us to a corner of the room. Carver, Anna and I are shoved up against the wall, our faces are pressed into it. The men spin us around, then push us down. My bound hands are cramping behind me, sending little darts of pain up my arms. Anton is watching us, sitting on a nearby crate, his stinger resting on his knee.

Carver's brow furrows. "I don't get it," he says, more to himself than to us. "There's no heat shielding on that thing."

"I know," I say. "They'll never make it."

"What's happening?" Anna says. "Why are they talking about old computer systems?"

Carver shrugs. "It's for the *Shinso*. But they'll burn up before they get halfway down. Why do you think nobody's . . ."

He stops. There's the strangest look on his face.

"What is it?" I say.

"The asteroid. That's genius."

Anna glances at me. "Do you understand a single thing he's saying?"

"They're going to use the asteroid as a heat shield," Carver says, his voice filled with wonder. "They're going to ride it all the way down."

53

Riley

"Is that even possible?" Anna says.

"In theory," Carver replies. "Something's gotta burn up. If they can go down asteroid first, then that's what'll catch fire."

"That's insane," I say.

"Hey," says Anton. Our voices must have risen, and he's looking over sharply at us. Carver subsides, shifting his shoulders to stop his bound hands hurting.

"What makes them think they can go back?" I say, barely speaking above a whisper. "What do they know that we don't?"

Carver shrugs. "Beats me."

Anna leans in. "But if they've figured out a way to survive on Earth, why haven't they taken it to the council? Why do they need to *hijack* the asteroid catcher?"

Carver grimaces. "Because we can't fit the entire station into the *Shinso*'s escape pods."

We stare at him.

"Think about it," he says. "They can use the asteroid as a heat shield, but they'll still be travelling a billion miles an hour. They'll never be able to land the ship. Their only shot is to bail out."

Of course. Asteroid catchers have escape pods, but there aren't that many of them. They're designed to carry the small crew of the asteroid catcher, maybe a few more. You could get everybody left on Outer Earth onto an asteroid catcher, but only a few of them would make it to the ground. These people – Mikhail and Anton and the rest of them, along with Okwembu now – are just putting themselves at the front of the queue.

"Earthers," Carver whispers.

"What?"

"That's what we should call them. They want to get back to Earth, right? So they're Earthers."

Anton's become bored. He's still sitting on his crate, but he's fiddling with his stinger, slipping the clip in and out with a rhythmic clicking. Our legs aren't bound, but there's no way we're going to slip past him.

Anna sees me looking. "If we're going to get out of here, we need to get these cuffs off," she says, keeping her voice low. She shakes her shoulders, frustrated with the bonds. "See anything?"

I look around, hunting for something we can use. Might as well try and teleport away – there are no tools within reach, no scissors or knives we could use. Not that Anton would let us try anyway.

I lean over a little too far to my right, and overbalance. I almost fall on my side, only just managing to pull myself back. As I do, I catch sight of the wall.

It's made up of interlocking metal panels. The panels are old, dented, and the edge of the nearest one is bent outwards a little. It's not sharp, but it's rough and rusted.

I scoot across, lifting my backside up to move myself along. Anton is still tinkering with his stinger.

"Riley," Carver says from behind me. "What are you doing?"

I push my back up against the edge, my bound wrists against it.

"Using friction," I mutter.

I brace myself, and begin moving my arms up and down, sawing the zip tie against the edge as fast as I can.

"*Really?*" says Carver.

Anton looks up.

I freeze. My wrists are still tightly bound. I can feel his eyes on me. *He's going to see you've moved. It's over.*

Anton grimaces, as if our presence offends him. He goes back to his stinger.

I keep sawing, trying to go as fast as I can without making too much noise. I grit my teeth as the spot between my wrists heats up. As I do so, the zip tie snaps. Blood rushes back into my hands, pins and needles dancing under the skin.

"You're crazy," Carver says. It comes out as a hissed whisper.

"It's our only shot."

Anna is shaking her head. "Shot is what we'll be, if we go through with this."

Anton is picking something out of his teeth now. There's no point doing this slowly. If I'm going to take him down, I have to cross the gap before he can call for help. A pressure-point strike should do it. Right on the back of the neck.

The pins and needles swell, shooting up my forearms. I grit my teeth, flexing my fingers, waiting until the pain subsides. I don't know what's worse: the pain, or making myself wait.

Thirty seconds goes by. I get my legs under me, get up on one knee. Anton still hasn't noticed.

"Riley," Carver hisses again.

I spring forward, rocketing to my feet. I'm trying to stay quiet, but Anton looks up almost immediately. His eyes widen, and I see him raising the stinger, lifting it towards me, his mouth opening to cry out.

But I'm way, way too fast for him. I cross the gap in seconds, whipping my right fist around in a long arc, driving it into the back of his neck, aiming for the pressure point.

It doesn't work.

Anton squawks in surprise, clapping his free hand to his neck, toppling off the crate, upending it and spilling its contents. Soil explodes across the ground with a muted hiss. Anton is already getting to his feet, already trying to bring the gun around. I don't give him the chance. I dart forward, driving a knee into his chest. He coughs, hot air blasting into my face. Then I roll off him, and swing my hand a second time into the back of his neck, following it up with a jab to his throat. Nerves and oxygen – shut down.

It disables Anton completely. His eyes roll back, his body twitching.

I lie next to him, breathing hard, waiting for him to move again. He doesn't.

A hand shoots into view, so suddenly that I almost lash out at it. It's Carver – he pulls me to my feet. The world tilts sideways for a second, the blood rushing back to my head. Anna is working on her bonds, sweat beading her forehead as she burns through them on the metal.

Her wrists snap apart. She doesn't waste time, jumping to her feet, and gesturing at us to hurry. Carver pulls me along – I have to blink a few times to get the world to stay put. I glance down at Anton, still on the ground. He's breathing – shallow and irregular, but it's there. A thin line of drool has leaked out of his mouth, staining the floor.

I glance at the overturned crate. It wasn't just filled with soil – there are tiny plants dotted in the debris, half grown, each one sprouting immature bean pods.

My stomach rumbles. We should get out of here while we're still alone, but none of us has eaten for hours, and, if we do make it out, we're going to need food. Working quickly, I strip the beans from the plants, stuffing them into my pockets.

"No time," Carver says.

"Just a second," I say, grabbing another handful of beans.

"We gotta *go*."

We run. We're in the shadow of the kilns now, slipping from one to the other in short bursts. My heart is firmly lodged in my throat. When we reach the end of the line of kilns, I have to stop, just for a second. There are crates stacked here, lined up on wheeled pallets. How are they planning to get this – all of this – onto the *Shinso*?

"Where's the exit?" I say to Carver.

But he's not looking at me. Instead, he's looking back down the line of kilns. Where a child is standing, staring at us. A young girl, frozen in mid-step.

Everything stops. Even the noise from the crowd fades away.

The girl opens her mouth. I can see her getting ready to scream, can feel Carver tense alongside me. But then she tilts her head, her eyes narrowed, looking right at me. "You're the lady who blew up her dad."

My eyes go wide. It's Ivy. The girl from the Caves.

"That's right," Anna says, giving Ivy a radiant smile. "She's the lady who blew up her dad. I'm her friend Anna, and he's Aaron. It's nice to meet you."

The girl nods, as if all of this was the most normal thing in the world. "I got bored with the grown-ups," she says, rocking back and forth on her heels. She stops, looks from me to Anna, then back again.

There's a yell, over from where we were sitting against the metal sheeting. Anton. His voice is hoarse, but unmistakeable. *Shit*. I should have squeezed harder, knocked him out properly.

I turn back to Ivy, on the verge of telling her to run as fast as she can, when the first of them comes around the crates. He

232

starts to yell, a noise which is cut off as Carver jabs him hard in the throat. He goes down, heaving, banging his head on the side of the opened crate as he does so. It overbalances, then topples off the pallet, spraying more soil across the floor.

Ivy is pushing up against the wall. I'm not sure what's open wider: her mouth or her eyes. More running feet, charging towards us. They'll be on us in seconds. And they're coming from *both* directions – from where we were up against the metal sheeting, and from over by the entrance. Hemmed in by the crates and the kilns, we're in a bad place to run from.

Anna is in a half-crouch, one hand hovering over the floor, outstretched fingers just touching it. "We split up," she says. "Go in three different directions."

"Won't work," Carver says. "Too many of them."

Anton comes round the corner.

His face is pale, the skin on his throat a blotchy red. But he's awake, and angry. He's at the head of a pack, all of them armed with lengths of lead pipe or small blades. In a few seconds, they're going to be on top of us.

So I do the only thing I can think of doing.

I drop to one knee in front of Ivy, and put a hand on her cheek. Her skin is smooth under my touch, as warm as a kiss.

"Honey," I say. "We're going to play a game. OK? No matter what happens, remember it's just a game."

Before she can react, I scoop her up, hoisting her to shoulder height. I wrap my left arm around her neck, pushing her throat into the crook of my arm, just like I did with Anton.

Then I pull tight.

54

Prakesh

Roger stands in the dim light, looking around him. Prakesh tries very hard not to move a single muscle.

Seconds tick by. Prakesh becomes exquisitely aware of every part of his body, down to his fingertips, which are just touching the grimy floor. He stopped breathing some time ago, and his chest has begun to ache.

Roger scratches his nose. Then he actually yawns. Prakesh has to suppress the urge to bolt from his hiding place and throttle him. He has to push it back, telling himself to stay put.

Roger turns and walks away. "Nothing here, either," he shouts, as if he'd spent the past few moments looking in a completely new area.

He walks out of sight. Prakesh waits ten seconds, counting them off. It's agony, and his mind can't help racing ahead of him, constructing a scenario where Roger and Julian and the rest of them are watching the gap in silence, waiting for him to make a move.

But he can't stay here. Sooner or later, one of them is going to think about looking on the other side of the metal sheet, and then it's all over. He has to get to the exit.

He allows himself two quick breaths. Then, with his blood hammering through his veins, he takes the gap. He runs bent over, doing everything he can to keep his footsteps silent, not daring to look round. He keeps his eyes locked on the barrel.

He's almost there when Julian spots him.

Prakesh hears him yell out from the other side of the hangar, quickly followed by the sound of running feet. His body doesn't react fast enough, and slams shoulder first into the barrel. It's empty, *bonging* as it bounces away from him. A shot from Julian's stinger rings out, the bullet ricocheting off the ceiling above him. How many bullets does the man have left? No time to find out, no time to do anything except sprint for the exit.

Prakesh can hear them behind him, all of them running, all of them coming straight towards him. They've got the advantage – with the plasma cutter, they'll have all the light they need. He can see his shadow spread out, its arms blurring as he runs, but most of the way ahead of him is cloaked in darkness. If he hits another metal sheet, or runs into one of the pieces of scaffolding . . .

"Get back here!" Julian sounds like he's lost his mind. He tries to fire again, but this time there's nothing but an audible click. He's out of bullets. Not that it matters: he couldn't hit anything anyway. And if Prakesh doesn't get out of here soon, these people are going to catch him and beat him to death. He's as sure of this as he is of his own heartbeat.

A shadow, darker than the rest, looms in front of him. He doesn't have time to see what is. He hurdles it, the toe of his right shoe just brushing its surface. If he were Riley, he'd probably tuck into a roll on the landing, preserving his momentum. But he's not Riley, and he lands awkwardly, very nearly falling flat on his face. His throat is a parched desert, cracking under the searing wind of his breath. *Come on, come on, come on.*

A figure lunges at him from a set of scaffolding on his right. Prakesh only just manages to duck under the man's arms, lashing out blindly. He feels his fist hit an arm, hears a soft grunt of anger.

There. The exit. Prakesh can just make it out, can just see the tiny green light on the keypad next to it. He sucks in another acid breath, and runs even faster. There's a giant crash behind him, as if one of Julian's men has run right into one of the stacks of metal pipes.

And as Prakesh reaches the door, as his hand finds the keypad. *Riley's birthday.* He punches in the numbers, 2104, fingers fumbling on the keys.

The keypad gives a dull beep. Incorrect code.

He wants to laugh. It's absurd. He made the code so it would be easy to remember.

The footsteps behind him fill the world, thundering closer. At the very last second, Prakesh realises what he's done. He switches the code, punching in 0421, slamming his hand on the ENTER button.

With a whining hiss, the door begins to slide back, letting in an intensely bright ray of light from the Air Lab.

Prakesh doesn't wait for it to open fully. He squeezes through the gap, blinking against the harsh light. He's vaguely aware of people on the Air Lab side, but doesn't have time to look. He reaches for the keypad on this side of the door, punches in the numbers, hits ENTER.

Nothing happens.

Prakesh's already overstretched mind nearly snaps in two. The door continues to slide away, and it's only after a second or two that he realises it has to go all the way before he can close it again.

He looks up, without wanting to. Julian and Roger are sprinting for the door. Fifty feet away, closing fast.

Prakesh can do nothing but watch them. As the door clicks into its fully open position, his hand is already on the keypad, his fingers jumping to the numbers. He hits ENTER, and the door begins to shut, closing agonisingly slowly. There's no way it's going to shut in time. Prakesh tells himself to move, but his feet have stopped listening to him. All he can do is watch.

55

Riley

"Riley, what are you doing?" Carver says.

I don't know. I'm making it up as I go along. Anna is looking at me like I've gone insane, her eyes darting between me and the approaching Earthers.

I can feel Ivy's throat pulsing in the crook of my arm. She's dead still.

Anton comes to a juddering halt, the men and women behind him nearly knocking into him.

"Stay back," he says over his shoulder. His eyes are locked on me and the girl, shot through with fear and fury.

"Gods, she's got—"

"Let her go."

I raise my chin, staring them down. "Listen up," I say, raising my voice so that it fills the room. "Everybody back off. We're walking out of here, and I don't want to see anybody in our way."

Ivy is still frozen. I can't tell if she's scared solid, or just playing along.

Mikhail arrives, pushing his way through the crowd, thunder

on his face. He ignores the girl, focusing on me. "Put her down," he says slowly.

"You think I'm joking?" I say, hefting her higher, using the surface of my arm to lift her chin. "I'll do it." Somehow, I manage to keep the trembling out of my voice.

A man falls out of the crowd. It's Jamal. There's anger on his face – anger, and a terror so raw it takes my breath away

"Please," he says. It's the kind of whisper that stops everyone speaking. "Please don't hurt her."

"She won't."

Okwembu steps out behind Jamal – the latest arrival to our little game, calm and composed. Mikhail tries to speak, but she places a hand on his arm. Carver and Anna have drawn closer to me, almost touching on either side, their bodies tense.

"Neither of them will," Okwembu says. "They don't have it in them."

She turns Jamal's face towards her, and smiles gently. "Your little one is going to be fine."

Her words snap Carver out of his trance. He steps in front of me. "Only if everybody locks their feet to the floor," he says. "We're going to walk out of here. If anybody gets in our way, we'll kill her."

A small part of me burns with revulsion at his words, but I ignore it. There's no other way out of this.

Okwembu's smile gets even wider. "Two of the young people in front of you have never killed before," she says to the crowd. "The other one, the one holding the girl, is Riley Hale. You probably know her. She *has* killed before – she murdered her tracer crew leader, and then own father. But she did it to save Outer Earth, and she feels so guilty that she'd rather die before taking another life."

She turns to face me. Her expression is completely neutral. "Did I miss anything, Ms Hale?"

Right then, Ivy decides she's had enough.

Maybe she realises that it isn't a game, or that it's not fun to play-act any more. She screams. And it's the kind of high-pitched scream that makes you want to put your hands over your ears and scream back, just to shut out the noise.

I let her go. I don't put her down – I *drop* her, not meaning to, but watching it happen anyway, horror rising inside me. The girl's face goes from surprise to terror in about a third of a second, and then she slams knees first into the ground. Jamal goes from standing to sprinting in the same amount of lime, running for his daughter.

Mikhail steps in front of Okwembu and points at us. The anger on his face is like steam trapped in a broken vent.

"Take them."

56

Riley

We run. Back down the line of kilns, ahead of the mob. A hunk of metal bounces off the ground in front of me, and another smacks me in the small of the back. I don't dare look around.

Carver is alongside me, his breathing hot and hard. Anna is just behind. We're nearing the back of the hangar, which either means we're going to have to double back or go all the way around, outpacing the mob.

We come to the back wall, and hang a hard left. There's an old slag container pushed up against the wall – big and clunky, open at the top, as tall as I am.

"Over there," I shout, pointing. Carver follows my gaze, then looks at me like I've gone mad.

"We can't hide in there!" he shouts back.

"She means above it," says Anna.

He looks up. Hanging over the container is a claw-scoop, the kind that looks like a giant, stubby fingered hand. The arm attached to it extends upwards, a mess of thick cables and pneumatic sections. The arm reaches its apex about twenty feet up, before curving down and terminating in a control cab,

241

bristling with levers and dials. But a few feet above the top of the arm is the metal frame of the gantry.

Before Carver can argue, I scrabble up the side of the container. I take a split second to get my feet on the rim – the crowd is closer now, shouts coming from everywhere, Mikhail's voice roaring above them – and then I jump.

My fingers snag one of the cables on the crane's arm. For a horrible moment I can't get a good grip. Then I lock in, and the rounded part of the scoop slams into my torso. My legs swing in space, but I use the momentum as they come back to push myself higher, my shoes scrabbling for purchase on the metal. The joints above me groan in protest, like an ancient monster, woken from its sleep. I'm moving as fast as I can, trying to climb, trying to make space for Carver. He jumps, and there's an enormous bang as he grabs the scoop. It lurches, swinging like a pendulum, the metal under my hands vibrating.

Anna cries out in alarm. I look back and down over my shoulder – they've got her. Two of them, Hisako and a man. He's holding her around the chest, pinning her arms to her sides, and Hisako is trying to capture her thrashing legs.

I don't know what to do. If I drop down now, the mob will be on me before I can get back on the crane arm. But I can't just leave her there.

Anna solves the problem for me. She twists her body to the side, slipping out of the man's grip, lashing out with her foot. She connects with Hisako's stomach, and I hear the woman's breath leave her body in a pained *whoop*.

Anna stumbles away, dropping into a fighting stance. Hisako and the man are between her and the crane arm. They're trying to flank her, sidestepping, Hisako rolling her shoulders like she's been waiting for a fight. And there are others coming up behind her.

Anna looks around, then up at us. "Keep going!" she shouts. "I'll find you."

With that, she launches herself at one of the nearby stacks of crates, scrambling onto the top of it. Then she's jumping along them, the pallets rocking under her weight. Angry shouts follow her, trailing in her wake. She takes one last look back. Then she's gone.

I was never the best climber. That was always Amira. She could get up a sheer wall, given a little time and a good pair of shoes. But she did teach me a few things. Even as I start to climb, I'm spotting handholds, seeing parts of the arm I can slip my fingers over or jam a foot into. The route unfolds like a puzzle. Someone fires a stinger, and I hear the bullet *ping* off the wall. I'm less worried about being shot than I am of falling, but it still makes me jump.

I hear someone yelling to go round the other side, to get the ladders.

"There's a *ladder*?" Carver says.

"Shut up and climb!"

My fingers nearly slip off one of ledges on the metal tube, the rust scraping across my skin. I hiss with pain, and my left leg swings out into space, threatening to take my body with it. I put everything I can into stopping the swing, pulling it back onto the arm. I'm breathing too fast, and I have to force myself to find the next hold, to keep going.

The arm starts to curve as I climb, bending inward on its arc. It makes things easier. The gantry is almost within reach now, although I don't dare to look further down it. If I see people running along it towards us . . .

Carver is right behind me, climbing so close that he has to wait a half-second for me to lift my feet so he can use their positions as handholds. I'm at the apex of the arm, steadying myself, when I feel him slip.

243

Time slows, then all but stops. He's clear of the arm, holding onto nothing. He has the most indignant expression on his face, like he can't *believe* the handhold betrayed him.

Usually, when you're climbing something, it's just you and the wall. Nothing else matters. Every so often, when you're high above the ground and balancing on a knife edge, it's just you and the hold you're reaching for. Everything else is blackness, and silence.

Right now, right this second, there's just my hand, and Carver's.

I reach for him. I put every ounce of power into it, but my hand is too far away and it's stuck in its own gravity well, drained of momentum.

His fingers touch mine. Move inch by inch up my hand. Every muscle in my arm is its own entity, hanging in space, burning with power.

And then his hand is gripped in mine, and he's swinging, transcribing an arc under the crane. The noise rushes back and his enormous weight pulls my stomach into the metal, knocking the air out of me. He's screaming, a yell that is half adrenaline, half terror, so heavy he nearly pulls me right off the crane. Somehow, I manage to hold on, using my thighs and the tops of my feet to anchor myself to it.

I swing him back, aiming for the downward part of the arm, and he snags a cable. His chest is rising and falling with jagged, jerky motions. When he lets go of my hand, my arm starts shaking uncontrollably. But he starts climbing straight away, and in moments we're balanced on the gantry, our feet planted on the metal railing.

I look up, and my heart sinks. The ladders weren't tall enough to reach the gantry, but they're tall enough to get to the top of a stack of slag containers, piled high in a corner of the hangar. There are already people on the top, and they're pulling up one of the ladders – intending, no doubt, to use it to reach the gantry. The crane we climbed is at the back of the room, towards the centre, and the ladders are being positioned ahead of us. I spin round, nearly losing my balance, and put a hand on the metal to steady myself.

"You OK?" I say to Carver, who looks more unsteady than I do.

He nods. We start heading down the gantry, away from the ladders, moving in a weird half-jumping gait that keeps us on the struts. There's no sign of Anna on the floor below us. Under our feet, I can feel the gantry vibrating as our pursuers finally climb onto it. We keep moving, and before long we've reached the wall closest to the entrance. But it's a dead end – the gantry runs up against the wall, and there's no way down, no handy claw-arm or ladder in sight.

Real panic starts to build inside me. I think of Mikhail's face again, of steam trapped in a vent, growing hotter and hotter.

The miniature train car. The one on the gantry tracks that was hanging over us when we were brought in. It's at ninety degrees to us. That part of the gantry is separate from ours, too far away to jump to, and the car itself is all the way down the other end.

But that's not what gets my attention. It's the car's power line: a single cable, thick as my wrist, sheathed in black rubber and connected to a power box, a foot or so above our heads.

Carver sees where I'm looking. "If we climb along it, it'll snap in two."

"Better idea."

I squeeze past him, nearly overbalancing, and put my hands on the power box. The cable goes right into it, into a slot bracketed by thick plastic. I grab the cable and pull, as hard as I can; he joins in, his muscles bulging.

The gantry under our feet has started to sway slightly,

bending as too many people converge on one spot. I hear Mikhail shout something, and realise that not only is he up there with them, but that they're closer than I thought.

"Riley, please tell me we're not doing what I think we're going to do," Carver says. We're both wiggling the cable, teasing it out of its socket.

"I'll hold onto you, OK?" I say. "You're heavier."

"Oh, *thanks*."

Another shot rings out. This one is closer, ricocheting off the power box itself. Slowly, ever so slowly, the cable gets looser, like a rotten tooth coming out of a gum. I can see the black edge of the rubber peeking over the white plastic.

There's a scream from behind us, and a second later there's a sickening thud from below. Someone took a plunge.

"Careful," Mikhail shouts. He sounds like he's right on top of us. This time, I do steal a glance over my shoulder. He's a few feet away, his arms out, trying not to overbalance. There are three men behind him, all armed with stingers, all pointed at us.

"You've got nowhere to go," he says. The words are a growl.

The cable snaps out of its plastic socket. Carver yanks on it twice, making sure his grip is steady. I wrap my arms around his waist. Mikhail's eyes go wide, and he takes a wobbling step forward.

I close my eyes. Carver jumps.

57

Riley

It feels like we free-fall forever. Like the cable in Carver's hands is attached to nothing.

That doesn't last long. The cable goes taut, snapping so tight I nearly lose my grip on Carver, and then we're swinging, just like Carver did under the claw-arm, only much faster. The train car on the gantry squeals in protest. I force my eyes open, and see the ground rushing towards us. The cable is too long, and if we don't let go at exactly the right second, we're going to slam into it at full speed.

"Now!" I shout. A split second later, five feet above the ground, Carver lets go of the cable.

I twist my body sideways, letting my right shoulder take the impact. As I roll, I do everything I can to keep my legs out of the way, tucking them up. It hurts like hell. I tumble, pummelled by the ground, and then I'm on my feet, adrenaline fizzing in my veins, sharpening everything in my vision.

We've come down a few steps away from the entrance. Carver is getting up, unsteady on his feet. He's actually laughing, although his eyes are still back on that gantry. Mikhail is ordering his men to the ladders, his face in a rictus of fury.

There are others on the floor, running towards us, but they're some distance away. "Time to go," I say to Carver. I focus the adrenaline rush, my eyes on the big door set into the wall. It's on a roller, way too big for us to push – and right now it's shut tight.

"Where's the door release?" I say.

"Hold them—" Carver says, then stops and tries again, steadying his voice. "Hold them off."

He sprints away, leaving me pushed up against the door, facing down the approaching Earthers. Six of them – two men and four women. No stingers that I can see, just lengths of pipe, and they're approaching cautiously. One of them has a limp, favouring his right ankle, and one of the women looks barely out of her teens.

Janice Okwembu is nowhere to be seen. Not surprising – she always vanishes whenever the action starts.

I step forward, squaring my shoulders. "The first person to try it gets one of those pipes wedged in their throat. Any takers?"

The group stops, hovering a few steps away. The young woman takes a step forward, her face set. Above and behind her, I can see Mikhail's group racing across the gantry, heading back towards the ladders.

"You think we'd just let you go?" says the woman. She's got one of the pipes, and, as she takes another step forward, she grips it in two hands to steady herself. "After what you did to Jamal's girl?"

I step forward to meet her. She refuses to step back. The others, emboldened by her example, line up on either side of her.

Better hurry, Carver.

The door gives a huge rumble, and begins to move on its

rollers behind me. The woman sucks in a breath – like she really, really didn't want to have to do this – then hefts the pipe and swings it at me, in a horizontal sweep. I was looking back towards the door, and only just catch the swing out of the corner of my eye. I dodge back, and the pipe whooshes by me, grazing my chest. The woman curses, tries to bring the pipe back, but I'm already running, with Carver on my heels, out of the door and away.

The Earthers chase us, shouting at us to stop, but we're in the open now – and there's no way they're outpacing a pair of tracers in the open. Their cries grow fainter and fainter behind us. It's impossible to work out where we are – the corridors around us could mark anywhere on the station. It's only when we emerge onto one of the stairwells that I realise we're in New Germany. The Caves are below us, and the Tzevya border is off to our left.

The power's off in the stairwell, and there's that stench again, wafting up from the bottom. We stop on a landing, breathing hard. The light is out, but as we arrive it flickers back on. An old woman is leaning up against the wall, dead eyes locked on the ceiling. Resin has sprouted out of her mouth like an obscene afterbirth, almost gluing her head to the wall.

We look away, and I catch Carver staring at me.

"What?" I say.

He shakes his head, as if banishing unpleasant thoughts. "Where did Anna go? She's not still in there?"

"I don't know. She'll be OK." I can't say whether this is true or not.

"Right," he says. "And we need to get back to your psycho doctor anyway."

I can feel the incisions in my knees throbbing. Part of me is amazed that I'm still whole, that Knox hasn't died yet. "What do we do then?"

"We get him to Apex. We warn them about the Earthers."

"Do you think Anna was right? That they're behind Resin?"

He shakes his head again "No idea, Ry."

Without another word, we start running again, pushing our exhausted bodies further, heading back down the ring.

58

Knox

Morgan Knox doesn't know how he gets hold of the syringe. But it's in his hand, his thumb resting on the depressed plunger. It takes all his effort just to remember what he's supposed to do with it.

Tube thoracostomy. That was it. He's got to drain some of the fluid on his lungs.

Every breath sends a constricting black corona into his vision, and, with each one, the corona gets bigger, narrowing his sight down to a small, bright circle.

He's lying on his back on the surgery floor, holding the syringe up to the light. It's a black shape, the needle appearing to grow before his eyes. He flips the cap off with trembling fingers, then lowers the syringe to his side. He's going to have to punch right through his tunic.

His right index finger feels out a space. There – between the second and third ribs on his right-hand side. He'll be able to get the needle into the pleural space, the area between the lungs, draining off some of the fluid. It'll buy him some time to address the underlying pathology, assuming he can stay awake to do it.

He doesn't know if it'll be enough. But if it doesn't do something, he'll fade away, and he can't allow that. Not while Janice Okwembu is still walking around.

The needle rests against the fabric of his tunic. Knox can't take enough of a breath to prepare for it, so he doesn't bother. He just pushes the needle in, right through the skin.

It's the worst pain he's ever felt in his life, slicing right through his chest cavity and out the other side. He can't scream. He can't do anything. It takes him a moment to get up the strength needed to pull the plunger back, and when he does so, the agony is almost unbearable.

He pulls until the plunger stops, then rips the needle out. There's another feeling now, beyond the pain: a searing stab of cold, right into the centre of his being. It's air, travelling in and out of the tiny hole he made. He holds the syringe up, pushing back against the darkness in his vision. The space in the syringe is filled with greyish-black ooze.

He lets it go, his hand dropping to the floor. He should do it again, withdraw more fluid, but he can't face going through that pain again. He concentrates on getting as much oxygen as he can from the tiny breaths he's able to suck into his lungs.

The corona leaps forward, driving his sight to a hot pinpoint of white light. Then even that vanishes, and Knox is gone.

59

Prakesh

Julian only just makes it through the doors.

He has to turn sideways, jamming his body into the crack. His one hand – the one not holding the stinger – lashes out at Prakesh. His face is contorted with rage.

Roger's hands enter the crack, wrapping around the frame, trying to push the door back. The motor starts complaining, grinding as it pushes against the obstacle. Julian growls in fury, swinging his arm again, his fingers hooked into claws.

It's impossible not to think of what happened to Oren Darnell. He was crushed by the massive doors leading to the Core, caught between them while trying to chase down Riley. This isn't the same thing: the door and the motor behind it aren't strong enough to do permanent damage to Julian. And, Prakesh can see, it's not enough to hold him either. Julian is pushing through, inch by inch, the growl turning to a groan as he fights through the gap.

Prakash starts to back away. It's only after he's taken a few steps that he remembers that Julian is out of bullets.

The realisation floods through him, an electrical storm

253

crackling through his muscles. Julian wants him? Fine. Prakesh strides towards him, grabs his upper arm and *pulls*.

With a squeal, Julian pops out of the door. Prakesh collapses backwards, and Julian lands on top of him, his skin hot and greasy, stinking of adrenaline. Prakesh sees, with unsettling clarity, the door close on Roger's fingers. He hears a cry of pain, and then the fingers are gone and the door clicks shut.

He tries to push Julian off of him. He's rewarded by Julian's fist driving into the side of his face, cracking against his cheekbone. The world flashes grey. Prakesh is dimly aware of another pain at the back of his skull, where he must have impacted with the floor after Julian hit him. He has just enough time to process this when Julian hits him again.

This time, the man's fist lands right on Prakesh's upper lip, splitting it open. Blood, hot and bitter, coats his tongue.

Julian's hands wrap around Prakesh's neck, thumbs digging into his throat. Julian is shouting – a sound filled with insane fear. Prakesh realises this distantly, almost academically, as if Julian is a plant specimen that has developed an interesting characteristic. Another thought follows it: he can't breathe. Can't get enough oxygen into his lungs. It's important, Prakesh knows it is, but he doesn't know what to do about it. Julian's face is inches from his, spittle flying from his mouth.

Prakesh can't feel the pressure on his throat any more. He's at the bottom of a deep, dark hole, looking up at a dwindling circle of light.

Something appears in the light, above Julian. No, not something. *Someone.*

With the same distant recognition, Prakesh sees that it's Suki. She has a fire extinguisher in her hands, a squat, red cylinder, heavy and rusted. She holds it horizontally, one hand gripping its nozzle assembly, the other holding the base. Prakesh notes all this, and wonders what she plans to do with it. There's no fire, and that's what you use fire extinguishers for . . .

With a desperate cry, Suki slams the extinguisher down onto Julian's head.

He stops shouting, and the most curious expression crosses his face. Part surprise, part anger. He doesn't look around, not even when Suki hits him again. The second blow turns him into a ragdoll, and he collapses on top of Prakesh, spasming.

The fingers around Prakesh's throat loosen and fall away. Oxygen comes rushing back, and, with it, reality. He shoves Julian off him, and the tech thumps onto the floor.

Suki raises the extinguisher again, tears falling down her face. She's shouting, too, as if Julian's fear fled his body and found a home in hers. Just before she brings the extinguisher down, Prakesh grabs her wrists. He doesn't remember getting off the floor, and the extinguisher bounces off his chest. It hurts.

She tries to shove him aside, tries to bully past him with the extinguisher. He still has hold of her wrists, and he grips them even tighter.

She drops the extinguisher. It lands nozzle first, and shoots out a spurt of white foam as the handle makes contact with the ground. Prakesh lets go of Suki's wrists, more in surprise than anything else. She yelps, then covers her mouth with her hands. Above them, her eyes are enormous.

"It's OK," Prakesh says. They barely count as words: his throat is a piece of rust-caked metal. His skin feels as if a steel band is locked around his neck, hot and constricting. He tries again. "It's OK, Suki. You're all right."

She wavers for a moment, then hugs him, burying her face in his shoulder. A part of Prakesh doesn't believe any of this is real. The lights are too bright, every sensation magnified.

"What about the others?" Suki says, her voice muffled in the folds of his lab coat. "Roger? Iko?"

255

"Trapped. They're not getting out of the Food Lab." He looks over towards the door, half expecting to see Roger forcing it open with his fingertips. But it's shut tight, the light on the keypad blinking a reassuring red.

Suki pulls apart from him. She opens her mouth to speak, but she's interrupted by the sound of cheering. She and Prakesh turn, and see the other techs charging across the floor towards them.

Prakesh tries to speak, tries to raise his voice. He wants to tell them that it isn't necessary, that any of them would have done the same thing. He wants to point them towards Suki, tell them how she saved him. But as they surround him, as they pound him on the back and reach for his hand, laughing with relief, shouting his name, he wonders if that's true. For the first time in forever, Prakesh Kumar feels like a hero.

60

Riley

Knox has got worse.

I can hear him breathing the moment we enter his surgery. There's a guttural quality to it, like his larynx is falling apart. The dark skin of his face is pallid as a block of tofu, stained with dark drips of Resin. He's managed to crawl halfway into the surgery.

Carver fills up a canteen with water while I examine Knox. I fold my jacket underneath his head – it helps still his ragged breathing a little.

"Here," Carver says, passing me the sloshing canteen. As I drink deep, he nods to Knox. "We should go. The people I've seen like that . . . they don't last too long."

I take a slug of water. "How long?" I say, trying to keep the tremor out of my voice. Almost manage it, too.

He shrugs. "An hour. If that."

"I can't get him another shot of the drugs in an hour. I wouldn't even know where to start."

"There's plenty in Apex."

"That's a two-hour run. At least. And that's without having to carry someone. What about the monorail?"

257

For a moment, Carver's eyes flicker. Then he sighs in frustration. "Not running, last I heard. We could find a train car at the top of the sector, but it could take us most of an hour if there isn't one nearby. And if we don't luck out, we won't have time to do anything else. Is there any way we could get those bombs out of you?"

I shake my head. "He said that if anybody but him tried to take them out, they'd blow." I suddenly have a picture of a bomb – a big one, a real monster – with all its tangled wires.

"How sure are you?"

"I'm sure, all right?" I say, anger flaring, thinking of Kev. I force myself to walk away, leaning my hands on the operating table. "Get out of here, Carver. If you stick to the top level, you should get to Apex before—"

"I'm not leaving. Not when you're like this. Not when you're making stupid decisions."

I stare at him.

"I'm not just talking about this death wish of yours," he says. When I don't respond, he shakes his head. "The kid, Riley."

"I am *not* going to have you be angry with me for what happened back there," I say. "We've got other things to worry about."

He kicks the leg of the operating table, hard. The bang echoes around the room. His voice follows it, raised in an angry shout. "You almost strangled her!"

I can see the fury building in his face. I'm reminded of how much he keeps hidden away – when I told him about Amira's death last year, he nearly throttled me.

"How could you do something like that?" he says. "She was a *kid*." He turns away, rubbing the back of his head, his other arm on his hip. It's such an exaggerated posture of frustration that I almost laugh, but then he turns back to me and the look on his face kills the laughter.

"I was *bluffing*," I say.

"We should have come up with something else. If I'd had two more seconds . . ."

"We didn't have two seconds."

"You're out of control. You're not thinking straight, and you're not letting us help you. This whole time, you've been trying to handle everything yourself. Remember what Amira taught us? Crew first, Riley. Dancers over everything."

"Amira *betrayed us*."

"And that makes everything she did null and void, does it?" He shakes his head. "You don't get it. Amira was the greatest teacher anybody could ever have, but she went bad, and she went bad because she didn't trust us. She bottled all her feelings up inside, just like you're doing now."

"I'm not her." The words are hissed through gritted teeth.

He talks over me. "She took it all on herself. All that responsibility. You're doing the same thing."

I turn away from him, trying to shut him out. It doesn't work.

"But – no, *listen to me*, Riley – you're not responsible for what happened to Kev. Amira was self-defence. And your father?"

"Shut up, Carver."

"Nobody should be in that position."

"*Stop*."

There are a million things I want to say, and a million more I don't even want to think about. Around us, the station is horribly silent.

"You don't get to send me off and die by yourself," he says. "Not happening. Not ever."

And then I'm kissing him. Hard.

My lips land on his with such force that it nearly knocks him over. I wrap my arms around his neck and pull tight. My tongue finds his, slipping past his open lips. It's only when he starts to return the kiss, a shocked second later, that the full knowledge of what I'm doing comes rushing in.

And yet, I can't stop. I don't want to. I know it's wrong, but the need for human contact, the need for something *normal*, is impossibly powerful. It's all I want. I want to bury myself in his arms and forget about everything. I soak up the kiss like water, like I've been wandering thirsty for months.

It's Carver who pulls away. He does it gently, leaving just a hint of warmth on my lips. It takes him a moment to speak. "Riley . . ." he says.

My cheeks are burning with guilt. All I can think of is Prakesh, lying next to me in our bed in Chengshi, his eyes closed, his mouth slightly parted as he sleeps. I can see the image clearly, as if I'm right there next to him.

I hear Carver suck in a quick intake of breath. My first reaction is to glance at Knox, but he's still out, his chest trembling. When I look back to Carver, I see a strange glint in his eyes.

"Carver, listen, I didn't mean—"

"All right, what if I had this thing?" he says, then stops. "But it's not ready yet," he mutters, more to himself than to me.

"What?" I ask, more confused than I'm willing to admit. I have to repeat myself before he looks up.

"The station's pretty empty now, right?" he asks.

I think of the thousands killed by Resin, and shudder. "It'll still take us too long to get to Apex."

"No, no, listen: anybody left alive – they aren't going to be hanging around in the corridors, are they?"

"Probably not, but what difference does it make?"

"It's perfect," he says. "I should have thought of this ages ago. Sorry about that."

He jerks a thumb at Knox. "Can you pick him up and bring him to the main corridor? I need to go and check on something."

I try to make sense of everything he just said, and come up with nothing. Carver doesn't wait for my response; he's already heading for the doors.

"Carver, wait up," I say. I only just manage to catch him before he runs into the passage. "*Carver.*"

"We need to get him to Apex in under an hour, right?"

"Yeah . . ."

"So I might have a way to do that." He starts to move again, stops. "Only: we might die."

"*Might?*"

"It's no more than a ten per cent chance. Twenty, tops."

"Excuse me?"

"But I think it'll work. Almost positive."

"Carver, now would be a great time to tell me what's going on."

Every second we stand still seems to make him more anxious. "OK, you remember I told you I was working on something big?"

A dim memory surfaces, of our conversation following Mikhail's arrest. "Sort of. Why?"

"Well, this is it. The thing that's big."

Without another word, he bolts.

"Get him to the main corridor," he shouts over his shoulder. "I won't be long."

"Carver!"

But he's gone.

With nothing else to do, I head back into the operating theatre. When I first woke up here, it was clean and ordered – Knox's perfect little world. But it's a mess now, with bottles and medical supplies scattered across the floor.

My mind keeps coming back to the kiss. Every time it does, I push it away. I can deal with it later. I have to. If I give it any attention right now, I'll collapse completely.

It takes me a few minutes to work out how to move Knox. I find myself wondering if it's even safe to move him, if that'll just add to what Resin is doing to his lungs, but it's not like I have an option.

He's my height, but he's heavy. It's impossible not to think of the expression *dead weight*. I have to psych myself up into hoisting him, getting my arms under his and linking my hands across his chest. He moans as I lift him up, and a thin streak of black drool trickles down his chin. I almost let him go, desperate for the slime not to touch my hands, but I force myself to hold on. My legs protest as I drag him out of the room, and his rubber-soled shoes screech as I drag them across the floor, his legs bouncing whenever he hits the edge of a metal plate.

If I wasn't so exhausted, if my neck wasn't starting to hurt from looking back over my shoulder to see where I was going all the time, this would almost be funny.

Somehow, I manage to get through the corridors surrounding the operating theatre. By the time I reach one of the larger corridors, my entire body has become a conductor for pain, a magnet for it. Aches and stinging and a needling itch in the back of my knees.

I drop Knox, and he groans again as his head thumps off the metal. The corridor is deserted. No Carver.

I sit up against the corridor wall, relishing the chance to let my body do nothing for a few minutes, keeping an ear out for any sounds. If the Earthers come, I want to be ready. But outside of the rumble of the station, the only sound is that of a flickering light further down the corridor, the filament buzzing and clicking. After a few moments, it sputters out, leaving that section in darkness.

Knox isn't the only reason to get to Apex quickly. If the Earthers get to the ship dock, if we can't get the people in Apex to mount a defence, they'll overwhelm the remaining stompers, and take the *Shinso*. I still don't know how Okwembu, and her knowledge of old operating systems, is going to help them. If we can't defend the dock, it won't matter.

There's a sound. One I can't place. I open my eyes.

It's a rumbling – distant and dull, like a mythical creature at the bottom of a cave. Is it the Earthers? I bend down to grab Knox and drag him to a hiding place, but then I stop. The rumbling isn't human. It sounds almost like a monorail car. But that's not possible – there's no monorail down here.

The rumble gets louder, revealing details of itself, unfolding into a high-pitched, whining growl. It's not static – it ebbs and flows, revving like . . .

Like an engine.

Carver.

The blackness further down the corridor is obliterated by a blinding white light as *something* comes round a corner.

The rumble becomes deafening, and it changes to a squeal as the light rushes towards us. Gaping, I flatten myself against the corridor wall. If this isn't Carver, then my life is about to get even more complicated than it is already.

Just as the light seems like it'll swallow us, it swings round, revealing what's behind it. The roar cuts off, grinding back to a low rumble as whatever it is skids to a halt, turning sideways in the corridor. It's Carver, and he's on top of a machine so strange that I have to focus to take it all in.

It has to be seven feet from front to back, with four black wheels. They're huge, each of them a foot and a half across, bracketing a crazy collection of piping and wires and cables, jumbled together like a child's puzzle. At the centre of it all, a massive, grooved steel block. A pipe shooting out of the back spits black blurts of smoke.

Carver straddles the body, his legs splayed out alongside

him. His hands are gripping a control stick. He's grinning like
a madman.

He shouts over the rumble of the engine: "Like I said. I was
working on something big."

61

Riley

I don't get a chance to say anything. The thing's engine gives a massive, grumbling belch and cuts out, spitting a final blast of smoke out of the tailpipe. The corridor stinks of oil, and the silence is almost as loud as the engine was.

Carver thumps the engine block with his foot. "No, no, *start*, you stupid thing."

He reaches down and yanks on a cord, pulling it once, twice. The motor gives a tiny puttering cough, but fails to catch.

"What. The hell. Is this?" I say.

"When it works, I call it the Boneshaker." He's off the vehicle now, crouching down, doing something clanky to its innards.

"*When* it works?"

"Yeah, well, I sort of only turned it on for the first time ten minutes ago."

"Carver . . ."

"I know what you're thinking," he says, without looking up. He's gone back to his tinkering, his hands jammed deep in the machinery. "How did he manage to build a working four-wheeler in six months? Ow!"

He pulls his hand back with a start. There's a small gash in his thumb, already bleeding. He sucks on it briefly, and plunges it back in.

"Actually, I was thinking that you've finally gone insane," I say.

He continues as if I hadn't said anything. "I just wanted to see if it could be done. I got tired of building little gadgets. I knew I had to work on something bigger."

"So you built *this*? Where did you get the parts?"

"Here and there," he says. "Trade for this, bribe someone for that, steal the other."

I open my mouth to speak, then decide that there's nothing I could say that would sum it all up.

I settle instead for hauling Knox upright. Unbelievably, it feels like he's got even heavier. When I lift him up, he starts coughing, his unconscious body shuddering as his throat tries to get rid of the gunk in his lungs.

I have to shout at Carver more than once to get him to help. We manage to get Knox sitting on the machine. His body is barely upright, his head lolling on his chest. I step back, my skin caked with sweat.

With a muttered prayer, Carver gives the cord another abrupt tug. This time, the motor jumps into life. Carver yanks his hand away, and then the thing is running – coughing and spluttering, but running. Carver pumps his fist and vaults onto the machine, landing in front of the comatose Knox. He tweaks the throttle and backs the machine up, lining it up straight, and then jerks the throttle, revving the engine.

"Climb on," he says. He has to raise his voice to be heard above the roar.

I jab a finger at Knox. "You sure he can ride this thing? It might make him worse."

"It's the only shot we've got. This is the fastest way up the ring."

"You'll never get through the crush!"

"There *is* no crush!"

I stare at him. Because he's right. There isn't. Not any more. The crowds of people that normally clog every public space in the station are gone. They've barricaded themselves inside their habs, shutting themselves away. For the first time in forever, the corridors and galleries are empty.

Before I can stop myself, I'm on top of the machine. *Boneshaker* is right – the vibrations from the motor travel up through my body, rattling my skull. With Knox and Carver on the thing, there's barely enough room for me – my backside is hanging right off the body.

Tracer routes unfold in my mind, corridors and passages that I've run a million times. Jumps I've done, walls I've climbed, stairs I've leapt down. My favourite spots. The ones I always try to avoid. All spread out in my mind, like a map on a desk, one I can run my finger over and plot the best route.

I reach forward and wrap my arms around Carver's midsection, sandwiching Knox between us. He trembles, and I feel a dot of Resin speckle the skin of my arm.

"We'll need to go up through Tzevya," I say. "We don't have time to go the long way round. Go to the end of the corridor, then hang a left."

"What about if we go down by the air exchangers?"

"My way's faster."

Carver guns the throttle and the world goes blurry.

62

Riley

I've never moved this fast. Not on a monorail car, not when I ran the Core, not on my fastest, most effortless sprint, when it feels like a fusion reactor is powering my legs. The speed is intoxicating, a thing of raw power, exploding through my body as the Boneshaker bucks and shudders underneath us.

I have to use my feet to stay on, hooking them into the guts of the machine, desperately trying to keep my balance. For a few seconds, I forget everything: Knox, Resin, Royo, Okwembu, the Earthers. Prakesh. I'm laughing, a furious, joyous howl that I couldn't stop even if I wanted to. I don't know if Carver can hear me, and I don't care.

We shoot out onto one of the catwalks, high above the New Germany gallery. There's nobody in sight. My mind is racing ahead of us, and my laughter cuts off abruptly as I realise where we're heading.

"Whoa, whoa, Carver, stop!" I shout.

He looks over his shoulder. The movement travels down into his hands, and the Boneshaker jerks a little. "What?"

"I forgot! This'll take us down the stairs."

"It's the only way. Trust me!" He twists the throttle harder. The machine surges ahead, and it's all I can do to keep my grip while holding Knox up.

The entrance to the far corridor looms, and then we're through it, in blackness for a few seconds before we emerge into a lit part of the corridor. Carver jerks the stick to the side, and it's only when the right wheels jerk upwards and rumble over something that I realise why. We just ran over someone. A body. I flick a glance back over my shoulder, but the corpse is nothing more than a shadow, fading fast.

Carver shouts over his shoulder. "Hold on tight!"

I lift my ass off the seat to get a better look. The stairs are short, no more than ten steps, but steep, and coming up fast. Carver twists the brake – until now I hadn't realised that there *was* a brake – but then changes his mind and guns the throttle again. I barely have time to process what Carver is doing before we're airborne.

We're going so fast that, for a moment, we don't actually fall. We just keep flying forward, and it's only when we're about to collide with the ceiling that the Boneshaker drops. The thought comes to me – much too late – that we should have slowed and then driven down the stairs. I feel the ceiling just touch the top strands of hair on my head. In a weird way, I'm too fascinated to be scared – everything is moving at light speed and in slow motion, all at once.

Carver leans back, pulling the nose up. We slam into the ground with a bang that shakes the corridor. The wheels squeal as they try to keep contact. Carver is screaming, fighting with the control stick. I see him tweaking the throttle, desperately trying to speak to the skid – and then we're out of it, running straight, zooming down the corridor and laughing so hard with relief that I think we're going to fall right off. I'm astounded that Knox hasn't snapped out of his unconscious state; then, I wish I hadn't thought about it.

"Next time," I shout, "go *down* the stairs!"

"How about next time you take us somewhere where there *are* no stairs?"

"I'll try. You know where to go from here?"

He nods. "You're not the only tracer on Outer Earth."

As the words leave his mouth, the Boneshaker's engine gives an almighty cough, bucking so hard that it lifts me off the seat. It sputters and dies, and we coast to a halt at a T-junction, bumping up against the wall.

"Shit, shit, shit," Carver says. He slams his foot down on a lever on the side, then does it again, but each time the motor refuses to catch, giving a sullen clicking sound before fading. The Boneshaker has left enormous, curling black lines on the floor, like question marks.

"Told you we should have gone down slowly," I say, dismounting. My legs are trembling.

"And where's the fun in that?" He follows me, bending down to ram his hands into the motor. The metal is steaming slightly.

It takes me a few moments to realise that Knox has lifted his head. He's staring at me, his eyes rheumy, almost clouded. Little black bubbles pockmark his cheek and lips, dotting his pale skin.

He opens his mouth, the words dropping out it like hanging spit. "Wuh. Wuh. Where. Where are wuh."

"He speaks," Carver says, not looking up.

I try not to meet Knox's eyes. "Getting you to safety."

"Wuh-why?"

"You die, I die, remember?"

He doesn't have long left. I close my eyes, trying not to pay attention to the hot, itching stitches. "Carver, we're running out of time," I say.

"I know, I know. It's the batteries."

"Just fix it."

"I'm trying."

That's when I hear the voices. They're distant, and it's impossible to make out the words, but it sounds like they're coming from behind us.

"Carver?" I say.

"I hear 'em."

The Boneshaker gives another roar, briefly catches, then dies. That nasty clicking sound ratchets out of the engine, followed by more curses from Carver as he gets ready to try again. I drop down into a combat stance, my hands at my sides, ready to take whoever comes first. *Buy some time. That's all you can do.*

It's a gang. I see it the second they come round the corner, colours out, vibrant purple, splashed across bandanas and tattoos. I don't know them, but it's easy to see what they've been doing. They're carrying boxes of stuff – food, parts, batteries. I guess it's easy to go looting when the station's locked down.

The leader is a short, stocky guy, with a shaven head and an ugly, badly healed facial tat in the shape of a scythe. He comes up short, staring in confusion at the Boneshaker. Then he grins and turns to his buddies, barking something at them in a language I don't understand. The ones carrying boxes put them down, and start to saunter towards us. They don't have any weapons that I can see, but I can tell they're ready to fight, and that they know how to do it.

Right then, the Boneshaker catches and holds. Hot smoke swirls around my legs, and I leap back on before I can think about it, wrapping my arms around Carver a split second before he guns the motor.

I'm sitting a little forward this time, squashed against Knox, but I feel hands brushing my back, scrabbling for a hold.

The front of the Boneshaker rises upwards, like an ancient beast rearing to attack. For one insane second I think I'm going to fall right off it. Then I see that the gang leader has grabbed onto the back edge of the Boneshaker and is being dragged along. His boots judder as they fly along the floor, bouncing off the metal.

I reach back to push him off, but Carver jerks our ride to one side. The man swings around, smashing into the corridor wall with a sound like a melon splitting open. He tumbles away, lifeless.

We're heading back the way we came – the Boneshaker came to a halt facing the wrong direction, and Carver didn't get a chance to turn around. "We're going the wrong way," I say.

"Better hang on, then."

Leaning to one side, he tweaks the brake, twisting the control stick and spinning the Boneshaker so fast that it nearly pushes us right off. Somehow, I manage to keep both Knox and myself on.

The gang is back on its feet ahead of us. There aren't that many, but they crowd the corridor. Carver shouts something, his words lost in the roar of the engine, then twists the power so hard that the grip almost comes off in his hand. The Boneshaker surges forward, its vibrations threatening to shake me apart, and we head right for the middle of them.

At the very last second, the gang scatters, diving out of the way.

One of them doesn't move fast enough, and the Boneshaker rumbles over her ankle. Her scream drills into my ears, but it's gone almost as soon as it starts. I expect to hear stinger fire, but we've knocked them down, and soon we've left them behind.

"Whatever you did to the batteries, it worked!" I shout.

Carver nods. "How's our patient doing?" he says.

I lean forward, studying Knox. He's unconscious again. The drool on his face has dried to a thick crust.

63

Riley

The power failures have grown worse – there are large parts
of the station in darkness now, whole corridors blacked out. I
think of the cities back on Earth. Or, at least, how I imagine
them to have been. Huge buildings, towering to the sky. Thin
streets winding between them like pieces of string, pulled tight.
Easy to imagine them teeming with millions of people. What's
hard is to imagine them empty, after the nuclear war. It must
have been like Outer Earth is now.

The closer we get, the more scared I feel. It's impossible to
know how Knox is doing, or how long he has. There's no telling
whether more of the drug will even help him. Maybe it's something you can only take once.

Don't think about that.

There are more bodies, and the sickly sweet smell of decay
is thicker, ebbing and flowing through the corridors. But there
are no more gangs, and nobody stops us. It's not long before
we cross the border into Tzevya.

Ahead of us, the corridor becomes a T-junction. Someone
has scrawled a message on the wall in black ink, and, as Carver

slows to take the corner, I see it clearly. *Resin? Turn back we shoot on sight.*

They might *shoot on sight*, but so far Tzevya looks deserted. I'd expected to find the corridors blocked by debris or something, but they're wide open, although the doors alongside remain closed.

We trundle down a short flight of stairs onto the bottom level. There's another corridor ahead of us, long and empty. Most of it is in darkness, but here and there a few lights flicker, still holding out.

I feel Carver hesitate for a moment, as if reluctant to go back up to full speed. But then he guns the Boneshaker. The wheels squeal, spitting up smoke, and we speed down the centre of the corridor.

We're about halfway down when I see it.

It's so fleeting that I'm almost ready to believe I imagined it, but then it catches the light again.

"Stop!" I scream at Carver.

He turns to look at me, his eyes narrowed in confusion. We're still going way too fast. I hurl myself forward, pressing up against Knox, scrabbling for the brake. Carver yells in surprise.

The Boneshaker starts to skid. Its wheel clips the wall, and we nearly unbalance as the vehicle lurches the other way.

My hand is on the brake, pulling it hard, my feet gripping the body of the Boneshaker in a desperate attempt to hold on. Carver is screaming, trying to control the machine, his hand fighting with mine for the stick.

I feel the machine tilt . . .

We come back, slamming into the ground and ending in a screeching, grumbling halt in the middle of the corridor. The engine cuts, leaving nothing but the sound of our breathing.

Carver starts to turn around, on the verge of asking me what I was doing—

And stops dead as the wire strung up across the corridor just touches the side of his neck

I still can't believe I saw it. I can barely see it now – it's only really noticeable through the impression it's leaving in the skin of Carver's neck, a thin channel just to the right of his Adam's apple. Somewhere, very distant, an alarm is blaring.

Very slowly, Carver leans backwards. His finger searches for the wire, finds it, twangs it gently. The light dances off it, zipping up and down its length.

"Like I said," I say. "Stop."

When he looks back to me, his eyes have gone huge.

Right then, what feels like every door in the corridor bursts open. There are people everywhere, ripping us off the Boneshaker and throwing us to the ground.

I try to stand, but I'm forced down by a foot in my back. I see Knox fall to the ground on my right, see a strand of dried Resin gunk fall across the floor.

Shoot on sight.

Before I can even articulate the thought, they've spotted the strand. Their angry shouts coalesce, turning into cries of "He's sick!" and "Do it!" I try to scream, but there's a gun barrel jabbed deep into the back of my neck. I see one being put to Knox's head, forcing it down.

My heart flash-freezes. It just cuts off mid-beat. I can't take my eyes off the stinger against his head, against the finger round the trigger. I can see every groove, every wrinkle. The joint is scarred, filigreed with white lines, and a thin silver band shines at its base. The finger begins to squeeze.

All at once, I remember where I've seen that ring.

"Syria!" I shout.

The finger pauses, just for a second. The hand holding the gun is shaking ever so slightly.

And then there's a voice, cutting above all the others. "Riley?"

The gun is lifted off my neck, and I'm pulled to my feet. My heart kicks back into gear, and it feels like the Boneshaker starting up: all noise and vibration. Part of me is still waiting for the gunshot that will end Knox's life, but it doesn't come.

Syria turns me to face him, both of his hands on my shoulders. He's wearing a medical face mask – gods know where he got it from. Greasy hair sticks to the mask in sticky strands, and the eyes above it are grim.

Anna is standing behind him.

Her expression dances between joy and confusion, shouting at the others to stand down. They stare at her, not sure whether to put the guns away, and it's only when she gets between them and me that they start to lower them. Syria is staring at me, recognition dawning.

I have a million questions – how Anna escaped the Earthers, how Syria ended up in Tzevya, what happened to the Caves. I don't have the energy to ask any of them. Behind me, I hear Carver hauled to his feet, shouting at the others to get off him.

From somewhere on the floor, Knox gives a hitching cough.

"He's sick," someone behind me says. "No exceptions, remember?"

The words kick the crowd back into gear. Syria steps forward, raising the stinger.

"*No*," Anna says, inserting herself between us and the crowd. "This one comes in."

"You giving *me* orders now?" Syria says, elbowing her aside.

"And who put you in charge, Caver?" one of the others says.

"Shut up. All of you," Anna says. She points to me and Carver. "I'm immune, so I'll take him – me and them, too. We'll put him in the hospital, in one of the iso wards."

"Out of the way, Anna," says a woman at one side of the corridor. She has a face mask, too, and short black hair that sticks up in untidy spikes.

"No, listen." Anna looks right at the woman. "Walker – you know me, and you know I'd never ask you this if I didn't have a good reason."

Walker raises an eyebrow. Anna looks over at me, then back at her.

She points a finger at my chest. "If he dies, so does she."

Silence in the corridor. Anna senses the hesitation, and presses home her advantage. "Donovan. Rama. Shanti," she says, looking at each of them. "Please. You have to trust me."

I badly want to say something – to tell them just why Knox's death means mine as well. But if I mention that I'm a walking bomb, it could disrupt the precarious position we're in. And even if Anna succeeds, what then? I need to get Knox to Apex. It's the only way he survives.

"Isolation ward," says the woman Anna called Walker. "We'll clear a path. But if one more person dies, it's on you."

Anna nods, then squats down next to Knox. I follow, lowering my head to hers.

"Anna, you don't understand," I say, but then I stop talking. Because Anna has reached in her pocket and drawn something out.

It's a tiny vial, no longer than her palm. It's just like the one Carver and I took from Apex – the furosemide-nitrate. The drug compound.

"We've still got a little left," she says.

64

Riley

The Boneshaker won't start. Anna, Carver and I have to carry Knox through the sector – Carver and I on each arm, and Anna on the feet. A squad of Tzevyans clears the way for us, ordering people back into their habs.

We'd never have got through Tzevya on the Boneshaker anyway. Most of the corridors are blocked off, guarded by people in makeshift face masks. They've done a good job; the wire that nearly cut Carver's head off was an early-warning system, attached to a home-rigged alarm somewhere else in the sector. It was never meant to be a weapon, even if it came horribly close.

Tzevya has drawn into itself, shutting off contact with the outside, hoping Resin will burn itself out. I don't know what world they thought they'd emerge into after it did, but it's a relief to be somewhere where the smell of decay isn't syrupy-thick.

The hospital is deeper into the sector, a few minutes from the border with Apex. Our honour guard peels off as we get there, as if they don't want to be near the place. It's small, with a narrow central corridor bordered by a few wards and offices. I expect it to be full, heaving with Resin patients, but the beds are empty. The wards are a mess, too, with upturned furniture and equipment scattered across the floor. As if they were the sight of a brawl.

Shoot on sight, I think, and shiver.

We put Knox into one of the isolation wards at the back of the hospital, a brightly lit room with a single bed and a keypad-locked door. By now, he's dosed up on furosemide-nitrate, and he doesn't wake up when we heave him onto the bed. There's no telling how effective this second dose will be. No way of telling how long I have left before Knox's body loses the fight.

There's no point taking him to Apex now, but we still need to warn the council about the Earthers. We can't let them take the *Shinso*. It's not just the fact that they'll be leaving us behind – we *need* that asteroid. It's the source of our minerals, our building materials, the things we need to keep this place going. The things we'll need to rebuild.

Walker, the only one of the Tzevyans to have seen us all the way here, volunteers to guard Knox's ward. Anna smiles thanks, and she and Carver and I make our way back through the hospital.

"We should go," I say. My voice sounds like it's coming from someone thirty years older. "Get to Apex."

Carver gives me a sideways look. "Shouldn't you . . . I don't know. Stay here with him?"

"Would it make a difference?"

He looks helpless. "I guess not."

Anna clears her throat. "It'll be tough to get inside. I'll get us some reinforcements."

I grind my teeth together. "They'll slow us down."

"You go up to Apex by yourself, or even if it's just us three, and they'll arrest you like they did the last time. You think they'll pay attention to anything you have to say? It'll be safer if we have an escort."

"Right," says Carver. "I'll get the Boneshaker fixed."

"Is that what you call that contraption?" Anna says. "Can you not just leave it here?"

"Leave it alone with a bunch of Tzevyans? Do you have any idea what the gangs up here would do to get their hands on that thing?"

Anna rolls her eyes, then turns to me. "What do you want to do?"

There are a few scattered chairs in the main lobby, and I sit down heavily in one of them. I don't have much choice – it feels like my legs are going to give out. "Think I'll just sit here for a minute," I say. "Come and get me when it's time to go."

"Right," Anna says, dragging out the word. She's about to say something more, but Carver shakes his head. They jog away, and the hospital doors close behind them with a hiss.

I lean back, rolling my shoulders, trying to sort through my thoughts. On the one hand, we need to get to Apex as soon as possible, before the Earthers do. On the other, they've got heavy equipment, supplies, and it'll take them a little while to get up there, even if they hurry.

There's got to be a way I can keep Knox alive. Maybe they've got something new in Apex – a more advanced drug compound, perhaps. But, really, what good will it do? Even if one exists, it's just delaying the inevitable.

At that moment, I feel the same way I did when I almost threw myself off the broken bridge. It would be so easy to go and find a high place, with no stompers around to stop me. One last run, and then it would all be over.

The thought is calming. I hold on to it, pull it close. If it comes to it, that's what I'll do.

I don't know when I fall asleep. The first I know about it is when I jerk awake, my head snapping forward. I was dreaming about my father again – I don't remember the dream, but I can feel it, like it's left some kind of psychic residue. My mouth is covered in sticky saliva. How long have I been out?

I stand up, surprised to find that my body doesn't just give up and fall apart at the seams.

With my legs aching in protest and my body pleading with me to go back to sleep, to sink into oblivion, I force myself to get up. I need to find Anna and Carver.

Although I've been to Tzevya before, I'm not as familiar with it as I am with the other sectors, and pretty soon I realise I'm lost. I'm on the top level, in a darkened corridor bordered by hab units. There's a hissing nearby, like steam escaping a trapped pipe.

I see a man at the end of the corridor. He's hunched over, adjusting something on the enormous stack of old crates that make up the blockage. Maybe he'll know where the sector hospital is.

I take a step towards him, and my leg gives out.

I don't realise it's happened at first. The next few seconds are a series of quick jerks, like I'm jumping forward in time between each awful moment. Then I'm down, crumpling to the ground, damn near bouncing off it as I skid to a halt, screaming.

The bombs. Knox is dead. Knox is . . .

But when I look down, I see that my legs are still in one piece. No bloodstains on the fabric of my pants, no splinters of shattered bone poking through. And it's only my right knee that's in pain, bright and sharp. The muscles are acting up, complaining about what I've put them through.

I feel pressure under my arms, and then I'm lifted right off the ground. The man is there, pulling me up with a strength that his wiry frame shouldn't possess.

"Easy now," he says. I have a moment to register that his accent is the same as Anna's, crisp and sharp, and then he's pushing open the door to one of the habs running alongside the corridor. He uses his foot, nudging the door open and turning sideways to pass through. My own foot bounces off the frame, and I bite my lip as the shock travels up my leg, like a finger twanging a taut wire.

The light in the hab is low – nothing more than a dim bulb on the ceiling. I have time to make out two cots, a double and single, before I'm lowered onto the bigger one. I put my head back, waiting for the numb feeling in my knee to pass.

"Any permanent damage?" he asks.

My face is prickly with sweat, but the pain has come down a little. For a long moment, I'm too relieved to speak. I really thought the bombs had gone off. I was so sure.

"Fine," I manage to get out. I try to sit up, but he puts a hand on my stomach.

"Easy," he says again. "Your body's just telling you to take a few minutes out. From what I've been hearing, you've had quite a journey."

He stands. "There's some water in Jomo's hab, I think," he says. "I'll be back in a minute."

Before I can reply, he's gone, the door clicking closed behind him.

I can hear my heartbeat in my ears, loud and insistent. I lay my head back on the pillow. As I do so, I catch something out of the corner of my eye, on the wall by the single cot.

I raise myself up on my elbows, getting a better look at the hab as I do so. There are stacks of clothes on the thin shelves running along the wall, lined up neatly next to a small pile of wrinkly apples. The single cot has been neatly made up, its threadbare blanket positioned carefully on the mattress, its pillow just so.

The thing I saw is a drawing. The light's too dim to make it out from where I'm sitting. Slowly, I swing my legs off the bed, waiting to see if they can take the pressure.

They can. I walk over to the single cot, squinting in the low light.

Whoever did the drawing is pretty good. It's executed in black ink: a single figure, running down a cylindrical passage, its walls delicately shaded. There's someone, the outline of a person, standing at the far end, and the central figure is running towards them. Looking closer, I see that the figure is female. Her hair streams out behind her, and she's wearing a jacket that looks like . . .

The picture snaps into focus. The passage is the Core, and the figure at the end is Oren Darnell. And the one at the centre . . . there's no mistaking it. Whoever did the drawing got my dad's old flight jacket perfect.

Very slowly, I reach out. My finger is about to touch the ink when I hear a voice behind me.

"Best not. It's murder to get off your hands."

The man has come back. He's holding out a canteen to me, and, as he moves into the light a little, I realise that he's Anna's father.

There's no mistaking it. The skin on his face is shot through with a filigree of lines and wrinkles and tiny scars, but his eyes are the same as his daughter's. He sees me staring, and raises his eyebrows quizzically.

"I brought you that water," he says.

I want to say something, but the words won't quite come yet. The water is delicious – cold and clear. I nod thanks, wiping my mouth and passing the canteen back.

"Frank Beck," he says, thrusting out a meaty hand. His grip is dry and firm.

"Riley Hale," I say, amazed that I can get the words out.

Frank steps past me, pointing to the picture. "I'd almost forgotten that was there. Used to it, I guess."

"Anna did that?"

"She's quite good, isn't she?" he says. "She drew that after the whole Sons of Earth thing calmed down. She wouldn't stop talking about how you ran the Core. Went on about it so much that Gemma – that's her mother – she told her to use some of the old matt-black we had lying around and . . ."

My voice feels like it's made of old glass. "Matt-black?"

"Oh – chemical residue stuff left over from water processing. I work down at the plant, you know. Anyway, she drew, er . . . well, this."

He raises his hand, sweeping along the length of the drawing.

I'm transfixed by it. I expect it to stir old memories, bad ones, but it doesn't. Instead, I find myself picking up the smaller details: the pattern on the bottom of my shoes, the way the figure at the end of the Core has the same hulking profile as Oren Darnell. She's even drawn the gloves I had on, which I used to fight off the freezing temperatures in the Core.

"I don't understand," I say to Frank Beck. "Anna and I – we don't exactly get along most of the time."

"Really?" he says, his brow furrowed. "I'd never know it from the way she talks about you. There was a new story every day when she was growing up, even before that bastard Darnell. Riley Hale ran New Germany Level 3 faster than anyone ever. Riley Hale jumped all the way off a gallery catwalk and survived. Riley this, Riley that. Said one day she was going to be faster than you."

"You're kidding."

"Not a bit of it."

I shake my head, still staring at the drawing, then sit down on the single cot. "But *we don't get along*. At all. We never have."

I think back to the first time Anna and I met – how she got in my face, challenging me to a race then and there.

Frank shrugs. "She's always refused to be second best at anything. She was running with a crew of lads up here, but she jumped at the chance to go and work for the stompers – mostly because she'd finally get to run with you."

"Was it you who taught her to use the slingshot?"

He gives a small smile. "Anna's always wanted to be the fastest person on Outer Earth, but it doesn't take much to see that her real talent is shooting. Drawing, too, but mainly shooting. I made that damn slingshot for her when she was a girl, and I don't think there's another sharpshooter in the six sectors who can aim like she can. I remember once when we . . ."

"Dad, you in there?"

Anna appears in the doorway. Frank Beck smiles. "Hey, sweetie," he says. "I was just helping your friend Riley here."

Anna steps inside. She briefly hugs her father, then turns to me, not looking at the drawing (*her* drawing) on the wall behind us.

"Carver's machine won't start," she says. "He's got one of the guys helping him on it, but it'll be a while."

Frank Beck holds his hand out. I take it, and he pulls me up off the bed.

"I've got some people together," Anna says. "Safety in numbers, right?"

I take a deep breath. "OK," I say. "Let's go."

65

Riley

We're halfway across the Tzevya gallery when the lights go out. This time they don't come back on.

We all stop, just for a second, waiting. The Tzevyans have been pretty good at keeping their sector clear of Resin victims, but I can still smell the dead here, the sickly-sweet scent of decay sticking in my nostrils.

"Any time now," says one of the others – Walker. But the lights stay off.

Syria clears his throat. "Let's go," he says, pointing to one of the corridors leading off the gallery floor. The lights are still on there, flickering gently.

There are ten of us, walking slowly up towards Apex. Syria leads the way. He's barely said a word to me. Every so often, I'll catch him looking in my direction, but when my eyes find his, he looks away. I don't mind. I'm not sure I know what to say to him. No one's said a word about the Caves, but I only have to look at Syria's drawn face, at the bags under his eyes, to know that the news isn't good.

It feels strange to be moving through Outer Earth in a big

287

group. More than that, it feels strange to be moving so *slowly*. I'm used to taking the corridors and catwalks at a run, not at an infuriating trudge. I bite back the urge to shout at them, to tell them to hurry. It'll just piss them off, and, right now, I need them on my side.

"Hey, tell me something, Hale," says Walker. "These people want to take the *Shinso* back to Earth, right?"

"Yeah?"

"How're they even planning to get on board? I mean, they take a tug, OK, but then what? The crew isn't just gonna open up and say, come on in, right?"

"They're using Okwembu to do it," I say. I'm thinking hard, trying to get my thoughts in order. "She knows something about the ship's operating system. I think they're going to use her to gain access."

Walker points to the floor. "What makes them think there's anything down there? Whole planet is a wreck."

I shrug, thinking back to Okwembu and Mikhail, back to the facility that served as the Earthers' base. "I don't know. They didn't exactly tell us their plans."

Walker is silent for a moment. Then she says, "Why don't we let them?"

"Why don't we let them what?"

"Take the ship."

"You're full of shit, Walker," says a man at the back. He's Donovan, I think.

"I'm serious," she says over her shoulder. "There's still the *Tenshi Maru*. Isn't there?"

"Way too far out," Syria mutters.

"And hang on," Donovan says. "You're proposing we let these people take one of our two remaining asteroid catchers, and just leave? What about the rest of us?"

"I just—"

"No. Not happening. Besides, we *need* that asteroid if we're going to have any hope of surviving."

"I'm just saying. These people want to try dropping this thing into Earth's atmosphere without heat shielding? Good luck and good riddance."

Donovan scoffs.

"They're going to use the asteroid as heat shielding," Anna says.

"Bullshit."

I shrug. "Actually, it makes sense. They'll have to be damn careful, though."

Walker ponders that. "But you said they didn't tell you anything about their plans."

"They didn't," I say. "Carver worked it out. He . . ."

I trail off. Something is jogging my memory, something I saw when we were captured by the Earthers.

It slips away, back into a mess of thoughts. There are still far too many loose ends, too many things we don't know.

"They've got weapons," I say. "They're ready to fight their way into the dock. The people in Apex need to know they're coming."

Walker shrugs. "People in Apex need to find out what this Resin thing is. That's what they need to do."

"Got that right," says Donovan. Syria huffs, flicking an irritated glance in his direction.

Anna falls into step alongside me. For once, her beanie is off, tucked in her jacket pocket. Her blonde hair is stuck to her forehead in untidy strands. Was she right about Mikhail? Is he the connection between us, the reason we aren't sick?

And if he is, does that mean that he and the Earthers cooked up Resin?

That thought again, flickering at the back of my mind, vanishing before I get a fix on it.

When we do reach Apex, it's a relief to see that most of the lights are still on. Of course, the doors are shut – huge slabs of steel, blocking off the wide entrance corridor.

Anna stops, resting her hand on the door.

"Now what?" says Syria.

"Why don't you knock?" Walker says.

"Wow. You're a genius, Walker," says Donovan.

"And you're an asshole."

"Yeah, well," says Donovan, walking over to one side of the door and dropping to his haunches. "I'm an asshole who's going to get us inside."

He's pulling at a panel on the wall – trying, I realise, to get to the wires behind it. He thinks he can short-circuit the doors somehow. I want to tell him not to bother – this is Apex, where if they want you outside, you stay outside.

At that moment, the doors give a massive mechanical whine and begin to slide open.

Behind them is a stomper, stinger up, aimed right at us. Syria swears, dropping the stretcher and scrabbling for his own. Walker, Donovan and the others already have theirs out.

The stomper is huge – a heavily muscled woman, not tall but built like a human version of the Boneshaker. Her name comes to me out of nowhere: Jordan. She was there when Royo sent Carver and me into the pipes outside the Recycler Plant.

The eyes buried in the black beetle-mask of her respirator are cold. "Don't move," she says. "Not a damn step, you hear me?"

"We're not sick," Anna says, raising his hands.

There's a second stomper now, coming up behind the first. I see his eyes widen. "It's Hale," he says to Jordan. He notices Donovan, still crouched by the side of the door, and trains his stinger on him.

"Get her into a brig somewhere," Jordan says. "Rest of them

can go on their way." She looks at Anna and the others. "Thanks for the delivery."

"Step aside, stomper," says Syria.

Jordan raises her stinger and fires. The bang is enormous, the bullet burying itself in the ceiling. We duck on instinct, and two of the people in our party take off, bolting away from Apex.

"Next one won't be a warning shot," Jordan says. "Hale – come with us."

"Just *listen* to me," I say. "Do you think I'd come back here if there wasn't a damn good reason?"

She doesn't lower her stinger. *I was wrong.* I thought I could negotiate with them, get them to give us passage. But none of this is working out like I planned.

"You've got one minute," she says.

I let out a shaky breath. "Is Royo—" I begin, but Jordan cuts me off.

"Still alive, for now," she says. "I'm in command. Now talk."

It takes less than that to tell them all about the Earthers. But when I'm finished, the stompers don't put their guns away. "Crap," Jordan says.

"But . . ."

"No. It's crap. I don't believe a word of it. Now you—"

There's an enormous roar, and then the Boneshaker bursts into view behind us. Carver is leaning back, as if trying to control a rampaging beast. Both the stompers are staring at the Boneshaker.

In the next instant, two things happen.

Donovan explodes off his haunches, moving faster than he has any right to. He shoulder-charges the nearest stomper, sending him sprawling.

The move distracts Jordan for a split second. I use it. I dart forward, jabbing at her gun arm. The heel of my left hand

smacks her on the back of her wrist. The heel of my right hits
the stinger itself.

It's a move that could get me killed if I miscalculate it, but
it works. Jordan's stinger goes flying, ripped out of her hand
before she can squeeze the trigger.

The Boneshaker comes to a screeching halt, rocking from
side to side. Carver cuts the engine. He looks at me, then at
the stompers, then at Anna, then back at me.

"What'd I miss?" he says.

66

Riley

After the tangled mess of Tzevya, Apex feels sparkling clean. The brightly lit corridors and white surfaces are free of the smell of decay.

Jordan and the other stomper are in the middle of our little group, their stingers confiscated, their arms held tight. Jordan's colleague got hit by Donovan in the scuffle, and blood is caked on his upper lip. Both of them are silent. We all are – we wouldn't really be able to hear each other anyway. Carver drives the Boneshaker behind us. He has the motor at just above idle, but in the tight corridors the noise is amplified. Every so often, Jordan looks back at it, a confused look on her face.

Apex is smaller than the other sectors, but it'll still take us a few minutes to reach the council chamber. I'm on the lookout for more stompers, and I can see Anna doing the same thing. Last thing we need is to run into an ambush. But there's no one around. Even Apex, it seems, has drawn into itself, like a freezing body diverting all its blood back to the core organs.

We're starting to get into a part of the sector that I recognise. It takes me a moment to work out where we are. A couple of levels below us is the main control room, where everything happened with my dad. Thinking of it is like touching an open wound.

Anna signals me to head down a corridor to our right, and that's when the Boneshaker cuts out again. The engine gives a giant, choking splutter, replaced by a resigned hissing noise, spraying clouds of noxious steam. Carver groans in frustration, his voice rising to a high whine. "Come *on*, you bastard, *come on*."

"Just *leave* it," says Syria.

Carver looks up at him. "Screw you."

Suddenly, everybody is shouting at everybody else, long-held tensions spilling out. Even I'm raising my voice, yelling for calm. At this rate, we're not going to get into an ambush – the stompers are going to come right down on top of us.

Somehow, Jordan's eyes find mine. I've walked into the fray, and I've ended up next to her. I can hear her voice clearly through the chaos "What are you doing, Hale?" she says.

I ignore her, but she keeps talking. "*Even if* these Earthers did exist," she says, building up steam. "*Even if* they actually managed to hijack the *Shinso*, they're not making it back to Earth. That thing's got no way to make it through the atmosphere without burning up."

I don't bother to tell her about the asteroid heat shield, and she doesn't give me a chance to. "Not to mention the fact that there are zero provisions left on that ship. They've been out there for nearly two years. I have to keep telling them that we can't send a tug, which is pissing them off because they're cooling their heels in Outer Earth orbit. So unless your *Earthers* have food of their own stashed away, they're not going anywhere."

I turn my head to tell her to shut up, and stop.

She stares at me. "What's wrong, Hale? Run out of lies to tell?"

But her voice sounds very far away. My mind is racing, connecting the dots faster than I keep track of it.

Jordan's words.

What I saw in the Earthers' camp.

The idea, dancing on the edge of my mind, steps into the light. I see everything, like when Anna's drawing suddenly snapped into focus.

And I really, really don't like what I see.

"Hey!" Anna says, all but bellowing the word. Finally, everyone stops talking. I barely notice. I'm rolling the idea around in my mind, desperately trying to find a weak spot in it, something I missed that will puncture it and sink it.

"Carver: leave it. We have to keep moving. Riley . . . Riley, what's wrong?"

Getting my tongue to form words is almost impossible. "You go on ahead," I say.

Anna narrows her eyes in confusion. "What?"

"I just . . ." I'm moving away, turning, breaking into a run. "There's something I have to do," I say over my shoulder.

"Riley!" Carver says. But I've already left them behind.

67

Riley

Doctor Arroway is slumped across the table in his office, his head resting on his forearms, slightly turned to one side. He's discarded his face mask – it's on the table in front of him, crumpled up. I can see the nail marks in its papery surface, as if he held it tight and scrunched it up before throwing it onto the table.

His office is at the back of the hospital, a messy room that looks as if someone has been living in it for the past few days. He probably has. I can still hear the sounds of the hospital – the moans of the patients and the barked commands of the few nurses and doctors that still remain – but they're muted here, and they're cut off completely when I shut the door.

Arroway jerks awake. He looks around him, and when he turns his face towards me I see that his eyes have sunk into his face, swallowed by huge black circles. He wavers for a moment, then realises who I am, and explodes out of his chair.

"No, no, no. Get away," he says, staggering backwards. His foot catches the chair leg as he does so, sending it crashing over. I can see him looking around for a weapon, something he can use against me.

He must think I want revenge, for not examining me when I told him about the bombs, back when I was captured at the broken bridge.

"Relax, Doc," I say, raising my palms. "I just want to talk."

"Talk?" Sweat beads on his forehead, and his eyes won't stop moving, still hunting for a weapon.

I force a smile. "Calm down. I'm not here to hurt you, or anyone else. I promise."

It feels like I do a pretty good job of keeping the nervousness out of my voice, considering. It feels like I'm hanging over a giant pit, dangling from a frayed rope, with a new strand snapping every minute. My earlier realisation is like a monster waiting in the pit, skulking in the shadows. I don't dare look at it, or even think too hard about it, or I'll fall from the rope.

I push on, using the words to strengthen my grip. "When you tested me – when you tested my blood. You didn't find anything useful, right?"

He's still looking at me like I'm going to lunge forward and bite him. After a few seconds, he gives a tight nod.

"I've got something for you," I say. "I think—"

My throat suddenly goes very dry, as if it doesn't want to say the words. I force them out. "I think it might help you figure out where Resin came from."

Arroway's eyes narrow. "How did you even get in here? They told me they sealed the sector."

"Never mind that. Here."

I dip my hand in my pocket. In the second before I pull it out, I pause. *You could leave it alone,* I think. *Just turn and run. Pretend you don't know anything.*

Then I take my hand out my pocket, and place what I'm carrying on the table.

The beans are a drab green colour, thin and curled. They're the ones that I took from the Earthers, thinking that I might need them as food further down the line.

"I don't understand," Arroway says. "What is—"

"Just test them." I've already got one hand on the door, pulling it open. The noise from the hospital floods back in. "Then come and find me. I'll probably be in the main council chamber."

Arroway stares at me, as if he still isn't sure whether I'm a dream or not.

"Come and find me," I say again. Then I'm gone, pushing my way through the hospital, not looking back.

I try to quieten my mind as I run through Apex. It's just as well I don't run into any other stompers – I'm so wired I'd probably try and take them head on. I try to sink into the movement, let the rhythm take me away, but dark thoughts tug at the edges of my mind.

It's not hard to find the council chamber. I can hear Syria bellowing from three corridors away, his voice ringing out, turned metallic by the corridor walls. "You're cowards! All of you!"

I step up my pace, breaking into a jog. Someone tries to answer Syria, but he cuts them off. "I don't care. You're just gonna let them take it? I swear to my gods, you walk out that door, and I'll use it to take your head off."

I've never been in the council chamber before, but I've seen it plenty of times on the station comms screens – the council leader would occasionally broadcast messages to the station from here. Okwembu did it all the time. It's smaller than I thought it would be, and, right now, it looks awful. The big centre table is strewn with detritus: discarded food containers, wrinkled jackets, tab screens. A glass of water has been knocked over, spreading a puddle across the middle of the table that nobody has bothered to mop up.

Syria is still shouting, threatening violence if anybody leaves. He, Anna, Carver, Donovan and Han Tseng are on one side of the conference table. Walker is on the other side, along with the rest of the Tzevyans. Jordan and her colleague are seated in one corner, sullen and silent.

Syria pauses for breath, and Walker cuts in, jabbing a finger at him. "We've been through plenty worse before. You think we can't survive a couple more years without asteroid resources?"

"I think you're a coward, that's what I think," Syria says.

Tseng looks as tired as Arroway was. There's no sign of his functionaries. "I absolutely forbid you to leave," he says to Walker. "If these people are really coming, then we can't let them leave. They are *not* taking that asteroid catcher."

Anna tries to cut in. "Everybody just—"

Tseng talks over her. "I order you to go down to the dock, and start fortifying it. You hear me?"

That causes laughter from everyone on the other side of the table. Walker tilts her head, looking Tseng right in the eyes. "Not a chance."

I hover in the doorway, not sure whether to intervene or not. I guess Walker had more supporters than she thought. But as I stand there, I think how easy it would be to agree with her.

It would be incredibly difficult to survive without the resources from the asteroid. That's our building material, our soil nutrients, everything. With the *Shinso* and its cargo gone, we'd have to rely on the one last ship out there: the *Tenshi Maru*. It might be months, even years, before it finds a suitable asteroid to capture and bring home. But we could hold out – especially now that there are far fewer of us left.

It's an uncomfortable thought, and it brings another. If the Earthers really want to take the *Shinso*, why should we risk our lives trying to stop them? Let them take the damn ship. If they think they can survive on Earth, then Walker is right: good riddance.

Anna sees me, and gestures me inside. Syria has started shouting again, and this time Walker has had enough. She and the others start picking their way across the room, heading for the door. One of them catches my eye, and half smiles, like we're both in a private joke.

Tseng has his hands flat on the table. For a tiny instant, I can see him as a council leader. It's a strange sensation, and I'm brought back to reality when he shakes his head furiously, making his greasy hair flick from side to side.

"They can't take the *Shinso*," he says. "We can't let them. We need to fortify the dock *right now*."

Walker ignores him, pushing past me with a muttered apology. Syria is shaking his head, as if he can't believe what he's seeing.

That's when Tseng really loses it. He hammers the table, once, twice, three times. "Don't you idiots understand? This isn't just about *holding out*. If we don't get that asteroid, this entire station is finished. It's over."

Something in his voice stops all movement in the room. Walker and her companions turn to look at him. Tseng falls silent, a deep expression of worry crossing his face. Like he's said too much.

At that moment, the lights in the room flicker, plunging us into darkness. Another power failure, identical to the dozens I've seen over the past few weeks. After a moment, the lights kick back on again in sequence, *click click click*. All of us look up at them when they do.

"What," says Syria quietly, "is so important about that asteroid?"

Han Tseng's indignant exterior has cracked. What's underneath is pink and tender, and he swallows, his Adam's apple bouncing.

"If we lose the *Shinso*'s asteroid," he says, "we lose the fusion reactor. If we lose the reactor, everything stops working. No heat. No air. Nothing. Outer Earth dies."

68

Riley

The silence feels like it has weight, like it's an actual presence in the room.

It's Anna who breaks it. "The tungsten," she says, her eyes wide.

Carver stares at her. "Holy shit. Of course."

His hands grip the top of a chair, and a deep growl of frustration rises in his throat.

"I don't get it," I say.

"I second that," says Walker.

Han Tseng sighs. "It's not the reactor per se. It's the shielding. It's made of tungsten alloy, which is ideal for absorbing the heat from the plasma core."

"This is just . . . *perfect*," Carver says

"The tungsten shields have degraded over time," says Han Tseng. "We've been throttling the power grid to reduce the strain on the reactor, but it's not enough. If we don't get the tungsten out of the *Shinso Maru*'s asteroid and repair the shields, then the reactor fails."

"Fails how?" Anna says.

302

"The second there's a shielding breach, it'll shut down. Just stop cold. Everything on the station that uses power is finished."

"What about backup systems?" Anna says. She's taken her beanie out of her jacket pocket and is knotting it in her hands.

Tseng gives a bitter laugh. "For an entire station? *Maybe* some of them are still working. Enough to power a sector or two, for a few days."

"Why didn't you tell people?" I say. "Why keep it a secret?"

Tseng notices me for the first time. "It would have caused a panic," he says. "And up until a few minutes ago, none of us was aware that the *Shinso* shipment was in danger. If everything had gone to plan, we would have had those shields fixed before anybody even noticed the power failures were a problem."

The question comes to the front of my mind, as if it was just waiting to be asked. "These people – the ones coming to take the *Shinso*. They think they can survive back on Earth."

Tseng shrugs, looking helpless.

"We *do* monitor the Earth, right?" says Carver.

Silence. Tseng won't meet anyone's eyes. After a long moment, he shakes his head.

The groan is involuntary, uttered by everyone in the room, brimming with disgust. Tseng swallows. "There's no point. Why spend time listening when we were never going to hear anything?"

Carver stares at him. "But you must have had software listening out. A sub-routine that would ping us if . . . tell me you had *something*."

Tseng gives a helpless shrug. "You don't understand. We listened for years. *Decades*. When we sent Earth Return down, we were monitoring non-stop." A note of defiance creeps into his voice. "But we heard nothing. It's dead down there, and we had to focus on surviving up here. There was no point hunting for transmission from a planet we were never going to go back to."

"So go and find out what changed," Walker says.

Donovan nods. "Yeah. Let's go and take a look. See what has these people thinking they can run out on us."

"*No*," says Syria. He looks thunderous. "Forget all that. It doesn't matter what these people know, or what they think they can do. We've *still* got a reactor, we've *still* got people, and we've *still* got our home."

Syria glares at us. "They could have come forward. They could have told him—" he jabs a finger at Tseng "—what they found. But they didn't. They wanted it for themselves. No way we're letting that happen. If we can really survive down there, then everyone deserves a shot at it. We need time to figure all that out, and time is one thing we don't have."

Tseng looks at me. "Is there any hope they'd listen to reason?"

I think of Mikhail and the Earthers. Of Okwembu, and how quickly she fell in with their cause. I think of the atmosphere in the old facility: that nervous tension, electric in the air. The stacked supplies, the shouted orders.

Slowly, I shake my head.

Tseng takes a long breath, lets it out. "I'll go and talk to the stompers. Maybe we can take these people down."

Syria shakes his head. "Not gonna work."

Tseng raises an eyebrow. "Excuse me?"

"We go on a hunting mission, we're going into unfamiliar territory."

"It's not unfamiliar," I say, nodding to Carver and Anna. "We were there."

"Right. But the rest of us weren't. And we know they're going to the dock – they'll need the tugs to get out the *Shinso*. They'll have to come all the way across the station, and when they get here we'll be ready. Why exhaust ourselves chasing them down when there's no guarantee we'll even find them?"

The room is silent again. Tseng is shaking his head.

Before anybody can say anything, there's the sound of running footsteps from the corridor outside. A moment later, Arroway comes round the door, moving so fast that Tseng has to make a surprised leap to the side.

At the sight of him, the fear that I pushed to the back of my mind scrambles into the light. I lick my suddenly dry lips, knowing what he's going to say. In that moment, I wish I could take it all back. I wish I had never given him the beans.

Arroway is out of breath, his shoulders trembling. He puts his hands on the conference table, tries to speak, doubles over with a cough.

"Doctor Arroway," says Tseng, his tone shocked, as if he can't believe that Arroway would just barge in like this.

"Resin," Arroway says. It's impossible not to hear the excitement in his voice – no, not excitement, more like joy. He coughs again, then straightens up. "We have the source. We know where it came from."

He points a shaking finger at me, a tired smile creeping across his face. "You were right. You are absolutely right. Those beans . . . how could we not see it?"

Tseng looks as if he's about to explode. "Doctor Arroway, *explain yourself.*"

Anna laughs, like she doesn't quite dare to believe it. "We can cure it, can't we?"

Arroway nods. "We've already isolated the components we need. It won't take long to start producing a cure – maybe not even an hour. We've already got all our production machines running full speed, for the furosemide-nitrate. Hell, with enough time, we could produce a vaccine for it. And it's all thanks to her." He nods in my direction, still smiling.

305

Everyone turns to look at me. I don't let myself pay attention to them. I march over to Han Tseng, and grab him by the front of his tunic.

"The Air Lab," I say.

"Let go of me."

"How do I unseal it?"

When he doesn't respond, I shake him so hard that his teeth clack together. "*Tell me.*"

"18623," he says. "The code is 18623. But I don't—"

I let go of him, already turning away, moving towards the door. I can feel a room full of shocked eyes on my back.

At the last second, I turn and point a finger at Arroway. "I want the first cure that comes off the line. You find me, and you give it to me."

"Ry, hold up," Carver says. "Ry!"

I launch myself out the room and take off down the corridor. Fear and guilt match every step I take.

69

Prakesh

The headache is cranked all the way up, and his throat still feels like it's being squeezed by a thick steel ring. But the soil under Prakesh's backside is cool. He digs his fingers into it, letting the grains collect in the fissures on the underside of his knuckles.

Ordinarily, he'd never do anything to compress his good soil. But, right now, all he wants to do is be close to it. He has his back to a tree trunk – the rough bark is uncomfortable and knobbly, but in a way he needs that, too. He's on one of the tree beds, a little way down from where he fought Julian Novak. The giant oaks tower over him, shade dappling his face.

At some point, he'll have to get up. Yoshiro's body will need to be taken care of. He's not relishing the task at all – every time he thinks of it, he feels a hot spike of anger towards Julian – but at least, he thinks, it's a task he knows he can do.

He feels a presence close to him, and opens his eyes. Suki is standing there, hands clasped in front of her. From this angle, she looks younger than she is. Her expression is slightly embarrassed, like she's interrupted a private ritual.

Prakesh smiles up at her, nods. "How are you doing?" he croaks.

She lets out a shaky breath. "Fine. Forget that – what about you?"

He waves the question away, nodding instead towards the part of the Air Lab where Julian almost choked the life out of him. "He under control?"

Suki flashes a pained smile. "Some of the guys took him back to the control room. Locked him in one of the storage units."

Prakesh feels an unwelcome flash of guilt. "He doesn't need to be looked at by a doctor, or . . ."

"Nah. He'll be okay. I don't hit *that* hard, you know."

She sits down next to him, as if she's had enough of waiting for an invitation. She crosses her legs underneath her, smoothing down her skirt.

"So what do we do now?" she says.

Prakesh shrugs. He starts to speak, but is interrupted by more cheering. A group of techs are crossing parallel to them, along one of the passages between the algae pools, and they're shouting his name. He raises a weary hand, flashes a smile. It satisfies them, and they move on.

"Carry on as normal," he says to Suki. "Although we need to set up testing protocols for whatever this disease is. Can't risk it spreading in here." He's already thinking ahead, thinking what needs to be done, of how best to isolate anybody who might be infected.

Suki puts a hand on his knee. "I'll take care of it."

"You sure?"

"Well, as we've already established from the extinguisher incident, you can't do everything."

"The *extinguisher incident*? Is that what we're calling it?"

"You can call it whatever you want. I still saved you."

"Yes, you did." He reaches over, squeezes her shoulder. His eyes find hers. "Thanks. I owe you one."

Before she can reply, he hears the sound from the other end of the hangar. The hissing of the door to the outside world.

Prakesh is on his feet before he can stop himself, stumbling towards it. The door is opening, and on the other side of it is—

Riley.

He breaks into a run. In moments, he's on her, pulling her into his arms. A part of his mind registers that she looks awful – run ragged, stinking of sweat, her stomper jumpsuit torn in a dozen spots. She's pale, her mouth a tight line. But he doesn't care. She returns his embrace, holding him tight, and that's all that matters.

"Is it over?" he asks, when they pull apart.

Riley looks up at him. And that's when he sees the fear behind the exhaustion. Sees that she's holding something in. Something bad.

"Riley, what is it?" he asks. "Tell me what's happening."

He grips her shoulders, pulls her close so they're face-to-face. "Gods, Riley, *talk to me*."

"Resin," she says. "It's you, Prakesh. Resin came from you."

70

Riley

Prakesh's eyes narrow in confusion. His head is tilted slightly to one side.

"I don't understand," he says. His tone is light, like I'm fooling with him.

I have to be the one to tell him. It's the only way I can handle this – if I know the news is broken by someone he cares about. But when I try to speak again, I can't find the words.

"Riley, what is this?" he says.

I force my voice to work. "You're behind Resin. You created it. Not on purpose," I say, when I see him about to interrupt, "but through what you were doing. It . . . it was an accident."

"Riley," he says, his voice even, calm, reassuring. "You're not making any sense. There is no way – *no way* – that I engineered Resin. Not even by accident."

The other techs have come up behind him, clustering in a loose semicircle. Above us, the Air Lab's trees stretch to the ceiling, the lights filtering through their canopies. We could be in an old story – one that takes place back on Earth, with mythical monsters hiding out in the dappled half-light. I wish we were. It would be easier to fight those monsters.

Slowly, I reach into my pocket, and pull out one of the beans. It's one I took from the crates in the processing facility, where the Earthers were camped out. I gave ones just like it to Arroway, so he could test them. Beans that come from seeds identical to the ones Mikhail had when Anna and I took him down – the ones in the cloth bag that spilled out of his pack.

I drop it into Prakesh's hand. He stares at it, using the fingers of his other hand to turn it over. There's a faded, pale stripe down the side of the bean, masked with thin hairs.

"This is from a previous batch," he says, then shakes his head. "Where did you get this?"

He turns the bean over and over in his hands, his calloused fingers running up and down it, as if trying to make sure it's real.

I try to keep things ordered in my mind. "Some of us weren't getting sick. Me, Carver, Anna. We hadn't contracted Resin. Okwembu hadn't either."

"OK . . ." he says.

"Remember how you told me that the defective batches couldn't be wasted? That it was being fed to prisoners?"

"They tasted terrible," Prakesh says. There's no humour in his words, just an undercurrent of fear, and it nearly rips my heart in two.

I keep going, telling him about the Earthers. How they weren't sick either. "I still don't know how they got hold of the beans, but my guess is that they stole them. They need provisions for the trip back to Earth."

"Trip back to – *what*?" Prakesh looks back at the techs. Some of them are shaking their heads in disbelief, but I can see the wheels turning, see them making the connections.

"Nobody in the Air Lab got Resin," I say. "Right?"

He's shaking his head, more in disbelief than refusal. "Riley, this is crazy."

"Because you were exposed, too. After all, you created them."

"It doesn't prove anything. There must be others on Outer Earth who aren't sick. Maybe some people just have a . . . a *natural immunity*."

"Maybe," I say, trying to hold back the tears and failing. "But, Prakesh, so far everyone we've seen who isn't sick has been exposed to those beans in some way. We've all come into contact with one of your previous batches. We either ate them, or touched them."

Prakesh slams the heel of his hand into his forehead, screwing it in, his eyes closed. "No, no, this is all wrong," he says. He's gone deathly pale, his walnut skin turning sallow.

I try to keep things ordered in my mind. It's hard, but I manage.

"When we were exposed to that batch, we got a low-grade version of the virus. It was like those flu shots we get sometimes – we build up antibodies, and then we don't get sick. Because we'd been exposed, we had antibodies that everybody else *didn't* have.

"The beans that came afterwards had a much stronger version of the virus. The rest of us – you, me, the techs, the prisoners – the antibodies we had kept us safe. We could fight the newer, stronger one off. Nobody else could, because they never had a chance to develop those antibodies."

I close my eyes. "The genetic engineering you did to the plants created Resin. You made the latest batch, thought it worked, put it on the monorail and shipped it out to every mess hall and kitchen in the station. People ate it, and they got sick. The only ones who didn't were those who had been exposed to a previous batch."

He actually takes a step back, like I'm going to lunge out and bite him. It takes everything I have not to reach out for him. But I can't do that – not yet. If I do, I'll just collapse.

Prakesh looks back at me. "A virus can't jump from plants to humans," he says, speaking to me as if I'm a child. "It doesn't happen. That's not how it works."

"Do you have any proof?" says one of the other techs. She's come up alongside Prakesh, her arms folded, fury on her face. "If you're going to come in here and accuse us of . . ."

"Suki, back off," says Prakesh.

"Boss . . ."

"I was in charge of production. This is for me to deal with. All right?"

Suki looks at him like he's gone mad, but nods. There are footsteps behind us, and I turn to see Jordan, along with Carver and a couple of other stompers. From the looks on their faces, I can tell that they've worked out what's going on. I gesture at them to wait.

"This can't be true," Prakesh says. "Tell me this wild theory has been tested, Riley. Tell me this isn't just a hunch."

And I do.

I tell him what Arroway found. How the link between Resin and the beans became apparent as soon as he began testing the samples I gave him. "They're developing the cure right now," I say.

A cure. Unbidden, the ghoulish face of Morgan Knox swims up from the depths of my mind. *I'm going to be OK.*

It takes me a second to realise that Prakesh is walking away.

He isn't running. He's just walking away from the group, his hands laced behind his head, his shoulders trembling.

"We need to take him in, Hale," says Jordan.

I didn't hear them come up behind me. I turn to face her. "What?"

"He's behind one of the most awful genocides in human history. Hundreds of thousands of people . . ."

"It was an *accident*."

"He's still responsible."

"So what are you gonna do?" I'm shouting now, but I don't care. "Lock him in the brig? In the dark? Make him invent, I don't know, time travel so he can reverse what happened?"

"Hale, listen to me."

"No, you listen. We're going to need everybody we have to defend the dock. You touch him, and you answer to me."

Prakesh is sitting up against one of the algae pools, staring into the distance. The techs are standing around, talking in hushed voices, looking as if they're not quite sure what to do.

"Go talk to him," Carver whispers. I look up at him, and he nods gently.

I walk to Prakesh. Every footstep echoes off the walls of the hangar.

He doesn't look at me, even when I slide down next to him. After a moment, I rest my head on his shoulder.

"It's too big," he says. "I try to look at all this, and I can't figure it out. It's like looking at the Earth. You can't see all of it at once. I keep looking at it from different angles, and—"

A single tear falls from his left eye, leaving a dark track on his cheek.

"I was just trying to stop people from being hungry all the time," he says.

"You weren't doing this alone," I say. "All the other techs . . ."

"Did what I told them to. I was the one who rewrote the genes of the plants. I mapped them, I coded them to make them grow faster. Maybe I didn't test them enough. But I thought I'd cracked it – all the others did was help the plants grow.

314

Not one of them could have seen this happening. None of them should have had to. It was my responsibility."

"I know what you're going through," I say, thinking of Amira and my father.

"Do you?" he says, finally turning to look at me.

I open my mouth to reply, and find I have nothing to say. The guilt I experienced after killing Amira and then my father was awful. Sometimes it felt like it was going to burn me up, turning my insides black and dry. But this? This is monstrous. I don't know what he's going through. What I know is only the barest fraction of it.

My mouth has gone as dry as frost on the station hull. "I don't care," I say. "You didn't do any of it on purpose. You were trying to help." I reach out and take his hand. "And none of this changes anything," I continue. "Not between us. I love you, and I'll always be here for you. No matter what you're going through."

But as I say the words I can't help but taste Carver on my lips. Feel his arms around me. That truth – if it is a truth – feels as enormous as the Earth itself. And like Prakesh said, I can't see all of it at the same time.

He gives my hand a squeeze. Very gentle, but it's there.

I hear the soft clinking of body armour, and look up.

"Time to go," Jordan says.

I want to bring the techs with us, thinking that we'll need all the manpower we can get. Jordan doesn't let me. "There aren't enough weapons," she says. "Besides, these geeks wouldn't know which end of the gun to hold."

Prakesh gives her a vicious look. I put my hand on his shoulder and his anger fades as quickly as it came. The sadness that replaces it is even worse.

In the end, we compromise: a few techs come with us, and the rest head up to the Apex hospital, where they'll help Arroway produce the cure for Resin.

"What do you want to do?" I ask Prakesh. More than anything, I want him by my side. I want him close to me, where I can keep him safe. But I know better than to voice these thoughts.

He takes a long time to answer. "I'll be along a little later. I need to think."

Without another word, he walks off across the Air Lab.

There's nothing left to do but head for the dock.

I've been here before, on a cargo run years ago. It's in Gardens, right on the border of Apex. The entrance is on the top level by the monorail tracks, with a massive corridor leading off it. One wide enough to allow big shipments of asteroid slag to pass through.

The doors at the front of the dock stopped working a century ago. Nobody ever fixed them. So as we're walking up, I can see right inside the huge, cavernous hangar, just as big as the Air Lab. I'd forgotten how enormous it is – and how hard it's going to be to defend.

On the far side are the giant airlock doors, bisected by a magrail similar to the one that powers the monorail cars. From the little bit of knowledge I have of how the dock works, the magrail extends outside, running along the hull. Tugs match the speed of the spinning station, then latch onto it so they can come inside the dock without having to worry about crashing.

The tugs are lined up along each wall, squat and menacing. There are only a few left – over the years, plenty of people have managed to steal one, desperately hoping it'll have enough range to get them back to Earth.

Tseng is nowhere to be seen. Can't say I'm surprised. The remaining stompers are gathered by the rusted hangar doors. Usually, there's a hardened group guarding the dock from intruders, so it's jarring to see such a small crowd there, dwarfed by the entrance. Anna, Walker and the rest of the Tzevyans are with them.

Syria is there, too. One of the stompers is looking down at him. He barely reaches the height of her shoulders. This time, she's the one doing the shouting, while Syria stands mute, with his back to us.

"Maybe you aren't understanding the maths here," she says. Her finger jabs his chest. Once. Twice. "*Six* crowd barriers left in this sector, and the entrance is about three times their length."

"I heard you," says Syria, slapping her hand away. Carver

317

glances at me, his eyebrows raised. Prakesh shakes his head. He hasn't said a word since we left the Air Lab, lost in his own thoughts.

The other stompers watch silently, their faces grim. Whatever they were doing before, it's like they've been drawn to this. Like they want to watch things coming apart.

The woman doesn't relent. "Unless you personally want to go dragging back the ones we've deployed already, we aren't going to be able to defend the dock. It's not going to happen. We're better off getting in one of the tugs and heading out to the *Shinso* ourselves."

"So you're just going to give up?"

"Stompers!" I shout. "Eyes on me."

Everyone looks me, eyes huge with surprise. It unbalances me for a moment – the words just burst out of me, and I'm still not quite sure what to say next.

Somehow, I find my voice again. "We are going to find a way to defend this dock, crowd barriers or not. Give me a headcount."

There's the oddest feeling coursing through my body. Like the feeling I get after a sprint, or a well-landed jump, when every muscle is humming with adrenaline. Carver has his chin to his chest, his eyebrows raised, looking at me with comical shock.

I glance at the woman who was complaining about the barriers. Her name pops into my mind from nowhere. "Officer Iyengar. Headcount."

She clears her throat. "Outside of the people you brought with you? Fifteen. That's all that's left."

I expect her to tack a snide remark on the end, but she just holds my gaze. My mind is whirling, thinking that we might have to pull some Air Lab techs from the hospital. But it won't help – much as I hate to admit it, Jordan was right about not

318

giving them weapons. Even if they know how to use stingers, and even if we have enough, we can't guarantee they'll stay cool-headed enough to make a difference. It'll be better if the majority of the people in the dock are stompers, or Tzevyans.

Right then, at that very second, I almost turn and run. As far and as fast as I can, away from everything and everyone. I keep my feet planted.

"All right," I say. I start pointing, jabbing my finger at each of them in turn. "You and you. We need every weapon we can get our hands on. Every stinger we can find. You: go to the hospital, see if anyone's responded to the cure yet, and get them down here. We need manpower. You three: start moving those crowd barriers. See if we can bottleneck these people."

Anna says, "Can we get word to the Earthers, somehow? Maybe if we tell them about the reactor, they'll . . ."

"Not a chance," Carver says. "They'll think it's a trick."

"It's worth a shot," I say. "We have to let them know what'll happen if they take the *Shinso.*"

"No," Iyengar says. "We don't know where they are. We could miss them entirely, and they might not listen to us if we find them."

I think hard, picturing the Earthers in my mind. "They've got weapons, and they've got heavy equipment with them, plus supplies. My guess is they'll be sending an advance force to clear us out, so they can take the tugs. There won't be as many of them, but they'll be heavily armed."

Behind us, Jordan shakes her head. "They'd be walking right into the line of fire. They'd have to know that."

"Maybe," I say, choosing my words carefully, aware of the need to have Iyengar onside. "But I don't think it'll stop them. They want to get off this station bad."

Without another word, I walk past her into the hangar, looking around for something we can use to create longer barricades.

An idea forms. "The tugs," I say, pointing at one of the ships. "Can we get them going? Position them in front of the entrance?"

Jordan interjects. "Flying a tug in an enclosed space? That's a bad, bad, bad idea. Not even seasoned pilots try that one."

"This is insanity," says Syria. "Why don't we just blow up the tugs? Hell, I've got demo experience – I could do it." He takes a step towards the nearest tug, but Carver stops him.

"If we survive this, we're going to need to get the broken-up asteroid inside for processing," he says. "We can't do that with disabled tugs."

Taking a deep breath, I turn to Jordan. "Find us a pilot. Somebody with tug experience. I don't care how dangerous it is – it's all we've got."

"I don't even know if there are any pilots left."

"Just look."

As she turns to leave, something else occurs to me. I call her back. "Find Tseng. Get him down here. And get on the line to the *Shinso*. Tell them to get as far away as they can."

Shaking her head, Jordan walks off. Syria and Anna follow her, leaving Carver and me standing by the tug.

"They won't have time, you know," says Carver.

"Who?"

"The *Shinso*. They're in orbit around us, and they won't be running their engines. They won't have time to get out of range of the tugs before this is all over."

"Doesn't matter. We need to warn them."

"Right." He lets out a long, slow breath, staring around the dock. "What about us?"

"What do you mean?"

"Well, Captain Riley's dished out orders to everyone," he says. "And hasn't left any for herself. Or her trusty sidekick."

Before I can answer, he says, "Listen, about earlier . . ."

I cut him off before he can remind me of our kiss, hating myself for having to do it, hating myself for not knowing what to think. "We'll deal with that later, OK?" I say. "After all this is over."

"Right," he says, a small smile crossing his face. "When we've saved the world. Again."

"From what I remember, *I* was the one who saved it last time."

The words are out before I can stop them. But when the memories come – Amira, my father, Okwembu – I'm surprised to find that they don't feel quite as sharp as before. Carver stares at me, and then bursts out laughing. "Of course," he says. "Sorry. Then this will be my first time. You can show me how it's done."

I hear my name shouted from across the dock. I turn and see a white-coated figure jogging across the floor towards us. It's a young woman, not much older than me, with golden-brown skin and a bob of dark hair.

At first, I think it's one of Prakesh's techs. I'm on the verge of telling her to get lost, but then I see that she's wearing the insignia of the station medical corps: two curved snakes around a vertical staff, the faded patch stitched onto the top pocket of the coat.

"You're Riley Hale?" she says, as she comes to a stop.

"What is it?"

She digs in her pocket. "Doctor Arroway told me to give you this."

My hand is moving even before she pulls out the vial of liquid. It's transparent, viscous and slimy, clinging to the walls of its tiny cylindrical container. "This is it?" I say.

"First off the line. Why did he want me to give it to you? He didn't say."

I tuck the cylinder into my pocket. "Never mind that. How do I give it to a patient?"

"You just inject it into any vein. But that should be done at a hospital, so I can't see what—"

I don't let her finish. I start moving, walking towards the dock entrance. After a few moments, I turn around and shout a thank-you in her direction.

I'm going to have to move very, very fast.

Carver jogs up alongside me. "Want to me to stay here? Or come with you?"

He's right. He should be helping prepare the dock. But I can't find it in me to tell him to go. I need someone next to me. What I have to do next is going to take every ounce of will I have.

"Come with me," I say.

He smiles. "Sure."

72

Knox

Beep.

Morgan Knox hangs on to reality by the thinnest of threads. He's awake, his eyes open, staring up at the ceiling of the isolation ward. Somewhere in the space below his neck, there is appalling, awful pain, as black and dry as space itself. He knows that if he pays attention to it, even for a second, it will overwhelm him, and he won't be able to hang on. Instead, he focuses on the sound of the EKG machine. As long as he can hear it, he's still alive.

Beep.

For the first time in what feels like decades, but must surely have been just a few hours, he's fully lucid. He knows where he is, and what has happened to him. And he knows that he doesn't have long left. Like the pain, he has to approach this thought at an angle, look at it from just the corner of his eye.

Beep.

If he had any strength left in his lungs at all, he would laugh. He set up his revenge so perfectly, executed it with the utmost precision . . . and then he was laid low by *this*. A disease.

Something he couldn't possibly have anticipated. If he'd put his plan into action only a few days earlier, he would have carried it off.

Beep.

It maddens him that he can do nothing about Janice Okwembu. But there is one bright point in the darkness: the little transmitter attached to his heart. The moment he dies, it will send out a signal to detonate the devices implanted in Hale. They will both die. But she's the one who will die screaming.

No.

It takes Knox a few seconds to register that the sound has changed. His eyes track down from the ceiling to the wall, and it's only when he gets halfway down that he recognises the sound he heard as human. Is someone with him?

No. You're not going to die.

Amira Al-Hassan is leaning up against the wall. She wears the same faded red scarf, and blood has soaked the front of her top, wet and black. She shouldn't be standing with a wound like that. She shouldn't be alive. But it's as if she barely notices it. She twists the end of her scarf in a clenched fist, and her eyes bore into Knox's.

He tries to speak, but barely has enough strength to move his lips apart.

No. Don't speak. Just listen.

She propels herself off the wall, moving with an uncommon grace. She walks to the bed and stands over it, looking down at him.

You think Riley Hale will suffer when you die? Sure, the explosives will hurt, but she'll bleed out fast. You know that, even if she doesn't.

Amira leans in closer. Her lips don't move when she speaks. *We could have been together, Morgan. We could have spent our lives together. She took that away from us. You think she should die quickly? It's not even close to what she deserves. Her death should take days.*

He reaches out to her, lifting his hand off the flimsy mattress. Trying to touch her.

Stay alive, Morgan. For me.

Beep.

He blinks. The movement seems to last an aeon. When he opens his eyes again, Amira is gone and in her place is Riley Hale.

73

Riley

It's a very good thing that Carver and I used to be tracers.

It means that we get back to the Tzevya hospital fast. We sprint across the sector, not talking, just running. I can feel the cure pressing against my hip, and some part of me thinks that every step is going to be my last, that we're not going to get there in time.

The hospital is still quiet, its beds empty. That won't last. Now that we've got a cure – or what might be a cure – they'll start distributing it quickly. Hospitals like this will become staging points, pulsing with energy, as Arroway and his colleagues start handing it out.

Uncertainty nags at me – we don't know how long we have before the Earthers reach the dock. We don't even know where they are, or how many there'll be in the first wave. But I can't defend the dock until I've dealt with Morgan Knox.

We find the isolation ward quickly. Knox's face is caked with strings of Resin, and he's still unconscious. But I can see him breathing, his chest shuddering as it expands and contracts. I don't waste any time. I grab a syringe from a nearby tray, then jam it into the steel mesh cap of the container holding the cure. Carver grabs Knox's arm, angling it towards me. With shaking hands, I inject every drop of the cure into his body.

Nothing happens.

"Is that it?" I say, watching Knox. There should be movement – when I injected him with the furosemide-nitrate, his entire body bucked and writhed as the medicine worked its way through him. Now, he's still. Comatose. My nerves feel like frayed cables, their strands pulled impossibly tight.

In that moment, I can feel the shape of the remote control, the one that would trigger the bombs. It's still in my jacket, wedged in its container. But I have it, and Knox doesn't.

I snap my fingers in front of Knox.

Nothing.

"Let me try," Carver says. Then he slaps Knox across the face.

He pulls the slap at the last moment. Knox cries out, a gurgling sound coming out of his throat. His eyes fly open, track across us, not seeing. Carver grabs Knox's chin, holds tight. "Wakey wakey," he says.

"Chest . . . . sore."

"They've got a cure for Resin," Carver says. I stop him with a hand on his arm.

I take a deep breath. I'm thinking back to that little girl, Ivy. The one I grabbed when the Earthers were almost on us. Carver was right. I shouldn't have done that. But I can draw on that same desperation, channel it into what I'm about to do.

And Carver's right. It's easier when you're not alone.

"You haven't seen people die from Resin, have you?" I say to Knox.

Carver picks up what I'm doing immediately. "We have," he says.

"You're awake for most of it," I say. "The last half-hour or so. People cough up their own lungs. They go blind. They die screaming."

None of this is true. But Knox doesn't know that. His breath is coming quicker now, rattling in his chest.

"They've got a cure," I say. "For Resin. You haven't been given it yet."

"So," he says, and coughs. It's as if he has to use every muscle in his body just to form words. He tries again. "So cure me. I die, you die."

"Yeah. But now you die in agony, too."

I catch the spark of fear in his eyes. It flares for less than half a second, but it's there. I lean forward, getting in his face. "And you don't want to die, do you? You never did. You want to *live*."

"Help me."

"No."

"Help me."

"You want that cure?" says Carver. "Let's trade. Her bombs come out, your lungs stay in. How's that sound?"

"Can't . . . operate. Too sick."

I keep my voice as steady as I can. "You're never going to touch me again. You're going to tell me how to remove them, and I'll find another doctor to do it."

Anger and fear and loathing combine on his face. It's one of the most terrifying expressions I've ever seen. I make myself keep looking into those eyes.

"You killed my Amira," he says.

"She wasn't yours, man," Carver says. "She never was. She belonged to us. She was a Devil Dancer."

He doesn't speak for a long moment. Then he says: "Left . . . wire."

I lean in. "What?"

"Cut . . . the left wire. My left."

"So that's it?" I say. "They open me up, pull out the bombs and cut the wire on the left? And what happens if they cut the wire on the right?"

He doesn't respond.

"Bullshit," Carver says. I look at him.

He returns my gaze. "He could be lying. The second those wires are cut, the bombs will go off."

"Telling . . . truth. *Please*."

But there's no way of knowing. He could tell us anything, and we wouldn't know until it was too late.

I lick my lips. "You help me, I help you. You prove you aren't lying, and I'll inject the cure myself."

A little strength comes back to him then. He bats at Carver's hand, trying to push it away. "I'm not lying," he says, each word punctuated by a breath. "Cut the left wire on each bomb when you remove it. That's all. Now cure me, because if I die, the transmitter on my heart dies, and it won't send the answering signal back."

His words dissolve into a coughing fit. Carver sits back on his heels, his brow furrowed. "I don't know, Riley. I'm not sure how we can—"

I reach forward and grab Knox by the shoulder. "What did you just say?"

He raises his eyes to mine. "What?"

"No, no. You said—" I pause, trying to get the words right. "You said that if the transmitter dies, it won't send a signal back. And that means the bombs explode. Right?"

He stares at me in confusion, then nods.

My heart is beating faster. "What kind of signal is it?"

He points to his ear.

All this time, it was right in front of me.

Carver sucks in a shocked, delighted breath. He's already way ahead of me. "I can do it," he says breathlessly. "Won't take long."

"You can duplicate the signal?"

"Oh yeah. Just have to find the frequency he's using, which I can do because—"

"You're a genius. Got it."

He flashes a huge smile, his eyes shining. "It'll take him out of the equation. Even if he goes under, the gizmos inside you will still get that answering signal."

He punches me on the shoulder. It hurts, but I don't care. I close my eyes, feeling relief too exquisite to describe.

"Come on," says Carver, pulling me up. "Let's get back to the dock."

We're halfway across the ward when Knox shouts after us, putting all the energy he can into his voice. "We had a deal," he says, and coughs again. "You have to cure me."

I look over my shoulder, at the broken man on the bed.

"I already gave it to you," I say. "You're cured."

Knox's scream of fury follows us all the way out of the hospital.

74

Prakesh

Prakesh sits on the edge of the roof, his feet dangling in mid-air.

Two techs are crossing the floor below him, six storeys down. He's amazed that they can't hear him breathing – to his ears, each inhale is as loud as an engine turning over, each exhale an explosion of exhaust. But neither of them look up, and, in moments, they're out of sight.

Vertigo takes hold, the floor rushing up to meet him. He blinks hard, then squeezes his eyes shut, tilting his head back.

"I have to think," he says.

The words come out as a confused mumble. But he's been thinking from the moment he left Riley, from when he dodged the other techs and found his way up here, from the moment he swung his legs out over the edge. The result is no different. It's as if something blocks the thoughts from forming, as if his mind is trying to protect itself.

What keeps coming up, what keeps pushing past the mental barricades he's hiding behind, are numbers.

Population figures. The number of canteens in each station sector. Batch numbers, stencilled onto crates of produce in big

331

black lettering. Monorail shipment times, printed in dull spreadsheets on his tab screen. There are strings of letters mixed in with the numbers, too. Cytogenetic locations: reference points for particular genes on particular chromosomes. Genes that he altered. Genes that he intuited would make the plants they belong to grow faster, bear more fruit.

The numbers don't matter. He can express the result in any equation he likes. He can rationalise it, tell himself that what he did made complete scientific sense. But at the other end of the equation is a single, stark figure. It measures in the hundreds of thousands, and it's growing by the second.

How could he have let this happen? How could he have been so short-sighted?

Nausea takes him. He clutches his stomach, appalled at the sick pain. He is desperate to throw up, but the tiny, clear section of his brain tells him not to. It would spatter on the ground below, attract people's attention, and he can't face that. Using every ounce of will he possesses, he holds the tide back, clamping his mouth shut, gritting his teeth.

Slowly, the feeling subsides. What's left behind is even worse.

Who is he kidding? He's not up here to think. He's up here because he saw what James Benson was planning to do – what James Benson *did*. He's up here because it's six storeys to the ground, a hundred feet up.

A bitter smile sneaks onto Prakesh's face. How could he have had that much hubris? Who was he to stop James Benson from taking his own life? He barely knew the man. That he could judge him, that he could try to control whether or not he lived or died . . . it's *obscene*. If Benson felt there was nothing left, that the rest of his life was beyond saving, then who's to say he wasn't taking the honourable way out?

And Prakesh's situation is far, far worse than Benson's. He

can feel it pressing down on his shoulders, an almost physical weight.

That number again. The one on the other side of the equation. Six figures, growing by the second. Because of him.

Riley would miss him, for a time. But he saw how she looked at him, when she delivered the news, and he knows that taking himself out of her life would be a mercy. And his parents . . . it will be hard for them, yes, but it's better this way.

Prakesh is suddenly aware of his fingertips, clamped onto the edge of the roof. He can feel the grainy surface, scratchy under his nails. It would take the slightest push. A tiny amount of force. And there'll be no Mark Six to catch him.

His fingers start to move, his hands pushing downwards.

Halfway through the motion, he opens his eyes. The floor rushes towards him, as if he's already falling, and vertigo locks his head in a vice.

It doesn't matter. He's almost off the roof, almost in the grip of gravity. In the next instant, it'll take him.

Prakesh lets out of thin cry of horror. His body is off the surface of the roof, on the edge of tilting into oblivion. He tries to pull it back, but he can feel gravity taking hold of his stomach. His fingers scrabble at the roof, his palms digging into it.

No good. He's falling.

With a panicked howl, he tries to dig his feet into the side of the building. His arms are the only things supporting him now, the elbows bent at a strange angle, wrists screaming with pressure, his feet kicking in mid-air.

Mastering every last ounce of energy he has, Prakesh swings his right leg up, hooking the heel on the lip of the roof. The motion is enough to shift his centre of gravity backwards. The edge of his ass touches solid metal. He teeters, every muscle straining, and then falls back onto the roof, slamming into it thighs first.

"Oh," he says. "Oh no. No."

He's barely aware of what he's doing: crawling away from the edge on his hands and knees. He goes ten feet before he collapses, hyperventilating. The nausea is back. This time, he does throw up, retching thin streams of gruel onto the roof.

The seconds tick by. With each one, he tells himself that he's still alive.

Killing himself would be the easy way out. That he could have thought otherwise amazes him. He would have regretted it immediately, cursing himself, horribly aware that there was nothing he could do to fix what he'd just done.

And, really, what would his death mean? It would just be another number in the equation, another victim of Resin.

Riley told him they were developing a cure. Resin won't last much longer. Prakesh can do nothing about what's already happened, but he might be able to change what happens next. He's responsible for hundreds of thousands of deaths; surely the only thing he can do now is to help save as many lives as possible?

He can go to the dock, make himself available, do whatever they need him to do. Maybe he can convince the people trying to take the *Shinso* that there's another way. And when it's all over, he can help distribute the cure. Not make it – he'll never set foot in a lab again – but he can get it where it needs to be.

He lies there for a few more minutes. Then he gets to his feet, his legs shaking with effort, and walks back to the stairwell.

75

Riley

The floor of the dock is humming with activity.

The stompers have returned, lugging crates, filling the room with the sound of clanking metal. They drop the crates with an enormous bang, and start pulling out weapons – not just stingers, but other guns, too. I see Syria rubbing his hands with glee.

Carver didn't come back with me. As soon as we left the hospital, he was off, saying he needed to find a working SPOCS unit and a soldering iron. Now I'm jogging down the middle of the floor, wondering how I'm going to fit into the chaos. I do a quick headcount of my own as I go. Fifteen stompers, excluding Carver, Anna and me. Plus nine Tzevyans. Just under thirty souls. It'll have to be enough.

"Hale."

Iyengar is waving me over. Han Tseng is with her. He looks even more exhausted than before.

"This man claims he can fly," she says.

I try to keep the surprise off my face. *"You?"*

335

Tseng shrugs. "You think I've been a councilman my whole life? I can fly a tug."

"Not for twenty years," says Iyengar, sniffing in annoyance.

He glares at her. "The technology's the same. You asked if I could fly? Well, I can fly."

"Yeah, but can you fly in here?" I say.

Tseng's eyebrows look ready to fly off his head. "In the dock?"

"We need those tugs—" I point to the ships along the wall "—over there." My finger jabs towards the door.

"You're crazy."

I smile and shrug, my eyes locked on Tseng's. For the first time in days, I feel alive. "Well, if you can't do it . . ." I say.

He folds his arms. "Young lady, I once flew one of these tugs through a field of asteroid slag debris, *and* it had a damaged thruster. I'm probably the only person who *can* do it."

Without another word, he spins on his heel and walks to the closest tug. "Just make sure nobody is standing underneath it when I turn the engines on," he says over his shoulder.

He walks to the back and reaches up, standing on tiptoe. There's a hiss, then a clunk as a ramp drops down from the back of the tug. Tseng pulls it down the last few feet, then clambers on board. The tug itself looks like an enormously fat man, with a bulbous nose and tiny fins jutting out of the sides. Even though it's in the smallest class of ships, it still dwarfs us.

Iyengar is shaking her head. I don't give her the chance to comment. "Make sure everybody has a weapon," I say, as Tseng appears in the tug's cockpit. "And make sure they've got something to hide behind."

"I can't do both," she says, sounding sullen and resigned.

"Then pick one, and find somebody to do the other."

With a guttural roar, the tug's engine springs to life.

Tseng might be right about the tech being the same, but the moment the tug lifts off the magrail, I find myself wondering about that little trip of his through the debris field.

All activity in the hangar comes to a screeching halt. Watching the tug jerk itself upwards, seeing it nearly clip the wall and spin out of control prompts a burst of horrified gasps from across the floor.

It doesn't help that the tug looks about as manoeuvrable as a chunk of rock itself. I can just see Tseng at the controls, his head visible in the cockpit, high above. I see him look down, then the tug slowly begins to drift forward, moving towards the middle of the dock. The roar of its engine is huge.

It takes me a second to notice that it's still rising. It's only a few feet from the ceiling, on the verge of clipping it.

"Look out!" someone yells. It's impossible to know whether Tseng hears them, but the tug drops, plummeting to the floor. Just as it's about to crash, Tseng gets it under control. It rocks from side to side, hovering over the magrail track, its engine thrumming with a sound like water being sucked through a distant pipe.

After a moment, Tseng starts to move forward, scattering the crowd which had gathered to watch. He brings the tug to a grinding stop near the doors – I can hear the metal keening as the tug judders to a halt.

I don't stop to watch him climb out. Moving is good. Moving means that I have to pay attention to my body, working out how to minimise the impact of each step to lessen the pain in my knees.

I'm at the entrance of the hangar, helping Iyengar move a crowd barrier into place, when I almost back right into Prakesh.

He's aged ten years. It makes my breath catch in my throat.

His face is haggard, his eyes red and raw. When I hug him, it's as if he barely has enough energy to squeeze back.

"How you holding up?" I say, as we pull apart.

He looks away, shrugs. At that moment, I want nothing more than to go back to our hab in Chengshi, curl up with him on the bed, and go to sleep. I want to pretend my kiss with Carver didn't even happen.

There are a million things I want to say to him. I want to tell him it'll be okay, even if it won't. I want to hug him again, and not let go.

Instead, I say, "We could use some extra hands. Can you help me with—"

"We can't do this, Riley."

"What?"

He waves at the rest of the hangar. "This. We can't let more people die. If I can go and talk to whoever is coming, try and convince them, then maybe . . ."

He trails off. I open my mouth, then close it again, not sure what words to use. We don't have time for this.

My eyes find his. "I know what you're saying, but we've met these people. They want off the station, and they're prepared to go through us to do it."

"They'll listen to reason. They have to."

"Kesh—"

"You don't understand," he says, pushing me away and holding my shoulders at arm's length. "This is the only way I can make it right. I *have* to help. Please tell everyone to stand down."

I take a deep breath. "No."

It's one word. Two letters. A single syllable. But in that instant, it's heavier than any word ever uttered. Prakesh's body sags, as if I'd just punched him in the gut.

"They won't listen," I say. I've never been more sure of

Rob Boffard

anything in my life. It's all too easy to see the weapons they were stockpiling, the determined look in Mikhail's eyes. "Either we stop them here, or they'll kill us all."

His shoulders sag. After a few seconds, he says, "What do you want me to do?"

76

Riley

The next twenty minutes are one big multi-stage cargo run.

Anna and I zip back and forth across the hangar, ducking and diving and dancing past anybody who steps into our way. We ferry stinger parts and help lift barriers and deliver messages from one end of the dock to the other. I break off every so often to direct operations.

The tension builds so slowly that it takes me a little while to realise that the friendly chatter has ceased. I can feel people becoming more harried, dropping things more often and cursing when they do.

After a while, there's not a lot left for us to carry. We rest for a moment, over by one of the remaining tugs.

"What are you idiots standing around for?" says a voice.

Royo. He's pale, haggard, and moving with increased care. But he's upright, being supported by Carver.

"Captain," says Anna solemnly, "you have an ability to take a beating that is nothing short of outstanding."

"Why, thank you, Beck," Royo says. "You have an ability to never shut up that I find similarly awe-inspiring."

340

His gaze finds mine. I can't describe what passes between us at that moment, but it's not something I have words for.

"Resin," I say. "Is it . . ."

"Getting there fast. Not everyone is responding to the injection Arroway cooked up – I think some are too far gone. But for what it's worth, yes, we beat Resin. Not that it helped ninety per cent of this station."

There's an uncomfortable silence.

"We'll deal with that later, Cap," says Carver. He reaches over, and passes me something. A SPOCS unit. It's been torn apart, and put back together again – when I jam it into my ear, it makes an uncomfortable fit.

"Is it working?" I say.

He nods. "Yeah. I think I got the frequency. But . . ."

"What is it?"

"Ry, there's no way of testing it. Not unless your friend Knox puts a stinger to his head. And it's a stop-gap at best – you'll have to keep it charged up."

"*Shinso*'s started moving," Royo says. "But they're not going to have nearly enough time to get clear, Hale. These tugs look small, but they've got plenty of range."

"It'll help," I say. "It has to."

Another wave of exhaustion slips through my barricades, and I have to bite my lip hard to get enough pain to fight it off.

Royo is eyeing us. "Where are your weapons?"

"We'll get there, Cap," Carver says. "Besides, who needs weapons when you have the Boneshaker?"

Royo raises his eyebrows. "You mean that thing?"

He jerks his head at the dock entrance, where the Boneshaker, black and hulking, is parked up against the wall.

"Run it right at 'em, and they scatter like bugs," Carver says, a huge smile eating up his face. "Riley's got her speed and Anna has One-Mile."

"Nope," Anna says. "Earthers took it." She casts a dirty look at the entrance to the dock.

As I look at her, an idea comes to mind. "Anna?"

"Huh?"

"Come with me."

Before she can say anything, I'm striding out across the dock floor, hopping over the magrail. I hear Anna following, calling my name, but it's drowned out as Tseng swings another tug overhead. I don't have to look up to know that I could probably reach out and touch the bottom of it.

I don't stop until we reach the weapons crates. The stompers are there, cleaning the stingers, and the bright smell of oil gets stronger as I approach. One of them looks up, then reaches down to get me a gun.

"Not one of those," I say, and he looks up, puzzled. I point to one of the other weapons in the crate. One I saw earlier, when they were first brought in.

"The long gun?" he says, his brow furrowed. "I was leaving that until last. I don't even know if it'll fire – last time this thing saw action was the Lower Sector Riots."

"Pass it here."

"Think you can handle it? It's heavy."

"It's not for me."

He shrugs, then lifts out the gun. Anna's eyes go wide.

It's long – as tall as I am, easily. A thin barrel, an extended stock, and, screwed onto the top, a scope. It stains my hands black, turning them gritty with oil.

She hesitates before grabbing it, like she isn't quite sure it's real. When she does, the expression of wonder in her face is just amazing. Anna hefts the rifle to shoulder height, jamming the stock into her shoulder and welding her cheek to it, squinting down the scope. When she lifts her head off, there's a black mark on her cheek. It's at odds with the white gleam of her smile.

"Do you even know how to use that thing?" asks the stomper cleaning the weapons.

Anna racks the breech, clicking it back, then glares at the stomper. When she speaks, her voice is a low growl. "Just give me the ammo."

77

Knox

The sheet on Knox's bed is stiff with dried Resin. He's been coughing for the past hour, and the fluid coming out of his lungs has gone from thin streams of liquid to sticky chunks. With each cough, he is able to breathe a little more easily.

And with each cough, his hatred for Riley Hale grows.

He curls on his side, tucking into the foetal position. Pain racks his body, and another round of coughing lodges a gluey hunk of Resin behind his back teeth. He sticks a finger in his mouth, fishes it out, and flicks it away. His head is clear – clearer than it's been in what feels like years. He knows what he has to do, and the sheer force of that knowledge, the clarity of purpose, is enough to make him swing his legs out from the bed.

He almost falls. He has to grip the mattress to steady himself, nearly pulling it off the bed. His nose is blocked, and, in the silence of the isolation ward, his breathing sounds harsh and hot.

He needs a weapon. Taking Hale on bare-handed is a non-starter. After all, her crew leader taught her to fight, didn't she?

From the door of the ward, Amira says, *That's right. She'll break you in half if you let her, just like she broke me.*

"I don't know where she is," he says. "I'll never find her."

You do know. Think back.

He pauses, his hand still gripping the mattress. That was it. Hale's friend, the blond one, said something important. *Let's get back to the dock.*

Knox runs a hand across his sticky lips, looking around him. His eyes fall on the wheeled instrument tray beside the bed. There's a syringe on it – the same one that Hale used on him, he's sure of it. Its plunger is depressed, and he can see a drop of liquid beading on the end of the needle.

He scoops it up, holding it in a two-fingered grip with his thumb on the plunger. Amira smiles, then turns and walks through the closed door. This bothers Knox for a moment, but then he pushes the thought aside.

He still feels horrible. Every muscle aches, every movement bringing agony. He makes himself walk, pushing open the door of the ward and shambling through the hospital corridors. Some of the lights are out, and he has to grope his way through. Several times, he bangs his shin or his hip into something in his path. Each impact feels like it vibrates his very bones.

He starts to hear voices, which grow clearer as he makes his way towards the entrance. He tightens his grip on the syringe. As he approaches the lobby, the voices grow clearer. There are two of them: two men, silhouetted in the main doorway, facing each other. They both wear the off-white uniforms of medical orderlies, and they look bone-tired.

From somewhere out of sight, Amira says, *Wait.*

The man on the left scratches his head. He has an untidy ponytail, and he keeps tugging at it. "How many we got coming?"

"Gods know," the other replies.

The first man yanks his ponytail again, his arm cocked over his right shoulder. "It's going to be a nightmare. How can Arroway expect two people to run this place?"

"Gods know," his partner says again. "You start setting up. I'll see if I can scrounge up some more volunteers."

"Seriously? You think you're actually going to find any?"

But the second man has already gone, his footsteps fading into the distance.

Ponytail shakes his head, then strides into the lobby. He's muttering to himself, and Knox can hear the words clearly. "Sure, sure, I'll just do all the hard work, why not?" he says. He starts clearing the main desk, shifting tab screens and food containers out of the way.

Now. Go, Amira says.

Knox crosses behind the man, trying to be as quiet as possible. He's almost at the door when he hears the man turn. "Hey. Whoa, hey!"

Knox doesn't look round. Ponytail pads up behind him, moving quickly across the floor. "Hey, you all right?" he says, putting a hand on Knox's shoulder. "You were inside? We've got a cure, so you can just hang out here and—"

In a single movement, Knox turns around and brings the syringe up, burying it in the man's eye.

He almost doesn't get there. The muscles in his arm feel like they're made of glass. And Ponytail sees the needle coming, tries to deflect it. But he's not fast enough.

He starts to scream, and Knox puts a hand over his mouth, shoving him backwards. They fall to the floor, the man bucking and writhing underneath him. Knox leans on the syringe, pushing it further in, and he feels the needle scrape bone. It isn't nearly long enough to penetrate beyond the eye socket, but it gives Knox the opening he needs.

He yanks the needle back, pulling it out of the deflating eye.

346

Rob Boffard

Ponytail is still trying to push him off, but his hands have strayed to his face, exposing the rest of him. Knox takes a split second to locate the carotid artery in the man's twisting neck, and then he stabs the needle downwards, again and again.

Soon, the man's struggles begin to get weaker. When they stop completely, Knox is drenched in blood.

He gives the syringe one final twist, then gets to his feet. He's shaking, and he knows that it was stupid to burn so much energy so fast. But his head is clearer than it's ever been, his purpose a bright shining light.

He looks down at the man one last time. "I'm discharging myself," he says, and keeps walking towards the doors, moving in long, loping steps.

78

Riley

It's while he's piloting the third tug that Tseng spins out of control.

He's put two of them across the entrance. The one he's piloting would block off the entrance completely, but when he tries to position the ship, it all goes wrong.

I'm running with Carver when there's an enormous grinding screech, and we look up to see the tug tilting forward. Its cockpit glass has smashed, and the ceiling of the dock has a huge black gouge ripped into it. Before I can process this, the tug lists to one side, and the stompers scatter as it smashes into the ground.

The ship bounces once before slamming into one of the tugs he's positioned across the entrance. The engine of Tseng's tug cuts, replaced by the crunching bang of the impact.

There's a stunned silence. I'm holding my breath, and Carver has grabbed my hand so tight that it's gone numb.

The hatch on the top of the tug snaps open, and Tseng crawls out. He tries to stand, and then topples off the top of the tug, his body falling out of sight. Two Tzevyans rush to his aid, and Royo immediately starts directing the other stompers to different positions across the dock.

"We are so screwed," says Carver, looking at the enormous gap in the hangar entrance between the wall and the parked tugs.

"Maybe not," I say, resuming our walk to the Boneshaker. Carver shakes his head, and follows. Glancing over my shoulder, I see Anna setting up behind some crates, with a clear line of sight down the entrance corridor. The long gun is balanced on the top of the crate, and she's got her eye glued to the scope.

When we reach the Boneshaker, Carver vaults onto it.

"How are you planning to use this thing?" I say.

"I'm gonna take them from the side. They won't know what hit 'em."

"Don't drive into the line of fire, then. OK?"

Carver flashes me a smile, then reaches out and pulls me into an unexpected hug.

"What are you going to do?" he says.

I point to the gun station, to one of the crates loaded with ammo.

"I'm a tracer," I say. "I'm going to run."

And without another word, I take off down the hangar.

I can feel the tension rising, crackling through the air. Stompers and civilians hunker down behind hastily placed cover. Stingers are checked, sighted, checked again. Everyone's eyes are on the corridor leading up to the dock. Royo's at the weapons table when I get there, talking to the stompers behind it. He's still pale, but seems more upright, somehow. By now, the combined noises in the hangar have become so loud that he's having to shout to be heard, but he stops when he sees me.

"Can't be more than a few minutes before they get here," Royo says. "You ready?" He hands me a stinger of my own, greasy with oil.

I don't get a chance to respond. At that moment, a rocket – a whirring, spinning projectile, propelled on a roaring cone of fire – comes howling through the entrance of the dock.

79

Riley

The rocket corkscrews through the air, detonating right above the middle of the hangar, sending out a cone of flaming, spitting shrapnel. One piece lands near me, charred black, crunching off the deck. Somewhere distant, there's a roar as Carver kicks the Boneshaker into life.

I dive behind a line of crates, my stinger out and trained on the doors. Two more rockets explode through the gap. One of them takes out a crane near the side of the dock, knocking two stompers sprawling. I see one of them skidding across the floor, a dark, smoking stump where his left leg should be. His face is a mask of pain and shock.

We're returning fire – I can hear the boom of the long gun, the spitting bang of stingers – but it isn't stopping the Earthers' advance guard from charging through. There are more of them than I thought, using plate metal as makeshift shields, dropping them to form cover.

I've never been a good shot – and that's under firing-range conditions. But I start shooting anyway, targeting the gap. One of them is running right at me – I fire once, twice, but hit nothing. As I get ready to fire again, I hear a thundering shot from my right. Anna: down on one knee, the long gun resting on a crate. She took down the Earther on the run, tracking his movement across the floor before shooting.

I don't have time to thank her. I keep firing. This time, I find my mark, my bullets taking one of the Earthers in the shoulder. She spins out, knocked backwards. The air is thick with acrid smoke.

More of them. Now they're using their own supplies as cover – crates on wheeled pallets, absorbing the gunfire, their surfaces denting as the bullets ricochet. Still more are breaking through the gap, running left, right, dodging out of the way. I hear Iyengar curse as a man she was aiming at vanishes behind cover.

There's no sign of Mikhail, or Okwembu.

I'm useless here. It's a damn miracle I hit even one person. I should be transporting ammo, keeping everyone else topped up. Frantic, I look around for the supply, spotting it a few yards away behind another barricade. I sprint for it, pumping my arms to push myself forward – and have to duck and roll as a length of metal pipe swings forward, nearly taking me in the face.

The Earther wielding it has come right through the lines, his eyes wild. The pipe is huge, so big that it looks like a roof strut, and he has to lean back to get enough force to swing it again. I feel rather than hear the pipe, like a sick vibration in the air. Just in time, I roll to the side, coming up as it bangs off the floor.

The Earther roars in anger, but I'm too fast for him, up in half a second and chopping him across the throat, right above his Adam's apple. It knocks him back – amazingly, he's still upright. Before he can regain his balance, I drive a knee into his stomach. That does the job.

Before he even hits the ground, there's a whooshing thud to my left. I look around to see that Iyengar is on fire.

One of the makeshift rockets hit her. She's screaming, tearing at herself in agony as flames bloom around her. With a horrible clarity, I see the skin on her face start to blister. Her fingers are stuck together. She falls face down, twitching.

Prakesh jumps to the front of my mind, and the feeling that comes with it is an impossible terror. I can't see him anywhere. I don't know whether that's good or bad. There's too much noise, too much drifting smoke. Royo is shouting, trying to regain control.

I feel the rumble of the Boneshaker before I see it. Then Carver is pulling alongside me, sweeping me onto it. He hands me a clip over his shoulder, the metal slick with oil.

"I'll drive, you shoot," I hear him say.

I don't have time to tell him that I'm a terrible shot. He guns the engine, and I nearly topple off the back as we scream off down one side of the dock.

80

Prakesh

"Get down!"

A hand on the back of his neck shoves Prakesh to the floor. Bullets whine overhead, the air rippling as it's pushed aside. The front of the makeshift barricades, where his head was a moment before, cracks and splinters as a volley of gunfire tears into it.

The man who shoved him down is peering over the top of the barricade, his hand still on Prakesh's neck. Prakesh can feel some sort of ring on one of the fingers, the metal cold against his skin. He looks up, the coppery taste of fear coating the inside of his mouth. The man has lank hair and an angular face. *Syria*, he thinks. *Riley called him Syria.*

There are two stompers alongside them, and, as they return fire, Prakesh gets to his knees. They're in a good position in the shadow of one of the tugs, but even as he raises his head, another bullet whistles past his ear and he ducks.

Syria moves with him, grabbing the front of his shirt. He pulls Prakesh close, all but snarling his words. "You gonna start firing any time soon?"

354

Prakesh is holding a stinger with both hands. He doesn't remember how he got it, who gave it to him, but he knows he hasn't fired a single shot. Every time his finger finds the trigger, he freezes.

Syria throws him aside, blind-firing over the top of the barricade. Another rocket detonates, filling the air with the hot stench of smoke.

What am I doing here? Prakesh thinks. A few hours earlier, he was in the Air Lab, outrunning and out-thinking Julian Novak, protecting his colleagues. Now he's in the middle of a firefight, asked to take even more lives than he has already.

"If you're not gonna fire, give me your ammo," Syria says, fumbling at the stinger in Prakesh's hands.

In response, Prakesh raises himself up, swinging his arms over the top of the barricades. He pulls the trigger once, twice, three times, not even aiming. He knows there is almost no chance of hitting anyone, and he doesn't care. He just wants it to be over, and the quickest way to do that is to drain his ammo. At any other time, the logical part of his mind would have protested this. But now, with the smoke invading his nostrils, it's all he can think to do.

His stinger clicks empty. In the instant before he ducks under the barricades again, Prakesh sees Riley. She's on the back of Carver's contraption, tearing across the floor, drawing fire from the Earthers.

81

Knox

Knox sees Okwembu first.

She's around the near side of the dock entrance, squatting on her haunches, utterly untroubled by the chaos going on around her. She wears the same prison jumpsuit she had on when Hale brought her to his surgery. She wears a thick jacket over it, the faux-fur collar bunched around her neck. There are other people around her, their heads bent close together. Knox can see their mouths moving, but he can't hear their words over the gunfire. One of them – a craggy, scarred man with long grey hair – is gesturing wildly, jabbing a finger at the dock.

There's a bang, and he ducks instinctively. He is on the other side of the dock entrance from Okwembu, leaning up against the wall. Whatever's going on here, whoever these people are, none of them has noticed him yet. They're focused on the battle, on pushing deeper into the dock.

He still has the syringe, its needle caked with dried blood and aqueous humour. He grips it tight. He'll walk across, come up on Okwembu, and jam it into the side of her neck.

No, says Amira, crouched next to him. *You won't get within ten feet before they cut you down.*

She's right. Of course she is. He shakes his head, angry with himself. He has to keep it together. He's still not strong enough – the walk over here has exhausted him, draining what little energy he has. His lungs are clear, but feel brittle, as if a breath that's too strong will crack a hole in them.

"You!"

Knox feels a hand on his shoulder. He tenses – his reactions might not be what they should, but he's still got the syringe, and he can still fight off whoever this is.

No, Amira says again.

Knox looks around. The man is tall, easily over six feet, with broad shoulders and a carefully trimmed moustache. He's clutching a tattered backpack in his hand, and he looks Knox up and down, his eyes narrowed. "The hell happened to you?" he says, raising his voice as a fresh volley of gunfire crackles through the air.

Knox tenses his fingers on the syringe. Whatever Amira says, he can't afford this delay. Hale is in there, he knows it, he just has to get to her. And he is acutely aware of how he looks, his face and clothing crusted with the evidence of Resin.

But the man's eyes are jumping, unable to focus, brimming with adrenaline. "Doesn't matter," he says, almost to himself, digging inside the backpack. "Take this. Stick to the left flank, and we should be able to take out a few more of them."

The stinger is black, home-made, the metal edges badly machined. Knox takes it with his free hand, palming the syringe with the other, leaving the needle sticking out between his middle and index finger. "Thanks," he says.

And looks up to see the man's shoulder explode with blood and bone.

Knox throws himself to the floor, out of the line of fire,

pushing the screaming man aside. He doesn't know where the shooter is, and he doesn't care. He crawls into the dock, staying as low as possible, heading for one of the wheeled pallets stacked high with crates. His hand is sticky with sweat, and he keeps a tight grip on the stinger.

Somehow, he makes it to the cover. There's a body behind it, curled in on itself, like it's trying to protect its stomach. Knox shunts it aside, tries to think, tries to form thoughts under the noise. He's lost his syringe somewhere – it must have fallen from his hand as he crawled. Doesn't matter. Amira is there, down on one knee beside him. A thin stream of blood issues from her mouth, trickling down her chin.

He takes two quick breaths, then raises himself up, sneaking a look around the side of the crates.

The dock is coming to pieces around him. The parts he can see through the drifting smoke are a tangle of muzzle flashes and sprinting bodies. He tries to stay calm, knowing that it's what Amira would do. *Hale. Where are you?*

He spots her at almost the moment the thought forms. She's on the back of the vehicle, the one they had him on earlier, tearing across the dock with her friend at the controls.

And as soon as he spots her, he hears Amira speaking in his ear, the anger in her voice as clear as a pane of glass. He turns to look at her, and sees that the blood coming from her mouth has covered her entire face. Her eyes are black holes in a sea of dark red.

There she is. There's the bitch. Kill her.

82

Riley

There are three Earthers crouched down behind one of the barricades. They've killed the stompers who were behind it, taking it for themselves. We're heading right towards them – a thought has just enough time to form in my head, a crazy jumble of words like *Can't* and *Aim* and *Impossible*. Then I'm firing.

I rise up off the seat to do it, aiming over the top of Carver's head. I don't even see where most of my shots land. But then one of the Earthers goes down, blood exploding out of a gaping wound in his temple. The other two turn, their eyes wide with shock, and then the Boneshaker is on them. The one on the left manages to get out of the way, diving right over the front of the line of the crates. The other isn't as lucky. I feel his body crunch under our wheels as we ride right over him, the vehicle bucking so hard that it nearly kicks us off.

Carver hangs a hard right, the Boneshaker screaming alongside the tugs barricading the entrance. As he does so, I get a good look at the dock. My stomach drops, and it has nothing to do with the speed we're moving at.

We're losing. It only takes me a second to see that. The few stompers and Tzevyans left are pinned down, hunkered behind the barricades with only the tops of their heads visible. I can't see Anna – just the tip of the long gun, standing upright. She's either reloading, or she's dead.

More Earthers come tumbling out of the gap. In seconds, my clip is dry, the slide slamming open. I raise myself up, putting one leg on the seat.

"The hell are you doing?" Carver shouts. He's pulled the Boneshaker to the right, shooting diagonally across the dock, crossing the gap while there's no gunfire from the others.

"Just keep going!" I shout. And at the moment where we zip by a tightly clustered group of Earthers, I hurl myself off the seat.

There are three of them, crouched low as they run, heading for cover. They turn at the sound of the Boneshaker, and I see the shock in their faces as I fly through the air towards them. My legs are tucked, with my knees pulled up to my chest and my arms out, elbows cocked back. In the split second before impact, I see that the one closest to me is Anton – the Earther who captured us back in Knox's surgery. His eyes are huge, his mouth open in horror.

I have just enough time to think the words: *I came back for you.* And then my shin takes him in the face.

I'm moving so fast that his mouth is still open when I hit it. There's a crunching sensation as his jaw shatters. It happens so quickly that he doesn't have time to cry out; he just drops.

I'm already tucking for the roll, the ground rising up to meet me, and when it does it's like sliding on oil, my body tucked in the perfect position. I rise up from the floor as the roll brings me up, striking out as I do so. Fist to stomach, elbow to chest. The last two Earthers go down.

Another *boom* followed by a crumpling sound behind me.

Another Earther – one I hadn't seen, a younger man with a trim beard – came up behind me. Now he's nothing more than a trembling body, his chest a dark, open wound.

I turn my head to see Anna flick me a salute. The barrel of her gun is still smoking. More rockets, shooting out from somewhere unseen in the entrance passage, exploding above us in a crash of noise and smoke. I start to run to the side of the hangar, away from the line of fire, when one detonates right next to me.

It's like someone took the world and yanked it away, leaving nothing but darkness and silence behind. Slowly, very slowly, flickers of light start to fade in, accompanied by a dull roar. My body has stopped responding: everything below my neck has checked out.

Amazingly, I don't feel fear. I don't feel anything.

I close my eyes.

I don't know how much time passes before I open them again. Some sounds have come back: the booming of gunfire, people shouting. But I barely notice them.

Because Morgan Knox is standing over me.

Somehow, he made it into the dock. He crawled out of the hospital, found his way here, wound his way through the battle. He's turned into something awful, barely a human being. His face is black with dried Resin. His mouth is open, and I see it's coated his teeth, filling out the thin gaps between them.

He's got a stinger. He's holding it in both hands, aiming carefully. It's less than four feet away. Impossible to miss.

Move, I tell myself. But the thought comes from far away.

Knox's open mouth forms a twisted smile. He sights down the body of the gun.

I try to form words, but I can't. I can only watch as he squeezes the trigger.

Rob Rolfrad

83

Riley

In the instant before Knox shoots me, I move.

It's more in desperation than anything else. I roll to the side, using my shoulders to wrench my body.

Knox fires. The bang slams my eardrums shut, and the bullet hits the floor right where my neck was. I can feel the vibrations travelling through the metal.

I let the energy in my shoulders travel. First to my torso, then my knees, then my ankles. I'm lying on my side now, my back towards Knox, and I kick out with my right leg.

My shin collides with his. He goes down, howling in fury. But as I roll back the other way, I see that he still has the stinger. He's up on one elbow, trying to get a bead on me.

I get to my knees, my head pounding, white heat burning in my throat. *Not fast enough.* He's going to aim and fire, and this time I'm not going to be able to stop him.

"Hey you."

Knox pauses, looks to his right.

Carver's boot takes him across the side of his head. He crumples instantly, folding in on himself. His head thuds off the floor, and the stinger spins away.

"That was for Kev," says Carver.

He stares down at Knox a moment longer, then looks over at me. "You OK?"

I'm too stunned to speak. Knox is still breathing, but he's unconscious, sprawled awkwardly across the floor.

"I'm fine," I say. We're off to one side of the dock, behind one of the tugs and out of sight of the entrance. The Boneshaker sits nearby.

"Can that thing still run?" I ask Carver, pointing to the Boneshaker.

He shakes his head. "Lucky shot hit the engine."

I point to Anna's shooting nest. Carver nods, and we sprint towards it, keeping as many barriers as possible between us and the entrance to the dock. Even so, we have to hit the ground a few times as bullets slam into them. There are bodies back here; too many of them.

Anna is crouched down when we get there. Her beanie is pulled down low on her head, and the eyes visible underneath it are glowing white-hot. There's no sign of Royo, or Syria, or anyone else we know. No Prakesh, either.

I lean up against the crates, breathing hard, feeling fury coursing through my veins.

"Are they *still coming*?" Carver shouts to Anna.

She nods, slamming the breech of the long gun shut.

"How many? I ask.

"Hard to tell," she says through gritted teeth. "A lot."

"Can we hold out?"

But even as I ask the question I know what the answer is. The dock is filling with smoke from the detonated rockets. Every breath burns, turning the back of my throat to acid. And everywhere I look, I see bodies. Stomper, Tzevyan and Earther, piled together. Even if we've taken down one of them for each of us, it's still not enough.

Carver grabs two nearby stingers, checks them, then tosses them aside with a snarl. "Empty," he says.

"Got anything else?"

Before he can answer, there's the rough whistle of another rocket. It detonates above us, and I go deaf again, the afterimage of the explosion imprinted on my retinas. Anna fires, her eyes just visible over the long gun's stock.

Right then, I get a glimpse of the back of the hangar, and my stomach goes into free fall.

Royo is sprawled out on the dock. The floor around him is slick with blood, gushing from a wound high on his right leg. His face is twisted with pain and fury.

Okwembu is walking towards Royo, a stinger of her own clutched in her hands.

But she's not firing. Because between her and Royo is Walker, swinging an enormous chain, daring Okwembu to take another step. She swings so hard and so fast that Okwembu has to dodge back, the thick chain striking the metal floor.

But none of that is what causes my blood to freeze.

It's Mikhail.

Royo hasn't seen him. Neither has Walker. But he's moving fast, coming up from behind them, his footfalls masked by the noise of battle. There's something in his hand. Something that catches the light from a rocket detonation nearby and reflects it back, turning the burning orange glow into something sharp and bright.

I boost out of my crouch into a sprint. I can feel from my screaming muscles that I'm moving faster than I ever have before, but it's like I'm running on the spot. The distance between me and the back of the hangar seems to grow, even as Mikhail closes it.

I try to shout a warning, but it comes out as little more than a husk of itself, thin and empty. My legs are still moving, and the sparks of pain shooting from them tell me how fast I'm going, but I'm not going to make it. I'm not even halfway there when Mikhail reaches Royo.

Walker is regrouping after her last swing, setting her shoulders to move the chain again, and Royo is almost catatonic, his hands dark with blood as they grip his leg.

At the very last instant, Royo sees Mikhail. He tries to raise himself up, an expression of astonished anger on his face. Okwembu is smiling, serene.

Walker whirls around, but it's too late.

Moving casually, almost gently, Mikhail puts a knee on Royo's chest. He hesitates, just for a second, and then he slides the blade into Royo's throat.

84

Riley

Royo goes still.

Walker screams in anger, lifting the chain high over her head. Before she can bring it down, Okwembu steps forward, and puts the stinger against her neck. I see her lips moving, but her words are lost in the wash of battle. Walker's shoulders slump, and she hurls the chain down, the links crashing to the ground.

Mikhail removes the blade, wiping it on the sleeve of his jacket.

The strength goes out of my legs, and I'm brought to a stop completely when Okwembu glances in my direction and pushes the barrel of her stinger harder into Walker's neck.

Mikhail raises the blade over his head. It must have been some sort of signal, because the gunfire coming from the entrance lowers, then stops completely. There are a few isolated pops from the remaining stompers, and a boom from Anna's gun, but then even those die away. Smoke drifts across the hangar floor. I can see Anna reloading. She hasn't seen what's happened to Royo.

"It's over!" Okwembu shouts, her sharp voice cutting through the fading echoes of gunfire.

Carver and Anna spin around, aiming their guns at her.

Okwembu flicks me a glance. "Careful, Ms Hale," she says, more quietly.

I realise I'm still moving towards her, and stop. I can't take my eyes off the gun at Walker's neck.

"No one else has to die," Mikhail shouts. "Not if you surrender yourselves."

There's silence in the dock. I look back across the floor, and I see with dismay that there are only a few of us left. Me, Carver, Anna, two Tzevyans, two Stompers. No: there are two more. Prakesh is over by the right-hand wall, leaning up against one of the tugs, his expression grim. Syria is with him.

But there are still at least a dozen Earthers, walking through the entrance to the dock. Mikhail brings the blade down, pointing it right at us. His eyes flash above it, green and clear.

And at that moment, one of the tugs at the entrance springs to life.

The Earthers around it scatter, and surprised shouts reach us across the dock.

Tseng. I can just seem him behind the controls. What is he doing?

The tug starts to rise. I look back at Okwembu, but she and Mikhail are frozen in place. It's only when Tseng tilts the tug towards them, its shadow growing on the ground as it rises, that they start to move, taking halting, panicked steps backwards, Okwembu pulling Walker with her.

One of the Earthers emerges from the entrance. It's Hisako – I remember her from when Carver, Anna and I were captured. I can barely make her out through the smoke. There's a tube on her shoulder. She points it at Tseng's tug, which is gathering speed, flying right across the dock towards us.

367

Okwembu sees it, too. "No!" she shouts.

Hisako fires.

The rocket hisses through the air, and hits the back of Tseng's tug with a bang that shakes my teeth. The tug lurches forward, propelled on a cone of fire. It starts spinning, whirling on its horizontal axis. Carver screams my name.

The roar of the tug becomes a tortured, metallic scream. I feel it pass overhead, and hurl myself to the ground. Its shadow passes on top of me. Mikhail and Okwembu bolt, sprinting towards the wall of the hangar, heading for the other tugs.

Walker runs, too. But not fast enough.

The tug hits the ground.

It's bouncing, breaking up, shedding pieces of itself like torn clothing. The cockpit vanishes, engulfed in a wave of fire which explodes from the tug's belly. Walker looks up, then the tug is on her. She vanishes in a whirlwind of torn, screaming metal.

Carver's grip on my arm is iron-tight. The destroyed tug is still going. The wrecked body is tumbling across the floor, heading right for the . . .

For the airlock doors.

They loom at the far end of the hangar. Big enough to let a whole tug through. Surely they'll withstand a hit – they're too big, too solid.

But the destroyed tug is coming in too fast.

It hits hard enough to shake the ground. Above us, the roof struts keen and screech, knocking loose dust and metal shavings. The boom is subsonic, catching in my bones.

The only thing louder is the silence that follows it.

When I look up, I see that the tug has smashed *through* the first set of doors, ripping right through the metal, knocking one door right off its tracks, coming to rest up against the outer doors.

Slowly, Carver and I get to our feet.

Rob Boffard

At that moment, the outer doors give off a low, metallic grinding sound. It's the sound of metal splitting. They're not holding – and beyond them is nothing but the vacuum.

"Oh gods," says Carver.

85

Prakesh

They used to tell stories about hull breaches when Prakesh was a kid.

They were scary stories – tales the grown-ups would weave while they gathered around, wrapped up in blankets while their parents sipped homebrew in the dim light. They would talk about the monsters lurking on the other side; how they would reach through the hole, open their giant mouths and inhale, sucking everything out in an instant.

Prakesh knows better now, and he wishes he didn't. Every fact about rapid decompression is flashing to the front of his mind. When those doors split, anything not nailed down will be dragged right out into space – including people. If by some miracle they manage to hold on, they'll have about ten seconds before the loss in air pressure rips consciousness away from them. Two minutes later, they'll be dead. That's if the whirlwind of flying debris doesn't kill them first

In a hundred years, it's never happened, not once. The solid steel skin of Outer Earth has never been cut.

They have to get away. They have to move now. But Prakesh

is already running the equations in his head, doing it involuntarily, size of the hole versus air speed versus tension on the station hull.

They'll never make it.

And, all at once, the idea is there, burning bright. Prakesh stands and runs, pushing past Syria, scanning the bottom of the tugs. *Come on, come on, where are you* . . .

There. The ramp access button, a bulbous red mushroom on the tug's underside. He hammers on it, and the ramp begins to drop, lowering down from the back of the tug. It's their only hope: get inside a sealed environment, away from the deadly effects of the decompression.

The ramp moves slowly, issuing a thin mechanical whine, and Prakesh has to suppress an urge to scream at it. Instead, he turns and cups his hands to his mouth. "Everybody! Get inside, now!"

Syria reacts first, his big feet hammering across the floor, his arms pumping. He gets there just as the ramp fully extends. He grabs Prakesh's shoulder, trying to pull him up the ramp. Prakesh twists away. "You go," he says. "I'll get the others on board."

Syria wavers, then bolts up the ramp, using the handholds on the inner walls to pull himself along. Prakesh turns, and sees Janice Okwembu sprinting towards him. There are Earthers with her, some of them still clutching their weapons.

He almost stops her, then shakes it off. He has to preserve life now, no matter whose life it is, no matter what they've done. He gestures them onwards, urging them to hurry, and they sprint past him, pounding up the ramp. It bends and creaks under their weight. There's no time to open any of the other tugs' ramps – he'll have to get as many people into this one as he can.

Prakesh's heart is pounding, every muscle tense, waiting for the airlock doors to give way. He tells himself not to hold his breath if it happens – his lungs will rupture if he does. Every instinct he has is to get into the body of the tug himself, but he stays at the bottom, looking for more people he can save.

Riley. Where's Riley? Prakesh shouts her name, but he can't see her.

86

Riley

The airlock doors give another grinding screech. An alarm blares in the distance. The smoke in the hangar clears for a moment, as if it wants to give us a full view of what's coming.

The doors give off another keening groan. The hangar is a grey nightmare, glowing orange in places from dozens of tiny fires.

Anna is with us, appearing as if from nowhere, her eyes wide and panicked. And I can't see Prakesh. I don't know where he is any more. I'm pulled in a thousand different directions.

"Can we seal the hangar?" I say to Carver.

"It won't work," he says. "The doors, remember?"

I can't even see the entrance to the hangar – it's vanished behind a curtain of smoke. But then Carver's words sink in: we can't seal the place off. The doors don't work – and the tugs won't block the entrance completely.

I hear my name being shouted, and see Prakesh. There he is, through a gap in the smoke. He's over on the other side, underneath one of the tugs. Somehow, he's managed to get its ramp open, and he's waving people on board. Okwembu and Mikhail move past him. They're all getting onto one tug. The thought of him on board with *her* . . .

"Come on," I say. Carver and I start running, and it's only a moment later that I realise Anna isn't following. I look back to see her still standing there, the long gun by her side. I don't like the way her mouth is hanging open, or the distant look in her eyes.

Ignoring Carver's protests, I run back to her, grabbing her by the arm. "Anna, we have to go."

She pulls away from my grip. "I can't leave."

"What?"

"My family. They're still here. They're still in Tzevya."

"You'll never make it."

She gives her arm a vicious shake and knocks my hand away, her eyes blazing, every moment of her sixteen years radiating out. "I *said* I'm not going."

"Anna, please," I say, and I'm startled to feel tears staining my cheeks. There's another groan from the outer airlock doors.

Anna puts her hands on my shoulders, letting the long gun fall to the floor. She stops being sixteen, just for a second. The distant look in her eyes has vanished, replaced by an eerie calm.

"You never gave me that race," she says, and then pulls me into an embrace, her small arms tight around my shoulders.

"You'd never have beaten me anyway," I say, my words muffled as I hug her back.

I want more than anything to pull her along with us. Instead, I whisper words into her ear. Words Amira might have said to me, in another time and place.

"Run. Faster than you ever have before. Watch your take-off spots on the jumps, tuck your arms for the rolls. Make sure you're always looking ahead."

Anna nods, tears of her own touching my skin. She breaks away, gives Carver a brief hug, and is gone, sprinting towards the dock entrance. She moves fast, vanishing down the corridor.

"Time to go," Carver says.

And at that moment, the airlock doors give way.

87

Riley

The rush of air knocks me off my feet.

I'm tumbling, my body slamming into the ground, skidding across it. The smoke turns into huge curls as it's sucked towards the breach. The roar is enormous.

Carver grabs my hand. He's got hold of one of the tugs, his feet planted on the floor and the fingers of his other hand gripping a handle on its underside. I swing my other hand up, gripping his wrist. He starts to pull, his eyes squeezed almost shut. The muscles in his arm stand out like power cables. He jabs at the tug's body with his elbow, and then the ramp is coming down, the whining of its motor cutting through the roar.

With a horrifying clarity, I see the drops of sweat on Carver's face wicking away, sucked off his skin by the force of the breach. One touches my own cheek, a tiny spot of wetness, gone almost instantly.

I don't feel fear. I hardly feel anything – just a thin, burning need to survive. I can't get any air into my lungs, and blackness starts to creep in at the edges of my vision. I catch a split-second glimpse of the airlock doors – or where they used to be. The space beyond them is endless.

Movement. Coming right at me. I duck just in time for a spinning crate to shoot past. If I hadn't, it would have taken my head off.

The pull of the air is like an arm around my chest, refusing to let go. Someone – Earther, stomper, no way to tell – shoots by us, tumbling out of control, their scream fading as they're sucked towards the breach. I want to look to the side, to find Prakesh, but I know that if I take my eyes off Carver I'm done for.

Then one of my feet is on the ramp. I finally risk a glance over to the other side of the hangar. I can't find Prakesh's tug – they all look identical, lined up along the far wall, entrance ramps shut. With a sickening lurch in my stomach, I see that they're rocking on their magrails.

I'm barely conscious now, with no oxygen in my body, moving by sheer force of will. I propel myself forward, dragging myself into the tug. There are handholds just above the ramp, and I wrap my fingers around them, the tendons in my arms screaming in protest. There's a push from behind, Carver's hands flat on my back, and then I'm sprawling across the floor. I hear Carver come in behind me, grunting with the effort. The ramp starts to close, its electronic whine louder inside.

The ramp shuts with a loud clack. I take a breath, but there's no oxygen. Nothing at all. It was all sucked out the moment the ramp began to open.

The blackness closes in completely.

I don't know how long I'm out. I know it can't be more than two minutes, because if it were I'd be dead. An alarm is blaring, the speaker painfully close to my ear, and a calm, mechanical voice is saying, over and over again, "Danger. Pressure Loss. Emergency O2 activated."

I roll over, trying to inhale as much air as I can. My lungs feel like they're being burned away, and each breath stokes the fire. I concentrate on the motion of taking each breath, pushing back against the pain. The world has shrunk to the space around my lungs, blacking out everything else.

Slowly, the fire recedes, the oxygen trickling into my system, my lungs finally settling back into a rhythm. We're in a small rectangular loading area in the middle of the tug. Readouts and storage lockers, some the size of a grown man, line the walls, and everything is bathed in a low red light. I get to my feet, struggling to hold myself upright. I'm trembling, but quickly realise it isn't just me: the whole tug is shaking, straining at its coupling.

Carver is already on his feet, stumbling past me. "Move, move, move, move!"

I get to my feet, unsteady but spurred on by adrenaline, nearly falling as the tug lurches to one side. There's a grinding noise from below, and as I duck through the low doorway into the cockpit, I can feel it shuddering through the tug.

There are two chairs made of bucket plastic, low to the floor, surrounded on all sides by switches and glowing readouts. Carver is already sliding into the left-hand seat, throwing switches and tapping readouts. Two control yokes jut out above the seats at chest height – for a second I can't help thinking of the Boneshaker.

I follow Carver, slipping into the seat next to him. I'm not sure what's louder: the hammering of my heart, or the terrifying grinding sound from the tug's coupling. Carver gives an experimental pull on his yoke, and mine matches its movement, nearly taking me in the chest. Someone has tied a slip of paper to the handle; I get a glimpse of the message written on it as the yoke is pushed back. *Alison – fly safe, fly straight. I love you. Kamal.*

It takes a few seconds for me to tear my eyes away.

There's a glass screen in front of us, curving around the tug's body. My breath catches as I look through it. The dock is a nightmare world of flying debris and whirling smoke. Bodies spin through the air, grab hold of something, are wrenched away.

On the other side, a tug has lifted off its railings and is moving towards the breach. There's no way to tell if its engines are on, or if it's being dragged by the force of the vacuum. My heart feels as if it's being physically pulled out into the dock, as if it can find Prakesh's tug all on its own.

Carver punches the air as our tug rumbles to life. Needles jump and skitter behind their transparent housing, and the yokes shudder with the force of the engine. "Strap in," he says, reaching behind him and fumbling for a belt. I scrabble for mine, finding it above and behind me; it goes down over my shoulders and between my breasts, clicking into a buckle between my legs. As soon as I slide it home, the straps pull tight, forcing me into the seat and knocking a little breath from me. Another tug is moving, tumbling clumsily across the floor, spitting sparks as it scrapes across it.

Carver has his hands on the yoke, staring intently at the readouts.

"You *can* fly this thing, right?" I say.

"Sure," he says. But he doesn't move, his fingers still wrapped around the yoke. Below us, there's another metallic growl as the tug strains at its magrail.

I close my eyes. "You can't fly it, can you?"

When I open them again, Carver is staring at me. There's a small, apologetic smile on his face.

With a final, fatal wrench, our tug tears loose of its coupling, and we're spinning and crashing towards the void.

88

Knox

Morgan Knox comes to just as the airlock doors breach.

For a few confused seconds, he doesn't know what's happening. He's pulled across the dock, and his lungs feel like they're being crushed in a vice.

Stop, he thinks.

But he can't. His hand snags something, one of the wheeled pallets the Earthers were using for cover, but he's pulled away almost immediately. His head collides with the floor, and brilliant sparks explode across his field of view. A second later, a whirling dagger of metal buries itself in his thigh. He has no air to scream with, can only watch in horror as the shard is ripped out by the pressure, trailing a fan of blood.

He can do nothing. He is a small child in the grip of a giant. The world around him is a roaring nightmare, a maelstrom of debris and bodies.

And then it . . . *changes*.

The sound dwindles, then vanishes. Knox is out of the storm, and he's looking at Outer Earth. It's huge, bigger than he could have ever imaged. He can see it curving away from him, see the glittering convection fins on its hull. Beyond it, the blackness of space is split by a billion tiny pinpricks of light.

Time slows to a crawl.

He can't breathe. He can't do anything. But as he looks at Outer Earth, Morgan Knox is gifted a moment of clarity. He realises what's happened, realises that Outer Earth has suffered a breach. And that's when the real fear grips him, pushing past the confusion.

Because he knows what's going to happen next.

He feels it on his tongue first. A prickly sensation, like a mouthful of iron. It's the moisture boiling off. His face is swelling, the skin stretching and warping. His eyes . . . oh gods, his eyes. The pressure is unbelievable.

And yet, he can still see. His vision has shrunk to two small circles, but it's enough to see Amira Al-Hassan, floating in front of him.

Morgan, Amira says.

And then she screams.

The sound tears Knox apart. What's happening to him is happening to her as well. He can see her skin starting to stretch, the tissues in her face swelling up. Her limbs contort, bending into impossible positions. She's dying, she's dying again, and there's nothing he can do about it.

Morgan, help me!

He tries to move. But his body has stopped listening to him. He needs air, needs oxygen, but there's nothing he can do.

Amira's eyes are horribly distorted, swollen red bulbs with a misshapen iris at the centre. She stops screaming, and suddenly her voice is full of scorn. *You can't do it, can you?*

He tries to speak.

You failed me.

Then she vanishes. Like she was never there. Like she never existed in the first place.

Knox's vision shrinks to a pinprick, then vanishes completely.

382

89

Riley

If we weren't strapped in, we'd be smashed to pieces in the tug's insides. The entire body shakes as we roll end over end, slamming again and again into the walls and floor of the dock. Another tug looms in the cockpit glass, but I barely register it's there before we hit it. The bang throws me back into my seat again as we spin off.

I get a split-second glimpse of the airlock doors, of torn and shredded metal. And then, all at once, we're out.

The only sounds are the tug's humming engine, and my own shaky breathing. We're still tumbling, with debris flying past us, but it's now against a backdrop of inky blackness. Every few seconds, the side of the station swings past, huge and dark.

"Yeah. OK. All right," Carver says, more to himself than to me. He's got hold of the yoke again, and is hesitantly reaching out to the instruments, flicking switches and running his finger along labels. I look away from the spinning hell outside the window, trying to ignore the lurching in my stomach.

Something hits us, bouncing off the roof with a dull boom.

When I open my mouth, my voice is louder than I intended. "Get us under control."

"I'm trying."

"Try harder!"

"Why don't you stop giving me shit and look for the thruster controls?"

I start scanning the dials and digital readouts, but it's like I'm looking at another language – one made of numbers and arrows and strange symbols. My finger hovers over the controls, and I have to exert real effort to move it. *Zero-G. We're in zero-G now.* It's impossible not to think back to when I ran the Core, a year ago. When I fought Oren Darnell in the microgravity.

"Got it!" Carver says, and twists a knob on the control panel. There's a low groan as the tug jerks itself into life. The spinning world outside the window is slowing, coming to a rest. For some reason, I expected everything to be darkness – for the blackness of space to be total. But it's as if we're floating in a chamber bathed in brilliant light. Objects slowly rotate, catching the light and holding it: a crate, a discarded stinger, the arm of a crane. A little way away, another tug spins gently, the cockpit dark and empty.

And then Outer Earth comes into view, and my mouth falls open.

We're about a mile away from it. Part of the station is cloaked in shadow. But the rest of it is awash with sunlight, gleaming like a jewel. The convection fins on the hull are huge, glittering slabs. The core at the centre is a mess of protruding cylinders, all radiating out from the central reactor. I can make out the tiny puffs of fire as the hull lasers open up on approaching objects, vaporising them, preventing them from damaging the station.

"No," Carver says, sucking in a horrified breath. I follow his gaze, and a breath catches in my throat.

The dock. It's as if a deity, angry and vengeful, made a giant fist and punched out the side of the station. The breach has torn a hole right through, a jagged wound that must reach into Apex itself. There's a cloud of glittering debris above the breach.

"Anna," I say, and it's a full second before I realise I've actually said her name. I turn to Carver, tearing my eyes away from the station. "Do you think she . . ."

"Don't worry," he says. "She'll have got clear."

But his eyes say something different.

He rotates the tug – I can hear the thrusters shooting off, like compressed air. The station swings away. The glow of the Earth, far below us, is just out of sight.

"There!" Carver shouts, pointing out of his side of the cockpit. I raise myself up as high as the straps will allow, my body assisted by the low gravity.

The asteroid is so big it takes my breath away. I know it's smaller than a single sector on Outer Earth, but at that moment it looks impossibly large. It's steady against the blackness, pitted and pockmarked, with shadowy craters and a trailing veil of ice reaching out behind it.

And on one side, dwarfed by its cargo and only just visible: the *Shinso Maru*. A tiny speck, connected to the asteroid with dozens of thin, silver threads. Each one of them will be a flexible carbon-fibre cable, twenty feet across.

It's hard to believe that the Earthers' plan will work. I try to picture them entering Earth's atmosphere, coming in behind the asteroid, using it as a shield against the intense heat.

"How far away are they?" I say.

"Close enough," Carver replies, pushing the yoke forward. I can feel the thrusters kicking in. The rumble comes up through my seat.

I push myself up out of my seat again. "I don't see the other tug."

"They got a head start."

"Or they didn't make it at all."

"Calm down, Ry. They'll have got there. Prakesh'll be OK."

He tries to make the words sound comforting, but doesn't quite get there. What comes out sounds almost mocking, and I can see that he knows it, refusing to meet my eyes. The memory of the kiss surfaces, and won't go away.

"Did you see any kids?" Carver says.

"Kids?"

"The Earthers – they had children with them, back in that mining facility."

We fall silent as the implication sinks in. The children have been left behind – every one of them, including Jamal's little girl, Ivy.

"Hey, look on the bright side," says Carver. "Your bombs haven't exploded. Guess my solution worked after all."

I touch my ear, without meaning to. There's no way Knox survived a dock breach. I guess Carver's right.

Against all odds, I feel relief. Sweet, beautiful relief. I hold onto it, just for a moment.

Carver corrects the tug, pulling down on the yoke, but it just slides the other way, nearly vanishing below us. "I wish I knew how to read this thing's instruments," he says. His forehead is shiny with sweat, his mouth set in a thin line.

We fall silent. My gaze drifts to the ship, larger now. It's in the full glare of the sun, and what I see takes my breath away. It's like something from a distant galaxy; from a civilisation much older than ours, one that has been around so long that they've evolved in a completely different direction. The ship is a huge, slowly rotating cylinder, half a mile long at least. It looks awkward and ungainly, with enormous thruster cones jutting off its body. The surface isn't a uniform grey like I thought at first. It's mottled blue and brown, too, with an almost plant-like texture. It's a little below us, off to the left. I point to it. "Can you bring us around?"

Carver pulls the yoke down, but nothing happens. His brow furrows, and he does it again, harder this time.

"Carver?" I say, trying and failing to keep the nervousness out of my voice.

"The thrusters." He breaks off, pulling the yoke towards him again. "They're not responding. They must have been damaged when the airlock blew."

I grab my own yoke and pull. A strange image comes to mind: a picture I saw years ago, in a school lesson I thought I'd long forgotten. A boat of some kind, the couple in it rowing hard against an unforgiving ocean current. When I pull the yoke down, the tug remains locked on its course, the hum of its engine steady. If we stay on our current course, we're going to shoot right past the *Shinso* and its asteroid, with no way to make it back.

"Can we fix them?" I say.

"Sure," Carver says. "If we had a few hours and I actually knew something about tug engines."

He's pulling at the yoke now, hurling it in different directions, the asteroid looming large in our field of view. "Come on, you piece of shit, work," he says. "Come on. Come on!"

90

Prakesh

It's all Prakesh can do to hold on.

They're flying away from Outer Earth, stars whirling past the cockpit viewport. Movement inside the tug is practically impossible. They might be floating in zero gravity, but there are at least twenty people inside, and there's hardly an inch of free space. Earthers and Tzevyans mingle together, huddled in the dim red light.

One of them floats past Prakesh, a knee half an inch from his nose, and he pulls back reflexively. He bangs his head on the wall, and gasps, tightening his fingers on the handhold. The lack of gravity is tearing his stomach apart – some of the others couldn't take the pressure, and there are already chunks of vomit floating in the stale air, glistening, catching the light.

He keeps seeing the airlock doors give way, keeps hearing the terrible roar as the air was sucked out. He doesn't know if the station can survive a breach that big. Riley will be OK, he knows it, refuses to think otherwise, but what about his parents? They're still on board.

He makes himself focus. He's near the front of the tug, near

388

the two pilot seats. They're taken up by Okwembu on the right, and Mikhail on the left. They've managed to strap themselves in, and Mikhail is fighting with the control stick.

"Everybody hold on," Okwembu says. "It's all under control."

"*Under control?*" Syria's voice comes from the back of the craft. "You just blew a hole in the side of the station."

"It's the only chance we have," Okwembu says. Prakesh stares at her in silent wonder – she sounds calm, almost bored, like the breach was part of her plan.

He makes himself speak. "We have to go back. We have to help them."

"Help who, Mr Kumar?" She doesn't turn to look at him. He wants to reach out and grab her by the hair, shake some sense into her, but he can't seem to remove his hand from the wall. His fingers have stopped listening to him.

"Everybody on Outer Earth," he says. "They're still there. We can't just *leave them*."

Now she does turn to look at him. In the red light, her eyes look like black holes.

"We can, and we have to," she says.

He feels anger, real anger, at the thought of following Janice Okwembu into anything. But, then, what choice does he have? What choice do any of them have?

Preserve life, he thinks, and grips his handhold even tighter.

Sweat is pouring down Mikhail's face. "All right," he says to Okwembu, almost mumbling the words. "We should be in range."

"Where is it?" she replies.

"Jacket pocket. You'll have to reach over."

Prakesh sees Okwembu shut her eyes, just for a second, then lean over to Mikhail. She's exhausted – he can see that now. Despite her calm demeanour, there are dark shadows under her eyes. She sticks a hand in Mikhail's jacket, and it emerges holding a small tab screen, a bulky antenna jutting out of it.

"You know what to do?" says Mikhail.

Okwembu mutters something unintelligible, tapping her way through the opening menus.

"*Hey*," Mikhail says. "You make it work. That's the only reason you're still alive."

He doesn't see the look Okwembu flashes him, and the pure poison on her face is enough to make Prakesh's eyes go wide. In that instant, she doesn't look human.

But she says nothing, turning back to the tab screen.

"What's happening up there?" Syria shouts.

"Yeah," comes another voice. "We can't see anything."

Okwembu is using a program Prakesh hasn't encountered before: all green backgrounds and sparse text. "It's going to take a few minutes," she says. "I haven't used Ellipsis since I was at the Academy."

"I thought you said you could do it," Mikhail says.

She rounds on him. "I can. I'm the *only* one who can. You should remember that. You just need to give me time."

And Prakesh understands.

They crew of the *Shinso* would never let them on board. They'd know what was happening on the station, and they'd have been told to get as far away as possible. So the Earthers are using Okwembu to override the ship, using her experience of the *Shinso*'s dated operating system. It wouldn't take much – all she'd have to do is force the ship's airlocks to activate, to let them dock.

And, on cue, the *Shinso Maru* slides into view, a tiny speck in the void, shadowed by the giant asteroid behind it.

91

Riley

Before I realise I'm doing it, I'm unbuckling my straps. They whiz back into the seat, and I float upwards, my stomach rolling uncomfortably. Carver stares at me in disbelief. "Where are you going?"

I don't have time to respond. I'm trying to bring to mind everything I know about moving in zero grav, remembering my journey through the Core. There are hand grips on the wall, awash in the red light from its interior. I use them to pull myself up, wincing as I bump into the ceiling.

Each move you make sends you in a new direction. Go slow.

It takes an enormous effort not to rush. Carver has unstrapped, too, floating behind me, his feet tapping against the cockpit glass. When I look back, I see that he's left a smeared boot print behind.

It's hard to pick out details in the hellish red light. I don't even know what I'm looking for – I half hope that there'll be an escape pod of some kind, but I know even before I get to the back that there's no way there'll be one on a ship of this size. My eyes rove over the back of the tug, looking for anything that might help us.

"Riley?" Carver says. It comes out a nervous shout, the cramped space amplifying the word, hurting my ears. But I don't reply, because right then I see the lockers.

The man-sized ones. The ones I passed on my way in.

My breath is coming in quick gasps as I tug on the handle. The locker opens with a creak of metal hinges, and inside . . .

"Are those what I think they are?" says Carver.

I grab onto a hand grip to steady myself, a stupid grin plastered across my face. There are three space suits inside the locker, each with the block letters SCC stitched on the chest. *Space Construction Corps.*

Carefully reaching into the locker, I pull the first of the three space suits out, and push it towards Carver.

"Riley, it won't work," Carver says, even as he spins the suit, looking for the seals. "There's a procedure for putting these on – you're supposed to check each other for breaks, spend an hour depressurising."

"Carver, now is *not* the time."

My own suit is made from what feels like grainy rubber, inflexible and tough. There are arches of plastic on the shoulders, one on either side, bracketing the space where my head will go. Here and there, dotted across the body, are tiny vents edged in hard plastic. It's dusty, too, the grains hanging in the air before me. How long have these suits been here? Will they still work?

My fingers find the seal running down the torso, and even as I yank it open I'm trying to recall what I know about the construction corps suits. The one-piece units are supposed to be easy to use – or easier, at least, than the ones our ancestors wore. The backpack unit has air, and power thrusters that let you move around – those must be the vents. I can't think of anything else, so I just concentrate on getting inside it.

Legs first, then arms. The inside is made of the same rubbery

Rob Boffard

material, and it rucks my jacket sleeves up as I jam my arms in. Working as fast as I dare, I close myself inside the suit. My hands feel as if they're made of lead, the fingers numb and clumsy in the thick gloves. The suit hisses slightly as the single long seal closes. It's tight around my neck, and like four small vices across my wrists and ankles. In the gloves, my fingers feel as if they're welded in place.

"Helmets," I say to Carver. "Where are the helmets?"

For a horrible moment, I'm sure that they're back on Outer Earth somewhere – that the suits will be completely useless. Carver looks like some kind of freakish doll that has come to life, moving his hands up and down his suit, patting the rubbery surface. There's a hiss, and then out of nowhere, his helmet appears: flexible plastic, sliding through grooves in the arches on his shoulders, shooting up from behind his head and over it before locking into place at the front.

He grabs my arm and jabs at something on my wrist. A small control panel, set into the suit – I hadn't seen it before. There's a loud whoosh, right by my ears, and my own helmet shoots over my head. As it seals into place, the ambient noise vanishes, and I hear nothing but the tiny hiss of the oxygen supply. That, and my own breath, coming in terrified hitches.

"—crazy." Carver's voice is tinny and faint, but there.

I try not to think about what he's saying. "How am I hearing you?"

"I don't know. Must be a frequency the suits are locked into."

"Get the ramp open," I say to Carver.

"If we go out there without pressurising properly—"

"You have a better idea?"

"There's got to be an airlock in here. We can—"

"There's not enough time!"

His fingers find the button, caressing it slowly, buoyed by the lack of gravity.

393

"Ry . . ." he says, and the fear in his voice is unmistakeable. "Do it!"

Carver hits the button.

Nothing happens. The ramp stays obstinately shut. Carver jams the button a second time, a third. I don't dare take a look out of the cockpit window. I just close my eyes.

There's a deep click, and then the whine of a motor as the ramp starts to open. I have just enough time to catch Carver's eyes – wide with fear, just like mine – and then we're tumbling, crashing into each other, sucked sideways by the loss of air pressure.

We both hit the ramp at once, almost becoming stuck as our bodies tangle in the gap. It's like the dock breach all over again – the same rushing sensation, the same sense of panic. But this time there's no seat to strap into. No metal cocoon.

I have time to shout Carver's name, just once. And then we're pulled free of the ramp, rolling end over end, into space.

92

Prakesh

They're coming up on the *Shinso Maru* way too fast.

Its hull looms in the viewport. There's a muted bleeping sound, and a calm voice warns them of a proximity alert. Mikhail grips the stick, pushing it gently. The hull slides away as the tug tilts downwards.

Everybody inside the tug watches the movement play out. Prakesh's mouth has gone completely dry. His world has shrunk down to that cockpit viewport. It's like they're trying to sneak up on a gigantic beast, get close to it without touching it.

Could he take over the tug somehow? He and Syria could rush the cockpit, overpower Okwembu and Mikhail, turn this ship around and . . .

And what?

He grits his teeth, furious with himself. Without wanting to, he thinks of Riley – she would know what to do. She always has a plan, always has something she could try.

She's not here, a voice in his mind says. *It's just you.*

"Steady," says Okwembu.

"I was a tug pilot for ten years," Mikhail says, speaking a little louder than he should. "I know how to fly."

He flicks a quick glance at Okwembu. "How much longer?"

The tug's comms system crackles. "Unidentified tug ship," says a man's voice, crisp and efficient. "This is Captain Jonas Barton of the *Shinso Maru*. You are not authorised to—"

Mikhail fumbles at the control panel, snapping off the transmission. It's immediately replaced by another soft beeping. "Warning," says the tug's electronic voice. "Fuel at five per cent."

"Gods," says someone behind Prakesh. He can't tear his eyes away from the viewport.

"Are you in?" Mikhail is almost shouting now.

"Nearly there," says Okwembu. She's navigating across the screen at a blazing speed, her fingers opening and closing windows faster than Prakesh can track.

"Nearly isn't good enough," Mikhail says. He's sweating so hard that it has started to drip off his face, forming opaque globules in the air in front of them. "We dock now, or we don't dock at all."

"Almost got it."

Mikhail pulls back on the stick. Prakesh's stomach lurches as the view swings upwards, the hull rushing towards them. Mikhail hits a few more controls, and the tug stabilises. They're really close to the hull now – so close that Prakesh can make out the details on its surface. The ancient warning labels, the handholds, the vents. He can see man-sized crusts of ice adhering to the hull, jagged and grey.

The thrusters on the side of the *Shinso* fire, all at once. At first, Prakesh thinks that they're trying to get away, to increase their velocity. But the angle is wrong. The thrusters are at ninety degrees to the body.

Mikhail peers out. "What are they doing?"

"Don't worry – that's me," Okwembu says. "We have to stop the *Shinso*'s rotation if we're going to attach to the airlock."

"That'll disrupt the on-ship gravity."

Okwembu ignores him. And – *there* – the airlock. A huge, round port in the side of the ship, with three scalloped hinges around the edges. Easily the size of their tug.

Without warning, Mikhail swings the tug around. This time, Prakesh almost does throw up – he feels bile climb into his throat, feels his mouth flood with saliva. The *Shinso* disappears, replaced by a backdrop of stars. What the hell is Mikhail doing?

He looks over. Mikhail's eyes are fixed on a screen set into the main console. It's a camera on the back of the tug. The feed is glitchy, but Prakesh can see the airlock. Mikhail is going to back them in, docking so that the ramp can lower and they can enter the ship.

"I'm going in," Mikhail says. He starts to reach for the thruster control.

"No," Okwembu says, and a note of fear has crept into her voice. "I don't have access yet."

"If we don't dock now, we'll run out of fuel."

"It won't accept us. You have to give me time."

Prakesh closes his eyes. He tries to picture Riley, and his parents, and Suki. He tries to think of the Air Lab, of the light filtering through the tree canopy, of the quiet, cool algae ponds.

"Warning," the electronic voice says. "Proximity alert."

One of the Earthers starts to scream.

"Proximity alert."

Without wanting to, Prakesh opens his eyes. The *Shinso*'s airlock fills the screen on the console.

"Got it!" Okwembu says.

There's a *thud*, reverberating through the tug, shaking its occupants. The lights flicker. Whoever was screaming stops abruptly.

A second later, the tug's ramp hisses open.

93

Riley

My suit has gone completely stiff, like I'm encased in ice. All I can hear is my breathing, thick and rapid, causing condensation to form on the inside of the helmet. There's no other sound.

I'm upside down, looking at the tug as we fly away from it. It's so small – a little metal bubble, nothing more, vanishing into the distance.

"—ley, get—" Carver says, his voice crackling in and out.

"What?" I shout. My eyes are locked on the tug.

"We need to— away. The thrusters—"

I collide with Carver.

I didn't even see him. He just slams right into me. We're knocked away from each other, tumbling out of control. My breathing has never been so loud. I can hear the details of every inhale and exhale, and each one tastes sour in my mouth.

There's another fizz of static, and then Carver's voice comes again. "—losing you. We—"

"Carver, can you hear me?"

"—sters!"

"Carver! Where are you?" I can barely get the words out.

Outside my helmet, the world is a spinning nightmare. I see him, just for a second, and then he's gone, spinning out of view.

I breathe deep, sucking in the damp-smelling oxygen, refusing to let myself throw up. I have to get control of my movement. Carver mentioned thrusters . . .

Slowly, I force my arm to lift, bringing it into view. The control panel is the size of a man's hand, nestled into the suit on the back of my wrist. No readout, but at least a dozen big buttons – ones you can hit with the thick-fingered gloves. They have writing on them – but it's like reading another language. *Trans. Mix. Gauge.* But one of the buttons is labelled *Thrust*. With fingers that feel huge and fat, I jab at it.

It's like getting kicked all over my body, all at once. Shoulders, shins, the centre of my chest, the small of my back – all of them feel a sudden, silent pressure. An image appears on the inside of my helmet: a small diagram of a space suit, with the six points highlighted by small circles.

I can't see the *Shinso*, or even Outer Earth. I don't even know which direction I'm facing. The blackness stretches around me – I've shrunk to a tiny speck, dwarfed by it, swallowed by it.

A piece of debris shoots past me, propelled by the dock breach. I barely get a fix on it before it's impossibly distant, tumbling away from me at light speed. It's as if I'm hanging over a bottomless pit, with nothing between me and an endless fall.

My stomach is a rolling ball of nausea, vertigo twisting it back and forth. I shut my eyes, focus on my breathing, wait for the thruster to stabilise the spinning stars.

"Riley?" Carver says, his transmission suddenly crystal-clear.

"I'm OK," I say, only just managing to get the words out. My mouth feels foul. The rapid breathing has crusted on my tongue.

"I can't see you. I'm heading over to the *Shinso*. Can you make your way to me?"

I look at the display on my helmet. It's just above my right eye, and as I look closely I can see the small circles indicating the thrusters are different sizes – some big, some small.

"How?" I say.

"Move your hands to your stomach. You'll find a little stick there."

I move my hands down, fumbling with my clumsy, unfeeling fingers. The inside of the gloves is soft and padded, but the outside might as well be moulded metal, and my skin burns from the effort. Somehow I do it, and my hands close around something thick and solid; my helmet's position won't let me see what it is, but it must have popped out when I activated the thrusters. And all at once I understand what Carver means.

Incredibly, Carver laughs. "I see you!" he says. He starts to say something else, but then his voice vanishes in a painful burst of static.

94

Prakesh

The crew of the *Shinso Maru* don't stand a chance.

Okwembu's hack stopped the ship spinning, removed its artificial gravity. They're nauseous, disoriented, not prepared for the sudden rush of bodies out of the airlock. If they'd been smarter, they would have set a trap, but they simply weren't expecting this many people.

Prakesh is one of the last out of the tug, in front of only Mikhail and Okwembu. The noise in the narrow corridor leading from the airlock is atrocious. The *Shinso*'s crew are trying to hold out, blocking the passage, fighting off the Earthers with fists and feet. But every movement sends them flying in the opposite direction, and they're not used to controlling themselves in the low gravity. Neither are the Earthers, but at least they have a few more minutes' practice.

Prakesh comes to a halt, one hand on the roof, the other on the wall, staring in horror at the assault. One of the Earthers fires a stinger, once, twice, her body slamming back into the floor. Blood spreads out across the corridor.

If he tries to wade into the melee, he'll just get himself killed.

He hates being a spectator, hates feeling so helpless – especially when people are dying in front of him. Another stinger shot rings out – it's in the hands of one of the crew, but the bullet goes wide, and it's ripped from his grasp.

There's a hand on Prakesh's shoulder. It's Syria, and he's gripping hard enough to dimple the flesh under Prakesh's shirt. His face is pale.

"Wait!" The voice comes from the other end of the corridor. "We surrender. Please."

Slowly, the movement in the corridor begins to subside. As it does, Prakesh starts counting, without really wanting to, working out how many people still live. There are six bodies, Earther and crew, dead from gunshot or stab wounds. One crew member has a broken neck, his head tilted at an impossible angle.

Four crew dead. Two Earthers. The remaining two crew members are cowering, floating in an almost foetal position, their palms out. A man and a woman, gaunt from years spent in space.

Okwembu pushes past Prakesh and Syria, her face expressionless. She doesn't seem bothered by the lack of gravity, her arms akimbo, fingers just brushing the walls. "Put the bodies somewhere out of the way," she says, propelling herself down the corridor. She stops when she reaches the two frightened crew members.

"I'm sorry that had to happen," she says. She's speaking quietly, sincerely, so much so that one of the crew members actually nods. "You need to take us to the bridge now."

The other crew member isn't swayed so easily. "Why are you doing this?" he says. "You're a councillor. You're supposed to be on the station."

"I *was* a councillor." A note of impatience has crept into Okwembu's voice. "Not any more. The bridge. Now."

95

Riley

"Carver!"

There's nothing. The panic starts to creep in again, tightening my chest and forcing the air out of my lungs. I'm not cold inside the suit – this is nothing like Outer Earth's core – but a chill creeps in nonetheless.

I tell myself to focus, to concentrate on getting the suit under control. I push the stick up, towards my stomach. Nothing happens

For an awful moment, I think my thrusters aren't working. Then my fingers feel buttons on the stick – one on the front, one on the back, perfectly cupped by my thumb and forefinger.

I hit the one on the back. My chest thruster puffs out a cloud of gas, and I feel myself moving backwards. Experimental pushes to the left and right make the circles on the corresponding legs and shoulders grow bigger as the others diminish. *Stick for direction. Buttons for thrust.*

Scanning the blackness for the ship, I push the stick down again, spinning in a slow vertical loop.

My hands are completely numb inside the space suit gloves,

and they're *hot*, as if all my blood has drained into them. But after fumbling for a few moments, I spot the *Shinso*, shining in the void as it reflects back the light from the sun. My breath catches – the distance is impossible to judge, but the gap between me and the ship feels like it stretches for miles.

I jam the thruster controls on the stick. My thumb is aching now, throbbing with pain, but I feel the kick at the base of my spine.

My eyes are drawn to a green bar, positioned alongside the thruster display in my helmet. It's filled to about two-thirds, and, as I look at it, it ticks down another measure.

As if my fuel is being used up. Or my oxygen.

Will I have enough to make it to the *Shinso*? No way to tell. It doesn't even feel like I'm getting any closer. I breathe as slowly as I can, taking small sips of air, trying with every ounce of will I have to control the frustration. If I was on Outer Earth, I could run this distance in minutes, just sprint across the gap.

I grit my teeth, keeping my thumb pressed down on the controls, ignoring the pain.

Slowly, ever so slowly, the ship creeps closer. Details start to resolve, shadows becoming clear on the surface.

There's a crackle over the radio. "—ley, come in! Do you hear me?"

"I'm here."

My words come out in a rough whisper. I clear my throat, and try again.

"Gods, I thought you were . . . Listen, don't come in too fast. You won't be able to stop in time."

I'm almost on top of the ship now, its hull swelling beneath me.

I see him. He's got his back to the ship, as if he's lying prone below me. Incredibly, he manages to wave: a single movement, long and languorous.

"We don't have much time left," he says. "I don't know how much juice you've got in your thrusters, but I've burned half of mine."

We glide above the surface of the ship. I can only see the edge of it, peeking over the bottom of my helmet.

"Shit," Carver says.

"What?"

"How are we going to get inside?"

"We go in the airlock," I say, confused.

"And how do we get them to open it for us?"

I open my mouth to reply – then stop. How could we be so stupid? The sensation in my mouth has got worse. When I lick my lips, my tongue is utterly dry.

"How are you doing for fuel?" I ask, stealing a glance at mine. One-third left, assuming it *is* fuel, and not my air supply.

"Almost out," he says, his voice steady. "Can you see their tug?"

"Where?"

"Down there, near the front of the ship."

I tweak the stick, just a little, and spot the tug even before he's finishing speaking. It's docked with the ship, clinging onto it like a bug. Its front end points outward; the ramp at the back must be connected to an airlock.

Relief floods through me – Prakesh made it. He's alive.

I push down harder on the button on my stick. We move towards the *Shinso* in slow motion, and I want to curse with frustration.

I don't. It would just waste air.

"It's stopped rotating," Carver says, puzzled.

"Let's go for the tug," I hear myself say. "Maybe we can get inside it."

We keep moving, pointing ourselves towards the front of the craft. We're almost there, the tug looming large in front

406

of us, when the white cone in Carver's thruster sputters and dies.

"No juice. I've got no juice," he says. I can hear him trying to keep the panic out of his voice. He's a little ahead of me, to the left.

"Hang on," I say, angling myself towards him. I have to slow myself down. If I overshoot and have to come back for him, I'll run out of fuel myself.

Almost there.

Almost . . .

I slam into Carver, taking him around the waist, pulling him along with me. My meter has started to blink red, a flashing beacon at the edge of my vision.

I can only just see past Carver's torso. His hand floats in front of my face, and just beyond it I can see the surface of the tug.

"Steady," says Carver.

"You need to guide me. I can't—"

"Riley, reverse! Reverse thruster!"

We're skidding above the tug's surface – too far above it. If I don't stop now, we're going to overshoot. I lift my finger – slowly, so slowly – and force it down on the second stick button. I feel a juddering in my chest, and Carver's body, pressed close to it, is pushed upwards. He grabs my hand, stretched out above me, and I can hear his breathing in my helmet. It sounds like water rushing through a pipe.

We come to a halt.

When I look down, I see that my foot has caught on a cable that stretches along the outside of the tug's body. If it hadn't been there . . .

Slowly, my muscles aching with the effort, I pull Carver down, onto the surface of the tug. Soon we're both kneeling on it, hooked onto the cable. There's almost no fuel left in my tank.

"Shit," Carver says again. This time, it comes out in a long, slow exhalation.

"Too close."

"Yeah."

"Can we disconnect the tug? Go in through that airlock?"

"No good. It'd take too long. Let's see if we can go round to the other side."

I was hoping he wouldn't say that. I steel myself, getting ready to pull Carver close to me and inch along the tug's body.

There's a sudden pressure in the small of my back. "I've got one of your thrusters," Carver says. "I'll hold, you pull."

"Letting me do the heavy lifting, huh?"

"Yeah, well, you can handle it."

There's another handhold a little further along: another cable, lifted slightly off the surface. I reach for it, using tiny taps of my shoulder thrusters to keep me steady. When I manage to get a grip on the cable, the sweat on my face is so thick that it's started to float off, coating my helmet. I can barely see out of the smeared surface.

"Keep going," Carver says.

But when I look up, I see there are no more cables. Nothing to hold onto. The back of the tug sweeps away from me, and I know that if I try to climb down it with Carver in tow I'll drift away. Beyond the tug's body, there's nothing but space.

"It's no good," I say. "We're out of holds."

"We can't be out. Keep looking."

"Carver, I'm telling you, we need to find another—"

I stop. As I speak, my free hand – the left one, the one not gripping the cable – drifts into view, and with it the wrist control. There's one button I hadn't noticed before. The writing on it reads: PLSM.

"These are construction suits, right?"

"Yeah, why?"

"I've got an idea. Is there something you can grab onto?"

"Hold on."

The pressure in the back of my suit takes an age to fall away. I force myself to stay still.

"OK, I'm holding onto the tug's body."

My right hand sweeps towards my wrist control, and thumbs the PLSM button. Another display pops up in my helmet: another bar crossing horizontally across the bottom. Words flash beneath it: *Plasma cutter arming*.

At almost the same instant, there's a flash of blue on the back of my left wrist. A nozzle has appeared; it flicked up from the suit with a tiny rumble of motors that I can feel in my chest. The light sparks, vanishes, then appears again: a thin streak of blue-white flame, reaching out beyond my hand. There's no sound at all.

Plasma cutter ready.

Carver whoops with joy. "Easy," I say, wincing at the burst of noise

"Sorry," he says, at a more manageable volume. "Good thinking."

I bring the flame down towards the surface of the tug. My wrist has locked in position – a safety measure, presumably, to stop me from bending it and cutting through my own suit. When the flame makes contact with the metal, there's a silent spray of sparks, drifting upwards and winking out instantly.

"I just tried my own cutter," Carver says. "Not getting anything. Keep going."

The metal has started to glow – first red, then white. I've been holding my breath, and let it out in a thin whistle.

"You holding on to something?' says Carver. "There's going to be a pressure blowback when we cut through, so we'd better—"

A section of the metal suddenly pops outwards like it's been hit by stinger fire. I'm still caught on the cable, but for a moment the whoosh of pressure knocks me off balance. The flame lifts off the metal, traces an arc through the vacuum—

—And cuts across Carver's chest.

Neither of us speak. I can see his eyes, wide with confusion, then horror. I've stopped breathing again. There's a burn mark on his suit, slicing across the middle of the letters SCC.

I hear him breathe over the radio. "I'm OK," he says. It's more question than statement. "Just . . . I'm OK. There wasn't much contact."

Slowly, I bring the flame back around. I start cutting again, trying not to look at the readouts in my helmet, stopping every so often to adjust my hold on the cable. My hands are impossibly numb. I cut in a rough rectangle, big enough for us to slip through in our bulky suits. The initial rush of air has stopped; the inner airlock door must have sealed. The inside of the tug is starting to become visible, awash with red light.

My gauge is only a quarter full now. I'm about to start cutting the final side of the rectangle, already thinking about how I'll push the cut panel away from us, when Carver says, "Riley, there's something wrong."

I force myself to keep the torch in contact with the metal. "What is it?"

"I'm getting a warning. On my suit display," he says. The words come out in chunks, like he can't put them all together. Or like he's finding it difficult to breathe. "Some kind of . . . oh gods, Riley, it's a pressure warning."

The plasma cutter. The burn mark on his chest.

"Don't worry," I say, not daring to look at him, moving the cutter as fast as I can. "We'll be inside soon, OK? Just hold on for me."

"Lot of warnings popping up here, Riley."

"I know, I know."

Eight inches to go. Seven. I try not to think of what we were taught about the physics of space. And what happens to the human body in a vacuum.

"My tongue. I can feel it on my tongue."

Five inches. "Carver, we're nearly there." Four.

Suddenly he's screaming in my ears. "It hurts, Riley, make it stop, *make it stop!*"

96

Riley

The next few moments are a confused blur.

I cut through the final edge and grab hold of Carver's suit, only just remembering to shut off my plasma cutter before I do. Carver has stopped screaming.

The chunk of metal that I cut out of the tug's body drifts away. Somehow, I manage to haul Carver through the opening. I'm fighting against the lack of gravity now, forgetting that I have to control my movements. But then we're inside the tug, drifting in the red-washed interior. I'm yelling Carver's name, and getting nothing, nothing but the crackle of the radio back.

I manage to get us over to the ramp, which leads down to the airlock. The thought occurs to me that there might be a welcoming party on the other side, but there's no way I'm staying in this vacuum a second longer than I have to. Not with Carver passed out, the pressure being sucked from his suit. I might be too late.

Don't you think that.

I hammer on the release, and pull Carver through into the airlock space – he feels light, like there's nothing inside the suit. The outer door closes. I hear the hiss of the airlock pressurising, and then the second one opens and we're moving through.

I grab at Carver's wrist panel, fumbling with it, and when his helmet shoots back into the suit I see that his face is almost drained of blood. His lips are a horrific shade of purple.

I shout his name, loud enough that it hurts my ears inside my own helmet.

I stab at my wrist, retracting the helmet, not caring about the change in pressure. It's like someone is jabbing hot needles into my ears. The familiar nausea is back. I groan with pain, but somehow I manage to keep my eyes locked on Carver.

I reach out, pushing past the pain, my suited hand finding Carver's face.

He doesn't move. Doesn't speak, or open his eyes.

I'm trying to form words, but they don't quite make it out of my throat. I try to slap him, but in the low gravity I can't get enough force. My hand just taps his cheek. I bite my lower lip hard enough to bring a trickle of blood, tasting the coppery tang of it, the sting taking attention from the horrible feeling in my ears and stomach.

"Carver," I say through gritted teeth. "Wake up. Please, Carver, wake up."

I take in a huge breath – the air tastes stale here, and dry – and scream into his face. "Carver, *don't leave me!*"

At first, I think I've imagined it. But then his lips move again, very slightly. I hold the movement in my mind as I would a very fragile piece of glass in my hand.

Carver coughs, then sucks in a huge *whoop* of air. He does it again and again.

"Riley . . ." he says, his voice barely a whisper. And then I'm burying my face in his chest, pushing us right into the wall.

"I think you can start calling me Aaron now," he says.

413

I can feel my tears falling away from my face, drifting past us. His arms go around my body, and although they don't pull me close, I can feel them there.

Good enough.

After a few moments, he whispers, "You need to let go."

"Not ever."

"No, you really do." He pushes me away, turns to the side and throws up.

I try not to look at the vomit; the slick globules hang in the air, splitting and turning, as if they're floating in a glass of water. The pain in my ears and stomach has dropped a little. Now that I have a chance to actually look at the surroundings, I can see we're at the end of a long passage. It's smaller and more cramped than the corridors on Outer Earth. There are banks of bright white lights in long lines across the ceiling. Somewhere, very faint, there's a buzzing sound, like a machine starting up.

"How you holding up?" I ask Carver, as I pull him along.

"Feels like someone hit me in the stomach with a steel pole," he says. "Eyes, too."

"Try swallowing. It helps a little."

"I can barely talk, you want me to swallow?"

"Make an effort."

He smiles a little, then groans in pain. I'm worried he's going to throw up again, but he gets it under control.

"Come on," I say. "We've got an Earth trip to cancel."

"You need to—" he stops, steeling himself. "You need to go on ahead."

I stare at him, confused. "I'm not leaving you."

"I can barely move two feet without wanting to spill my guts. I'll just slow you down."

"Aaron . . ."

But I see his hand gripped tight to the wall hold, and I know he's serious. I swim back towards him and hug him again, resting my head on his shoulder. "Promise me you'll try to get somewhere safe?" I say.

"Not a chance. I'll be right behind you, soon as my stomach stops trying to crawl out of my mouth."

I kiss his cheek – his skin is like ice. Then I'm gone, moving away before I have a chance to think about it.

97

Prakesh

Prakesh has never been on the bridge of an asteroid catcher.

It's enormous, far bigger than he would have expected for a crew of six. It's arranged like an amphitheatre, with three tiered levels. The captain's chair is right in the middle of the bridge, tilted slightly back. Workstations surround it, and there are dozens of other screens positioned around the walls, Prakesh can only guess at some of their readouts. He's floating near the back wall, doing what he can to keep the contents of his stomach in place.

What captures his attention is the front of the bridge. It's taken up by a huge viewport: a curving, rectangular sheet of toughened glass. Through it, Prakesh can just see the edge of the Earth.

What's down there? What have the Earthers found that makes them think they can survive?

The bridge is packed. The two remaining crew members have been pushed down into their seats, each of them surrounded by a group of Earthers. Okwembu is bent over one of them, her body twisting as she floats in mid-air, clutching her tab screen. Prakesh catches snippets of conversation, and realises they're trying to restart the ship's thrusters, get it spinning so that they can get the gravity back. He hears them talking about their course – they're going to put the ship into orbit around the Earth, plan their next move.

He feels someone slide in behind him, and then Mikhail is whispering in his ear. "Don't even think about it," he says, his breath hot and dank on Prakesh's skin.

Anger floods through him, but it's a weary anger. He turns himself around to face Mikahil, putting his hand on the wall to steady his body. "Think about what?"

"Doing anything stupid." Mikhail's eyes bore into his. "You think I don't know who you are?"

For a horrible moment, Prakesh is sure that Mikhail knows about Resin – that he'll tell everyone. But instead, the Earther leader says, "You fought against us, back in the dock. You try and get in the way here, and I'll break both your arms."

Prakesh almost laughs. What is he possibly going to do? Take out a bridge full of armed Earthers by himself? Even if he enlists Syria – currently against the back wall, fighting against the nauseating effects of the lack of gravity – he'd end up dead.

"Get the hell away from me," he says.

"You just—"

"I said, get away from me." He shoves Mikhail in the chest. They fly apart, Prakesh bumping into the ceiling. A couple of the Earthers cry out in alarm. Before they can jump in, Prakesh raises his hands, meeting Mikhail's thunderous gaze. "I'm not going to do anything. Just leave me be."

Mikhail looks as if he wants to break Prakesh's arms right there and then. Instead, he pushes himself off the wall and floats back onto the bridge. "One move," he says, as he passes Prakesh.

But Prakesh doesn't respond. Because he's looking at something over Mikhail's shoulder.

It's on one of the screens at the back of the bridge. It's filled with fast-scrolling text, the background the same sickly green as Okwembu's tab screen. The text is too far away to read, but Prakesh can just make out the enlarged writing in the giant, blinking text box superimposed over it.

PRESSURE LOSS IN AIRLOCK 3A. OUTER DOOR COMPROMISED. DO NOT USE.

Prakesh stares at the screen, thinking hard.

It takes a hell of a lot for airlock doors to fail. Short of a speeding tug smashing through them, it's extremely rare to get something like an unplanned pressure loss. When they came in the airlock, it was a clean entry. The seal was good.

Could the tug have dislodged? Could there be a problem with the seals? It's always a possibility, but Prakesh doesn't think so. Someone else is trying to get through that airlock.

Riley.

It's impossible. His mind is playing tricks on him, letting him believe something is true when there's no possible way it could be. He's only setting himself up for a disappointment, and he's had about as much of that as he can handle.

And yet . . .

Prakesh looks around, taking in the bridge. No one is paying attention to him – not even Mikhail, who is talking with Okwembu.

There's no way he can take back the *Shinso*'s bridge.

But that doesn't mean he can't go find out what's causing the pressure loss in airlock 3A.

Moving as quietly as he can, he swims over to the bridge doors, scraping his fingers against the floor. Halfway there, he looks up to see Syria's eyes on him, narrowed in confusion.

Rob Boffard

Prakesh shakes his head, very gently, side to side. Then with one last look back over his shoulder, he pushes his way out through the doors.

98

Riley

Moving down the corridor is easy. I shoot from one handhold to the next, ignoring the nausea still bubbling deep in my stomach.

There are no doors along the walls to break the monotony of the steel panelling. There aren't even any signs or power boxes – and certainly no graffiti, like you'd see on Outer Earth.

The corridor takes an abrupt left turn, heading deeper into the ship itself, and I push my way around it. The buzzing sound is still there, but now it's joined by others: the slow, creaking groan of the hull, louder and more insistent than Outer Earth's. The low rumble of the engines, felt more than heard. And somewhere deep in the *Shinso*'s guts, there are voices. Almost impossibly distant, but there.

Guts. The word feels right; the corridor seems to go on for miles, like the intestines of some enormous creature. One that's spent its entire life in the deepest reaches of space.

Somewhere, deep in the bowels of this thing, is Okwembu. And with her: Prakesh.

I screw my eyes shut. *No*. He's not with her. He might have helped her and the other Earthers inside a tug, but that's just how he is. He wouldn't have let them die. There is no way that he'd have helped them beyond that. He would have tried to stop them. They could be holding him prisoner right now. They could be torturing him. They could—

I make myself stop.

I can't just run in without a plan. If I take off, if I try to save Prakesh, I could get myself captured. I have to be careful. I don't know what condition Outer Earth is in after the breach, but I *do* know that if anybody is still alive there, they need that asteroid.

More than anything else, I have to stop the ship. That might mean going in the opposite direction to Prakesh.

I have to trust him. Trust that he'll be OK.

After an age, the corridor opens up into a spherical chamber, with other passages leading off ahead of me, and to the left and right. The voices are louder now – ahead of me, I think – but I still can't hear the words.

There's a sign set into the wall at the entrance to each passage. I move around to the one on my left. The words are grimed over, their cleaning neglected by astronauts who know their way around the ship blindfolded.

I rub the dirt off to read them, and the granules hang suspended as I knock them off. Some of the fine particles drift up my nose, and I sneeze – the motion pushes me back, sending me into a fast tumble, and I have to grab a handhold on the floor to steady myself. I'm hyperventilating, the air coming and going so fast that I'm suddenly light-headed. The sign I was cleaning swims in front of me, upside down now. I'm angry at myself, furious that I'm not better in zero gravity.

It takes me a few minutes to get my head right. The sign indicates a corridor heading to *Mining, Astronautics, Engines.* Moving around as carefully as I can, I get my bearings. I can go straight ahead to *Ship Bridge*, or drop down the passage to the right, to *Crew Quarters, Mess, Gym, Reactor Access*.

Bridge is out. Sure, I could stop the ship from there, but not without fighting through Okwembu and her Earthers.

So what, then?

My eyes drift back to the other signs – and settle on *Reactor Access*.

At the very edges of my mind, a plan begins to form. Before I can poke holes in it, I'm pulling myself down the right-hand corridor.

If anything, the passage is even narrower here. I find myself drifting towards the ceiling, and more than once I get caught up against it, the impact jarring my stomach and sending little shocks of nausea up my throat.

It's not long before the passage opens up again – this time, into a dimly lit hallway lined with six closed doors, three on each side. In the middle of the hallway, there's an abandoned plastic food carton, slowly rotating as it hangs in the air. There's a tiny slick of something brown in one of its corners.

I move past it, glancing at the doors as I do so. Each one has a name stencilled onto the wall next to it, in block capitals: DOMINGUEZ, LEE, BARTON, OLAFSON, SHALHOUB. Right at the end, perched on top of KHALIL, someone has drawn a surprisingly detailed grinning cartoon devil, looking over its shoulder at me, pulling down black pants to flash a bare ass. Next to it, in black ink, someone has written: *Rashid, the demon of the Asteroid Belt*.

The passage gets narrower again, and this time the lights fade entirely, either dead or turned off. I can just see by the light of the crew quarters behind me, and, at the far end, there's another glimmer of white light. By the time I reach it, pulling myself out into another spherical chamber, a spiky fear has joined the nausea, jostling for space in my stomach.

There's a passage in the floor this time, dropping down into darkness. There's a big sign next to it, laid out in more stencilled letters:

REACTOR ACCESS

WARNING AUTHORISED PERSONNEL ONLY.

I grapple towards it, steeling myself for the darkness, when I happen to look up and see something strange.

There's another passage, heading off to the right. According to its sign, it leads to the *Mess*. At first, I think that there's just a lot of grime covering the wall, but I stop myself, my body half in the lower passage, and take a closer look.

It's not grime. It's too thin, too wet looking.

Almost without realising it, I'm pulling myself out of the passage, heading towards the mess hall, wanting to know and desperate to get as far away as possible. The splatter I saw is blood. There's not a lot of it – it wasn't shed by anyone living.

And when I get through the passage – when I pull myself out the other side – I find them.

Four bodies. All *Shinso* crew. Suspended in mid-air, loose-limbed, with eyes that are glazed and dead.

99

Riley

I turn away, pushing myself tight into one of the walls, my cheek against the cool metal. It's at least a minute before I have the strength to look at the bodies again.

My gaze drifts along the wall. There are seats built into it, with heavy straps that would go across the chest. I guess if you're eating in zero gravity you need your hands free. There are lockers running along the wall opposite me, and there's debris floating around the room, too: half-empty, opaque pouches of liquid.

The bodies are clustered together in the centre of the room, their loose limbs bumping up against each other. Two men, two women. One of them is facing me, and I can see the gaping stinger wound in her chest.

There's nothing I can do for the crew now, but perhaps there's something in the lockers that would come in useful. I pull myself along to them, swimming across the bottom of the room to avoid the bodies. When I get upright again and spring the lockers, the items inside tumble out, joining the cloud of debris scattered across the room. More food pouches, bars, pressurised water canisters. An entire sealed plastic container of straws tumbles out of one and drifts away, its contents bouncing around inside it.

There's a knife inside the locker, velcroed to the back. For a moment, I'm confused – you don't use knives and forks to eat in zero gravity – but then I see that it's more like an old hunting knife. I've seen a few like it on Outer Earth – heirlooms, objects from the planet below us. This one has a wooden handle, worn smooth, but the blade has been kept good and sharp. It must have belonged to one of the crew. I reach out and grab it.

Now I have a weapon.

I tuck it into my belt, telling myself to make sure it doesn't drift loose. Then I take two deep breaths, and pull my way out of the mess hall.

I've nearly reached the spherical chamber leading to the reactor when there's a voice not ten feet away.

"You think they got aboard?"

I choke back a breath, not letting a single sound escape, and push myself against the wall. My hand just touches a slick of blood, and I have to force myself not to yank it away again.

In the chamber, the owner of the voice floats past, his back to me. He's with another women, moving slightly above him. Both of them are Earthers – I recognise them from the battle in the dock. How many made it on board? Those tugs aren't big enough to fit more than a dozen people – maybe twenty, at a push. Strange to think that of all the Earthers I saw, only a tiny fraction made it here.

"Of course they got on board," says the woman. "You saw the airlock alert."

"I'll push 'em back out if they're still there."

"She wants them alive. You know that."

They've headed back into the passage, moving towards the crew quarters. I can't risk following them. Even with the knife in my belt. I wait for a beat, two, three, until the voices are gone completely. Then I slip out into the chamber, and pull myself into the passage leading to the reactor. I go feet first, and the darkness swallows me.

There's a ladder running down the one side of the shaft. I fumble more than once, cursing under my breath as I lose my grip on the rungs. But there's a light at the bottom – a tiny, bright, yellow glare – and it keeps me centred. Before long, I'm pulling myself out of the shaft into the passage at the bottom.

It's at right angles to the drop, the ceiling low and cramped. The metal here is rusted in spots, coated with a kind of yellowish rime. The floor below me is a grate, laid on top of a tangled mess of pipes and wires. The sounds I heard earlier are muted – all except one. The buzzing noise. I'm closer to the machine now, and the sound has become a growl, so low it rattles my insides.

I have no idea what I'm going to do when I get to the reactor. I know it's a fusion core, like the one on Outer Earth, only much smaller. It'll have shielding, but there's got to be a way inside.

I have to disable it somehow – it'll stop the *Shinso* in its tracks, cut all power to the engines. Of course, I might blow it, and myself, into the next world. And it might cut power to everything else, too, including the life-support systems. But there should still be enough air to breathe for a while, and if I can get Carver and Prakesh, if we can then make it back to the tug . . .

I stop counting the ifs and the mights. Instead, I look around the cramped passage for a handhold, and pull myself along it, heading in the direction of the buzzing noise.

I'm expecting another airlock at the end of the passage. There is one – but it's been left open, the doors recessed into the wall. Good. That means there won't be any alarm triggered when I go through. I can see part of the reactor chamber on the other side, bathed in a clinical white light.

The room is laid out in a circle, like a rotunda, and the floor slopes away from me, with strips of light leading to the machine in the middle. It rises in a giant cone to the ceiling, twenty feet above me. Like its bigger brother at the centre of Outer Earth, its body is cocooned in cables.

I push myself off towards it, looking around the room for a control panel. I'm half hoping that it'll be as simple as telling a computer to shut the reactor down, but there are no controls anywhere. The only thing that disturbs the shape of the walls are several metal storage boxes, each one five feet long, held to the walls by more velcro.

As I get closer, I can see the body of the reactor underneath the tangle of cables. Thick steel plates, the joins between them sealed with thick, grey rubber. The same substance runs around the cables where they meet the body.

I circle it, running my hands along the plates and the seals, looking for a weak spot. Nothing. No panels, no screens, not a single thing that will let me get inside. I make my way over to the boxes, hauling them open. They're all empty. No tools, save for a small screwdriver, strapped down inside one of them. Useless.

And it doesn't help that I know almost nothing about fusion reactors. Assuming I do get inside, what would I see? I picture a glowing ball, hanging suspended in its own nest of cables, and curse myself for not knowing, for not asking Carver if he knew what to expect.

I pull the knife out of my belt, and jam it into one of the seals as hard as the low gravity will let me. It only just pierces the rubber-like material. I wiggle it back and forth, feeling the sweat pop out on my forehead, but I only manage to get a little bit deeper into the seal. It'll take hours to get through.

Could I cut into one of the cables, maybe? I throw the idea out almost as soon as it occurs. Which one? And how would I do it without frying myself?

I've left the knife caught in the seal. As I watch, it comes loose, spinning slowly in the space in front of the reactor. After a few moments, the blade is pointing right at me.

I freeze, unable to look away from it. Because, right then, I get another idea. But this one is like a poison of its own, seeping right through me, corroding everything it touches.

I can't cut through the steel plating, or the rubber seals.

But what if I could blow up the reactor?

100

Riley

I turn away from the knife, determined not to look at it again.

But I can't stop my mind from weighing up the possibilities. They stretch outwards in my mind, three steel cables stretching away from me in different directions, pulled taut, like the cables tethering the asteroid to the *Shinso*.

Along one, I fight my way through to the bridge. I manage to avoid being captured, or killed, somehow, and I take control of the ship. I turn it around, bring it home. The station gets the tungsten it needs to shore up the reactor. Outer Earth survives.

But that cable snaps in an instant. Getting past the Earthers by myself? Taking every single one of them out of commission with no backup, no gadgets from Carver, and no idea of the bridge layout? It's a possibility so remote as to be almost non-existent.

Cable two. I try to get to the bridge. I'm captured or killed, and the *Shinso* continues its journey. There's no asteroid slag, no tungsten for the station's reactor. Outer Earth dies. Anna, and everyone else, dies.

Along the final cable, I . . .

I cut into myself. Knox told me how to get the bombs out – *cut the left wire*. I somehow do it without dying from blood loss, or passing out from the pain, or blowing myself up. I get the bomb out – it'll have to be one; the thought of cutting more than once causes my gorge to jump – and use it to blow up the shielding around the ship's reactor. Knox said the bombs were sensitive to impact – I can use the storage boxes to detonate one of them.

The blast probably won't be enough to disable the reactor entirely, but it might let me get inside, assuming I'm still conscious or coherent enough to do something about it.

Let's say I do it. It'll be just like back in the Recycler Plant – I simply have to put the bomb in the right place. The *Shinso*'s power dies. Those aboard it have no option but to make for the tug, and head back to Outer Earth. The chances that we can stop the *Shinso* from drifting too far and bring it and its cargo back into station orbit are slim, but still there.

No. I won't. I can't.

I'm already thinking about all I've been through. Everything I've survived. I'm thinking about Kev, and Royo, and everyone else who has died to stop this ship from leaving. I think about what I had to do to my own father to save my home. I'm thinking about Anna and her family. About Jamal, and his daughter Ivy. About everyone I know on Outer Earth.

A voice drifts up from a very dark place in my mind: a place I'd almost forgotten about. A little black box where I put the things I never want to think about again.

There's nothing you can do to save it, Amira says. *It's finished. We were never supposed to live this long.*

And somewhere else, a tiny thought crystallises. It glows like a star, full of immense power, but so far away that it's nothing more than a pinprick of light in a black void.

I'm not you, Amira. And I never will be.

I turn around, gripping one of the cables to spin my body. The knife is bumping off the body of the reactor. Slowly, I reach out for it, gripping its wooden handle.

101

Riley

I'm up near the ceiling, next to the cables that run from the reactor. I've got a cable around my right arm, hooked into the armpit. I've jammed my left ankle into a cable further along, tilting the back of my knee towards me.

It's an awkward position, and a tight fit – the cables push at the back of my neck and head. I've torn a strip off the bottom of my shirt, pulling it tight around my left leg, midway up my thigh. I have no idea if that's the best place for a tourniquet, but I know it has to go on somewhere. I've already taken one of the storage boxes from where it was velcroed to the wall. If this works, I'm going to need to hit the bomb with something to detonate it. The box floats next to me, gently rotating.

I've pulled up the leg of my jumpsuit. The air in the reactor is chilly, and I can feel it prickling my skin. I take a look at the stitches again, running a finger along them and fighting back the dry taste in my mouth. The stitches form a puckered line, running across the flesh at the back of the knee. Most of the stitch, save for the spiky ends, runs under the skin. I think back to the words Knox used: *popliteal fossa*. A gap in the muscles.

I run my finger across the part above the stitch. The thought of cutting into it is enough to bring more cold sweat out across my body. It's all too easy to imagine never being able to run again, miscalculating the cut, damaging the muscles themselves . . .

I can't do this. I can't.

Several deep breaths later, the blade is a few inches above the skin. If I can cut along the line of the stitch, it should open up a little. I should be able to see the bomb.

And remove it without blowing myself up.

Around me, the buzzing of the reactor feels softer, as if the machine is waiting to see what happens. I can hear my own heartbeat, and my breathing, exquisitely precise.

The knife hovers, trembling.

And before I can do anything, my hand acts on its own, jamming the knife into my flesh.

I let out a shocked gasp, staring at the blade sticking out of my flesh, coming out at an angle. *There's no pain. There's no—*

Blood wells up around the knife, floating in huge bubbles. And it's then that the pain comes. A giant, searing bolt. I throw my head back and scream.

Surely the bombs can't be worse than this. It feels like someone is holding a red-hot brand to my leg: holding it and twisting it.

Tears double and triple what I see, but I can still make out what I have to do. The knife has cut through the part of the stitch closest to the bone on the left. If I keep going, I can go right through the stitches, and open it all up.

My right hand, gripping the handle of the knife, is trembling so hard that I have to use my left to steady it. I grit my teeth, and begin pushing it outwards, sawing gently up and down, cutting through the stitches.

My back aches from having to twist my body, but I barely

notice – compared to the pain from my knee it's almost nothing. Every single movement brings a stab so intense that it greys out my vision. Every cut stitch brings such a wave of relief that I nearly cry out, and every one seems to be more painful than the last. By the time I sever the final stitch, my legs and the space around them are a red hell, and the grey at the edge of my vision has turned black.

But I can see the bomb. I can see it.

The wound is open now – a gaping purple-red mouth, with ragged edges. I can see the muscles and the gap between them, just visible under clouds of blood. And *there*: a metal casing. A flat, dark-green square, half an inch across, with a raised circular segment in the middle. It looks impossibly small – there's no way something that tiny could do any damage.

I think back to Kev, think back to the bloodstain spreading across his shirt.

I need to see more. And I need both hands to do it. Somehow, I get the knife away from the wound, and put the handle between my teeth. The blood that stains it is still warm, coppery on my tongue, and that alone is almost enough to make me pass out. I bite down on the handle, and use my shaking fingers to gently pull the gaping mouth open some more.

This time, I do pass out.

When I come to, the knife has dropped out of my teeth and is floating in front of my face. I don't remember what the pain was like; I just remember it being *there*, so enormous that I couldn't even comprehend it.

I snatch the knife out of the air and look back down at my destroyed knee. My head feels clearer now, as if it's been wiped clean by the pain.

I grip the bomb between thumb and forefinger, and begin to slide it out from the gap.

Knox was wrong. Anyone could have removed it. It would have been better if it—

Something pulls at my muscle, something between it and the bomb. I freeze.

Working as gently as I can, trying not to touch the edges of the wound, I slip my finger underneath the bomb. Wires. Two of them, sheathed in rubber and slick with blood, running from the body of the bomb to the muscle itself. *Attached* to the muscle, wired into it. Had I kept pulling, I would have ripped them right out. In the haze of pain, I'd almost forgotten Knox's words. *Cut the left wire. My left.*

The knife is already back in my hand, and, working as slowly as I can, I slip it back under the metal casing. I feel it touch the wires, and the thought of cutting the wrong one is enough to make me gasp.

I make sure the blade is right between the two wires, resting against the bomb casing. My hand is trembling so hard that I can hear the tapping of metal on metal. His left would be my right. So I have to cut the right-hand wire. I rest the blade against it, ready to cut. I need to do it in a single movement, yanking the blade across and cutting right through.

What if Knox was lying?

Out of nowhere, a memory surfaces. The memory of being ambushed by the Lieren, back when I was just a tracer. They had me pinned against the corridor wall, and one of them had a blade at my face. He was going to cut off one of my ears. He was flicking the blade left, right, left right, trying to decide which one.

Each breath is shaking now, barely making it out of my lungs. I have to decide.

I flip the knife, angling it towards the other wire.

Then I flip it back, and cut the first one.

102

Riley

I scream.

It lasts for perhaps half a second, cut off as my throat slams shut. The knife is through. It skidded off the edge of the cut, but I barely felt it, the adrenaline knocking away the pain.

I did it.

I slice through the remaining wire, and then I'm holding the bomb in my hands.

The entire casing fits into my palm. I'm laughing now. It's a horrible sound, lumpy and angry. My entire body is drenched with sweat, and my knee . . . I can't even look at my knee. When I lift my arms from around the cables, pulling myself out, the muscles in my upper body scream in protest.

I swim towards the reactor as if in a dream. With every beat of my heart, darkness pulses at the edge of my vision.

You will not pass out. Not now.

Time skips forward again. I'm in front of the reactor. The bomb is suspended there, nudging one of the rubber seals. The storage box is positioned on my shoulder like a rocket launcher. I'm aiming it right at the bomb. One hit. That's all it'll take. I have enough presence of mind to throw the canister, rather than swing it – no telling how big the explosion will actually be.

There's a voice. The words hang in the air as if caught in the low gravity themselves, and it takes me a few moments to understand them.

"Riley, what have you done?

Very slowly, I turn my head.

Prakesh is floating in the open door of the airlock, his eyes wide with confusion and horror.

I try to say something, but the words won't come. He puts a hand on either side of the door, and launches himself into the room, heading right for me.

No – not for me. For the box I'm holding on my shoulder. I grip it tight, ready to launch it at the bomb.

"Stay back, Prakesh," I hear myself say.

He's grabbed hold of a cable, pulling himself to the stop. "Ry, you're hurt – we need to get you some—"

"I said, *stay back*."

"OK," he says, raising a hand. "I'll just talk then. All right? I'll just talk."

He can't keep his eyes off my knee, a thin stream of blood still trailing from it. When it touches the metal on the reactor, it spreads out, so dark it's almost black.

"We're too far away now," he says. "If you blow the reactor, we'll never make it back."

I say nothing.

"They know you're here – I only just managed to get ahead of them. Come back with me. Please."

I don't hear the rest. I'm looking past him. All the way to the reactor airlock.

Okwembu is there, along with Mikhail.

They've got Aaron. Mikhail has an arm around his throat, and a stinger pressed to the side of his head.

103

Riley

I can't move.

I have to blow the bomb. But if I do that, Aaron dies.

All I can see is the stinger, jammed up against his head. He's barely conscious, and there are dark rings under his eyes, standing out against his pale skin.

"Better put it down," says Mikhail, pulling his arm tighter around Aaron's throat.

"I didn't want it to come to this," Okwembu says. She's moved into the chamber, a few feet away from Prakesh. "But Ms Hale, you need to do what he says."

"I can't."

I'm crying now, the tears spurred on by the waves of pain coming from my knee. They fall out of my eyes, drifting in front of me.

Okwembu speaks slowly, as if carefully examining every word. "Outer Earth is lost. It's finished. Even if we somehow repair the Core, we've lost too many people to Resin."

I think of Anna, her father, all the others left behind. "You're wrong."

But it's as if she doesn't hear me. "The only thing that matters now is that humans survive. And the best chance of that is this ship."

"Don't listen to them, Riley." Aaron's voice is almost inaudible under the noise of the reactor, but there's still some strength in it. "Just . . ." His words are choked off as the arm pulls tighter around his neck.

"Riley, please," says Prakesh. "Just do what she says. Do it for me."

I stare at him, not understanding his words. When comprehension comes, it's as if a bullet has gone through my own head. "You're with them?"

"You know I'd never want this. Any of it. But I can't let anyone else die. Not you, not Aaron, not anyone else in this room or this ship. And if you blow that bomb, that's what'll happen."

"And Outer Earth?" I say. "What about them?"

The regret on Prakesh's face is infinite. "We can't help them, Ry. *I* can't help them. I never could. The only thing I can do is protect what we have now. I can help keep this ship safe."

"Prakesh—"

"You have to let me do this," he says.

Is he telling the truth? Would Prakesh lie to me? It's impossible to think. It feels as if there are more people in the room than the five of us. Kevin is there, and Yao, floating just out of sight. Royo, his dark eyes locked on mine. Amira, right behind me, whispering in my ear.

My father is here, too, with my name in orange letters over his face. I can't quite see his eyes.

"I'll give you three seconds," says Mikhail.

Okwembu glances at him. "No, Mikhail. I have this under control."

"Three!"

"Riley, I love you, but you have to stop," says Prakesh.

"Two!"

"Mikhail, *stand down*," says Okwembu

"One!"

"Do it, Ry," Aaron shouts. "Do it now!"

I throw the box.

104

Riley

But not at the bomb.

Instead, I throw the box away from me, so hard that it bounces off the floor with a dull boom. The bomb floats in front of the reactor, its wires just touching the surface.

Silence.

Relief is written on Prakesh's face. "Good. That's good, Riley."

I look down at my hand. Somehow, the knife is back in it. I don't know how – I can't even remember seeing it since I used it on myself. And, right then, it's as if all the voices, all the people crowding the reactor chamber, the buzzing of the reactor itself, just vanish. My mind is wiped clean. There's just me, and the knife.

And Janice Okwembu.

She's floating in front of me. Her eyes sparkle with triumph. Everything that's happened, all of it, from my father to the Devil Dancers to Resin to the dock to Morgan Knox . . . all of it is because of her. The chain of events she set off, by bringing my father back, put us here: on a hijacked vessel, with the station in ruins behind us, and hundreds of thousands of people dead.

She's the origin point. She's responsible. She wanted power, and control, and it tore Outer Earth apart.

I'm barely aware of what I'm doing. I feel my hands grab hold of something, and use it to spin me around. I move my right leg, the undamaged one, swinging it around so that my foot is in contact with the surface of the reactor. The knife is pointed upwards, gripped tight in my hand. Its blade is crusted with dried blood.

I push off the reactor in what feels like slow motion, but somehow I know that I'm moving faster than I ever have before. Everything I've gone through coalesces, simmers down into those two things. The triumph fades from her eyes, replaced by fear.

And the sight of it, that naked terror in her eyes, is wonderful.

Someone grabs me around the middle. The world comes rushing back – Aaron, Mikhail, the reactor, all of it. The knife is gone, flying away from me. Okwembu, too, pulled back by Mikhail. He throws Aaron aside as he does so, sending him flying.

I'm shouting, hammering on the arms that grip me tight. It's Prakesh. We slam into the wall of the chamber, and my knee flares with impossible pain. He just pulls his way up my body until he towers over me, pulls me into an embrace, locks me in it. My words turn to nothing, to incoherent screams.

I fight to get away from Prakesh, but there's no strength left in my arms. Eventually, all I can do is stare at him. Betrayal, hatred, love, pity – I feel every single one of them.

"No more deaths, Riley," he says. "No more. Not even her. It's over."

105

Riley

There's food, water and a room with very bright lights. The *Shinso Maru*'s medical bay – I don't really remember how I got here, but Aaron is with me, strapped into one of the other beds.

I can't feel anything below my left knee – the man working on it puts a huge needle into my leg, and the pain simply melts away. I'm strapped down, held in place by wide velcro straps, but my arms float freely. I can barely move them.

The man is muttering to himself as he works on the cut. "You did this to yourself?"

"There was a bomb in me," I say. "I took it out."

I hear him pause for a moment, as if waiting for more. When it doesn't come, he goes back to work.

"There's another one," I say. I barely recognise my own voice. "Other knee."

His eyes go wide. Then he shakes his head sadly. "I don't . . ." he says, and trails off.

"Please. You have to take it out."

"Dominguez was our medical officer," he says. "I'm doing what I can, but I'm out of my depth here. I'm sorry."

443

He's right. Better to leave it where it is, for now. As long as that transmitter in my ear stays charged, I'll be OK.

It's then that I notice the patch on his chest, faded and frayed, but still legible. KHALIL, ASTRONAUTICS OFFICER.

"The demon of the Asteroid Belt," I say. I don't know if he hears me. I'm drifting down a long, dark tunnel, shot through with flecks of fire. I expect to see my dad, with my name obscuring his eyes, but I'm way too deep for that.

When I wake up, Khalil is gone. In his place there's one of the Earthers, floating by the door. I vaguely remember him from the attack on the dock – a giant man, with a face that looks as if he hasn't smiled in years. "Are you here to make sure I don't kill anybody?" I ask. My throat feels as if it's filled with razor blades.

He doesn't say anything. Lifting my head, I get a look at my knee for the first time. It's wrapped in bandages; a swollen ball of white fabric, dotted with blood.

I rip off my velcro straps. Using the wall for control, I move over to Aaron's bed. He's flat on his back, his eyes closed. The glaring lights show up the purple circles underneath his eyes. There's a drip stuck into his arm, hooked up to a bag of yellowish liquid.

"They said not to wake him yet," says the man by the door.

I put a hand on Aaron's shoulder, and squeeze. Instantly, the man is by my side, moving between me and the bed. I didn't realise how big he was – my head barely reaches his shoulders.

"Best do what you're told," he says, staring down at me.

I return his gaze. "What are you, then? My bodyguard?"

"Mikhail says to keep you in here. He'll figure out what to do with you later. You and your friend."

I'm already working out how to take him down, working out the best way to disable him in low gravity. Then I realise

I've only got the use of one leg, and that my other limbs feel like thin glass. I've as much chance of taking him down as I have of surviving in space without a suit. I turn and push myself back to my own bed, pulling myself down onto the edge of it, strapping myself back in.

Sometime later, I look up to see Prakesh.

His eyes are drawn, but he tries to smile as he moves towards the bed. The bodyguard floats between him and me, his hand raised.

"Let me see her," Prakesh says.

The man doesn't move. Prakesh's eyes flare with anger. "If I was going to try something, I would have done it by now. *Let me see her.*"

After a long moment, the giant lets him past. Prakesh pushes himself around him towards the bed.

I can't look at him.

I keep seeing Okwembu. I was so close. And *he* stopped me, pulled me away just before I could have my revenge. For Outer Earth, for my dad, for everything.

I should hate him. I want to.

But as he reaches the bed, as I see the pain in his eyes and feel his hand on my shoulder, that hatred cracks and crumbles.

I can't blame him for not wanting anyone else to die while he stands aside and does nothing. How can I turn him away, when he's in so much pain? It would be the worst thing possible.

I reach out for him, and we embrace. I bury my head in his shoulder.

Neither of us speak. We don't need to. We just hold each other tight. Both of us have made mistakes. Both of us are broken, in our own way.

I don't mention what happened with Aaron. I don't know how.

"What's it like?" I say. "Up on the bridge?"

He rests his forehead on my shoulder. "They're working out how to shape the asteroid. It has to be structurally sound for re-entry. They're going to need to go outside to do it."

"That's enough," says the guard, appearing behind Prakesh. I squeeze him tight. "Go," I say. "I'll be all right."

"You sure?"

In answer, I squeeze even harder. I don't tell him the real reason I want him to go. It's because Aaron is awake, and watching us, and the confusion in his eyes is too much to bear.

"I'll come back, OK?" Prakesh says. "I'll come and get you."

He looks back at me one last time.

"I love you," he says.

"I love you, too."

He leaves, and the door slips shut behind him. The guard doesn't say anything as I unstrap and float over to Aaron's bed. He's sitting up, drinking from a pouch of water through a straw.

"Guess we're going to Earth then," he says, pulling the straw from his mouth.

"I guess."

He shrugs. "Gonna be interesting to see how they do it. Even after they get through the atmosphere, they'll still be going a billion miles an hour. I'm thinking they'll use the escape pods, bail out . . ."

He trails off as I wrap my arms around him. It's all I can do not to start crying again. He hugs me back, then lifts my head to his, his lips brushing mine.

I pull away.

Gods help me, I pull away.

His eyes meet mine. "I just thought – after all we've been through, we could . . ."

"Please don't ask me this, Aaron. Not now."

I reach up to touch his cheek, but he pushes me away, anger

blazing on his face. "I was there for you. This whole time, I've been right alongside you. Back at the hospital in Apex, the Boneshaker, the fight in the dock, the tug – all of it. Doesn't that mean anything?"

His words echo my thoughts about Prakesh. My heart feels like it's about to shatter, like a single tap on chest would kill me. I have to fight back the tears.

"You really still love him?" Aaron says. "After all that he's done?"

It comes out as a whisper. "I don't know."

"Then why did we kiss? You tell me that. Why?"

When I speak, each word is like a weight being hung around my neck. "I wanted to be close to someone. I wanted something normal."

"Excuse me?"

"I shouldn't have done it, Aaron. It was wrong. You're my *friend*."

He's crying too now. "You don't understand," he says. "You two have each other. Who do I have, Riley? Who do I have?"

I can't answer him. I wouldn't know where to begin. I don't know what I'm becoming, or what to think any more.

The door opens behind us. I hear Prakesh's voice. "You're OK to come through to the bridge, if you want."

"Don't go with him," Aaron says in a whisper. "Stay with me. Please."

But I don't.

We leave the medical bay, Prakesh and I, the bodyguard floating along behind us. He hasn't said a word. I take one last look back at Aaron – only for a second, because any longer and I'll crack in two. He's turned away from us, facing the wall.

On the bridge, banks of glowing screens are lined up like soldiers. A giant screen hangs from the ceiling; it's displaying what looks like a projected course, the *Shinso* a tiny dot in the top right corner. The Earthers are here – at least twenty of them, floating in small groups. Syria is there, too, huddled by the wall. He doesn't look at me.

The far wall is transparent. I can see the Earth. The sun is just peeking over the far horizon. A band of colour spreads out from it, dark blue becoming crimson and orange and white.

That's when I see Okwembu.

She and Mikhail are floating just below the window, deep in discussion. Mikhail's body has been caught by the sun, but the top half of Okwembu's body is cloaked in shadow. She turns to look at me, and her face is a black hole, silhouetted against the light. It's impossible to see her expression, and she doesn't move – just stares at me, her chin slightly lowered. I get a ghost of the anger I felt in the reactor, when it was just me, her and the knife. Prakesh seems to sense it, and holds me tighter.

We're not done yet, I think, looking at Okwembu. *You and me. Not even close.*

It's Mikhail who comes forward, using the railings that buttress each level to pull himself towards us. I expect him to be angry, but as he comes towards us he actually smiles. "I'm glad to see you up," he says.

I flinch from him, doing it before I can tell myself not to. He stops, and raises his hands. "You have nothing to be afraid of. Not from us. You understand that we have to keep a watch on you—" he gestures to my guard, still floating behind me "—but I hope you will help us when we reach our destination."

I'm shaking my head, and when I speak I struggle to keep the rage out of my voice. "Destination?" I say, jabbing a finger at the window, at the black mass under the sun's band. "There's nothing there. Nothing and nobody. We destroyed it, remember?"

"You haven't told her?" Mikhail asks Prakesh. He shakes his head.

448

"Told me what?"

Mikhail gestures to the big man. My bodyguard. "Alexei. Bring the recording."

"What is this?" I ask Prakesh.

"You need to hear it," he says.

As Alexei moves to the other side of the bridge, Mikhail turns back to us. "It's true that most of the Earth is a wasteland. The nuclear bombs saw to that."

"Then what—"

"Don't interrupt. The climate on maybe ninety-eight per cent of the planet's surface is completely destroyed. But we've discovered a part of the Earth where it's starting to clear."

I'm shaking my head, not quite believing it. "OK, so what? Starting to clear isn't the same as completely clear. You still don't know what's down there. If it's even habitable."

Alexei comes back. He has an ancient recording unit, no bigger than my hand. Mikhail takes it, and presses play. Static hisses out of the tinny speaker. Around us, the room has gone silent.

"I don't see—" I start, and then a man's voice is coming out of the speaker, so crackly I can barely make it out. I have to listen hard, but soon I hear the tonal vowels, the clipped words.

"It's Chinese," I say.

Mikhail nods. "The English message will come in a moment. We think they're broadcasting in different languages to reach as many people as possible."

"We haven't had any communication from Earth in fifty years. Not one."

"That is correct," Mikhail says. "And so we stopped listening. That device in your ear—" he points to my SPOCS unit, still there despite everything I've been through "—it runs off cell frequencies, as you know, which means it can't pick up old radio transmissions."

And all at once, it clicks into place.

449

The static. The bursts across the SPOCS line. The interference that Aaron could never fix, that hurt my ear whenever they came through.

I remember the thing I saw in the old mining facility that the Earthers had taken over. The device with the old-fashioned screens, displaying the strange shapes.

We weren't listening. The Earthers were. They found something – something that convinced them that they could survive on Earth. They didn't tell the council because they knew that only a few people would ever be able to return to the planet. They wanted it to be them.

There's a pause in the recording, and then it switches into English.

"If anyone can hear us, we are broadcasting from a secure location in what used to be Anchorage, Alaska. There are at least a hundred of us here, and we have managed to establish a colony. We have food, water and shelter. The climate is cold, but survivable. If you can hear us, then know that you're not the only ones out there. Our coordinates are—"

Mikhail turns off the recorder.

"Do you see now?" he says quietly.

I can barely find the words. "It's an old message. It has to be."

Alexei shakes his head. "At the end of it, he gives a date. One which was only two months ago."

"They live," Mikhail says. "The broadcast was meant for survivors on Earth, but we heard it, too. And we're going to find them."

It feels like everyone in the room is watching me. Okwembu hasn't moved – her face is still cloaked in shadow. Slowly, I raise my head towards the window.

The world looks back at me, dark and silent, with the sun coming up over the horizon.

Acknowledgements

Thank *you*, for reading this book. I hope you stick with Riley for the next chapter. Her story is far from over.

And to everybody who ever got in touch about Riley and Outer Earth, who talked about the books online, who bought copies and mouthed off about the books to their friends . . . too many good people to name, but you all rock.

This book is dedicated to my mom and dad, Ken and Vee Boffard. I love them more than I can say, but that's not the only reason I'm singling them out. For this story, they went the extra mile, lending me their considerable medical expertise. Thanks, too, to my sister Cat, who was totally unfazed by our family WhatsApp group filling up with discussions about the best way to stab someone in the eye.

For further scientific and medical advice, I'm grateful to Professor Guy Richards (Wits University), Andrew Wyld, who advised me on radio and cell frequencies, and the incredible Dr Barnaby Osborne (University of New South Wales). That asteroid re-entry plan? Totally his idea. You don't think I come up with this stuff on my own, do you?

Errors are my fault, in all cases.

To my friends Rayne Taylor, Dane Taylor, Chris Ellis, Ida Horwitz and George Kelly, who gave me magnificent feedback.

Ed Wilson is a fantastic agent and a rock-solid drinking buddy. His early comments and encouragement made this happen.

Anna Jackson edited the hell out of this one. Nobody does it better.

To my Orbit Books crew: Tim Holman, Joanna Kramer, Felice Howden, Gemma Conley-Smith, James Long and Clara Diaz. Also Devi Pillai at Orbit US. We did it again.

Thanks, too, to Richard Collins for the copy-edit and Nico Taylor for the killer cover.

When *Tracer* was published, Nicole Simpson was still my fiancee. By the time you read this, she'll be my wife – and by some margin the best thing to ever happen to me. It behooves me to mention her family: James, Bettina, Trisha, Lotte and Hardy. Thanks for letting me stick around.

The story continues in

IMPACT

by
Rob Boffard

A signal has been picked up from Earth.

The planet was supposed to be uninhabitable. But it seems
there are survivors down there – with supplies, shelter and
running water. Perhaps there could be a future for humanity
on Earth after all.

Riley Hale will find out soon enough. She's stuck on a space-
ship with the group of terrorists who are planning to brave
the planet's atmosphere and crash-land on the surface.

But when the re-entry goes wrong, Riley ends up hundreds
of miles from her companions Prakesh and Carver, alone in
a barren wilderness. She'll have to use everything she
knows to survive.

And all of them are about to find out that nothing on Earth
is what it seems . . .

extras

extras

about the author

Rob Boffard is a South African author who splits his time between London, Vancouver and Johannesburg. He has worked as a journalist for over a decade, and has written articles for publications in more than a dozen countries, including the *Guardian* and *Wired* in the UK.

Find out more about Rob Boffard and other Orbit authors by registering for the free monthly newsletter at www.orbitbooks.net.

if you enjoyed
ZERO-G

look out for

LEVIATHAN WAKES

The Expanse: Book One

by

James S. A. Corey

If you enjoyed

ZERO-G

look out for

LEVIATHAN WAKES

The Expanse: Book One

by

James S. A. Corey

Prologue: Julie

The *Scopuli* had been taken eight days ago, and Julie Mao was finally ready to be shot.

It had taken all eight days trapped in a storage locker for her to get to that point. For the first two she'd remained motionless, sure that the armored men who'd put her there had been serious. For the first hours, the ship she'd been taken aboard wasn't under thrust, so she floated in the locker, using gentle touches to keep herself from bumping into the walls or the atmosphere suit she shared the space with. When the ship began to move, thrust giving her weight, she'd stood silently until her legs cramped, then sat down slowly into a fetal position. She'd peed in her jumpsuit, not caring about the warm itchy wetness, or the smell, worrying only that she might slip and fall in the wet spot it left on the floor. She couldn't make noise. They'd shoot her.

On the third day, thirst had forced her into action. The noise of the ship was all around her. The faint subsonic rumble of the reactor and drive. The constant hiss and thud of hydraulics and steel bolts as the pressure doors between decks opened and closed. The clump of heavy boots walking on metal decking. She waited until all the noise she could hear sounded distant, then pulled the environment suit off its hooks and onto the locker floor. Listening for any approaching sound, she slowly disassembled the suit and took out the water supply. It was old and stale; the suit obviously hadn't been used or serviced in ages. But she hadn't had a sip in days, and the warm loamy water in the suit's reservoir bag was the best thing she had ever tasted. She had to work hard not to gulp it down and make herself vomit.

When the urge to urinate returned, she pulled the catheter bag out of the suit and relieved herself into it. She sat on the floor, now cushioned by the padded suit and almost comfortable, and wondered who her captors were — Coalition Navy, pirates, something worse. Sometimes she slept.

On day four, isolation, hunger, boredom, and the diminishing number of places to store her piss finally pushed her to make contact with them. She'd heard muffled cries of pain. Somewhere nearby, her shipmates were being beaten or tortured. If she got the attention of the kidnappers, maybe they would just take her to the others. That was okay. Beatings, she could handle. It seemed like a small price to pay if it meant seeing people again.

The locker sat beside the inner airlock door. During flight, that usually wasn't a high-traffic area, though she didn't know anything about the layout of this particular ship. She thought about what to say, how to present herself. When she finally heard someone moving toward her, she just tried to yell that she wanted out. The dry rasp that came out of her throat surprised her. She swallowed, working her tongue to try to create some saliva, and tried again. Another faint rattle in the throat.

The people were right outside her locker door. A voice

was talking quietly. Julie had pulled back a fist to bang on the door when she heard what it was saying.

No. Please no. Please don't.

Dave. Her ship's mechanic. Dave, who collected clips from old cartoons and knew a million jokes, begging in a small broken voice.

No, please no, please don't, he said.

Hydraulics and locking bolts clicked as the inner airlock door opened. A meaty thud as something was thrown inside. Another click as the airlock closed. A hiss of evacuating air.

When the airlock cycle had finished, the people outside her door walked away. She didn't bang to get their attention.

They'd scrubbed the ship. Detainment by the inner planet navies was a bad scenario, but they'd all trained on how to deal with it. Sensitive OPA data was scrubbed and overwritten with innocuous-looking logs with false time stamps. Anything too sensitive to trust to a computer, the captain destroyed. When the attackers came aboard, they could play innocent.

It hadn't mattered.

There weren't the questions about cargo or permits. The invaders had come in like they owned the place, and Captain Darren had rolled over like a dog. Everyone else — Mike, Dave, Wan Li — they'd all just thrown up their hands and gone along quietly. The pirates or slavers or whatever they were had dragged them off the little transport ship that had been her home, and down a docking tube without even minimal environment suits. The tube's thin layer of Mylar was the only thing between them and hard nothing: hope it didn't rip; goodbye lungs if it did.

Julie had gone along too, but then the bastards had tried to lay their hands on her, strip her clothes off.

Five years of low-gravity jiu jitsu training and them in a confined space with no gravity. She'd done a lot of damage.

She'd almost started to think she might win when from nowhere a gauntleted fist smashed into her face. Things got fuzzy after that. Then the locker, and *Shoot her if she makes a noise.* Four days of not making noise while they beat her friends down below and then threw one of them out an airlock.

After six days, everything went quiet.

Shifting between bouts of consciousness and fragmented dreams, she was only vaguely aware as the sounds of walking, talking, and pressure doors and the subsonic rumble of the reactor and the drive faded away a little at a time. When the drive stopped, so did gravity, and Julie woke from a dream of racing her old pinnace to find herself floating while her muscles screamed in protest and then slowly relaxed.

She pulled herself to the door and pressed her ear to the cold metal. Panic shot through her until she caught the quiet sound of the air recyclers. The ship still had power and air, but the drive wasn't on and no one was opening a door or walking or talking. Maybe it was a crew meeting. Or a party on another deck. Or everyone was in engineering, fixing a serious problem.

She spent a day listening and waiting.

By day seven, her last sip of water was gone. No one on the ship had moved within range of her hearing for twenty-four hours. She sucked on a plastic tab she'd ripped off the environment suit until she worked up some saliva; then she started yelling. She yelled herself hoarse.

No one came.

By day eight, she was ready to be shot. She'd been out of water for two days, and her waste bag had been full for four. She put her shoulders against the back wall of the locker and planted her hands against the side walls. Then she kicked out with both legs as hard as she could. The cramps that followed the first kick almost made her pass out. She screamed instead.

Stupid girl, she told herself. She was dehydrated. Eight days without activity was more than enough to start atrophy. At least she should have stretched out.

She massaged her stiff muscles until the knots were gone, then stretched, focusing her mind like she was back in dojo. When she was in control of her body, she kicked again. And again. And again, until light started to show through the edges of the locker. And again, until the door was so bent that the three hinges and the locking bolt were the only points of contact between it and the frame.

And one last time, so that it bent far enough that the bolt was no longer seated in the hasp and the door swung free.

Julie shot from the locker, hands half raised and ready to look either threatening or terrified, depending on which seemed more useful.

There was no one on the whole deck: the airlock, the suit storage room where she'd spent the last eight days, a half dozen other storage rooms. All empty. She plucked a magnetized pipe wrench of suitable size for skull cracking out of an EVA kit, then went down the crew ladder to the deck below.

And then the one below that, and then the one below that. Personnel cabins in crisp, almost military order. Commissary, where there were signs of a struggle. Medical bay, empty. Torpedo bay. No one. The comm station was unmanned, powered down, and locked. The few sensor logs that still streamed showed no sign of the *Scopuli.* A new dread knotted her gut. Deck after deck and room after room empty of life. Something had happened. A radiation leak. Poison in the air. Something that had forced an evacuation. She wondered if she'd be able to fly the ship by herself.

But if they'd evacuated, she'd have heard them going out the airlock, wouldn't she?

She reached the final deck hatch, the one that led into

engineering, and stopped when the hatch didn't open automatically. A red light on the lock panel showed that the room had been sealed from the inside. She thought again about radiation and major failures. But if either of those was the case, why lock the door from the inside? And she had passed wall panel after wall panel. None of them had been flashing warnings of any kind. No, not radiation, something else.

There was more disruption here. Blood. Tools and containers in disarray. Whatever had happened, it had happened here. No, it had started here. And it had ended behind that locked door.

It took two hours with a torch and prying tools from the machine shop to cut through the hatch to engineering. With the hydraulics compromised, she had to crank it open by hand. A gust of warm wet air blew out, carrying a hospital scent without the antiseptic. A coppery, nauseating smell. The torture chamber, then. Her friends would be inside, beaten or cut to pieces. Julie hefted her wrench and prepared to bust open at least one head before they killed her. She floated down.

The engineering deck was huge, vaulted like a cathedral. The fusion reactor dominated the central space. Something was wrong with it. Where she expected to see readouts, shielding, and monitors, a layer of something like mud seemed to flow over the reactor core. Slowly, Julie floated toward it, one hand still on the ladder. The strange smell became overpowering.

The mud caked around the reactor had structure to it like nothing she'd seen before. Tubes ran through it like veins or airways. Parts of it pulsed. Not mud, then.

Flesh.

An outcropping of the thing shifted toward her. Compared to the whole, it seemed no larger than a toe, a little finger. It was Captain Darren's head.

"Help me," it said.

Chapter One: Holden

A hundred and fifty years before, when the parochial disagreements between Earth and Mars had been on the verge of war, the Belt had been a far horizon of tremendous mineral wealth beyond viable economic reach, and the outer planets had been beyond even the most unrealistic corporate dream. Then Solomon Epstein had built his little modified fusion drive, popped it on the back of his three-man yacht, and turned it on. With a good scope, you could still see his ship going at a marginal percentage of the speed of light, heading out into the big empty. The best, longest funeral in the history of mankind. Fortunately, he'd left the plans on his home computer. The Epstein Drive hadn't given humanity the stars, but it had delivered the planets.

Three-quarters of a kilometer long, a quarter of a kilometer wide — roughly shaped like a fire hydrant — and mostly empty space inside, the *Canterbury* was a retooled colony transport. Once, it had been packed with people, supplies, schematics, machines, environment bubbles, and hope. Just under twenty million people lived on the moons of Saturn now. The *Canterbury* had hauled nearly a million of their ancestors there. Forty-five million on the moons of Jupiter. One moon of Uranus sported five thousand, the farthest outpost of human civilization, at least until the Mormons finished their generation ship and headed for the stars and freedom from procreation restrictions.

And then there was the Belt.

If you asked OPA recruiters when they were drunk and feeling expansive, they might say there were a hundred million in the Belt. Ask an inner planet census taker, it was nearer to fifty million. Any way you looked, the population was huge and needed a lot of water.

So now the *Canterbury* and her dozens of sister ships in the Pur'n'Kleen Water Company made the loop from Saturn's generous rings to the Belt and back hauling glaciers, and would until the ships aged into salvage wrecks.

Jim Holden saw some poetry in that.

"Holden?"

He turned back to the hangar deck. Chief Engineer Naomi Nagata towered over him. She stood almost two full meters tall, her mop of curly hair tied back into a black tail, her expression halfway between amusement and annoyance. She had the Belter habit of shrugging with her hands instead of her shoulders.

"Holden, are you listening, or just staring out the window?"

"There was a problem," Holden said. "And because you're really, really good, you can fix it even though you don't have enough money or supplies."

Naomi laughed.

"So you weren't listening," she said.

"Not really, no."

"Well, you got the basics right anyhow. *Knight*'s landing gear isn't going to be good in atmosphere until I can get the seals replaced. That going to be a problem?"

"I'll ask the old man," Holden said. "But when's the last time we used the shuttle in atmosphere?"

"Never, but regs say we need at least one atmo-capable shuttle."

"Hey, Boss!" Amos Burton, Naomi's earthborn assistant, yelled from across the bay. He waved one meaty arm in their general direction. He meant Naomi. Amos might be on Captain McDowell's ship; Holden might be executive officer; but in Amos Burton's world, only Naomi was boss.

"What's the matter?" Naomi shouted back.

"Bad cable. Can you hold this little fucker in place while I get the spare?"

Naomi looked at Holden, *Are we done here?* in her eyes. He snapped a sarcastic salute and she snorted, shaking her head as she walked away, her frame long and thin in her greasy coveralls.

Seven years in Earth's navy, five years working in space with civilians, and he'd never gotten used to the long, thin, improbable bones of Belters. A childhood spent in gravity shaped the way he saw things forever.

At the central lift, Holden held his finger briefly over the button for the navigation deck, tempted by the prospect of Ade Tukunbo — her smile, her voice, the patchouli-and-vanilla scent she used in her hair — but pressed the button for the infirmary instead. Duty before pleasure.

Shed Garvey, the medical tech, was hunched over his lab table, debriding the stump of Cameron Paj's left arm, when Holden walked in. A month earlier, Paj had gotten his elbow pinned by a thirty-ton block of ice moving at five millimeters a second. It wasn't an uncommon injury among people with the dangerous job of cutting and moving zero-g icebergs, and Paj was taking the whole thing with the fatalism of a professional. Holden leaned over Shed's shoulder to watch as the tech plucked one of the medical maggots out of dead tissue.

"What's the word?" Holden asked.

"It's looking pretty good, sir," Paj said. "I've still got a few nerves. Shed's been tellin' me about how the prosthetic is gonna hook up to it."

"Assuming we can keep the necrosis under control," the medic said, "and make sure Paj doesn't heal up too much before we get to Ceres. I checked the policy, and Paj here's been signed on long enough to get one with force feedback, pressure and temperature sensors, fine-motor software. The whole package. It'll be almost as good as the real thing. The inner planets have a new biogel that regrows the limb, but that isn't covered in our medical plan."

"Fuck the Inners, and fuck their magic Jell-O. I'd rather have a good Belter-built fake than anything those bastards grow in a lab. Just wearing their fancy arm probably turns you into an asshole," Paj said. Then he added, "Oh, uh, no offense, XO."

"None taken. Just glad we're going to get you fixed up," Holden said.

"Tell him the other bit," Paj said with a wicked grin. Shed blushed.

"I've, ah, heard from other guys who've gotten them," Shed said, not meeting Holden's eyes. "Apparently there's a period while you're still building identification with the prosthetic when whacking off feels just like getting a hand job."

Holden let the comment hang in the air for a second while Shed's ears turned crimson.

"Good to know," Holden said. "And the necrosis?"

"There's some infection," Shed said. "The maggots are keeping it under control, and the inflammation's actually a good thing in this context, so we're not fighting too hard unless it starts to spread."

"Is he going to be ready for the next run?" Holden asked.

For the first time, Paj frowned.

"Shit yes, I'll be ready. I'm always ready. This is what I *do*, sir."

"Probably," Shed said. "Depending on how the bond takes. If not this one, the one after."

"Fuck that," Paj said. "I can buck ice one-handed better than half the skags you've got on this bitch."

"Again," Holden said, suppressing a grin, "good to know. Carry on."

Paj snorted. Shed plucked another maggot free. Holden went back to the lift, and this time he didn't hesitate.

The navigation station of the *Canterbury* didn't dress to impress. The great wall-sized displays Holden had imagined when he'd first volunteered for the navy did exist on capital ships but, even there, more as an artifact of design than need. Ade sat at a pair of screens only slightly larger than a hand terminal, graphs of the efficiency and output of the *Canterbury*'s reactor and engine updating in the corners, raw logs spooling on the right as the systems reported in. She wore thick headphones that covered her ears, the faint thump of the bass line barely escaping. If the *Canterbury* sensed an anomaly, it would alert her. If a system errored, it would alert her. If Captain McDowell left the command and control deck, it would alert her so she could turn the music off and look busy when he arrived. Her petty hedonism was only one of a thousand things that made Ade attractive to Holden. He walked up behind her, pulled the headphones gently away from her ears, and said, "Hey."

Ade smiled, tapped her screen, and dropped the headphones to rest around her long slim neck like technical jewelry.

"Executive Officer James Holden," she said with an exaggerated formality made even more acute by her thick Nigerian accent. "And what can I do for you?"

"You know, it's funny you should ask that," he said. "I was just thinking how pleasant it would be to have someone come back to my cabin when third shift takes over. Have a little romantic dinner of the same crap they're serving in the galley. Listen to some music."

"Drink a little wine," she said. "Break a little protocol. Pretty to think about, but I'm not up for sex tonight."

"I wasn't talking about sex. A little food. Conversation."

"I was talking about sex," she said.

Holden knelt beside her chair. In the one-third g of their current thrust, it was perfectly comfortable. Ade's smile softened. The log spool chimed; she glanced at it, tapped a release, and turned back to him.

"Ade, I like you. I mean, I really enjoy your company," he said. "I don't understand why we can't spend some time together with our clothes on."

"Holden. Sweetie. Stop it, okay?"

"Stop what?"

"Stop trying to turn me into your girlfriend. You're a nice guy. You've got a cute butt, and you're fun in the sack. Doesn't mean we're engaged."

Holden rocked back on his heels, feeling himself frown.

"Ade. For this to work for me, it needs to be more than that."

"But it isn't," she said, taking his hand. "It's okay that it isn't. You're the XO here, and I'm a short-timer. Another run, maybe two, and I'm gone."

"I'm not chained to this ship either."

Her laughter was equal parts warmth and disbelief.

"How long have you been on the *Cant*?"

"Five years."

"You're not going anyplace," she said. "You're comfortable here."

"Comfortable?" he said. "The *Cant*'s a century-old ice hauler. You can find a shittier flying job, but you have to try really hard. Everyone here is either wildly under-qualified or seriously screwed things up at their last gig."

"And you're comfortable here." Her eyes were less kind now. She bit her lip, looked down at the screen, looked up.

"I didn't deserve that," he said.

"You didn't," she agreed. "Look, I told you I wasn't in the mood tonight. I'm feeling cranky. I need a good night's sleep. I'll be nicer tomorrow."

"Promise?"

"I'll even make you dinner. Apology accepted?"

He slipped forward, pressed his lips to hers. She kissed back, politely at first and then with more warmth. Her fingers cupped his neck for a moment, then pulled him away.

"You're entirely too good at that. You should go now," she said. "On duty and all."

"Okay," he said, and didn't turn to go.

"Jim," she said, and the shipwide comm system clicked on.

"Holden to the bridge," Captain McDowell said, his voice compressed and echoing. Holden replied with something obscene. Ade laughed. He swooped in, kissed her cheek, and headed back for the central lift, quietly hoping that Captain McDowell suffered boils and public humiliation for his lousy timing.

The bridge was hardly larger than Holden's quarters and smaller by half than the galley. Except for the slightly over-sized captain's display, required by Captain McDowell's failing eyesight and general distrust of corrective surgery, it could have been an accounting firm's back room. The air smelled of cleaning astringent and someone's overly strong yerba maté tea. McDowell shifted in his seat as Holden approached. Then the captain leaned back, pointing over his shoulder at the communications station.

"Becca!" McDowell snapped. "Tell him."